Henri

Seventeen Short Stories

Douglas Bosack

STONEWALL PRESS
PAVING YOUR WAY TO SUCCESS

Printed in the United States of America

ISBN: Paperback: 978-1-948172-24-0
           eBook: 978-1-948172-23-3

Library of Congress Control Number: 2018936506

STONEWALL PRESS
PAVING YOUR WAY TO SUCCESS

Stonewall Press
363 Paladium Court
Owings Mills, MD 21117
www.stonewallpress.com
1-888-334-0980

In memory of Dianne

The Stories

A Victim of Circumstance

*I*t was getting dark when Frank Martin stepped off the porch of his beach house. His deck shoes sank deeply into soft sand as he headed for the shore. Walking up a small dune covered with tall grass and reeds, he passed through an opening in an old hurricane fence.

The beach was still warm from the day's blazing sun. Frank took a seat in the sand. He'd brought along an empty bottle from his car, the last remnant of years of self-destruction. Rolling the bottle in his palms, he stopped to look at its label, Johnny Walker Red, his favorite.

It was a clear night with a bright moon in the eastern sky. Small waves, accentuated by moonlight, rippled across the bay. The peaceful quiet of the beach, enhanced by the rhythmic lapping of water on the shore, was an inviting setting for Frank.

Gazing out over the harbor, his eyes settled on a red light atop a large buoy a few hundred feet out. He spoke to himself, "I can't believe I didn't see that thing. I must have really been trashed."

Frank was a lobster boat captain, employed at a marina just a mile up the coast from his home. In addition to setting lobster traps, his job entailed taking summer tourists out on a run once a week. On those days, he would often cruise by his property, pridefully pointing out his beautiful home to his guests. Two months ago, while motoring by in a boat jammed with vacationers, he had smashed into the buoy, tearing a hole in the bow of his rig.

He'd been drunk, as he was every day—so drunk he hadn't even noticed the approaching buoy in the bright, midday sun. Terrified tourists had screamed as their captain frantically headed for shore, beaching his craft in shallow water. No one was injured. Nonetheless, Frank's boss gave him a two-month suspension and an ultimatum, "Ya got two months to soba up, Frank. Or don't botha comin' back!"

Reports of the accident and details of the captain's drunkenness were splattered all over the *Bar Harbor Times*, such an event being big news in the small resort town.

Relentless gossip followed; talk about the drunken lobster boat captain who had nearly killed a bunch of tourists shot through the city's native community. Over ensuing weeks, Frank was plagued by embarrassment, shame, and self-reproach—emotions he had drowned out for years with alcohol.

Frank stood and walked to the water's edge, moonlight reflecting off the empty liquor bottle he gripped in his hand. "It's now or never; this is my last chance."

Heaving the bottle out over the bay, he symbolically aimed at the distant buoy. The bottle flipped end over end and fell to the water with a splash, landing far short of its target.

Frank walked back to his home, passing through clumps of sand shrubs, canary grass, and cattails dotting the dunes. In the dark, he didn't see his neighbor, Walter, walking down the beach.

"How ya doin' tonight, Captain Mahtin?"

Frank turned to the old man. "Hello, Walta. I'm doin' fine. "Weatha says there's a nor'easta comin' in. Gonna hit tomarra mornin', so they say."

"That so?"

"Shore is, Franklin. Ya best be careful if ya goin' out for lobsta." "Thanks, Walta. I'll keep that in mind."

Returning to his empty house, the house he hated, Frank was flooded by good memories—memories that only added to his loneliness and despair. The beach house had been such a lively place, so full of laughter, love, and happiness. Frank, having cherished his family and his life, had been a happy, contented man until a tragic day six years ago.

For years hence, he had been full of hatred and disgust for the drunk driver who took his wife, his children, and his will to live from him. The driver, a young man, a mere boy, still sat in prison, paying for his offense, the same offense Frank had since committed countless times. "I hated him so much I wanted to kill him. Now I'm just like him. No betta than him, just as irresponsible 'n' dangerous."

He'd received many letters from the incarcerated youth, all conveying the young man's heartfelt sorrow and regret, begging for understanding and forgiveness. Frank had repeatedly ignored the man's pleas, never responding.

After the boating accident, his feelings changed. "I should talk with that poor kid in prison. I don't hate him anymore; I understand his pain. I feel his pain." He made plans to visit the prison the following week.

•

Frank changed clothes, drove to town, and entered an old church in the center of Bar Harbor. In the church's basement, he found a room heavy with the smell of fresh coffee and cigarettes. He took a seat at a long table surrounded by men, women, and a few teenagers. The moderator asked for introductions around the room. When Frank's turn came, he said, "Hello, I'm Frank. I'm an alcoholic."

He was to receive his thirty-day chip that evening. He didn't want it; in his mind, he didn't deserve it. Frank was different from the rest, or so he thought. Thirty days of abstinence meant nothing to him, and deep inside he knew it would never last. Thinking himself to be an imposter, a deceitful liar, he did not want nor believe he deserved recognition.

At meeting's end, with a look of embarrassment, Frank reluctantly accepted his chip, along with applause from the group and a hug from the moderator. He left the meeting consumed by shame and regret, emotions that weighed upon him—emotions that sent him looking for relief. He drove to a carryout.

Frank sat in his car, paralyzed by self-doubt, pondering his past and what he knew would be a dismal future. After thinking for a long while, he stepped out to the parking lot.

The following morning, the storm hit. Frank holed up in his house, fighting temptation, resisting the urge to go to his old friend in the cupboard, the bottle of Scotch he'd bought but hadn't opened. By evening, while the storm lingered, he succumbed to his desires.

Pulling the bottle from the cupboard, he recalled what his doctor had told him. *Frank, your liver enzymes are sky-high. You've already got cirrhosis, and the alcohol has weakened your heart. You must quit drinking!*

He paused, staring at the golden-brown contents of the capped bottle. "I don't care about my liver or heart; I've nothing to live for anyway." He opened it.

The scent of Scotch wafting from the bottle excited him. Frank reveled in the taste of the smooth liquor rolling over his tongue and down his throat. Within seconds he felt a familiar inner warmth and comfort. He stopped after only one glass, all that was needed to provide relief from his pain. Fear of a hangover on his first day back to work forced him to cap the Scotch and return it to the cupboard. He went to bed.

The next morning, Frank suffered shame from breaking his promise of abstinence. His failure to uphold his vow of sobriety to himself and his employer saddened him. It was the beginning of the vicious cycle he'd gone through so many times past: struggle to abstain; cave in; feel regret, shame, and remorse; and drink again to abolish those terrible feelings.

Ruining his one-month stretch of sobriety produced overwhelming pain, and he knew there was only one cure. He drank another glass and left for the marina.

At work, Frank, concerned his alcohol-tainted breath would expose him for the unworthy employee he was, craftily avoided talking with his boss. His first day at sea was uneventful; he took in a good catch. The following day he was to take out a group of vacationers.

That evening, Frank thought of how weak, worthless, and destitute he was. *I'm no good to anyone. I haven't done a good deed or helped another soul in years. I can't even help myself.*

He had three Scotch on the rocks before turning in for the night. As he lay in bed, Frank contemplated ways to end his misery, his disgusting life. He knew he'd do it sooner or later, either by drinking himself to death or by more active means. Sleep came to him reluctantly.

Wanting to prepare for his 8 a.m. tourist excursion, Frank awoke early. The sun was rising over the harbor, creating a spectacular array of colors at the horizon. He thought of how he and his wife had loved the early morning beauty of the bay—holding each other as they watched the sun rise. It was all lost on him now.

Recalling his thoughts from the prior night, Frank's feelings of despair returned. He wasn't looking forward to a long day dealing with tourists; with three runs scheduled, he wouldn't finish until six or later. Walking to the cupboard, he grabbed his Scotch and took two long gulps straight from the bottle.

•

Sandpipers ran along the beach as the captain loaded patrons on his boat. It was a beautiful morning with bright sunlight shimmering off a light chop on the water. Flat-bottom skiffs, sailboats with colorful spinnakers, and a few yachts decorated the harbor. Flocks of gulls and puffins cried out as they flew overhead.

Frank pulled his diesel-powered craft out of the marina as customers donned life jackets and positioned themselves on the aft deck behind the helm. Captain Martin turned north along the coast, heading for his beach house. As he approached, he carefully steered clear of the buoy in front of his home. After pointing out his property to his guests, he turned east, toward open water—hoping for a good lobster catch and maybe a whale sighting or two to entertain the guests.

After passing the buoy, he accelerated, the boat's prop creating a large wake behind. A young boy, far back stern near the transom, was struggling with his life jacket while his mother, not paying attention, conversed with friends. The child removed the jacket and leaned far over the transom, reaching out to the foamy water of the wake. The cruiser hit a large wave.

"Michael! He's fallen in! Oh, God, someone save him!"

Frank's head shot around to see a child already fifty to sixty feet behind the craft, floundering in the water. He cut the engine, ripped off his windbreaker, and dove off the helm, disappearing in the icy-cold water of the bay.

Kicking hard, he pulled furiously with what were once large, powerful arms. Frank, unaware of the toll years of alcohol abuse had taken on him, was surprised by how quickly he was sapped by the frigid water. Despite being depleted of energy, he endured and finally reached the youngster whose head was quickly pulled above the surface.

Looking back to his rig, Frank's heart sank. The boat had drifted farther out, leaving him terror-struck. Physically spent, certain he'd never make it back, especially with Michael in tow, Frank wiped his eyes and peered toward shore. He saw the buoy a short distance from them. It was gently swaying in the water, as if waving to him, inviting him to come over for a rest. To Frank, the buoy, his former nemesis, now seemed like an old friend. Elated by the sight of it, he wrapped an arm around Michael and set out, pushing hard with legs and feet churning furiously.

His clothing, heavy with water, was pulling him down. Frank kicked off his deck shoes and forged on, full of panic but determined to save the child. An intense burn weakened his muscles as he pushed himself, struggling to keep Michael's head above water.

Reaching out to the steel base of the buoy, Frank shouted, "We made it! We made it, Mike."

Mustering his last bit of strength, he lifted his frightened companion to safety on the buoy's large platform and told him hold on tight and wait for help. The shivering boy said he was okay and added, "I'm sorry for breakin' the rules, mister. Am I gonna be in trouble?"

Captain Martin smiled, "No, you're not in trouble, Michael. I'm just glad you're safe." As Frank clung to the side of the buoy, he looked back at his boat. A man was at the helm; a tourist had commandeered the craft and was coming to their rescue.

"Mike, look, they're coming to get us."

Michael turned toward the boat. Seeing his mother, who was now high up on the helm, he yelled, "Mom, I'm okay, I'm okay." His young voice was drowned out by the wind, the waves, and the roar of the diesel. "Mom, the captain saved my life, I'm okay."

Michael, turning back, smiled at Frank, "Thank you, mister."

Frank was about to speak when a crushing heaviness hit his chest; overwhelming weakness consumed him. As his hands instinctively clutched over his heart, he released the buoy. Feeling himself slipping down, Frank desperately reached out, grabbing for something, anything, to keep him above water. His arms, leaden and weak failed him.

Michael screamed as the captain's face went white.

Frank took a final, frantic breath as his head submerged, and water poured into his lungs. He lost consciousness and sank, slowly drifting down ten, twenty, thirty feet. When his motionless body reached the bottom of the harbor, gently settling on the floor of the bay, Frank's right hand floated from his chest, coming to rest on a discarded, sunken bottle lying in the sand—a bottle full of seawater, label reading Johnny Walker Red.

News of Captain Martin's demise during his heroic rescue of a young boy shot through the community of Bar Harbor.

A day later, the young man in prison read of Frank Martin's death, saddened he would never get his chance to make amends.

Steven's Education

He had lived on the street for years, ever since his wife had left him. Steven Hunter was a loner who always felt oddly, inexplicably uncomfortable, sometimes petrified around people. His progressive social phobia eventually cost him his marriage, his job, and any prospect for future employment. Steven's wife couldn't deal with him—his anxiety, his fears, and his weirdness were all too much. His unemployment was the last straw for their marriage. She divorced him and took off, leaving him horribly in debt and soon to be homeless.

It was late, time to turn in for the night when Steven walked to the end of the alley and crawled into his new home. He loved the closeness, the sense of security, and the privacy his cardboard box provided. He liked the scent of wet cardboard, which reminded him of his childhood and the many times he'd hidden in an old refrigerator box his parents had left behind the garage.

Steven had tried living with other homeless men, usually in abandoned buildings, but they'd always made him nervous and uneasy. He preferred being alone, isolated. Steven Hunter cherished solitude.

The city's newly elected mayor ordered a crackdown on street people and petty criminals, instructing the police to round them up. They took Steven to a shelter. He hated it. It was impossible for him to relax while sharing space in a dormitory setting. A few days later he ran away.

The police had no trouble finding him—living in the same alley and the same box. He was taken back to the shelter and given a warning.

"Mr. Hunter, if you run again, we'll be forced to put you in jail. You have to stay here!"

Steven couldn't understand why they wouldn't leave him alone. He kept to himself and never broke the law. He never stole, never vandalized, never destroyed property, and never bothered anyone. He was harmless.

That didn't matter to the mayor or the police; the city had to be cleaned up. Two days in the shelter was all he could take; he ran again. Two days he was back in jail.

The judge reluctantly sentenced him to ninety days at County. Steven, though placed in the facility's low-security section, was a nervous wreck. Being housed with other homeless men and some criminals, those convicted of minor offenses, turned Steven into a ball of anxiety. Minimum security had no cells; all occupants were placed in a large, dormitory-style room lined with rows of bunk beds. Stephen would have preferred solitary confinement.

A few inmates were in for misdemeanors or low-level felonies, such as larceny, drug possession, domestic violence, or repeat DUI. Steven's bunk-mate, William Comstock, was a thief doing his second stint for petty larceny. He'd been lucky, having committed grand larceny many times without being caught.

"Hey, man, guess we be bunk-mates," said William.

Steven was caught off guard by the comment. He hesitated. William continued. "What's wrong? You afraid to talk to a black man."

"Uh... no. I'm sorry. I'm Steve Hunter."

The man, a muscular guy with broad shoulders, extended his hand. "Glad to meet ya—I'm William Comstock, that's William, not Bill—just William, okay?"

"Sure, William."

For a few days, that introduction remained the extent of their conversation. Steven did his best to keep to himself while Comstock hung out with other prisoners. Eventually, the big man opened up to his bunk-mate.

"Hey, what's wrong with you, Hunter? Don't you ever talk?" Hesitating, Steven slowly responded. "Uh, yes... I talk sometimes. I'm kinda quiet, though. I... I like... I like privacy." "Privacy! How the hell you gonna have privacy stuck in here with over a hundred men? I can tell ya from experience, time goes by a lot quicker if you make some friends."

Steven thought about that. *Friends, I've never had any.* Comstock continued. "What you in for?"

"Being homeless."

"What? Homeless? Who gives a shit?" "The mayor."

"Oh, man. You get caught up in the mayor's city-sweep?" "I guess so."

"What a bunch a shit. Guy's homeless, his life stinks, and they stick him in jail. The mayor has a bug up his ass about crime. But the homeless? That ain't right."

"I agree."

William, like so many criminals, especially the unsuccessful ones, loved to tell of his lawless exploits. Steven found that an odd paradox, wondering how William, or any of them, expected to get away with crime if they talked their heads off about it. He concluded they were, like himself, immature, insecure men, whose fragile egos demanded recognition. He thought, *I bet the big boys of crime, like the mob, carefully avoid notoriety. But these guys, they thrive on being rebellious and having everyone know about it.*

William Comstock simply couldn't help himself; he loved to talk, and since Steven had no place to hide, he had to listen. Day after day, for hours on end, William bragged about himself. He told Steven how clever he was as a criminal, explaining all the tricks of his trade.

Over his three-month incarceration, Steven was told, in detail, how to be a thief. He learned how to pick locks, disarm burglar alarms, and break into private homes and stores without being detected. William explained how to quietly navigate through a dark house in the middle of the night, how to tell valuable jewelry from costume junk, and how to use a small penlight to locate purses and wallets. To his surprise, Steven became fascinated with the finer points of successful thievery. He enjoyed his talks with William, whom he found friendly, entertaining, and intelligent.

His gregarious associate told him how to quietly break window glass by first covering it with masking tape, how to avoid leaving fingerprints by wearing latex gloves, and how to drag your feet to prevent tell-tale

Without him, you'd be stuck with a bunch a hot shit and no money." Steven was curious. "How do you go about finding a fence you can trust?"

"That's an excellent question, my friend; I'm proud of ya. There's no easy way on the trust issue. You talk to people you know and you take your time. Cops are notorious for going undercover as a fence, just waitin' to nab nice guys like me."

Steven smiled. "You *are* a nice guy—in my opinion."

"Well, thank you, my man; I appreciate it. You keep that up, and I may have to make you an honorary brother."

Steven smiled again.

As the end of Steven Hunter's incarceration approached, William gave his bunk-mate the most important advice of all. "Steve, my friend and main man, I have one last recommendation for anyone wantin' to practice my trade."

"What do you mean, William? Surely, you're not talking about me, are you?"

William burst out laughing. "You, of course not. You're a great guy, but you ain't got what it takes to be in my line a work. I shouldn't be laughin', but you gotta admit—"

"I know, I know. Still, you scared me there for a second."

"Sorry 'bout that. I'm just talkin' in general, not 'bout you." Steven chuckled, "That's good."

"So, I was gonna say, if someone, not you, wants to be a successful thief, I have one very important recommendation for 'em."

"What would that be?"

"Never, ever, ever carry a piece. Anyone confrontin' a burglar is a very nervous individual. The sight of some asshole with a gun can put them over the edge—beyond the brink of rational thought. What I'm sayin' is they get crazy!"

"Crazy?" asked Steven.

William laughed. "Yeah, I think you got it, brother—crazy. He continued. "If they're armed as well, the homeowners that is, they gonna shoot your ass first and think 'bout what they done later. That's an especially important rule in rural households, out in the country, where shotguns are the rule. No one, but no one, wants to be taken out by a shotgun. Besides, I can't think of a single situation where a gun, or even a knife, would be of benefit."

"Yeah, I understand. Makes perfect sense to me."

"Steve, a thief needs to make his job as easy and safe as possible. Carryin' a gun is just plain stupid. If you're not carryin' and you're caught and convicted of *unarmed* robbery, you'll usually do easy time. But, conviction on *armed* robbery's a whole different ball game; it ain't nice. And, you pack a gun and get trigger happy, killin' someone, you can kiss your ass goodbye. You'll get life or, worse, the needle. No smart thief ever got life in prison or execution."

Steven, amazed at how interesting he found all of this, felt a surprising degree of respect for his friend. It was odd and difficult for Steven to explain, but he actually admired William, who seemed so clever, dedicated, and for the most part, successful at his trade. Furthermore, Steven appreciated William's commitment to do no physical harm.

"Steve, I been doin' jobs for a long time. I bet I know 'bout all there is to know 'bout stealin'."

"Sounds like it to me. I can't believe how much you've told me over the past months and how interesting it's been."

Two days later, Steven Hunter was released from jail. When William said goodbye, a tightness grew in Steven's throat. He nearly cried. He was leaving the best friend he'd ever had, probably the only friend—a big, black man he'd met in prison.

Steven felt pathetic, realizing how his introversion and isolation had ruined his marriage, caused years of loneliness, and deprived him of the pleasure of friendship, which he'd found in knowing William Comstock.

The county jail gave Steven cab fare and called a taxi to take him directly to the homeless shelter. When the cab pulled up in front of the shelter, Steven thanked the driver and stepped out. As the cabby pulled away, he stood and stared at the shelter's entrance. A moment later he turned and ran as fast as he could. He knew better than to return to his alley, where he'd soon be discovered by the police. Instead, he walked for hours, heading out of the city into the countryside.

For days, he slept in the woods, contemplating his future. He missed William and often wished he were back in jail with his friend.

He searched for food, finding barely enough to sustain him through his time in the woods.

Steven had nowhere to go—returning to the city would be pointless. The mayor's sweep crew would quickly find him. He needed money and considered trying to find a job but knew no one would hire him—a middle-aged bum just released from jail.

On his fourth day of hiding, the potential consequences of Steven's situation—the risks of another, possibly less inviting incarceration or, worse, being confined in a homeless shelter—induced him to make a promise to never, ever give up. Steven made a commitment to survive on the street, no matter what. He'd survive outside, in the world, by any means possible. If the mayor wouldn't let him live in the alley, he'd have to get more creative and find some other way to stay alive.

The next morning, while lying on a blanket he'd found in a dumpster, Steven Hunter, staring up at the sky, thought of William Comstock and was struck by a revelation—an awareness. Steven knew exactly what he had to do.

•

His first theft was a pen and pad of paper from a drug store. Steven was shocked by how easy and exciting it was to steal. It gave him a giddy feeling of being alive. Leaving the store, he broke out in laughter. "That was too easy. I can't believe it."

That afternoon, he stole some Twinkies and cupcakes from a carryout. Returning to the woods with his snack and his pen and paper, he wrote all he could remember about what his friend had taught him. The following day he went to work.

Finding a fence was the toughest part; it took him two weeks to find a trustworthy associate who could move his goods. A short time later, he had enough money to rent a motel room. A month later, he moved into an apartment. Soon after, using his apartment as a base of operations, Steven advanced his career, concentrating on very small but very valuable goods.

During one of his late-night heists, he had a thought, a realization. *I'm really good at this, and I know why. My whole life I've been quietly sneaking around, hiding, doing my best to avoid people. How ironic, my years of social phobia have trained me to be an expert thief. Finally, something good has come from my decades of misery.*

•

Two years after the mayor's decree, His Honor received an award for his efforts at ridding the city of what he called "disgusting, homeless bums and low-life criminals."

Leaning back in his recliner, Steven relaxed to read the paper. He chuckled as he read of the mayor's self-proclaimed success at cleansing the city of "street scum." Steven thought, *His Honor wouldn't be smiling if he knew he'd unwittingly transformed one of those disgusting bums into a wealthy, low-life criminal.*

Steven was living in a modest, two-thousand-square-foot home in the suburbs of the city. He had legally purchased his home, his furniture, his car, nearly everything he had, with cash—the cash he'd received from his fence. One notable exception, in honor of his old friend, was a pair of eighteen-karat gold candlesticks adorning his fireplace mantle. He'd stolen those.

He missed William, the man who'd led him to his new career and wealth. He longed to talk with him but knew, considering his friend's garrulous nature, it would be too risky. Despite their friendship, Steven was afraid William wouldn't be able to resist talking about his homeless bunk-mate turned thief and how he had taught him the trade.

Steven Hunter walked from his family room to his backyard. He needed to clean his patio in preparation for an afternoon visit from friends invited over for a pool party and barbecue.

As he vacuumed his pool, he thought of how wonderfully his life had changed over the past few years. Being so happy, he rarely thought of his prior social isolation. Steven's regrets over his wasted years had been erased by new friends, new relationships, and a busy, productive life. He could scarcely believe how many close friends he'd made since leaving the street—each of them trustworthy, all of them criminals.

For security, none of his friends were told his real name. He went by first name only. In the city's underworld, Steven was known as William, not Bill, just William.

Carl and Lynnette

ynnette was birthed in a trailer, outback Georgia, 1945. Her parents done chose Lynnette Rose for a girl, Robert Ray for a boy. The doctor come out from town for the delivery. There was complications. Years later, Daddy told Lynnette somethin' 'bout Mama havin' a small birthin' canal, a tiny pelvis with some kinda bad proportions. Lynnette's mama, Ginny, passed that very night, right there in the trailer. Doctor did all he could but there was just too much bleedin'.

Lynnie's daddy, Carl, took his wife's death real hard. Him and Ginny known each other since they was youngins: same age, same schoolin', married at sixteen, tried for years to have babies. Finally happened when they was in their late thirties; that's when Lynnette come along. Ginny's dyin' left a huge hole in Carl's heart. He filled that hole with Lynnette.

The neighbor folk couldn't hardly believe how Carl took to carin' for that baby. Seemed like Ginny's motherin' instincts done passed right over to her husband. Customers at the gas station could see how it was. They'd talk 'bout what a good man Carl was, he bein' so good at fatherin' and such. They'd recollect what he was like before that baby and how much he done changed after she come along. Lynnie was everythin' to Carl, and Carl was everythin' to Lynnette.

Carl's daughter was a precocious little thing, always years ahead of the other kids. She'd carry on with the station customers, talkin' just like an adult. Some come by just for the pleasure a chattin' with her. She was such a sweetheart.

Lynnie was a whiz in school, straight A pupil right from grade one. Her daddy drove her to school every mornin' and picked her up every afternoon. He'd close the station twice a day for those trips. Carl knew the school bus driver, and he known her to be a drinker. Weren't no way he was puttin' his baby on that bus. Best to close up shop than to trust his darlin' to that woman.

Lynnie was always rememberin' her daddy's birthday. Money was too darn scarce to be buyin' him a present, but she always give him a card. Havin' no way a gettin' to town for a store-bought card, she'd make one from notepaper, all pictured up with crayon drawin's. When she was 'bout ten years age, she fancied givin' her daddy a special birthday gift.

The rest facility in the station was real dirty. Lynnie fixed on makin' that a fine, clean room for her daddy. That room's sink was covered with greasy dirt, same was the door 'n' door handle. The floor was right filthy, and the toilet bowl was all stained up, rusty like, from well-water. Lynnie went to workin' on it the day right prior to her father turnin' forty-five. She cleaned all the greasy spots with Dutch Cleanser, made the mirror to sparklin', usin' vinegar 'n' water, washed that grimy floor and scrubbed all those rust stains out with a Brillo pad. Just 'bout the time she was finishin', her father come knockin' at the door. Lynnie cracked that door, just a bit.

"I'm sorry, Daddy, but you can't come in."

"I can't? Why not, honey?"

Lynnie smiled. "Cause you just can't right now. It's a secret."

Carl, seein' the smile on his daughter's face, reckoned there was nothin' bad goin' on in there. Anyhow, the chance a Lynnie doin' somethin' outta line was nigh impossible. Carl, quiet like, left and walked over to the trailer to use the toilet.

Next mornin', Lynnie made certain her daddy went in the station before takin' her to school. Carl found a big "Happy Birthday" sign posted on the restroom door. That room was spotless with clean towels hangin' over the sink and a glass vase a wildflowers sittin' on back the toilet. It was his best birthday gift ever. Carl never forgot that.

•

When Lynnie was in grade six, her daddy let her work the station's cash register after school. Carl Conroy's place was the only fuel for a good ten-mile-stretch a' road, and business was right steady. Lynnie tendered cigarettes, soda 'n' candy, and some grocery items like bread 'n' milk. She could make change in her head quicker than her daddy could workin' on a scratch pad.

Her help give Carl needed time for fixin' automobiles in the garage. He was a good, honest mechanic who always charged a fair price and never fixed nothin' didn't need fixin'. His customers knew that, and they was right loyal.

Carl liked havin' Lynnie round the station as long as she was careful. She wasn't never allowed in the garage; he was strict 'bout that. He wasn't takin' no chance on her gettin' hurt. When she was a bit older, he did let her tend to the pumps. Lynnie loved pumpin' gas, and her customers loved watchin' such a young girl handle those big machines. They got a kick outta that.

Lynnie was good at it, too—good at pumpin' gas. She was always attentive and courteous to her customers.

In all her years workin' those pumps, she had but one run-in. Carl clearly recollected that—that day some big shot come by the station for a tank a petrol. Lynnie was 'bout twelve years age back then. Carl was in the garage when some man pulled in, an out-a-towner on his way to Atlanta, drivin' one a' those big luxury sedans.

Lynnie, excited 'bout seein' that car, run out to care for her customer. Carl still recollects her callin' out, "I'll get it, Daddy." The driver, dressin' in a suit 'n' tie, looked to be somethin' important, maybe some kinda lawyer. He told Lynnie to "fill her up."

When she finished pumpin', she accidental like dribbled a bit of gasoline down the side a that shiny black automobile. Carl, hearin' a commotion outside, went to see what was goin' on. He found Lynnie sittin' in the dirt, lookin' real scared, with that man yellin', "You little hillbilly trash. Look what you did to my car."

When that fella bent over, lookin' to slap Lynnie, he was cut short by a mighty grip on the scruff of his neck. Before he knew it, his face was smashin' down on the trunk a that luxury vehicle. When Carl let 'im go, he run like a rabbit to his car door, yanked it open, and sped away—gas cap still sittin' on top the pump.

Carl hadn't no concern 'bout him not payin' for the gas. Gettin' him away from Lynnie was all he wanted. He can still recall how terrified his girl looked, sittin' there on the ground, all teary eyed. Later on, she told Carl she was mostly scared 'cause of her daddy's anger, not the man yellin'. Carl never forgot that.

•

By age thirteen, Lynnie could darn near run the station by herself, course not the garage. She knew better than to get caught messin' round in there. Even so, cause she was so darn smart, she knew just 'bout everythin' there was to know 'bout cars, just from watchin' 'n' talkin' 'bout it with her daddy.

Lynnette seemed to pass from a little girl to a young woman overnight. One day Carl was watchin' her work the register. She was wearin' a T-shirt 'n' jeans and was leanin' over the counter. He could see his baby wasn't no child no more, and it made 'im kinda sad. His daughter was growin' up fast, and he weren't sure he knew how to handle it. He was wishin' he could talk to Ginny. She'd know what to do—what to do 'bout the female things.

Unknown to Carl, Lynnette was feelin' just as awkward 'bout that as he was, but she was too embarrassed to talk 'bout it. Carl worried on this for a time, wonderin' what to do. What he 'ventually did to help Lynnie was a beautiful thing.

On a Saturday mornin' before Lynnette was up, her father put a Sears-Roebuck catalog on the station counter. Later on, she found that catalog opened to the pages on ladies' underthings, sittin' with a note.

> Lynnie,
>
> You can pick out what you like. This afternoon we can drive into town and fix ya up with clothes and what else you need.
>
> I love you, honey,
> Daddy

That note brought tears to that girl's eyes. She so loved her daddy for his kindness. She could feel his embarrassment in havin' to deal with this, and she loved him all the more for it. Lynnette never forgot that.

•

Lynnie flew right through middle school, and 'fore Carl knew it, his girl was in high school. Lynnette truly found her place there in high school; she loved it. She spent less time workin' the station and more time in the trailer studyin'. She hankered for knowledge, readin' every book she could get.

Knowin' her father was missin' havin' her round the station, Lynnie done her best to help him by workin' a few hours each day after school. She was real careful 'bout keepin' her clothes clean and not gettin' her hands dirty. Carl was glad to see her considerin' her looks that way.

Sometimes Lynnie'd be workin' 'til evenin'. If so, she'd study harder that night, even after her daddy was sleepin'. She'd switch on her nightlight and read 'til late in the mornin'. This was her secret. If her daddy known 'bout that, he woulda made her quit helpin' him. He knew her studies was more important than her workin' the station.

As years passed and Lynnette grew into a beautiful young lady, Carl reckoned he had to change his ways a bit, so as to not make his girl feel uneasy. Him and her had always been close, lots a hugs 'n' kisses. Lynnie seen the change in her daddy's affection. His hugs was less tight and his kisses was less regular. She understood and appreciated that.

Carl had another important bother 'bout his eye-catchin' daughter. He was hell-bent on keepin' her away from the local boys, most he knew to be no-count rednecks. One a those boys got fresh with Lynnie back when she was 'bout fifteen.

She was workin' the register when Carl come in from the garage and seen a boy reachin' 'cross the counter at his daughter. Lynnie jumped back when that boy tried slippin' his hand in her blouse. Later on, she told her daddy how thankful she was, hearin' his voice 'n' all.

"You git, boy! Git outta here, now!"

That punk boy turned to Carl and seein' him as a thin, old man, shouted back, "Says who? You gonna throw me out, old-timer?"

Carl smelled alcohol on that youngin. He knew him to be from a white trash family and he'd seen 'im round the station before. That boy was a sight big for his age, standin' 'bout six feet.

Size wasn't no matter to Carl. His glare was 'nough to scare that kid to runnin' for the door with old Carl right behind. Soon as they was out a Lynnie's sight, Carl set a hard kick to that no-count's rear. Done shot him right out the door and face down in the dirt. That boy jumped up and run away. Not Lynnie nor her daddy ever seen him again.

•

In high school, Lynnette shined in every way: academics, athletics, and after-school clubs. Senior year she was elected class president. Lynnie never thought much of her perfect grades 'n such a small, country school. Bein' number one in a class of thirty-two wasn't nothin' special, not like her valedictorian speech was. It was real special, a big event for her, her daddy, and her little town.

Her speech wasn't nothin' ordinary. It wasn't 'bout nuclear bombs. It wasn't 'bout the iron curtain. It wasn't 'bout all the poor folk in Georgia. No, it was somethin' different, and parts of her speech was written up in the back pages of newspapers all 'cross the South. Her speech was 'bout the very best thing in her life. Her speech was 'bout her father.

•

Lynnie's testin' scores in high school got her in the best college school in the land. She was goin' to Harvard on what they called a full-ride, all expenses paid. There was no way Carl coulda been more proud a his girl. Carl was right proud, and Lynnie was right terrified.

She had to go away and leave behind everythin' she ever known. Most hurtful of all, she had to leave her daddy. She had to leave his hugs, his reassurin' love, and his wonderful way. She was gonna miss all the little things—things like washin' his work clothes and doin' his cookin'. She was gonna miss his familiar scent—his smell a Old Spice, mixed with sweat, motor oil, and cigarettes.

She knew she was havin' to part with the man who been her strength, her sanctuary, her life—the wiry, gray-haired man who done took her from a fillin' station trailer baby all the way to Harvard.

She had no way out. No more tendin' the station, no more handlin' the register, no more doin' his bookkeepin'. Thinkin' 'bout it broke her heart. In all her eighteen years, she never been more than thirty miles from home. Now she was headin' for Boston, Massachusetts.

•

In early part a September 1963, a Greyhound bus pulled up front a Conroy's Garage. Lynnette had all her necessary items jammed in a single, tweed suitcase. She was wearin' a blue sundress and white sandals. She and her daddy walked from the trailer to the dirt road out front.

The bus doors swung open, and the driver, lookin' to be a middle-aged colored man, stepped out. "I'll be takin' that bag for ya, miss." Lynnette, outside her sadness, forced a smile as she handed him her bag. "Thank you, sir." When she turned to facin' her father, her eyes welled up with tears and a tight feelin' grew in her throat. The two a them was silent, standin' just inches apart when those tears started rollin' down Lynnie's cheeks.

"You know I love you, Daddy." "I sure do, honey."

"You know I have to go now, don't you?"

"Course I do. It's a wonderful thing, Lynnie. It's what I been hopin' for all these years, seein' ya go to college 'n' all."

"I know that, Daddy. I'll write every day."

"No, ya won't. I don't need that, honey. You're gonna have lots a workin' to do in college. Don't you be wastin' no time writin' to me."

"It's not a waste of time."

"You can write me once'd a month. That'll be plenty."

"Daddy, I'll want you to visit. I'm sure I'll have a lot of new friends, and I'll want them to see what a special person you are."

Carl thought 'bout that. He'd be a misfit, and he knew he could never go. In his heart, he knew she wouldn't be wantin' him there—garage man, done quit schoolin' at grade eight. "Sure, baby, we'll see." Carl felt a burnin' need to leave. He hugged his daughter. "Goodbye, hon; you be safe now. I know you're gonna make me proud." Lynnie's head fell when her father let go a his hug.

"I don't want to go, Daddy. I'm scared."

Carl spoke a stern but kind voice. "I think most everybody's scared, least at first. Being scared might be a good thing, Lynnie. I suspect it makes a person try harder; it keeps 'em outta trouble. You go now; you're gonna be fine."

He gently steered her to the door of the bus and added, "I'm gonna be fine, too. Don't you be frettin' none 'bout me." Then he, sharp like, turned and walked away, leavin' Lynnie standin' there, arms at her side, cryin'.

She felt a tap on her shoulder.

"'Scuse me, miss. We's got to go. I got a bus full a people waitin' here."

Lynnette climbed the stairs of the bus. She sat far back as she could, wantin' to see her father and the station long as possible.

Carl never looked back. He had a brake job waitin'. It was time to get to work. As he was nearin' the garage, he stopped. He wanted to turn for one last glimpse of his daughter, but he couldn't. A tear fell from his chin and, silent like, disappeared in the dry dust at his feet.

•

As Carl reckoned, he got a letter every three, four days. Lynnie was havin' the time a her life, and he was real glad to hear it. Regardless his bein' lonely and heartsick, he wanted the best for his daughter. He had to be strong. Life was gonna be different now that Lynnie was gone. He was gonna have to make it all by his lonesome.

In middle October, to Carl's sadness, an invitation come.

Hi Daddy,

It's parents' weekend next month, just before Thanksgiving. That's when all the students invite their parents to visit. I can't wait to have my friends meet you.

You're such a wonderful man. I know they'll all love you.

With love,
Lynnie

Carl was right shocked. Lynnie been there for more than a month and shoulda known by now that her daddy could never be fittin' in. He reckoned she must not be thinkin' straight—figured his small-town girl wasn't seein' things for what they was. *How can she want all those rich folk meetin' me, her gas-pumpin' father? It don't make no kinda sense.*

A further letter come one week later.

Daddy,

    I've made your bus reservation. You'll only have to close the station for a few days. I can't wait to see you.

All my love, your daughter,
Lynnie

Carl broke right into a cold sweat readin' that letter. *What's wrong with that girl?* He was so sure she'd be too darn ashamed to have him out there. He thought his girl must not know where she come from. She was so smart 'n all, with book smarts, but she didn't know the way people was. He'd have to bide his time. She'd be comin' to her senses if he waited a bit.

Bein' mighty relieved when no letter come for two weeks, Carl reckoned his baby was finally figurin' it out—figurin' her daddy was not the kinda man to be visitin' Harvard. Just when he was feelin' good 'bout the whole thing, a box come in the mail. It was a long, shallow box, return address: Lynnette Conroy, Cambridge, Massachusetts.

Carl, slow like, took the brown wrappin' off the box and opened it. An envelope sat on top some tissue paper.

Hello Daddy,

    I'm so excited about seeing you next week. I've enclosed your bus tickets.

    I hope I guessed right on the sizes.

Your loving daughter,
Lynnie

Carl pulled back on the tissue paper findin' a dark brown sport coat, white shirt, yellow tie and khaki dress pants. A fancy pair a real leather shoes was sittin' at the bottom. He looked at that box a clothin', shook his head, took up the letter 'n' tickets, and slid the box 'neath his bed. "How can I tell her I won't be comin'?"

Couple, three days later, Carl pulled that box from under his bed, figurin' he might well see how his outfit looked, even if he wouldn't be usin' it. He thought 'bout his old dressin'-up suit hangin' in the closet—hadn't wore it since Ginny's funeral—outgrown it years ago. He dressed down to his underwear and, not wantin' to soil his new duds, went to the sink to wash his hands.

Everythin' fit, even the shoes. Carl looked in his bureau mirror and couldn't help from smilin'. "I look pretty good, darn good for an old boy from Georgia." *An old boy from Georgia,* he thought. *I ain't no boy, I'm a man—a man who's gonna let his bein' 'fraid a those people hurt the most important thing in my life.*

He sat in his chair to ponder 'bout it. *Lynnie's happiness is the important thing, much more important than my fearin' bein' embarrassed 'bout myself.* He walked to the bureau and picked up the bus tickets.

•

Few days on, a Greyhound bus come to a stop in front a the station. Carl, wearin' his new clothes, walked out carryin' a quilted satchel. The same colored fella who done picked up Lynnie took Carl's bag and helped him aboard. Carl took the very first seat, waitin' on the driver to finish packin' his belongings.

Lookin' out the window at his station, Carl started havin' an odd feelin'. The station wasn't lookin' right. It was run down, lots more than he always 'visioned it. He was there every day, comin' and goin', drivin' Lynnie back 'n forth to school, and he never really seen the place.

The *C* in Conroy's Garage was hangin' crooked, and the pumps was lookin' old, rusted, and outta date. He'd done forgot 'bout the two junk cars and rusty oil drums sittin' out back. The place needed lots a cleanin' and paintin'.

Carl plucked a pen and pad a paper from his pocket to make a things-to-do list. Just when he started writin', the bus jerked forward and pulled off in a cloud a dust, blockin' his sight a the station. He was gonna have to finish that list when he got back home.

The bus was swayin' down the same old dirt road Carl been down a hundred times past. His view, ridin' high in that big bus, give the countryside a whole new look. He seen things he'd not saw before, and to his surprise, it give him some excitement 'bout the trip.

He was taken back by the beauty a the land with its blaze a colors glowin' 'neath a bright blue sky. There was green, tree-covered mountains with paths a orange, Georgia clay runnin' down the hillsides. Though he'd been goin' up and down that same road for years, Carl never truly seen how pretty it was.

In his entire life, he never been outta the state a Georgia. He seen the ocean once, years back, when his mama and daddy took their youngins to Savannah. That was the longest trip he ever done.

Lookin' down to the floor, Carl saw his shoes to be covered with dust. He snatched a napkin layin' next seat over, wiped his shoes to a shine, and gazed back to the blank notepad sittin' on his lap. Just the thought a doin' all that repairin' at the station left him tired. Lookin' up, takin' in more a the countryside and feelin' his excitement grow, he thought, *Maybe I might not have to do all that repair work.*

Carl thought, *I own the station outright. I never hardly thought a sellin', but right now it's seemin' like a good idea. Lotsa folk was offerin' to buy in the past. Sellin' would be easy, but then what? What would I do without the station, 'specially now that Lynnie's gone? Lynnie, all that way out there in Boston, out on the shore a that Atlantic Ocean. Seems darn far for gettin' to on a two-day bus ride.*

Carl started thinkin' 'bout the ocean and his trip to Savannah. When they was there, his family gone down to a pier where he recollected seein' a man catch a big ocean fish. He thought 'bout the charter fishin' boats he seen, those boats with their powerful inboard motors. He'd read 'bout those high-power engines in a few a his auto-repair magazines. Those ocean boats used them big Chevy 'n' Chrysler automobile engines. He could work on those; he was sure of it.

He never had much time for fishin', and he never done no boatin'. Still, Carl always figured it would be real good fun. He thought, *Maybe I could try fishin' durin' my time in Boston.*

Lookin' back outta the huge windshield a the bus, he saw they was in new territory. Carl never seen this part a the state and he couldn't hardly believe how thrillin' it was. Most of all, he couldn't quit thinkin' 'bout how much he'd love workin' on those boat motors.

Carl thought he might well get a boat for hisself if he sold the station. Then he thought better 'n that. *I'm gettin' right carried away. Sellin' the station would be a might big move. Maybe a might big mistake!* He was gonna have to reflect a bit, real careful like.

As that bus drove on through South Carolina, Carl fell to sleepin'. He woke a couple hours later, hearin' the driver announcin' their entry to the state a North Carolina. His head, cleared by that nap, led him to start to more thinkin' 'bout his life. Some reason, after restin' 'n' all, it was seemin' more right than ever to consider movin' on. *I can do it. I'm a man, not no boy. There's no reason me spendin' the rest a my days down in Georgia alone.*

Carl was right surprised' 'bout how good it felt, cogitatin' 'bout leavin'. Still, he knew he was gonna have to do some real hard considerin' 'bout this when he was back home. *Home*, he thought. *Don't seem like home no more with Lynnie gone.*

The bus cruised on through the afternoon 'n' night. Carl slept most a the trip.

•

Old Carl Conroy had quite a weekend in Boston. He couldn't understand it; all those folks was downright polite, treatin' him to be a gentleman. Him and Lynnie had a darn good time attendin' a party the school put on for the parent folk. Carl could scarcely believe how much drinkin' those rich folk did. He was no drinker, but he did help hisself to one glass a beer, just one. All in all, Carl was right dumbfounded 'bout the number a nice folk he come across at that gatherin'. He never forgot that.

Lynnie showed her daddy round Boston; he was taken by the sights, amazed there was so many college schools in that town. Carl was 'specially keen on seein' all the historical places from the olden times. He recollected learnin' 'bout some a them durin' his schoolin' years. He thought 'bout how he near made himself sick, frettin' over his trip to Boston. *I was worried so much 'bout comin' here. Now I'm havin' the time a my life.*

•

Back in Georgia, it didn't take Carl no time to make his judgment on all he done thought 'bout on that bus. Sellin' the station was easy, just like he figured. He sold it right quick, makin' a good bit a money— more than 'nough to start his new life.

'Bout three, four years later, Lynnette and her fiancé, a young college professor, gone on their first deep sea fishin' trip, just off the coast a Massachusetts. Lynnie caught a biggun, a twenty-pound striped bass, right there on her daddy's boat.

Some time on, Carl's granddaughters gave their Papa Carl some special birthday cards. Their mama told 'em what kinda cards he liked. They weren't no store-bought cards. No, they was special cards made from notepaper, all pictured up with crayon drawins'. Carl never forgot that.

Basement Monsters

I never should have turned out the light, but that's water over the dam, and there's no turning back.

It all started when I was old enough to hang out in the basement by myself, about eight or nine years of age. We had a nice basement my father had remodeled. One side was a recreation room with a pool table, a fireplace, a sofa, and a twin-size bed. The other side, which could only be entered through a door at the bottom of the steps, was the utility room. My dad had installed a bathroom with a shower on that side. He had a workroom down there, too, with a workbench against the wall across from the furnace and hot water heater. The washer, dryer, and wash tub were at the other end of the room.

The space beneath the steps had been enclosed into what my mother referred to as the fruit cellar, something I never understood. She never stored any fruit in there. It must have come from her days growing up in the woods of New Brunswick, long before refrigeration. The fruit cellar was a small room, no more than six by eight feet in size.

I don't recall spending time in the basement when I was really young, less than five, and I can't remember if I was frightened by the basement's dark spaces back then, but I bet I was. When I was a bit older, nine to ten, my buddies from the neighborhood would stop by to shoot pool or mess around with chemicals and other crap in the fruit cellar, my friends being the only real fruits in the place.

I have two siblings, an older brother and a little sister who's a real sweetheart. My brother built shelves and a counter-top in the fruit cellar, using it as an electronics laboratory. He liked to fiddle around with radios and televisions, seeing if he could electrocute himself.

That was common back in the late fifties and early sixties, not electrocution, but messing around with radios and old televisions. Later, after my brother left for college, I threw all his electronics junk in the trash and moved in with something more exciting and potentially more lethal, my chemistry set.

My friends and I liked to hang out in the cellar making stink bombs, messin' around with hydrochloric acid, and heating chemicals with my Bunsen burner. After we got bored with stink bombs and acid, we moved on to the real thing, pipe bombs.

Ceaselessly working to construct a pipe bomb that would actually explode was an exercise in futility. Years later, I realized the federal government had banned the sale of the compound essential to an amateur chemist's attempts at manufacturing gun powder. That compound was sodium nitrate, a substance not included in my Sears-Roebuck chemistry set.

So, our bombs, sans sodium nitrate, rather than explode, would fizz like a gigantic flare, shooting a myriad of colored sparks to the sky as we ran around screaming with delight. Despite their failure to go BOOM, the flares were pretty cool. Not only were they fun to watch, but you could do other stuff with 'em—stuff like jamming one under a neighbor's car tire to watch it melt rubber. We'd anxiously await the finale when the tire exploded with a big BANG.

I'm getting off track and should return to the point of this story—Basement Monsters.

•

In the evening, after my friends had gone home, the basement took on new, frightening characteristics. It could scare the livin' crap outta me. After dark, I'd often mess around on the utility side of the basement, dangerously close to the furnace.

Our furnace was a big, hulking thing, not one of the compact models you'd find today. It was an enormous, brown, sheet metal contraption that looked like a gigantic lunch box—a lunch box with huge ducts and pipes shootin' out of it. It stood about five feet high, three feet wide, and five to six feet long.

I'd hang out at my dad's workbench, screwin' around with his tools, especially his power tools, frequently turning toward the furnace to make sure the monsters weren't sneakin' out from the spooky, dark area behind. During the day, with sunlight coming through the basement windows, I was fine. Only at night would things get really creepy.

I'm familiar with the inside of that furnace. When I was a little kid, my father invited me to accompany him to change the furnace filter. He thought I might enjoy learning about the inner workings of a natural gas heating system. Opening a metal plate door, my dad revealed a two-foot by two-foot passage into the back of that giant lunch box.

Looking through the hatch to the bottom of the furnace, he said, "See those pipes down there, son? That's where the gas flows." Pointing to rows of small, cuplike flanges, each with a center hole, lined across the top of every pipe, he said, "See those whatchamacallits? That's where the flames shoot out to warm our house in the winter." He followed with, "Those little doodads are the reason our fuckin' heating bill's so high, especially since your mother insists on keepin' the goddamn thermostat set at a cool, comfortable, eighty-four degrees."

He locked the hatch, after which I thanked him for the lesson on forced-air heating. I was particularly pleased he had cursed so freely in my presence, using the real F word, instead of the modified "frickin'" F word.

Since my father was so blatantly free with his language in front of his seven-year-old son, I assumed he was giving me permission to speak in a similar way. Soon after, I altered my vocabulary, occasionally throwing in a new verb or adjective, saying such things as "Fuck this" and "Fuck that" and "Fuck you" and, my favorite, "Go fuck yourself" every half-hour or so.

•

Back to the monsters. Leaving the workroom to go upstairs for the night was the worst part of being in the basement. I'd take a deep breath, pull the cord hanging from the overhead, bare light bulb, and run like a rabid monkey to the other side of the basement, the recreation room, praying to God as I went, hoping I'd remembered to leave the game room light on.

If that light was on, I'd stop for a breather before switching it off and then burst up the steps, knowing for certain one or more of the Basement Monsters were close behind, just inches away, groping toward me, trying to grab me by the throat and drag me down to the depths, to their lair, most likely behind the furnace, where I would be devoured like one of those frickin' huge submarine sandwiches guaranteed to satisfy a hundred or more starving party guests.

If they didn't catch me, and thank God, they never did, I'd soon reach sanctuary at the top landing, which was illuminated by a ceiling light. I'd immediately stop to nonchalantly enter the kitchen as if I were as slick as Cool Hand Luke. Paul Newman was the man back then.

Sometimes, when I was in the basement and my mother was upstairs in the kitchen, she'd call out with what I hated to hear, something like, "Remember to turn the lights off, honey. We don't wanna be wastin' electricity now, do we?" I hated that shit.

•

One of the other spooky basement spots was under that damn bed. The twin bed, elevated about six inches from the floor, had a foreboding, shadowy darkness beneath. The bed, quite close to the pool table, often functioned as a sofa when my friends and I were playin' eight ball. Once again, Paul Newman's *The Hustler* comes to mind. All we lacked to be as cool as Paul was a Scotch on the rocks and a pack of Lucky's.

I wouldn't go near that bed when I was alone in the basement. Visions of monster paws, flyin' out from under the box springs, grabbing me by the ankle and dragging me down, induced me to give the bed wide berth, never getting closer than four or five feet, purposely detouring to the far side of the pool table to avoid walking past the bed and the dark monster cave below.

Another prohibited location was behind the basement couch, which was against the rec room wall, creating an eerie, dark area behind. No way on earth was I gonna sit on that couch after nightfall, truly believing some long, hairy arms would reach up from behind, grabbing me by the head, claws digging into my scalp, pulling me over the back of the couch to be torn limb from limb and eaten alive.

For terror-inducing creepiness, second only to the furnace, was the bathroom shower. Through my entire childhood, I took only one shower in that bathroom, and I lived in that house for sixteen years.

As I've previously said, my dad designed and constructed the basement bathroom—toilet and shower included. The shower was sort of a concrete block torture chamber, which my demure mother later painted in a color she referred to as titty pink.

She also, because of the chamber's small dimensions, put a sign outside, just above the shower curtain, reading, "Claustrophobics Beware!" She told me it was a jab at my father for making the damn shower so small.

To my chagrin, my dad never finished the job of putting one of those covers, the metal plate doo-hickey with holes drilled in it, over the drain. Hence, as a mere child, I was exposed to an open, four-inch-diameter pipe in the center of the shower floor. At age ten, I had my one and only experience in my father's pride, his basement bathroom.

•

Having little experience at showering, I positioned my little, snow-white body beneath the shower head before adjusting the water temperature. With excited anticipation, I turned the lever.

My mother, upstairs making my lunch, heard my screeching cries and whimpers as jets of ice-cold water quickly turned to pulsations of scalding-hot bullets. I screamed, "Holy Mother of God," and leapt from the shower, dancing around the bathroom floor to cool off.

To this day, I remember my mother calling out, "Sweetheart, are you all right?"

I didn't reply. She yelled louder, "What the hell's goin' on down there, you little shit?"

I yelled back, "I'm fine, Ma. Don't worry about it." Under my breath, I said, "As if she really gives a fuck."

Cautiously adjusting the water temp, I stepped back in the shower. Forgetting about the open pipe, I unwittingly put my toes directly down the drain hole.

Gasping with horror, I pulled my foot out, expecting to find chewed-off, bloody stumps instead of toes. To my relief, my toes were still there, wiggling away.

With disconcerting anxiety, I finished my shower having recurrent visions of giant hermit crabs crawling out from the drain, snapping my feet off with enormous pinchers.

In addition, my wild imaginings of Basement Monsters, the existence of which I believe to be an indisputable fact, went on as I pictured a huge, furry arm, shootin' out of the pipe, draggin' me down to the depths of the city's sewer system.

But I'll tell you what finally got to me, what kept me from ever using that shower again. It was something that honestly did come out of that drain.

Now you may think I'm overreacting like some impetuous little kid, but I don't think so. When that horrid, slimy, zucchini -sized centipede crawled out from that pipe, I said, "Okay, that's it; I've had enough."

Flinging my body outta the shower, I crashed, soaking wet, to the bathroom floor. Forcing myself up, I wrapped a skimpy towel around my waist, lest my mother embarrass me with some comment about by my tiny, hairless genitals, saying something like, "Honey, what a cute little package you have!"

I ran upstairs to the kitchen, screaming as I approached my old lady. "Listen, Ma, a kid's gotta draw the line somewhere, and I'm drawin' it right here. Monsters or no monsters, I just don't feel good about this whole thing." I emphatically bellowed, "Sorry, I just can't do it!"

My mother asked, "Do what, honey?"

"I can't... I refuse to take a shower in that fuc... uh, lousy shower with no drain cover."

After telling her of the centipede encounter, she said, "Sweetie, I'm sure you're exaggerating."

To which I responded, "Oh yeah, exaggerating, huh? Well then, I invite you to go down there and wrestle that freakish mutant back into the drain. I'm just not up to it today."

I was more than a little pissed about the oversized multiped darting around my bare feet, so pissed that I openly criticized my father in front of my mother, something I'd never done.

My state of shock from the centipede attack must have left me disoriented, causing me to lose all sense of reason as I addressed my mother, who had yet to learn of my father giving me permission to use what had become my favorite word. I blurted out, "Dad leaves the drain cover off, what a fuckin' dumbass!"

I recall a blur, followed by indescribable pain as the palm of my mother's right hand made contact with my left cheek. Her slap, delivered so accurately and with such force, sent me airborne, knocking me right out of my bath towel as my skinny, naked body crumpled to the kitchen floor.

I lay there moaning, spread-eagle on the floor, anticipating an ambulance ride to the emergency room to have stat X-rays of my cervical spine, when my mother, showing her deep level of concern, said, "Honey, what a cute little package you have!"

•

So, that's how it was with the Basement Monsters. Even years later, when I was thirteen years old, a full-fledged teenager, I thought I was the only one, the only guy my age who was still tearing around the basement like a hyena, screaming up the steps for fear of being ripped apart.

Not literally screaming, I'm using the verb as an act of high-speed running, in place of calling-out screaming, which I'd never have done, lest my mother hear me and later tell my father, saying something like, "The Basement Monsters were after him again." After which they'd both chuckle, and my father would spout off with, "I can't believe any son of mine can be such a pussy!"

As I've said, I was convinced I was the only one my age still afraid of Basement Monsters. That is until the night I caught my brother, my BIG brother, no less, flying up the steps like a rabbit in heat, screeching to a halt when he reached the landing, casually climbing the last two steps to the kitchen. Thank God, I just happened to be in the right place at the right time, sitting at the kitchen table.

I instantly surmised the situation, deducing the only logical explanation for his behavior—the Basement Monsters were after him, too! I couldn't have been more pleased. My older brother, *What a serendipitous observation*, I thought as I looked him straight in the eye and asked, "Did they almost get you?"

Blushing with embarrassment, mortified I'd caught him, and acting as though he had no idea of what I was talking about, he said, "You little fuck-moron, why aren't you in bed?" That was a night to remember. I felt fully vindicated.

A year or so later, a while after my fourteenth birthday, I was alone in the basement workroom, tearing apart my sister's bicycle, when the room's only light bulb flickered and went out.

Horrified, standing in the dark, just a few feet from the furnace, I took off like a bottle rocket, tripping over everything in my path as I tore for the stairway, cartwheeling up the steps, and falling flat on my face at the landing. Concerned I was still within eyeshot of the monsters downstairs, I crawled up to the kitchen floor, where I collapsed in a heap of trembling flesh.

I lay there, staring at the ceiling, counting my blessings, thanking God along with anyone else who came to mind: my parents, my siblings, my aunts, uncles and cousins, my hockey coach, even my smelly janitor friend from my old grade school, thinking each of them had at least once mentioned me in their prayers, invoking God to protect me from the massive jaws of the Basement Monsters, requesting divine intervention to keep all inhuman creatures at bay.

Struggling to my feet from the floor, I reveled with joy, realizing my parents, brother, and little sister had already gone to bed and were not in the kitchen where they would have witnessed my blatant display of utter cowardice.

•

Despite my concern about Basement Monsters, I'd often spend hours alone in the dungeon, the basement, messin' around on woodworking projects and tearing apart lawn mower engines or anything else I could get my hands on. It was tough being alone in my innovation laboratory, so close to the furnace and the creepy spaces behind.

Eventually, I decided to prove it to myself, prove there were no monsters, prove I simply had a wild imagination and was acting like a frightened child. I was a teenager now, a fourteen-year-old. Centuries ago, a guy my age could have had a wife and family. It was time to be a man.

I devised a plan to demonstrate that Basement Monsters simply did not exist, they being a figment of my and my chicken-shit brother's imagination. To confirm my hypothesis, I would tough it out in the dark, the real dark, the pitch-black darkness of the basement workroom.

As my memory serves me, it was eleven thirty or so, eleven thirty at night. My parents and little sister had gone to bed and my brother was away at college. The work area was lit by a single light bulb with a string hanging down. I stood under the light, took a deep breath, and pulled the string. The basement was blacker than black; I couldn't see a thing. My imagination, or so I thought, took off. I was sure I heard something sliding toward me. Terrified, my heart nearly popping out of my mouth, I yanked the light cord. Nothing there, absolutely nothing.

Letting out a sigh of relief, I said to myself, *This is crazy. Now I'm imagining noises!* Taking another breath, I turned out the light, determined, even if I heard something, to stay there in the dark for at least one heart-stopping minute.

While counting in my head, one thousand one, one thousand two, one thousand three, I heard the noise again—shoosh, shoosh, shoosh. Something was sliding across the floor, I was sure of it. I stood firm, motionless, letting go of the light cord so I couldn't pull it. I noticed a musty smell, like moldy bread… THEN IT HAPPENED!

•

Before I give you further details on just what happened, I'd like to emphasize one salient point. That point is this: what I'm about to tell you is the absolute truth. This is not fiction; it is pure fact. I'll proceed.

IT HAPPENED! Something grabbed me from behind, squeezing my chest with a vice-like grip. A thought flashed through my head, *Man, I really do have a wild imagination.* But it wasn't my imagination. I felt long nails jabbing my chest as fur-covered paws pulled me off my feet. I screamed hysterically while being dragged slowly across the floor in complete blackness. I had no idea what it was or where it was taking me. I couldn't see a thing.

Hearing an odd sound, the metallic sound of a turning handle followed by the squeak of a rusty hinge, I screamed, "It's the furnace! For the love of God, not the furnace!"

Kicking and screaming, arms and legs flailing, I frantically grabbed wads of coarse, thick fur, helplessly trying to free myself from the monster's death grip, certain my terror would send my heart into a fatal arrhythmia. I heard the hatch close as I was tossed to the bottom of the furnace, landing on the gas pipes and flame flanges I'd seen years ago with my father.

Moments later, my screams, echoing through the interior of the furnace, were interrupted by voices. Someone was in the basement outside the furnace. I stopped yelling and listened. It was my parents, calling out for me. They were in the workroom, just a few feet away, searching in response to the blood-curdling screams they'd heard just moments before.

I was about to yell to them when a huge, leather-like paw came from behind, wrapping around my face and mouth, stifling all efforts to alert my parents.

It started talking to me. Not really talking, more like putting thoughts directly into my brain without a sound. The monster's thoughts were saying, *Settle down. Fighting is useless. You belong to me now!*

Frantically struggling to call to my parents, my voice squelched by the heavy paw gripping my mouth, I heard the heartbreaking sound of my parents leaving, climbing the basement steps.

The monster, again communicating that there was no escape, went on to convey its delight, its joy in having finally caught me, it having been secluded and lonely for so many years. In addition, it communicated it was time for it to move on, and it couldn't leave before finding a replacement, such as me.

The monster—I think I'll call it The Thing—The Thing, apparently sensing my parents had left, removed its paw from my mouth. I immediately yelled, "What did you tell me? You want me to replace you? Are you out of your mind?"

Its thoughts kept saying, *You can't get out. You'll never get out. Be glad you're still alive. Others aren't so lucky. You get to survive, to take over for me. You should be grateful.*

•

After two days of captivity, it was more apparent than ever that escape was impossible. I belonged to the The Thing. During my first two weeks in the furnace, The Thing taught me all it knew about basement monstering, telling me, via thought transmission, similar to ESP, how much fun I was going to have scaring the shit outta my little sister, maybe even my older brother.

In the Thing's opinion, terrifying young children was the highlight of any monster's life, more exciting than I could ever imagine. At the time, having no knowledge of what was about to happen, I wrote The Thing off as a delusional, psychotic creature with little understanding of who I was. However, shortly after, to my horror, strange things, physical things came about.

That evening, while sitting on the gas pipes of the furnace, an odd sensation spread over my body. Soon I was covered head to toe with thick fur. My nails lengthened into sharp claws as my arms retracted into short, leathery stumps with large, hairy paws and fat, sausage-like fingers. My legs shortened and widened; my ankles retracted and my feet morphed into broad, flat paddles with stubby, webbed toes.

My head started to shrink down and broaden out as my neck disappeared, leaving a hump-like, fur-covered mass above my shoulders. I could feel my mouth widening as my ears shrank away, leaving only holes in the side of my flattened-out skull. My mouth, extending from ear hole to ear hole, became a mammoth opening lined with thick, broad teeth, between which protruded an enormous tongue, roughly the size of one of those snow-sledding saucers, hanging from my mouth, dripping thick, gooey saliva.

Incredibly, I didn't mind becoming a monster; in fact, I enjoyed it. Just as The Thing had said, the further my body transformed, the more I delighted in the prospect of scaring young children senseless.

The Thing's thoughts explained that children were rarely, almost never captured. Basement Monsters, having such short, squatty legs with broad paddle feet and compact, stubby arms and paws, could barely walk, let alone catch horrified children, bolting around in a dark basement like a mongoose. He told me he'd never have captured me if I hadn't been so stupid as to stand in a pitch-black basement, ignoring the approaching sounds of his flat feet sliding across the floor.

I thought about it, thought how I'd been so ridiculous as to test myself, but it didn't matter anymore. I was amazingly content, pleased to be living in the furnace, anxiously anticipating my first late-night adventure, when I would terrify those foolish enough to venture down to the basement by themselves after dark.

Soon after my transformation, I thankfully acquired the ability to convey thoughts between myself and The Thing. I say thankfully because I had lost the ability to speak. My broad, gaping mouth couldn't make a sound. The Thing informed me I lacked vocal cords, an evolutionary laryngeal change designed to keep monsters from inadvertently giving themselves away by crying out or moaning to spook children.

I mentally asked the Thing why I'd never seen a trace of it during the many years I'd spent screwin' around in the basement. It told me it was because all monsters possess an innate sensitivity to light. Their bulging, blood-red eyes cannot tolerate even the slightest smidgen of illumination. When struck by light beams, they instantly disappear, becoming invisible within a microsecond.

The Thing thought to me, *It's an automatic reflex we've developed over the millennia. If a photon of light enters either of our eyes, it immediately signals the invisibility sequence. That's why no one's ever seen a basement monster. If there's any light, we're invisible, and if you're in total blackness, you can't see us, even if we're standing right next to you.*

I transmitted a thought, *What about all of this spit and drool dripping from our humongous tongues? Why didn't I see tracks of slime all over the basement floor?*

It thought a response, *That's a good question. I'm pleased to hear you're getting into your new role so well. The junk dripping from our tongues evaporates the instant it hits the floor. You needn't worry about telltale, salivary tracks following you on your nocturnal excursions.*

It communicated that its favorite hiding places were under the bed, behind the couch, in the fruit cellar, and of course, behind the furnace. I couldn't believe it. They were the exact places I'd feared so much. It explained why that was.

We have the ability to broadcast our location to children. It really adds to the enjoyment, knowing they sense your presence, being scared mindless.

To further my education, I enquired whether Basement Monsters ever went upstairs. It thought, *We're allowed upstairs, but it's difficult for me to climb the steps, so I rarely go.*

I responded, *If that's so, why am I so afraid of going to bed, diving in from three or four feet away, crashing to the mattress, horrified by the monsters I'm certain are hiding beneath, waiting to grab my feet, dragging me down to their den, where I'd be mauled beyond recognition, later dying in my mother's arms, she questioning whether the bloody mass of flesh she's holding is really her son, her cute little boy? I was sure one of you guys was under there, beneath my bed.*

It explained, *No, it's not us. The space under your bed is alligator jurisdiction. I try to stay away from those lousy reptiles—they stink!*

Alligators! I thought. *I knew it!*

Thinking about the time I caught my brother in the act, blasting up the basement steps with a look of pure panic, I thought, *Are adults afraid of the basement?*

It conveyed, *As humans age, they usually, but not always, lose susceptibility to a monster's thought transmissions. Generally, they can't sense our presence.*

I sent a question, *Are my parents ever frightened?*

It transmitted, *I don't know about your mom; she always leaves the lights on.*

What a hypocrite, I thought. *What about my dad? Certainly, he'd never be scared.*

The Thing countered, *Hey, I've seen your old man really scoot when the lights go out.*

I conveyed hysterical bursts of laughter, picturing my father scurrying around the basement like a chinchilla in a fur factory.

After completion of my training period, The Thing informed me it would be leaving soon. A moment later it thought, *Please excuse me for a minute. I have to send a transmission to our executive director of relocation.*

As its transmission concluded, I enquired where the director resided and where it, The Thing, was being sent. It told me the relocation executive lived in the sewers beneath Paris.

When I communicated my surprise, it informed me Basement Monsters are worldwide. I thought about that for a second, at which point it responded, *I picked up your thought. You were wondering about foreign countries having homes without basements. If there's no basement, we're assigned to the attic. Humans with neither a basement nor attic are the fortunate ones who get to live in peace.*

I asked where its new assignment was.

The Thing responded it was being sent to a basement in Texas, which it looked forward to since a warmer climate would mean shorter winters and less time spent in the raging inferno of an operating furnace.

That last thought raised some concern on my part, to which it responded, *Don't worry; It's not too bad. Our fur has a natural flame retardant. It does get a little toasty at times, especially when your mom's been messin' with the thermostat. But you'll get used to it.*

A few days later, considering its long journey to Texas, it thought it better get going. At three a.m., in the blacker-than-black of the night, after my parents and little sister had gone to bed, it was time for The Thing to leave. It thought to me, *Hey, it's been a real pleasure meetin' ya. I mean it. I have a long trip ahead of me. I gotta run, or should I say waddle, all the way to Texas.* It added, *You be sure to hold down the fort for me, okay, pal?*

I assured it I'd do my best, at which point it slowly crawled out of the furnace. I crawled out right behind to watch it leave, hearing its broad, flipper feet slapping on the steps as it slowly climbed to the landing. It passed right through the locked door as if it were wide open and waddled onto the driveway, where moonlight struck its eyes, initiating the invisibility sequence. In a fraction of a second it was gone but still there, strolling down the drive, invisible to the world.

•

Of course, my parents never found me, and I'm sure they've forgotten about me by now. They were probably a bit upset at first. My name and photo must have been plastered all over the newspapers: *Sweet, young, innovative boy vanishes from basement. Police in search of kidnapper. Parents heard horrible screams coming from basement. Investigators dumbfounded by lack of evidence. City prosecutor orders interrogation of parents.*

They probably had my picture on television, too—the network invoking viewers to pray for the life of a tender, lovely, highly intelligent young man.

I hope the police didn't accuse my mom and dad of anything serious, saying things like, *We know you two are irresponsible parents. We know about the dangerous chemicals and the pipe bombs. We know about you, sir, teaching your young son to swear like a drill sergeant, allowing him to use the F word in casual conversation.*

Yeah, we've interviewed some of your neighbors, Mr. and Mrs. Jackson, for instance. They told us your son liked to ride his bicycle by their house, smiling and waving, calling out to the elderly couple, "Hi, Mr. Jackson. Hi, Mrs. Jackson. Both of you should go fuck yourselves."

We also know you exposed your child to a dangerous, insect-infested drain pipe in a closet-like, claustrophobia-inducing, homemade shower. Centipedes are highly poisonous; you two must know that.

I can imagine the officers saying, *Yeah, we know that and more. The two of you better own up to this. Where's your son's body? Tell us now, and things will go much easier for both of you murdering bastards.*

My parents would likely say, *No, no, you don't understand, officers. We loved our boy.*

The police, shocked by that admission of guilt, would say, *You 'loved' your boy? Why are you using the past tense? Is your son gone?*

My parents, not the sharpest tools in the shed, and definitely not experts on grammar, would reply, *What? What does anything have to do with tents?*

The police, exasperated with their suspects' stupidity, would say, *Never mind. Let's move on.*

My parents would gratefully reply, *Yes, please, let's.*

The police would go on with, *We know your son was a real smart-ass. We know how difficult he must have been for you, why you probably wanted to get rid of him, even kill him.* My parents, feigning bewilderment, would reply, *What?! What are you talking about? You can't be serious?!*

The police might continue confronting my father. *Sir, we also know you're not the brightest bulb in the pack. Excuse us for saying this, but we've heard your son referred to you as a 'dumb-ass'. We have experience with dumb people. Dumb-ass people do dumb-ass stuff—stuff like killing their children.*

My father would be shocked by that revelation, astounded his son would ever say such a thing. He'd probably ask my mother if it were true. She'd lie to cover for me. *Oh, honey, I can't imagine. He'd never.*

Continuing with their interrogation, the police would add, *We also know about you, ma'am. We know how you allowed your son to nearly scald himself to death in your husband's shower-chamber-of-horrors. We've heard all about your less than loving response to your boy's agonizing screams of pain, you calling out, "What the hell's goin' on down there, you little shit?" Yeah, we know that and more.*

We know you slapped your son hard enough to send him airborne, flying right out of his bath towel. Yeah, we also know you made fun of his tiny genitals and refused to take him to the hospital for an examination of his spinal column. We know all of it, and we're gonna keep an eye on you, a very close eye.

My parents would probably break down crying, not over me, but over the thought of spending the rest of their lives in prison, having to send my little sister to foster care. Of course, my brother would be pissed—pissed that Mom and Dad couldn't pay his college tuition from prison. He'd blame me for all of it.

•

It's been more than two years now. Last winter was kinda rough. It got pretty hot in here, making me anxiously look forward to spring and summer. My sister's now nine years old. She comes down here often, sometimes after dark by herself. It's been a lot of fun for me watching her tear around, flying up the steps like a horror-stricken chipmunk after turning off the light.

I hope she never tries to challenge the darkness, as I did. I'm not so sure I'd enjoy getting that close to her, actually touching her. She's such a sweetheart; I'd hate to give her a heart attack or something else, maybe a stroke. Of course, I'd never drag her into the furnace the way The Thing did with me. Apparently, that's only necessary when you need a replacement.

I think I'm gonna be here a long time. That's okay; I'm pretty content with my den in the furnace and my nightly rounds. There is one thing that annoys me though. I've developed a funny smell in my fur and on my breath. It's kind of a musty, moldy bread smell.

Sometimes people go down in their basement and notice a smell like that, thinking they may have a water leak or mold in the wash tub. That's usually not the case. Most often it's because one of us has been there. That's something you may want to keep in mind.

Ciao

Ciao is an excerpt from my novel *Caduceus*. Doctor David Barnett, a cardiologist, is a recovering alcoholic. Laura Conti is the widowed daughter-in-law of Carlo Conti, a disgruntled entrepreneur who harbors an irrational hatred for doctors.

Carlo, holding Barnett responsible for the death of his thirty-eight-year-old son, Michael, Laura's late husband, has hired attorney John Gallagher to prosecute Barnett for medical malpractice. Barnett was attracted to Laura when he first met her at the time of her husband's presentation to the hospital nearly two years ago. Having seen her in court today, despite the risk of her father-in-law's wrath, Barnett has boldly asked Laura on a dinner date.

David arrived at Ciao a few minutes ahead of time. Being anxious about his date, he didn't want to make any mistakes, such as showing up late. Ciao, a nicely decorated, moderately priced Italian restaurant on the north side of town, was a convenient location for both Laura and David. The place was comfortable with brocade upholstering, plush carpet, Renaissance-era appointments, and low-volume classical music. Most importantly, the food was outstanding. David thought it was a nice choice for a first date.

He entered the foyer, relieved to see Laura had yet to arrive. After confirming his reservation with the hostess, he took a seat on a long bench. The foyer was chilly, and he left his topcoat on. His hands and feet were cold from intermittent waves of winter air passing through the entry to the bar area—an area with which he was quite familiar.

After his divorce, David had spent many lonely evenings in there, diluting his brain cells to make his anguish tolerable. He'd often drink until closing and then stagger out to the parking lot.

David recognized a few faces of steady customers sitting at the bar. He hadn't been there for years. Despite that, he wasn't surprised to see many of the regulars he knew from the past. He didn't think poorly of his old friends, rather, they made him feel empty and sad—sad for them and sad for himself as he pondered his decades of alcoholism, realizing how it hurt had Susan, ruined his marriage, distanced him from his children, and damaged his integrity and self-esteem.

He was keenly aware of the daily turmoil his former drinking buddies were going through, reminding him of how fortunate he was to finally be out of that cycle of self-destruction. *I'm the lucky one*, he thought. *If it hadn't been for my career, I never could have afforded the expensive rehab program I attended.*

If not for that opportunity, he could easily be sitting at the bar right now, seeking oblivion from the pain of divorce, a pain that, fortunately, probably because of his sobriety, had long since faded away.

He was certain his old pals would love to see him, welcoming him back home with shouts of, "Look who's here!" and "Hey, Dr. B, where the hell ya been? Come on in, Doc. Join us. It's just like old times." David had a brief urge to do just that. He let it pass.

"Hello."

Barnett looked over his shoulder and quickly stood. "Hi, Laura. Did you have any trouble finding the place?"

"No trouble at all. Your directions were perfect."

"I'll take your coat if you want. It's a little cold in here, but I'm sure the dining room will be warmer." Barnett hung their coats in an adjoining cloakroom and walked with Laura to the hostess.

"Your table is ready, Doctor." "Great, thank you."

The dining room was warm and cozy. A stone-faced fireplace with a large fieldstone hearth stood in the center of the room. Its massive chimney extended high through a cathedral ceiling, which was crisscrossed with large, rough-hewn oak beams. Dining tables draped with white cloths were spaced throughout the room, and booths, cushioned with dark maroon leather, lined the far wall.

Crystal chandeliers, suspended high from above, gave the room a pleasant radiance, enhanced by a golden glow and crisp crackles emanating from burning logs in the fireplace. Plush, emerald-green carpet muted the noise of the restaurant, creating a pleasant acoustic quality of intimacy.

David and Laura took a moment to warm up in front of the fire. Their waiter, a rotund, middle-aged man with a heavy black mustache, seated them at a nearby table. Barnett was pleased with the waiter's choice, near the fireplace but not so close as to be hot, and isolated enough to provide privacy. The table was adorned with a candle centerpiece and a single red rose in a slender glass vase.

Laura smiled, "This is beautiful."

"I'm glad you like it. It's one of my favorites, and it's surprisingly nice considering the exterior, which doesn't look like much."

"I know what you mean. Looks kinda plain on the outside, but it's lovely in here. I was actually a little leery when I drove up."

David got caught staring at his beautiful date. She smiled and blushed just a little. There was a slight irregularity in her front teeth. He found it attractive, different from the perfect teeth, almost too perfect look common in the era of orthodontia.

The waiter introduced himself and left a menu and wine list. "I'll give you a few minutes to review our wines. Be back shortly."

"Laura, would you care for some wine?"

"Sure, I'd love some; gotta have wine with Italian food; don't you agree? You choose whatever you'd like, David."

A forlorn look draped the doctor's face. "Laura, I don't drink. I assumed you knew that."

"No, honestly, I didn't, but it's fine with me. I won't have any either. How's that?"

"I'd prefer you have some wine. If you don't, it will make me feel I'm imposing my problems on you."

"Is there a problem?"

He paused. "Yes, this is a little awkward for me, mainly because I was so sure you knew."

"I'm sorry, David. I don't follow. Knew what?" "Knew I'm an alcoholic."

"You are? Well, that's okay. You don't drink, right? So, I guess you're a former alcoholic. Who's to say, anyway? I mean, what makes you so sure you're an alcoholic or were an alcoholic?"

Laura was enamored with David, and despite this being their first date, she'd already fantasized about them in a long-term relationship. It hurt to hear of problems right off the bat, especially after what had happened to Michael. She didn't want more heartbreak and tried to ignore David's issue. She wanted him to be the way she saw him—she wanted him to be perfect.

Barnett looked her straight in the eye. "I'm sure I am—I'm sure I'm an alcoholic. Believe me, drinking was a big problem for me, mainly during my divorce. Laura, it's pretty much understood it's a disease that stays with you. You can stop drinking, but you're still an alcoholic, a recovering alcoholic, so to speak."

Laura remained hopeful. "Well, it's fine with me, David. You're not drinking now, and it sounds like you've got a handle on it. Why did you think I would have known about it?"

"Because of your father-in-law."

"Carlo? He never said anything to me. How would he know?" "I'm not sure how he knows so much about my past, but it all came out at the deposition. It was obvious he'd been told a lot about me." Laura interjected. "I wasn't at the deposition."

"I know. But I assumed Carlo would have talked to you about me. Unfortunately, I suspect my addiction will be a major issue in this malpractice case. Since Carlo was the one to initiate it, I figured he told you all he knew. At the deposition, John Gallagher asked me some pointed questions about it, my alcohol use, that is. Carlo never said anything to you?

"Not a word. He hasn't said much at all about this whole thing. He acts as if he has to protect me. That's why I wasn't at the deposition. He didn't want me there."

"Laura, this is about your husband. Why wouldn't Carlo want you involved?"

"David, the lawsuit is his idea. I had nothing to do with it. I feel bad about it, especially now."

Pleased with her statement, David was thinking it could be an indication of her interest, possible romantic interest, in him. He decided to pursue it. "You feel bad *now*? Is it okay if I ask what you mean by *now*? Has something changed?"

Laura blushed as her eyes went wide. "Come on, you know that's not a fair question, but I'll answer it anyway." She smiled, cocking her head slightly "'Now' means now that I've gotten to know you. I find you to be a nice man, a good person, and from what I saw of your work in the hospital, I think you're an excellent cardiologist." Smiling broadly, she added, "So there, Doctor Barnett. And that was a sneaky way to find out how I feel about you. But it's okay; I'm glad I told you. Now it's your turn."

In addition to beautiful, Barnett found Laura cute and witty. *My turn*, he thought. *That's perfect.* "My turn, great. I *want* to tell you my feelings, which I think are obvious since I'm the one who asked you out for dinner. Laura, I find you attractive in all respects: your appearance, your personality, your sense of humor, your intelligence—everything. I realize we barely know each other, but at this point, that's how I feel."

Laura, momentarily speechless, blushed again. "I'm flattered, David, and pleasantly embarrassed by your compliments. Thank you. I think I can confidently say I feel the same about you. That's the reason I'm so upset with my father-in-law. I wish he'd never started this whole thing. I should have stopped him a year ago."

"It's okay. You couldn't have stopped him anyway. He seems so bitter and determined. He would have found a way to sue me, with or without you."

"I suppose you're right. He loved Michael so much, and he's so alone now. He lives in a big, expensive house all by himself. I'm sure it's made him angry: his solitude, his wife, his children. It's so tragic. He blames doctors—he blames everyone else for his problems, everyone but himself."

"Laura, I'm not worried about it, the suit that is. If Carlo hadn't pursued this, we never would have seen each other again. I wouldn't have been happy with that, especially since I've been thinking about you ever since we first met at the hospital. Of course, under those circumstances, there was nothing I could do. But now, more than a year later, I think it's okay—it's more appropriate."

Laura, trying to hide her enthusiasm, smirked, and said, "Come on, Dr. Barnett; you're really pourin' it on. I may start thinking you're manipulating me. That wouldn't be good."

"No, it wouldn't. And it wouldn't be true." David thought for a moment. "I'm sorry. I'm being forward."

Delighted with what she was hearing, Laura also paused in thought. *I've had trouble forgetting him, too, especially knowing he's divorced and available.* After Michael's death, she was horribly lonely. It was easy to fantasize about meeting a new man, and David Barnett fit her dreams perfectly. She silently stared at her date.

David, with a sense of anxiety, changed the subject. "You mentioned Carlo's wife. Where is she?"

"David, Mrs. Conti, Marie, died three years ago. Michael was all Carlo had left after his wife's death."

"I didn't know about Mrs. Conti; I'm sorry to hear that. Why did you say, or imply, Carlo should blame himself? Blame himself for what?"

"He's fanatic about not seeing doctors—has been, at least since I've known him. Marie told me that after Cassie died, Carlo developed an irrational hatred for physicians, and he refused to let Michael or Marie go to doctors."

"That's crazy. But Michael went to a doctor; he saw Tamayo." "Yes, he did, but as far as I know, Tamayo was his first. I'm sure, when he was a child, he saw a pediatrician for the usual shots, immunizations, and such. Michael said he was never sick while growing up, not 'til now or, you know, when this all happened." Laura looked away.

Reaching across the table, David gently touched her hand. "Laura, maybe we should talk about something else."

"I don't mind. I'd rather explain this whole bizarre thing. I think we *should* talk about it, especially now, David. Maybe... maybe I could help you, you know, help you with your trial."

Barnett was pleased with her offer. His attraction to Laura grew in response to her kind gesture. "I guess it's possible. Maybe you *can* help me. I'd really like to know what's goin' on in your father-in-law's head. That would be helpful."

"David, I'm sorry this is happening."

"Please, you don't have to apologize. It's obvious it's not your doing, but honestly, I wasn't sure of that until now. I'd hoped you weren't in this with Carlo, and I'm pleased to hear you're not."

"Oh, my, I'm glad we're discussing this. None of this was my doing, It was all Carlo's idea, and he refused to listen to anything I said." "Laura, I don't understand his anger—what his complaints are.

I'm sure you remember what happened in the emergency room when Carlo got physical with me. I couldn't believe it; he was irrational. Weren't you shocked by his behavior?"

She leaned forward, closer to David as if to tell a secret, nearly whispering. "I wasn't shocked, not in the least. I've seen much worse from my father-in-law. Most of the time he's in control, balanced, but every now and then he'll explode. Never with me, never directed at me, but often in my presence. If Michael or Marie said the wrong thing or did the wrong thing—wrong in Carlo's mind—he would erupt. It was terrifying. I think he has a deep, inner anger; he's angry at the world, especially the medical world."

"Anyway, Laura, right now it looks as if John Gallagher doesn't have a case. However, who knows what could come up later in this trial. Fortunately, I'm not that worried about it. It's not the end of the world if I lose a malpractice case. Most cardiologists have at one time or another. I've got good insurance. It would be a blemish on my record, but as I've said, it happens. Two of my partners have lost malpractice suits, and they're both very good cardiologists."

"But you didn't do anything wrong, did you?"

Her question, like a ghost from the past, hit David's subconscious. Thoughts rose from deep within. *Did I do anything wrong? Was I drunk— am I a drunk?* He paused to compose an answer. Looking directly into Laura's eyes, he replied, "Laura, I feel bad about the situation. Honestly, at the time, because it took me longer than usual to respond, I felt a bit of guilt. It's my nature to be hard on myself. I wish I'd come to the hospital right away when Steve Goetsch called me the first time." David looked down at the table.

Laura asked, "Would it have made any difference? Any difference if you'd arrived earlier?"

Raising his head, he hesitated. "Laura, I don't want this to sound like an excuse; it's not, please believe me. The truth is, in my heart, I know it wouldn't have made a difference. Michael's coronary problems were so severe—he was truly in a hopeless situation. I know that logically, but it's sometimes impossible for me to avoid feeling shame."

"I believe you, David. I wouldn't be sitting here with you if I didn't."

David smiled and quickly, too quickly, responded, "Why *are* you here with me?" He immediately regretted his question, having put her on the spot for the second time. "I'm sorry; don't answer that. It's not a fair question. This whole thing is strange, isn't it? The way we met, your circumstances with Carlo, all of it. The truth is I don't care about the odd circumstances, Laura. I'm glad you're here, very glad."

She happily responded, "Me too."

At that moment, as if on cue, the waiter returned, placing a basket of bread and two glasses of water on the table. "I'm sorry I took so long. My apologies. How about a bottle of wine?"

David looked to Laura, "We never did decide, did we?" "It's your call, David."

"All right, would you like red or white?" "I'd prefer red, Doctor."

Pleased with her decision, he grinned and looked up to the waiter. "She'll have a glass of the California Cabernet. I'll have coffee."

The waiter filled their water glasses and took their dinner order. He was just about to leave when he turned back and addressed David. "Sir, please don't think I'm pushing wine sales. However, I always inform our customers of the cost advantages of buying a bottle. If you're going to have two glasses of wine, you'll have practically paid for an entire bottle. In addition, if the bottle isn't emptied, it's our policy to let you take the remainder with you."

David looked across the table.

"David, I'm sure I won't have more than one glass."

"It does make more sense to buy the bottle. You can take the rest home and have a glass tomorrow if you want." Barnett looked back to the waiter. "As per your suggestion. We'll have a bottle of the Cabernet."

"Very good, sir. I'll be right back."

•

John Gallagher finished his last bit of Scotch and set the empty glass on the table. Across the booth sat his business partner, Robert Saun-ders, who had driven to Toledo from Detroit to discuss an ongoing case in their firm.

"John, you gonna have another one?" "I might. How 'bout you?"

"Nah, I shouldn't. I've got a bit of a drive ahead of me. I better play it safe with the booze."

"Yeah, I should probably go, too; I've got an early day tomorrow." "You haven't told me what you're doin' down here. Anything interesting?"

"I'm in the middle of some half-assed malpractice case that's gone to a jury. I have to be in court at eight thirty."

"Eight thirty—sounds like you *should* get goin'. You ready to take off?"

"No, I think I'll have one more while I go over some notes. You ought to go, Bobby; it's gettin' late, and like you said, it's a long drive to Detroit."

"Okay, John, I'll give ya a call tomorrow." "Sounds good."

As his partner was about to leave, John Gallagher stood and reached for his wallet.

"Hey, don't worry about it, John. I've got it."

"Okay, Bob, thanks. We'll talk tomorrow."

Saunders grabbed his topcoat from a hook near their booth and walked out of Ciao. Gallagher, watching his friend leave, looked around the dining room. Caught off guard, he did a double-take. They were sitting together near the fireplace, barely fifteen feet away.

My God, he thought, *what in hell are they doing having dinner together? This is incredible.* The attorney leaned back in his seat to be out of Laura's line of sight. He whispered, "Now, I'll definitely have another drink."

•

Laura took a sip of wine. "This is good. Thank you."

"I know. I mean, I know it's good; I've had more than my share in the past. But coffee suits me just fine now. I really don't miss it, the wine that is."

"Good," she responded. "I'm impressed with your diligence." Barnett wanted to get off the topic of alcohol. "Laura, I'm still amazed the Conti family never had any medical care. Didn't Michael's mother complain?"

"David, Marie Conti was deeply in love with her husband; she told me so. He was very good to her, most of the time. But believe me, Carlo ruled the household, and we all accepted it."

"But she died. Didn't she go to a doctor? What happened to her?" "She died in her sleep. Everyone said it must have been a heart attack."

The thought of an autopsy popped into David's head. He didn't ask, thinking it would be too clinical, too intrusive. "Yeah, a heart attack, that's probably what it was. Was she sick before that? Did she ever ask to see a doctor?"

"She did. She told me about it just before her death. Carlo never knew. As far as I know, he still doesn't know. About a month or so before she died, she called Michael and told him she was tired all the time, having breathing trouble."

"Yes, sometimes those are the only symptoms; sometimes there's no pain, no chest pain."

"I know, but she did have chest pain or any kind of pressure in her chest—she told me that. I remember the word 'heaviness.' David, she was frightened. Marie planned to see a doctor somewhere around Detroit, and she made Michael promise not to tell his father."

Michael didn't tell Mr. Conti? And she died?"

"That's right. Michael never said a word. He'd always been dominated by Carlo, horribly intimidated by him. After his mother died, he figured it was pointless to mention it, knowing it wouldn't change things and would only anger his father."

"Anger his father! Wasn't *he* angry, Michael, that is?"

"Michael never got angry; I honestly think he was afraid to express anger or any other deep emotion."

David paused for a moment, contemplating Michael's psyche and the traumatic effects his father's ridicule must have had on his emotions. Laura, noticing her date's preoccupied look, waited. Once again, the doctor decided to change the subject.

"How about Carlo? He must have gone nuts when his wife died." "I'm sure he did, but I wasn't there. Michael and I were in Toledo, and

Carlo was up in West Bloomfield. By the time we found out about Marie, Carlo was surprisingly calm. Soon after, he refused to talk about it."

"He wouldn't talk about it?"

"No, not once since the funeral, and he was quiet, very reserved at the funeral home."

Once again, David thought of Michael. "Laura, how about Michael's health problems? Did he tell his dad he was going to see Tamayo?"

"No way, never. I had to twist his arm to make him go in the first place. He asked me to arrange the office appointment. I wanted to go along, but he wouldn't allow it. Carlo never knew a thing until afterward, you know, Michael and all."

Their waiter arrived with appetizers, *crostini al fungi*, and portabella mushroom. They resumed their conversation as the waiter served Laura a portion of the portabella.

"May I ask how you chose Dr. Tamayo?"

"I looked in our HMO pamphlet. We didn't know a single doctor in Toledo, and I didn't know what else to do. Tamayo was in the pamphlet; he also has a very large ad in the Yellow Pages. It said he was both an internal medicine specialist and board-certified cardiologist. It was just by chance really—his ad caught my eye."

David envisioned an expensive, full-page phone book ad, touting the varied talents of the spectacular Raymondo Tamayo. "Yes, I bet it did catch your eye."

"What do you mean, David?"

He hesitated, again regretting what he'd said, the remark suggesting a lack of respect for Tamayo. He didn't want Laura to blame her-self for inadvertently choosing a charlatan as her husband's physician.

"Oh, nothing. Tamayo's a good cardiologist. He's just a bit money oriented. I'm not surprised he has a huge ad in the Yellow Pages."

"Do you think I made a mistake? Could someone better, a different doctor, have saved Michael?"

Now, David *really* regretted his comment. He had to lie to convince Laura that Tamayo had been a good choice. "Absolutely not. Tamayo did all the right tests, just as he explained in court today. He's a very experienced and very thorough cardiologist. Believe me, Laura, you couldn't have changed a thing."

Sadness covered her face. Her head fell.

David assumed he hadn't been very convincing. "Laura, I'm sorry this happened. I'm sure you loved Michael very much."

Looking up, her eyes meeting his, Laura said, "I guess I loved him; I was never sure."

David was silent, shocked by her comment.

Laura continued. "I was once very much in love. It was before I met Michael. His name was Kent. We met freshman year at Hillsdale College. I was crazy about him, but it didn't work out. I guess it wasn't meant to be. He left me for another girl during our junior year. I was devastated, a total mess, and very vulnerable afterward."

"I'm sorry to hear that."

"That's when I met Michael. It was different with Michael. He was very kind, but it was different. Something was missing; I suppose it was the passion I so enjoyed with Kent. With Michael… I guess… maybe I was attracted to the security, his family, their wealth, you know. Don't get me wrong, David; I loved him, but it just wasn't the same."

David paused, choosing his words carefully. "I understand; there are different kinds of love."

Laura added, "He was a truly a good person, but he was so cautious, so dominated by his father. It was a problem."

"Yes, I get that impression. I'm sorry you had to go through all of that, Michael's death, I mean."

"Don't be, it's over now. It's all in the past, and I'm okay." Intrigued by her candor, David wondered, *Could Laura and I have real passion together?* He sat in silence for a moment, imagining making love to her—imagining what it would feel like to kiss her, caress her, touch her, and explore her body. He fantasized about them together in a lifelong romance. He wanted to talk about it, about the passion and love and excitement he craved. He'd gone without that for so many years, and he wanted to pursue all of it with Laura. For now, to simply delve into her mind, to excite her with romantic conversation would be satisfying.

"David, are you all right?"

Snapping out of his trance, he cleared his thoughts and smiled. "Sure, I'm fine. I guess I was lost in a daydream."

•

John Gallagher looked across the room just as the couple's waiter returned with dinner. Realizing he'd be staying longer than anticipated, the attorney ordered dessert and a cappuccino.

•

"Laura, when I asked about Carlo's hatred for doctors, you mentioned Cassie. Who's Cassie?

"She was Michael's older sister, Carlo and Marie's daughter, their first child."

"I didn't know they had a daughter. I reviewed Michael's medical records to prepare for this case. A sister was never mentioned."

"I know. He rarely spoke of her; it's kind of a forbidden topic, especially when Carlo's around."

"Hope you don't mind… what happened to Cassie?"

"I don't mind. Her name was Cassandra. She died on her fifth birthday. I think it was in the early fifties, fifty-two or fifty-three."

"Oh, no, so young, a five-year-old—what a tragedy. Was it some sort of accident… maybe a car accident?"

"No. It wasn't. Apparently, there was something wrong with her heart. According to Michael, she'd been sick for about two years; she had trouble breathing. Michael never knew all the details. His mother told him a few things, but his father refused to talk about Cassie. I once spoke with Marie about it. That was six or seven years ago. Marie said Cassie would have spells."

"What kind of spells?"

"I was told she complained of chest pain. She'd get short of breath and turn blue, sometimes to the point of passing out. They took her to a few doctors; some were specialists. The doctors couldn't find anything wrong. A cardiologist at Ford Hospital in Detroit suggested it was possibly an emotional problem. Marie said they took Cassie to a psychologist who thought she was faking the spells to get more attention."

"Oh, my God! Then she died?"

"Yes, died suddenly on her birthday. As you'd expect, Carlo and Marie were beyond consolation. Cassie's death took its toll. They were emotionally destroyed.

"I'm sure they were. This story is heartbreaking."

Laura continued, "Carlo never got over it. He never forgave the doctors for not saving her, and he despised the psychologist who said Cassie simply lacked attention from her parents. It's been over forty years, and Carlo still holds his hatred and resentment to this day."

"Wow, that explains a lot. I couldn't understand the deal with the family not seeing doctors, having no health insurance, the whole thing. It's so unfortunate; it's sad."

"I know. Marie told me Carlo went through a personality change after Cassie died. She said he'd always been somewhat of a free spirit. But he changed, he became a driven man; he wasn't content with his life. She even told me he swore he'd never have another child."

"How did Michael come about?"

"I guess Michael was an accident, not planned. Marie told me some very personal things, you know, two women discussing life, romance, heartbreak."

David gave a nod and smiled. "Yeah, I get it."

Laura continued, "Marie said she knew exactly when it happened—when she conceived Michael. It was New Year's Eve 1960. They'd both been out to some kind of fancy party and had been drinking. Marie confided in me that after Cassandra's death, Carlo became obsessed with Catholicism."

"Catholicism?"

"Yes, Marie, said about a month after Cassie's death, Carlo started attending church every day. Marie thought he was guilt-ridden about leaving the church years prior, before Cassie was born. She even told me Carlo thought his daughter's death was punishment from God, punishment for having left the church."

"No kidding. That's fascinating, although sad."

"Marie said Carlo followed Catholic dogma to the letter. That's why he refused to use birth control. She and Carlo used the rhythm method. I guess they weren't careful the night Michael was conceived."

"Well, that'll do it."

They both chuckled, and Laura said, "I guess it did."

David continued, "Laura, that's quite a story. As I said, Michael never mentioned his sister in any of his medical history."

"I'm not surprised. No one talked about Cassie, especially when Carlo was around."

David wondered about the child's death. *A five-year-old dying suddenly—sudden death is usually cardiac, but in a five-year-old? Maybe it was congenital.* He asked Laura, "You said Cassie had problems with shortness of breath and chest pain?"

"Yea, that's what Marie said."

"They didn't think it was asthma?"

"I guess not. That would be easy to tell, wouldn't it?"

"Yes, it should have been. I can just imagine their crippling agony, their young daughter dying suddenly for no obvious reason. No wonder Carlo's bitter. And then, to lose a second child, even at age thirty-eight; that's still young."

An image of Michael Conti's coronary angiogram popped into David's head. He became pensive, quietly thinking, *Michael had incredibly severe coronary disease for his age. No smoking history, no hypertension or diabetes. Tamayo testified Conti's cholesterol was better than average. It just doesn't make sense.*

"What are you thinking, David? You look concerned."

"No, I'm fine. I was just wondering about the Conti family. Their daughter had shortness of breath and chest pain and died abruptly at age five. Mrs. Conti died in her sleep, and since she'd sought medical attention, I must assume she had some sort of worrisome symptoms. Michael probably . . ." David paused, feeling he shouldn't discuss Michael's death anymore. He switched to Carlo. "Laura, does Carlo have any heart problems? I suppose he's never been to a doctor, but have you ever noticed anything?"

"Well, yes, I have. I've seen him put those little pills under his tongue."

"Nitroglycerin?"

"I guess. He tries to hide it, never talks about it, but I've seen him on two or three occasions."

"How'd he get nitroglycerin without a prescription?"

"Oh, Carlo's very self-sufficient. He'd find a way, even if he didn't see a doctor. What are you thinking, David? What are you thinking about their family?"

"It's probably not important, and it's just a wild hunch."

"What hunch? Come on, you have to tell me."

"Laura, it's unusual for a young girl like Cassie to have symptoms of chest pain and then die. There's a hereditary condition that runs in some families. It's rare, present in roughly one in five hundred people."

"What is it?"

"It's a genetic defect—it causes extremely high cholesterol levels, so high, in fact, young children, even infants, can die from a heart attack. It's called familial hypercholesterolemia, or FH for short."

"Wouldn't the doctor have checked Cassandra's cholesterol?"

"Not back then. They didn't routinely test for cholesterol in 1952. It wasn't until the sixties that the relationship between cholesterol and heart disease was recognized."

"But what about Michael? He didn't die as a child. Just because Cassie had a problem doesn't mean he had it, does it?"

"Laura, I'm just speculating. It's a rare condition, and I'm probably off base. Besides, Tamayo said Michael's cholesterol was okay, actually better than average."

Laura persisted. "What if he was wrong? What if the test was screwed up? David, can't that happen?"

"It's not very likely."

"But it could happen?"

"I suppose. I've seen some mixed-up lab results on occasion." He peered hard at Laura. She looked anxious, concerned. He regretted bringing up the whole issue.

"David, after we moved to Toledo, Michael became obsessed with his diet. He made me change the way I cook. He wouldn't eat any fat. I never understood why he was suddenly worried about his health."

"Well, did he have his cholesterol level checked after you moved here?"

"I don't think so. He never said so. How could he? He never went to a doctor. As I said, I had to push him to see Tamayo."

Laura thought for a second and continued. "He also started exercising like mad. I couldn't believe it. He was running every day and swimming at the gym. It was all new for him. I thought it was because he was so stressed out at work."

"He had a rough time at work? Did he like his job?"

"He hated it. Carlo forced him into it. Michael thought he was under qualified. He was conscientious to a fault and worried about everything. It was a high-level position his father arranged for him. He had to make a lot of important decisions, and it didn't agree with him. It was really a lot of stress."

Barnett took the opportunity to get off the cholesterol topic. "I bet you're right, Laura. The cholesterol condition I mentioned is un-likely. I doubt it's a factor. Perhaps your husband had lifelong problems with anxiety. It's been shown prolonged tension can aggravate atherosclerosis of the coronaries, you know, hardening of the arteries, so to speak." He added, "Laura, I'm sorry I mentioned heredity."

She reached across the table and touched Barnett's hand. "It's okay. You're right. There's no point in my getting upset. I don't want to ruin the evening."

Her touch was electrifying. David felt his pulse race. He looked down at the table as she slowly withdrew her hand. "How's your dinner?"

"It's excellent, David."

"Would you like another glass of wine?" "Maybe one more."

"Good, good, I like that. I'll have more coffee, but I better switch to decaf. I've got to get some sleep tonight."

•

John Gallagher finished his dessert. He was getting impatient and considered leaving but changed his mind when he saw the waiter bring their check.

•

"Laura, I've really enjoyed this. You're a great conversationalist."

"Oh, come on! I bet you say that to all your girls."

"All of my girls! What girls? I haven't had a date in years." Laura looked pleased.

Gallagher looked on as the pair continued talking. Another fifteen minutes dragged by. Laura finished her wine. David poured the remainder of the bottle into her glass.

"Oh, please, David, thank you, but I've had enough. I have to drive home, you know."

Barnett left cash for the tab, and the couple walked together to the coat room. "I'll walk you to your car. Where'd you park?"

"I'm pretty far back. The lot was full when I got here." "Okay. Let's go."

There was an awkward silence as they crossed the parking lot. The doctor was nervous. It truly was his first date since leaving rehab over two years ago. He pondered a goodnight kiss and thought, *If I'd been drinking, I wouldn't be so unnerved.*

On previous dates, he was usually emboldened by intoxication. This was something new. *Should I shake her hand and say it's been a fantastic evening, I'll call you some time?*

They approached her car. The air was brisk, cold enough to see your breath. Laura's auburn hair was beautifully highlighted by light from a nearby streetlamp. David concentrated on her face and eyes. Her cheeks were flushed by the crisp evening air. He was taken with her beauty.

"Well, Doctor B., I had a very nice time."

"So did I. Besides being fabulous company, you're incredibly beautiful."

"Oh, stop. You're much too nice."

"That's my opinion; I think you're gorgeous."

"Well, thank you very much. You're quite handsome yourself, David."

Removing her bag from her shoulder, Laura searched for her car keys. David took a step closer.

"There they are." She looked up to David just as he gave her a light peck on the cheek. Laura's eye's widened as her brows rose. "Thank you!"

In contrast to David, she was pleasantly intoxicated from two glasses of wine and wasn't the least bit nervous. "Why don't you try that again, but do it right here." Laura pushed her lips out in a kiss.

David wrapped one arm around her shoulder, the other around her waist, and kissed her firmly on the mouth. Her lips were full, soft, and sensuous.

Other than the couple in an embrace, the parking lot was empty and silent. When Laura stood on tiptoes to enhance their kiss, one of her high heels slipped off, snapping down on the hard, cold pavement with a loud click.

The sound, ringing out in the chilled air, carried to the periphery of the lot, where it was heard by John Gallagher who was intently observing, safely concealed by the darkness of night.

To Live Is to Suffer

To live is to suffer. To survive is to find meaning in suffering. Considering that, he closed the book, leaned back in the library chair, and contemplated his future.

For Sean McMillan, the idea of unavoidable suffering was absurd. Staring at the cover of Friedrich Nietzsche's, *Beyond Good and Evil,* he thought, *This was written in the nineteenth century, more than a hundred years ago. What did Nietzsche know about contemporary man of the future? Life was hard back then and his theories no longer apply. I've never suffered, and I don't intend to.*

So far, Sean's life had been smooth sailing. Of course, at the age of nineteen, he was a novice at living. Still, he didn't believe suffering was a mandatory component of being alive—or maybe he just didn't want to believe it. In either case, he figured by being attentive, vigilant at being safe—by always doing the right thing—he could avoid the adverse consequences of life: anxiety, worry, shame, guilt, regret, remorse, depression, illness, and pain. In a word, he would never suffer.

Sean McMillan made a personal commitment to a life of caution. *If I'm careful and never let my guard down, with a bit of luck, I can avoid the torment and pain of life. I'll eat the right food, take vitamins, never drink alcohol, never smoke or use drugs. I'll be a conscientious driver, buy a safe, quality car, never speed, and always wear a seat belt.*

Sean promised himself never to gamble and to do his utmost to avoid debt. He'd not participate in hazardous activities, such as skydiving, rock climbing, or scuba diving. In short, he and only he would be in control of his life, no one else.

Time passed slowly. Adhering to his vow made life uncomfortably boring. He started college and was happy, or so he thought.

Before you can love another, you have to love yourself. He'd read that in his psychology text and believed it. "Do I love myself? I'm not sure. I must… why wouldn't I?"

Compulsively suspect of his motivation for everything, Sean questioned the depth of his love for Courtney, the woman with whom he'd shared life for the first year of college.

She's beautiful, sexy, intelligent, kind, and level-headed—what's not to love? Over time, Sean and Courtney's partnership evolved into a romantic, loving alliance. After graduating college, Courtney went on for a master's degree in child education, and Sean entered law school.

In law school, a mere four years after vowing to consciously circumvent life's pain and suffering, Sean experienced what he considered the unavoidable adversities of adulthood. His vow to avoid suffering was overpowered by negative emotions. Financial worries, insecurity and fear over his plans to be an attorney, doubt regarding his devotion to Courtney, and anxiety over their engagement and anticipated marriage plagued him. Sean's previously painless, carefree life became a distant memory.

Having dated little prior to meeting Courtney, Sean questioned his intention to spend the rest of his life with the only woman with whom he'd shared intimacy.

Consumed by thoughts of the unknown, exciting thoughts of being with someone new, someone different, gave him a wandering eye and imaginings of pre-marital infidelity. Though he looked and fantasized, he never took action.

After Sean graduated law school, he and Courtney, not yet married, moved into a small apartment. He passed the bar exam and joined a large, well-respected law firm. She found employment as a special education teacher.

On a rare, work-free morning, just a few weeks after joining his firm, Sean awakened early and decided to relax at home for a few hours.

Sean kissed Courtney goodbye on her way to work and returned to the kitchen to finish breakfast. The young barrister sat drinking coffee, mentally reviewing his life. *Am I in love or simply in lust? I'm not sure.* Unable to distinguish between the two, he queried his motivation for marriage. *Maybe I'm making a mistake. Maybe we're both making a mistake.*

Sipping the last bit of coffee in his cup, he thought, *I'm crazy about Courtney. Besides, I doubt I could ever be totally content with any woman.*

Realizing the grass is always greener, gave Sean a satisfying reassurance about his commitment to Courtney. Knowing his or anyone's desire for change, for something new, was often a misguided fantasy, reaffirmed his decision to be cautious and always do the right thing, believing he could control, even create his future by molding his life through diligence, devotion, and discipline.

Recalling his college psychology course, Sean drew some conclusions about the nature of life. *Most lives are replete with wishes, pipe dream illusions created by the mystery of an unknown, unpredictable future.* He thought, *Satisfaction in life is hard to come by, fleeting in nature, and beset with unfulfilled yearnings. We often want what we can't have. I want more, but more of what? I don't even know; it's ridiculous.*

Sean, thinking of his readings on existentialism, recalled the writing of Soren Kierkegaard, Albert Camus, and Franz Kafka. *They were right; life is meaningless. You're born, you struggle through life with recurrent pain and suffering interspersed with fleeting pleasures, and you die—kaput, you're gone. What's the point?*

Continuing his mind games, he thought of Nietzsche. *I've relentlessly tried to avoid pain—avoid suffering. It's so much work; now I know it's impossible. Nietzsche was right, but I don't want him to be right—I hate being in pain.*

Striving to suppress thoughts of other avenues, other paths through life, especially other women, one in particular, a young para-legal at his office, Sean had a revelation. Walking to the kitchen window, he spoke, "What makes me such a special catch? Nothing! There are plenty of guys out there just like me; I'm no better looking, intelligent, or talented than thousands of men in this city."

Knowing he'd come to a crossroad, knowing he had a critical, potentially life-altering decision to make, Sean considering his reading of Scott Peck's, *The Road Less Traveled*, thought, *I did what he said. I chose the hard path, the road less traveled, and it hasn't worked. It just hasn't worked.*

At the kitchen counter, he poured more coffee and returned to the window. Two squirrels were playing in the yard. The smaller one scurried up a tree to its nest with the other close behind.

Sean spoke, "Deep inside I know I'm lucky to have Courtney. And, incredibly, she loves me; I'm sure of it. If I call this off, sooner or later, I'll be sorry. If I screw it up, she'll leave and never look back. I'd be crushed. It would be crazy to leave her. I'd have to be insane." Thinking of what he'd just said, *I'd have to be insane*, Sean whispered to himself, "My God, that's it. I've spent ten years of my life desperately trying to do the impossible, and it's been a complete waste of time. Now, I'm cracking up. Maybe I'm crazy—maybe I'm going insane.

From nowhere, something, an unrecognizable, indefinable something, invaded Sean McMillan's mind. Frightening confusion filled his head. He trembled, his heart raced, he perspired. The kitchen walls moved in; the ceiling dropped; the room was squeezing in. Paranoia grabbed him.

Fearing he'd pass out, he took a seat at the table. Minutes crept by. Terrified, afraid to move, Sean's thoughts, like a sandstorm whirling through his head, defied organization. He could not think. He could not construct a single, meaningful thought.

Slowly, gradually, the storm cleared, and the strange unknown vanished as quickly as it had come. "Whoa, what the hell was that?"

A frightening image of an old, demented man in an infantile state flashed through Sean's head. He gasped, "Oh, my God, I think I need a psychiatrist."

Pondering his situation, the event he'd just experienced, and his recent, all-consuming worry, Sean spoke to himself. "My mother saw a psychiatrist. Could this be hereditary? What if it comes back? What if it keeps happening? What if it becomes permanent? I'll lose my job... I'll lose Courtney... I'll lose everything."

Sean thought, *I shouldn't mention this to her or anyone. I'll keep it to myself. I can't let Courtney know.*

Minutes after realizing the benefits, the security, the joy of intimately sharing life with a partner, Sean McMillan was back to keeping secrets.

Five days later he was sitting in the office of psychiatrist, Dr. Arthur Fitzgerald. The doctor, after hearing his new client's soliloquy, compassionately addressed Sean's issues.

"Mr. McMillan, I find your story fascinating, especially your intent to avoid pain and suffering throughout life. I can't recall ever hearing of anything even remotely similar."

Sean asked, "Is that a good thing or a bad thing?"

The doctor smiled. "It's neither. However, I feel your aspiration, your ideal, albeit noble, will be difficult, perhaps impossible to achieve. You need to know that."

"Doctor, you're the only person I've ever mentioned this to, and at the moment, it seems juvenile, an almost childish objective. I'm a bit embarrassed."

"Don't be, Mr. McMillan. Your goal may be unrealistic, but it's not without merit. I certainly won't criticize your attempt to, as you put it, 'always do the right thing.' Even if the vagaries of life do occasionally get in the way, I admire your virtue. Which brings me to the good news."

Smiling, Sean asked, "There's good news?"

"Sure, there is. I think your episode in the kitchen was due to prolonged stress, the pressure of desperately trying to perfectly control your life. The event you described sounds like a bout of acute paranoid claustrophobia, probably due to burdening yourself with control issues, trying to direct every facet of living."

"I hope you're right, Doctor—I guess... Is that 'paranoid claustrophobia' a serious thing?"

"Not as serious as it sounds. Mr. McMillan, you can't control everything; I'm sure you realize that. Honestly, people can't control most of what happens to them. In some ways, that's what makes life exciting and worth living."

Sean hesitated, absorbing what he'd just been told. *Living a controlled life may eliminate some of the danger, but at the same time, it eliminates the excitement, the mystery of the unknown, the unpredictability of the future—the future being right at this moment, with each second, every minute that ticks by, every hour, tomorrow, a month from now. I've been missing the joy of being alive. No wonder I'm depressed!*

"Doctor, you're right. I'm sure you're right… I just realized it. Dr. Fitzgerald, you're incredible." Sean looked at his watch. "In less than forty-five minutes you've changed my entire outlook on life."

Fitzgerald smiled. "Thank you. Every so often, I get it right." Sean continued, "I feel so relieved. I can't believe it."

"Be careful, sir. Sudden revelations can be euphoric, but euphoria is fleeting—it won't last. The important thing is to address your chronic rumination, your worry about everything. In consideration of what you've just described, your revelation, I'm confident things will improve."

The psychiatrist pulled a card from his coat pocket. "Here's my number. Why don't you make an appointment to see me in a month; after that, if you're feeling better, you won't need to return."

"That's it? No pills, no sedatives, no Xanax?" Don't you think I need some medication?"

"No, I don't. Medication's the last thing you need. Just relax and accept life as it comes. If you stop trying to control your life, I believe your anxiety will stop."

"I hope so."

"As I've said, it's noble to do the right thing—you just need to expand on what the right thing is. You're missing out on the exciting adventures of life. Ride a bike, get on a plane, take Courtney with you to see the world. You're an intelligent, successful man, Sean. You should take advantage of what you've already accomplished. Learn to accept life's occasional pitfalls in stride. Perseverance in the face of pain takes courage. Courage is gratifying and self-fulfilling."

"Courage, I like that. Thank you so much, Doctor. I'll see you in a month."

Outside, sitting in his car, Sean made a decision, *I'll surrender to my heart, instead of my mind.* A weight was lifted from his shoulders. He'd do everything possible to make a successful, loving partnership with Courtney, the beautiful woman who dearly loved him. They would share each other, splitting worry, dividing it between them.

Sean thought, *That's it, that's what mutual love and trust are all about. Having a partner can cut your problems in half. You share each other's problems… you talk, each provides reassurance, safety, security, trust… you function as a team, a single unit, a single being, joined together... two people melded together as one.*

He couldn't believe how good he felt. *Fitzgerald's right. The stress of worry has been wearing me down. I've gotta relax and accept life as it is. I should marry Courtney—I have to marry Courtney.*

Looking at the car's clock, he spoke aloud, "I'm gonna be late; gotta go. I can't wait to see everybody at the office. I love my job… I love my life. That shrink is good." He sang along with the radio as he drove to the office.

•

After their wedding, Sean and Courtney settled into a daily routine; they worked, saved money, and were soon able to buy a house. It was an old, red-brick house built in the 1920s—a large, two-and-a-half story home with leaded glass windows, a slate roof, limestone inlays, and green shutters.

Many of the neighboring homes were occupied by young professionals who planned to renovate and modernize their properties. Sean and Courtney had similar intentions.

Sean enjoyed his law practice; his partners liked him, and his income was climbing. Courtney loved teaching; she adored her young students. Everything was as Sean thought it should be.

The McMillan home renovation became a team project, occupying most of the newlywed's spare time. They worked together. They laughed. It made them close.

•

After two years of marriage, Courtney became pregnant. Elated by the idea of having a family, Sean's love for his wife deepened. In a word, Courtney was easy—easy to talk to, easy to please, easy to live with, easy to love.

Sean liked who he was; he liked his life, and importantly, he'd learned to love himself, a new experience. The world was a beautiful place.

A baby came, a girl they named Charlotte. A tiny human being, she was as homely as most newborns are, with a smooshed face, an oddly shaped head, scant hair, and a gummy smile.

Charlotte quickly blossomed into cuteness. Her face, enhanced by curly brown hair and green eyes, carried a perpetual smile. Her movement, mannerisms, expressions, and laughter all exuded a precocious intelligence. She was a joyful addition to the family.

Courtney, a spectacular mother, quit her teaching job to be a full-time parent, taking Charlotte everywhere she went. At two years of age, the child had never experienced a babysitter. Sean spent every spare minute with his wife and daughter. Life was good for the McMillans.

As his law practice grew, so did Sean's responsibilities and time spent at work. Fortunately, the firm, unlike most, appreciated the importance of a stable family life to the success of the business. Generous vacation time was the norm, and time spent with spouse and children was encouraged.

The couple, utilizing their free time to work on the house, decided they'd start at the top floor and work their way down. Knowing the renovation would take years to complete was of no concern. Looking forward to a lifetime together, they liked the idea. Sean, having learned the basics of many skilled trades from his father, had talented hands and soon became proficient at carpentry, plumbing, and some aspects of electric wiring. Charlotte, helping with the renovation as much as a young child could, loved being with her parents.

By the time the project reached the main floor of the house, Charlotte was approaching age five. Sean's birthday present for his daughter was a play area he'd secretly prepared in a spare room on the home's second floor. The surprise unveiling took place on July 7, Charlotte's birthday. The room had a large mirror for ballet practice, a tabletop video game of Ms. Pac-Man, and small furnishings designed for a young girl, including a painted, white-and-pink vanity, and much to Mom's approval, a study desk with a complete collection of an encyclopedia.

Mother and daughter loved it. Charlotte squealed with excitement. Courtney, almost as surprised as her daughter, told her husband how spectacular and talented he was. She kissed him and whispered something in his ear. He smiled.

•

Life went on; Courtney became pregnant again. The doctor said they would have a baby boy. Two months before her due date, she and Sean would celebrate eight years of marriage.

On the morning of their anniversary, they discussed plans for an evening out with a movie and dinner. Charlotte would be staying home, having her first experience with a babysitter.

That afternoon, Sean called home. Courtney, in anticipation of a night out, was taking a nap before getting ready for the evening. Charlotte had joined her. The phone, unanswered, went to voice mail. Sean left a message saying he'd be home soon.

Excited about an evening out with his wife, Sean left work early and picked up a bouquet of yellow roses, Courtney's favorite. Driving home, he noticed a line of dark smoke rising over his neighborhood. He thought, *Mr. Sheeny's at it again, burning brush in his backyard.*

Turning the corner of his street, he slammed on the brakes and yelled, "NO!"

Flames were shooting out of the roof and windows of his house. Dense black smoke filled the sky as fireman fought the blaze. Two fire trucks, numerous police cars, and an ambulance blocked the street.

Leaving his car askew at the corner, Sean ran to the house. As he approached, a police officer stepped in, "Mr. McMillan? Are you Sean McMillan?"

"Yes… my wife, my… my daughter, where are they? My God, they're in there sleeping. Get them out—please! Get them out!"

"Sir, we need to talk."

Sean, oblivious to the comment, ran right passed the officer. A fireman blocked his path. "Sir, you have to stay back. Please go with Officer Wagner."

Looking back at the house, Sean saw the front door smashed in. He hysterically screamed, "Where are they!"

Sergeant Wagner, thinking of his own wife and child, compassionately replied, "Mr. McMillan, please… please, sir, we have to talk.

The comment, like a knife through Sean's heart, made him scream even louder. "No, no, NO! This can't be happening. God, help them. Help me!"

Wagner, gently touching Sean's arm, softly replied, "Sir, please, you should have a seat in my car."

Sean gave the policeman a blank stare.

Wagner spoke. "I'm so sorry, Mr. McMillan, your wife, and daughter didn't survive.

An agonizing scream of utter helplessness erupted from Sean's mouth. His mind raced, *My partner, my love, my salvation is gone. My beautiful daughter is gone.* Remembering the pregnancy, he screamed, "My son, my baby boy! Oh, my God, no, no, no."

Sobbing hysterically, Sean was escorted to the front seat of the officer's patrol car. With tears streaming down his face, he quietly asked, "Can I see them? Please tell me they're not in the house."

"They're in the ambulance, sir."

"I want to see them. Please, can I see them?"

"Mr. McMillan, I don't advise it. I think it's best to wait… you know. We'll take care of your wife and daughter. You can view them at the hospital."

Sean, eyes fixated on the dashboard, gave a subtle nod.

The yard was crowded with firemen, policemen, and paramedics. An elderly woman, among a group of bystanders who had gathered across the street, approached the car. Over the past few years, she had developed a friendship with Courtney. She hugged Sean. They cried together.

•

Attendance at the funeral was incredible; the crowd was immense. Family, friends, teachers, lawyers, neighbors, even a few sympathetic strangers who had read of the tragedy were there.

A reception followed. Overwhelmed by the turnout of mourners, Sean's head reeled from the barrage of repetitive questions and comments: "Poor, Sean, were so sorry, so sorry, so sorry. What happened, honey? What caused the fire? Do they know how it started? She was so lovely, so beautiful. I heard she was pregnant. So, lovely, she was pregnant? Such a beautiful child, so smart, so cute. It's so sad, so sad, so sad. Sean, you must be devastated, crushed. We're so sorry. You poor man, devastated, crushed, need anything? Just call. Need anything? Just call… call… anything… call."

That night in a motel room, desperately trying to sleep, Sean Mc-Millan, tossed and turned for hours, his mind spinning—he was confused, consumed, tortured.

The motel alarm clock sounded at seven a.m., and Sean, having been awake all night, rolled out of bed, walked to the bathroom and looked in the mirror. "My, God, I look like shit."

After a shower, he called his secretary, instructing her to cancel all appointments for the remainder of the week. Sean had a court case scheduled that morning, a case he couldn't get out of. But his secretary could easily cancel any remaining appointments for that afternoon. After his court appearance, Sean returned to the motel and crashed in bed, sleeping soundly for hours.

The following day, he returned to the house, what was left of it. Courtney's car, still in the drive, was unharmed but both sets of keys had been lost in the fire. At Sean's request, the police had jimmied the door earlier that morning.

He looked inside. A silk scarf of Courtney's was lying on the front seat, along with one of Charlotte's coloring books.

Picking up the scarf, he held to his nose. The scent of Courtney's cologne, the cologne he'd given her years before, her favorite, the one she'd worn ever since, brought her back to him. Overwhelming memories took him to tears. He put the scarf in his coat pocket.

In the glove box, he found a hair brush and a pocket-book containing a lipstick, a checkbook, and a small bottle of the same cologne.

Taking all he'd found, he closed the car door and drove to his office. Even though his appointment schedule had been cleared, he still had a pile of backlogged paperwork to finish. He returned to his motel room late that afternoon.

After an interminable week of misery, Sean mounted the energy, the will, to call the head of the city's fire department, Captain Randolph Edmunds, who informed him the fire investigator's report was yet to be completed. Despite the chief's promise to contact him as soon as the report was available, Sean, anxious to know what had happened, questioned him about the possible or most likely source of the fire.

"Mr. McMillan, I want to extend my condolences; you've suffered a horrible loss." The captain continued, "Your house, being old, contained aged, dry lumber, layers of oil-based paints, and outdated electrical wiring. I'm so sorry, sir, but it doesn't take much to start a fire under those conditions."

"I feel responsible, Captain. I never should have bought such an old house. I'm sure newer construction is more fire resistant, isn't it?

Sir, don't, please don't punish yourself over this. New houses, old houses, it doesn't matter. Fires happen; it's an unpleasant fact of life."

Life, thought Sean. *I know about life. Life is pointless, meaningless, and riddled with suffering.*

"Are you there, sir?"

Yes, I'm here, Captain. One more question, if you don't mind." "Sure, go ahead."

"My house, the fire, I was told you were there. You saw the fire?" "Yes, sir. I did."

"Can you speculate on what caused that specific fire, anything at all you can tell me?

The captain, with reluctance in his voice, cautiously replied, "Not specifically, Mr. McMillan."

Sean pressed him, "Nothing? Nothing at all?"

Captain Edmunds relented. "Well, had there been any recent construction, any remodeling, new wiring?"

Hearing the word, remodeling, Sean felt sick. He remembered something—something he should have remembered months ago. A flash of terror shot through him. Overwhelmed by weakness, he couldn't speak.

"Mr. McMillan... are you there?"

Sean replied in a stuttering, shaky voice. "Uh, yes, Captain. Sorry... I have to... I've got to take an important call. I'll get back to you for the final report. Goodbye." He hung up.

Sean sat in his office, trembling, horrified, his head spinning. "I killed my family! It's my fault."

He remembered one specific electric outlet he'd installed in Charlotte's playroom. Being anxious to finish the project in time for his daughter's birthday, he'd allowed himself to break a personal rule, a rule to never cut corners—to never leave a project unfinished. In his haste, Sean, short one electric-outlet workbox and out of safety wire connectors, had improvised, promising himself to properly wire the outlet the following day. As his mind reviewed his quick fix, he was consumed by guilt. Out of supplies for his last outlet installation, he had used an old strip of electrical tape and twisted, poorly connected wires, which he jammed in place behind an ancient plaster wall. He moaned to himself, "It was supposed to be a temporary fix. How could I have forgotten?"

On his daughter's birthday, the jury-rigged outlet had worked; the video game was on, and all was ready for a surprise presentation to Charlotte. But, the following day, Sean forgot to properly finish the job. It never crossed his mind; he simply forgot.

Guilt, shame, and remorse shot through him. *How could I have forgotten something so important? I made a mistake. I'm not supposed to make mistakes. I'm not allowed to make mistakes—that was my vow, that was the plan, that's been the plan for years. My God, why was I so impatient? I could have waited; I should have waited. I've killed them, my wife and daughter. I've killed Courtney, the love of my life, my partner in life, my other half; we were supposed to save each other by sharing the pain. It was supposed to be okay.*

Mumbling to himself, Sean's head fell. "I'm alone… left to suffer… they were right. The fucking philosophers were right, 'to live is to suffer… life is meaningless'; life is pain, and in the end, you're gone, you're dead. Sean covered his eyes, placed his head on his desk and sobbed.

•

As anticipated, as predicted by Nietzsche and the existentialists, Sean's life became wretched misery. Intractable insomnia, interspersed with terrifying nightmares, became his nightly norm. Sleep deprived and depressed, he began failing at work as his performance deteriorated.

Within a short time, his irrepressible guilt led to alcohol, followed soon after by cigarettes. Sean's daily routine became wake up with a hangover; show up late at the office, or worse, late for a court case, thereby aggravating more than a few judges as well as other attorneys; leave the office early and head straight to a bar: smoke, drink, and occasionally eat, and then stagger out to the car for an intoxicated, illegal drive home.

As his drinking escalated, Sean's nightmares progressed to horrifying visions of his wife and child screaming for help, asking why he had killed them. Sickening dreams, like Technicolor movies of Courtney and Charlotte, filled his head.

He had images of Courtney, pleading, *Sean, why did you do this, honey? Why did you kill us? You killed our baby, honey. Did you make a mistake, Sean? Did you make a mistake? Is this your fault? Did you make a mistake, a mistake, a mistake?*

Recurrent dreams of Charlotte plagued him nearly every night. She'd be sitting on her grave, saying, *Hi, Daddy, I love you, Daddy. Why did you kill me and Mommy, Daddy? Why did you kill us?*

Sean's life became constant pain—he hated himself, hated life, hated being alive. Consumed by mental anguish, regret, remorse, and anger, his self-confidence and the ability to love himself, what had taken years to develop, quickly vanished.

Irrationally assessing the potential legal consequences of having killed Courtney and Charlotte, Sean, without even researching the issue, convinced himself he was guilty of manslaughter.

Thinking he had committed a crime added resolve to Sean's hesitation to call Captain Edmunds for the fire investigator's final report. With deranged thought processes, overwhelmed by negative, destructive emotions, Sean, foolishly thought he could be charged with a felony, even incarcerated.

The quality of the attorney's performance at work eroded further. He lost weight; his skin took on a yellow-grey hue; he was gaunt. His law partners, aware of his heavy drinking, tried to be understanding but, over time, became disgruntled.

In the early evening after work, Attorney McMillan, bringing along a leather shoulder bag of library books, would head to his favorite bar. The bar staff, waitresses and bartenders, became familiar with his routine of placing a stack of books on the bar next to his drink—a double martini or Manhattan. Sitting with drink in hand, Sean would read, pouring over philosophical texts and essays on the nature of man and the meaning of life until he became too intoxicated to comprehend.

Afterward, late at night, he'd reminisce about the past, torturing himself with memories of his wife and child.

In his motel dresser, he kept a box containing a tiny bottle of cologne and a lock of hair, hair from the brush he'd found in the car, strands of hair from both his wife and daughter—strands he'd wound together in a tiny braid, a braid with a lingering scent, a human scent, the unique scent of family, the scent of love.

Holding the opened bottle of cologne to his nose, Sean would go back. The nostalgia of Courtney's cologne, like a time machine, would take him back on a bitter-sweet journey of melancholia, a journey through both pleasure and pain.

After a long cry, he'd put the cologne and braid back in their hiding place where they'd stay until the next time he wanted to feel the joy and pain of his lost life, a life and a love he had personally destroyed.

•

Sean read the great philosophers, the existentialists, the fatalists, and the nihilists. Not surprisingly, his attempts to eliminate his misery through knowledge were fruitless.

Approaching six years of destitute loneliness, Sean McMillan was nearing the end. His drinking, his smoking, his sedentary life, and most importantly, his suffering, had taken a devastating toll on his appearance, his health, and his will to live.

Colleagues at work lost all patience with their debilitated partner. The hard reality of money and reputation became the bottom line, and Attorney McMillan was given an ultimatum—*quit drinking, clean up your act, and be the attorney you once were, or get out.*

Seriously considering, actually planning his suicide, Sean, for the first time in his life, reached out to God for divine intervention. He read the Bible.

Days later, having completed a sizable portion of the New Testament, slowly making his way, conscientiously reading, hanging on every word, Sean had a revelation—a memory, something most would consider minor, but for Sean, a memory, a thought he hoped would save his life. He would see Dr. Arthur Fitzgerald, the man who years earlier had so dramatically changed him for the better.

Amazed, stupefied he hadn't considered the option previously, and excited by the prospect, the adventure of again conversing with the compassionate, talented psychiatrist, Sean experienced a revitalization, a surge of energy.

Lying in bed, finishing the last verse of Paul's First Letter to the Corinthians, he gently closed the book and, thinking of Fitzgerald, was taken by an unexpected wave of dread. *What if he's retired? My God, he might not even be alive.*

Racing through the phone book, he grabbed his bedside phone and dialed. A recording came on, "You've reached the office of Dr. Arthur Fitzgerald. The office is closed now. If this is an emergency, please dial 911. Otherwise, please…"

Sean, his fear immediately replaced by comforting relief, hung up. The following morning an appointment was made. A few days later, he was sitting in the same office of the same man he'd seen many years prior.

Fitzgerald, who had aged well, looked older but more distinguished. To Sean, he had mellowed, speaking in a more relaxed tone. Despite not having seen his client for nearly fifteen years, the doctor readily recalled the unique nature of Sean McMillan's plan to consciously avoid life's suffering. He distinctly remembered him.

The psychiatrist intently listened to Sean tale of woe, his marriage to Courtney, their daughter, the remodeling project, the hasty outlet wiring, and the devastating fire. Sean conveyed his demoralizing, guilt-ridden conclusion—his presumption of guilt following his call to Captain Edmunds. He followed with a detailed description of his alcoholism and his mind's journey to the depths of hell.

Recognizing the irrational nature of his client's overwhelming guilt—irrational because the source of the fire was a complete un-known—Fitzgerald surmised Sean was blaming himself for some-thing that likely never happened and for which he no responsibility.

"Mr. McMillan, you seem certain you caused the fire."

"I know it was me, my carelessness, I just know—I can't explain it; you'd never understand how I feel."

"Honestly, I think I have a good understanding of how you feel. Sean, you've been your own judge and jury. You've convicted and imprisoned yourself for something you probably had no part in. You've gotta let yourself off the hook; you're killing yourself over something that never happened."

"Doctor, it's so painful. I know it's my fault, I'm sure of it."

"You *think* you're sure of it. Logically, you know better. I understand your pain, Sean… the pain's keeping you alive; without it, you'd be empty, no emotion, no energy, no will."

"That sounds crazy; I don't understand. Why would I need this torture?"

"You need it because you've put yourself in a long, disabling state of despair. All you have left is pain, and you dwell on it."

"Doctor, I accept what you're saying… I think. But I don't understand it."

"Sean, it's okay. Right now, you don't need to understand it. You need to replace it—replace your pain and suffering with something else, something good."

"How do I do that?"

"You start by facing reality, the reality that you may have unintentionally, unwittingly made a mistake, but also, you must accept the reality that the odds of this tragedy having anything to do with your mistake are incredibly remote."

Fitzgerald, contemplating a way to save his client from interminable misery, smiled. "Trust me, Sean, you're gonna get better."

Sean took a deep breath and sighed, "It's so hard."

"I know it is. But believe me, you will recover, and you will be happy; I promise."

His eyes welling with tears, swallowing hard, Sean replied with a faint, cracking voice, "I… I believe you. I don't know why, but I believe you."

Dr. Fitzgerald continued, "I happen to know Captain Edmunds. He and I went to high school together. If you'd like, I can call him for the investigator's report, his final assessment."

With a look of relief, Sean said, "Oh, that would help… that would help a lot. I'm so nervous; I'd be nervous calling… you know him, really? That's great. Thank you, Doctor."

"Good, I'll make the call. You need to schedule an appointment to see me in two days—no more than two. See me Thursday morning; I'll have the report by then. If you have any thoughts of hurting your-self, you can call me. Call me at home if necessary."

The doctor handed Sean his personal card. "Please don't give this number to anyone. I need to sleep now and then."

Sean smiled, thanked the psychiatrist again, and left the office.

•

Fitzgerald had lied. He had never met Randolph Edmunds, had never even heard of him. He didn't call anyone; there was no need. He would fabricate an answer, an explanation for the fire that would sound realistic but, most importantly, would exonerate Sean, freeing him from his self-imprisonment.

The doctor knew, if by chance the fire had been caused by the un-finished wiring project, Sean's life would be irreparably ruined. Even if the report concluded the home's old, outdated wiring was the culprit, Sean might blame himself for agreeing to buy such an old house. Fitzgerald's manufactured explanation had to rescue his client from any chance of self-incrimination.

As instructed, Sean returned Thursday morning. Dr. Fitzgerald was seated at his desk, waiting.

"Long two days, Mr. McMillan?"

"My God, yes. But I'm okay, Doc, so far."

"You look better. You must have gotten some sleep." "I did; I feel better, too."

The doctor paused.

After a moment of silence, Sean hesitantly asked, "Did you... did you call? What about Captain Edmunds?"

"Yes, Sean, I did call. Edmunds was out of town. I had his secretary pull the report."

"And?"

"And, it's not what you thought, not even close. The fire had nothing to do with the remodeling. They're sure of it."

More silence.

"So… so what did the report say?"

"Sean, this will hurt; what happened, so simple and so trite, will be painful, but it's a pain you can deal with. It's not your pain; you have no guilt to bear."

"Please, what did it say?"

"The fire crew found a cooking pot virtually welded to the stove top. They're convinced it's what started the fire."

"A pot on the stove?"

"That's right. You told me your wife and daughter were napping."
"Yes."

"She probably forgot about the stove being on. The report said the kitchen smoke alarm, being downstairs, may not have awoken someone sleeping upstairs. I'm sorry, Sean; apparently, your wife simply forgot. That's an easy thing to do."

An instantaneous flood of relief washed over Sean McMillan. For the first time in many years, he was free… free of guilt, shame, remorse, and self-hatred.

•

Sean's rapid recovery, fully anticipated by Fitzgerald, left him ecstatic but feeling foolish that something as simple as a phone call from him to Captain Edmunds could have prevented years of crippling guilt and suffering. Despite that, for the first time in countless years, he felt alive. He was happy.

No longer needing to numb his emotions, Sean immediately quit drinking. His withdrawal from alcohol, causing painful but tolerable mental and physical torment, lasted a couple of months, much longer than he'd expected. However, his abstinence was well worth it.

Cigarettes were a different proposition. Withdrawal from nicotine can be torture, and so it was for Sean. One of the most addictive substances on earth, nicotine is incredibly difficult to stop. It took many months.

Within a year, Sean McMillan was a new man, alcohol and nicotine-free. Years of progress ensued. Sean's work, finances, health, and attitude continually improved. Life, with the exception of one thing, was wonderful. That one thing was solitude. In the evening and on weekends, Sean was lonely.

•

He saw her at the grocery store, standing at the far end of the aisle. Instantly mesmerized, Sean stopped short. Partially hidden by a dis-play of sale items, he watched to appraise her beauty—*late thirties, blond-brown hair, beautiful face, well dressed, sweater, skirt, heels*—Sean was smitten.

Taking a deep breath to shake off his anxiety, he consciously bolstered his courage and strolled in her direction, formulating a plan as he went. He wished he had a cart, a basket, some implement of diversion, but it was too late.

She turned, looking down the aisle. Sean smiled, and kept walking, rehearsing things he might say, such as, *Hi, you come here often? Hi, what ya buyin'? Hi, I've never seen you here before. My, God, I'd sound like a teenager.* At the last second, the best comment, an honest comment, came to mind.

Stopping barely two feet from her, Sean said, "Hi, I purposely came down this aisle to talk with you. I'm single, you're beautiful, and I'd love to meet you."

Faintly blushing, she replied, "Wow, what a nice thing to say. You don't beat around the bush, do you?" She extended her hand, "My name's Sandra."

Sean, gently taking her hand, thrilled by its smallness, replied, "Hi, I'm Sean McMillan." He took a quick peek at her left hand. *No ring! Thank you, God.*

They went on a date, then a second, and a third. Within three months they were living together—in three more they were married.

Sean's self-doubts about love resurfaced. After years of shame and recrimination, once again, he had to learn to love himself in or-der to love his new partner. It took time, but over subsequent months, he gradually achieved his objective. His love for Sandra became firm and real.

The couple bought a house, a new house, new construction with all the associated safety features: fire-proof materials, smoke alarms, carbon monoxide detectors, radon detectors, and a security system.

A baby came, a girl they named Kendra. Just like her stepsister, Kendra was a tiny human being, as homely as most newborns are, with a smooshed face, an oddly shaped head, scant hair, and a gummy smile.

Kendra quickly blossomed into cuteness. Her face, enhanced by curly blond hair and blue eyes, carried a perpetual smile. Her movement, mannerisms, expressions, and laughter all exuded a precocious intelligence. She was a joyful addition to the family.

Sean's law practice was booming. Having regained confidence and motivation, he moved up the pyramid and, though working fewer hours, was bringing home more money. He and Sandra occasionally socialized with members of the firm. His partners found her delightful.

Sandra became pregnant with a second child. The couple, approaching their sixth wedding anniversary, looked forward to a baby boy.

That summer, deciding to take a vacation before Sandra was too pregnant to travel, the family flew to a resort on the gulf coast of the Florida Panhandle. The weather was perfect, the beach was beautiful, and their hotel was elegant.

Two days into the vacation, Kendra, having seen other children fishing from a dock, asked her father if they could try. The next day, waking early, the family ventured down to a nearby marina where Sean rented a fishing boat. With safety in mind, he rented a big boat, a classic, twenty-six-foot Chris-Craft inboard, with a cabin and a generous aft deck lined with cushioned seats. The boat was rigged for fishing.

A young Hispanic man, Manny, introduced the family to the rental, explaining operation of the motor and use of the fishing gear. He showed the family the cabin, complete with a galley, a table, and sleeping quarters for two. Manny, stepping back to the dock, handed Sean a bucket of fresh bait.

Sean started the engine. As he carefully pulled away from the dock, he called out to Manny, "Life jackets, Manny. Where are the life jackets?"

The young man yelled back, "Sir, they're up front in storage. They're under the bow, in storage, under the bow."

Sean smiled and called back, "Okay, thanks."

Having to leave the helm to retrieve the life jackets, Sean shifted to neutral. The Chris-Craft slowly drifted through the tight quarters of the marina. Sean heard a man calling out, "Move that cruiser— hurry up." He turned to see a sailboat briskly cutting through water. An old, grey-bearded man in a Greek sailor's cap, jeans, and a sun faded sweatshirt was frantically waving his arms. "Get movin', sailboats have right of way, you idiot. Move that goddamn boat!"

Sean pushed the accelerator; his craft jerked forward. The sail-boat, leaning hard to starboard, shot by, clearing the Chris-Craft's transom by mere inches. Sean accelerated and yelled out, "Sorry."

The old sailor grimaced and returned a few salty words.

Seeing more sailboats coursing through the marina, Sean was overcome with apprehension. His inexperience at boating sent him into a panic as the anxiety of the moment consumed his thoughts. He forgot all about the life jackets.

Desperately wanting to set out for the gulf, he cautiously steered his craft toward an exit in the marina's concrete breakwater. After slowly cruising past the barrier, he pushed the throttle and headed out to open sea.

For the first half-mile or so, the boat cruised through shallow water, only ten to twelve feet deep. It was a warm, clear day with a slight breeze creating a small chop on the water. The sun, beaming between scant, white clouds, highlighted the shallow, sandy bottom of the bay.

Kendra, wanting to get a better view of the seabed with its bright green vegetation and occasional starfish, sea-snail, or clam, asked her mother if they could stop for a better look.

Sandra, tapped Sean on the shoulder, and, yelling over the roar of the engine, asked to stop for a minute or two. As the boat slowed, Kendra and her mother leaned over the railing, spotting some small fish, a couple of clams, and a pink starfish.

Looking out toward the horizon, Sean noticed a freighter, a huge ocean-going ship, about a mile away, heading east toward the Atlantic. Minutes later, after Kendra had seen enough, they were on their way, setting out to deep water. Passing over a sharp drop off, the reflective, shallow sea bottom with its false sense of security vanished, being re-placed by an ominous, deep, blue-black sea and a chilling wind.

Sandra, sensing danger, called out, "Sean, the life jackets, we need the life jackets, honey."

He cut the engine to an idle. The Chris-Craft, freely afloat, turned sideways, bow pointed west, port side facing south. The boat, lapped by small waves, drifted slowly out to sea.

Sean entered the cabin and went fore to the bow. He opened the closet beneath the bow's deck. His mind raced, *Empty, no jackets, it's empty.* He yelled, "Shit."

A bleak gloom passing through him created an urgency to re-turn to the marina, to the resort, to their hotel room, to be snuggled in a warm bed with Sandra and Kendra. Sean desperately longed for a safe place.

An unexpected image of Courtney, Charlotte, and the fire flashed through his mind. He scrambled out of the cabin, back to his family.

Sandra asked, "Where are they, honey? Where are the life jackets?"

"They're not there. The damn jackets aren't—"

"Look at the big wave, Daddy."

Sean turned. A single, massive, six-to-eight-foot wave was approaching. He thought of the wake, the freighter's wake. "Hold on!"

The craft, struck broadside by a wall of water, violently rolled starboard, nearly capsizing. Sean, thrown off his feet, struck his head on the steel frame of the captain's chair. Sandra and Kendra were catapulted overboard.

Knocked unconscious, Sean McMillan was dreaming. He was lying in the sun, on a beach at a shoreline, being washed over by waves of cold water. A flock of seagulls flew overhead. The gulls were screaming for help. He heard them. They knew his name. "Help us, Sean; help us, please help us."

He awoke lying on the rear deck in a foot of water. Cut bait and a plastic bucket were floating nearby. Dragging himself up, he looked over the boat's rail. There they were, splashing, struggling. Sandra was desperately screaming for help, "Help us, Sean, help us," calling for him, husband and father, to come to their rescue.

The gulf's current quickly separated Kendra from her mother, dragging both of them away from the boat. Kendra, already fifteen to twenty feet from her mother, was crying, calling out, "Help, Daddy, help!" All three, father in the Chris-Craft, mother and daughter in the sea, were drifting apart.

Kendra, with a look of terror, arms flailing, head bobbing up and under, up and under, screamed, "Daddy, help me!"

Sandra, three months pregnant, was fighting to stay afloat, coughing, choking on water, calling out to her husband, "Sean, save us—save Kendra—get Kendra."

Sean turned the ignition key. Not a sound; the inboard motor was underwater. Stepping to the rear of the deck, he jumped up on the transom. About to dive in… he stopped.

A mere thirty seconds had elapsed from the moment the errant wave had crashed into the cruiser. In another half-minute it would be too late. Sean, imagining a future of unbearable suffering, was paralyzed by the impending tragedy.

Standing erect on the transom, blankly staring out at his drowning family, Sean McMillan, oblivious and confused, was overcome by a maelstrom of agonizing memories ripping through his brain.

He mumbled, "To live is to suffer. I tried to do the right thing. Life is meaningless. Life is pain. I was careful, but I made mistakes. I made a mistake, the life jackets, I didn't look. It's my fault—it's all my fault—it's always my fault."

"Daddy, please, ple . . ." Kendra went under, popping back up, gasping for air.

Sandra screamed, "Sean, my God, help us!"

His family's cries, muffled by the deafening cacophony of pain swirling through his head, seemed miles away.

He thought, *They're too far out. There's not enough time. I can't save both of them. I'm a good swimmer, but it's all happening too fast. I can only save one of them. Which one? Should I save Sandra... her and the baby... no, it should be little Kendra. She's young... I should save her... which one?*

Sean, eyes glazed, face expressionless, thought of the existentialists. Looking up to the sky, he whispered, "Which one do I save? How do I decide? For God's sake, help me."

Not detecting a bit of advice from the philosophers, Sean chose to abandon his lifelong heroes. For once, he would rely on his own instincts.

He thought, *There is no right thing. There is no meaning. There's only pain, nothing but pain. Life is pain and suffering, pain and pain and more pain.*

A yearning, an intense need for pleasure, for something nice and good, consumed him. Again, his mind wandered. He was with Courtney and Charlotte, sitting on the living room floor of the old house. They were playing a card game, a game of hearts. Courtney and he were laughing over Charlotte's cute giggle.

His memories changed to fantasies. Courtney's scented scarf drifted down from above, landing on his lap. He held it to his nose, savoring the fragrance, reveling in her essence. Leaning over, he put his nose to the nape of his wife's neck. He was taken by her precious redolence.

His daydream continued. Turning back to Charlotte, he saw her hair had changed from flowing waves to long braids tucked behind each ear. He gently lifted a braid and placed it under his nose. The exquisite scent of a child, the scent of family, the pure scent of love possessed him.

As always, Sean's joyful dreams were pushed aside by painful, agonizing thoughts. He snapped awake to the screams of his drowning family. *I must be careful. I must do the right thing.*

A drip fell from his chin. Glancing down to the transom, he saw blood; a drop of blood had fallen from the injury to his head. His eyes shifted, focusing on the terrifying blackness of the water. Sean recalled something Dr. Fitzgerald had told him. *It takes courage, Sean. Courage is gratifying and self-fulfilling. It takes courage.*

Looking out to his wife and child, he made a decision. For the first time in Sean McMillan's life, he knew exactly what he had to do.

The Short-Order Cook

From early childhood, Larry Reynolds suffered from coprophagia—a compulsion to drink his urine and eat his feces.

After graduating high school, Larry found a job as a cook in a newly opened restaurant, a small place serving breakfast and lunch.

He caught on quickly, enjoying the challenge of running the kitchen by himself. Business picked up fast, and the owner was pleased with Larry's performance and cooking skills.

Day after day, Larry fought temptation, consciously burying his illicit urges deep inside. At two months' employment, he caved, succumbing to his desires.

At first, he only urinated in the soup. Soon after, he decided the salad dressings could use a tune-up. His position as sole cook made it easy to hide his disgusting activities.

Months went by, business was good, and the owner was elated. By then, Larry was peeing in everything: soups, dressings, gravies, sauces, any item that would readily accept and conceal his deposits.

In addition to urine, Larry's compulsion included the occasional consumption of his excrement. At first, potential shame and guilt, along with fear of making someone sick, prevented him from adding any to his culinary creations. However, his obsession ultimately got the best of him.

To avoid detection, Larry only added small quantities retrieved from the toilet. One or two teaspoons full could be neatly disguised by dark colored soups and brown gravies. He kept a close eye on the restaurants clientele. To his relief, no one complained, and no one got sick.

The owner, who was rarely at the restaurant, being so pleased with his cook's performance, gave Larry a big raise and a nice perk— full health insurance. Life was going well for Larry Reynolds—until one fateful day.

Dropping by on an unannounced visit, the owner entered through the rear of the kitchen. He caught his cook standing at the stove, apron slung over his shoulder, zipper down, adding a little flavor to a large pot of pea soup. Larry was immediately fired.

A day later, a new cook came on board. Over ensuing months, business gradually fell off to the point that closure was imminent. Unhappy customers complained the food had lost a certain zing since Larry had left.

In desperation, the owner placed a call to Larry Reynolds, begging him to come back, offering another raise. Larry accepted.

On his first day back, an elderly couple, regulars at the restaurant, stopped by the kitchen to visit. "Larry, honey, my husband and I are so pleased to have you back. The food here has lacked that special pizzazz ever since you left."

The cook politely smiled, thanked the aging couple for the compliment, and thought, *That special piss-azz would be more accurate.*

Within weeks of Larry's return, business was booming.

An Observation on Self-Esteem

I think I'll start with Bart Jenkins, follow with Tommy, and then tell you a little about myself.

Bartholomew Franklin Jenkins, quite a heady name for one so undeserving. I know his middle name only because of his incessant talking about his favorite topic—himself. Bart came from Pensacola, a true Southern boy with the drawl to prove it. Back then, in the sixties and seventies, people down there were part of the Deep South, not like now, the South being so diluted by northern transplants.

Sergeant Jenkins, having suffered through so much ridicule of his funny name at the hands of grade school classmates, hated being called Bartholomew. He preferred Bart, or Black Bart as he often called himself. Black Bart was an appropriate nickname, not in reference to his skin tone—he was white—but as a description of his soul, if he had one.

His only friends in our platoon, two sycophants, were allowed to call him Blackie. No one else called him that, at least not to his face.

His so-called friends were his protégés, two losers who looked up to Sergeant Jenkins as a role model, someone to emulate. The rest of the platoon found the sergeant intolerable. Bartholomew Jenkins offended everyone he met; it was simply his nature, and it was beyond his control. I think he came by it honestly, being the product of an in-credibly abusive family. He wasn't abused himself; instead, his father taught him how to abuse others. Bart's daddy, as he often called him, a career officer at the naval base in Pensacola, taught his son how to physically and emotionally destroy others for his personal benefit.

Black Bart openly hated everyone and made no bones about it. An incorrigible bigot, he loathed anything foreign, anything and any-one who wasn't just like him, which meant he hated everyone. There was no one else in the platoon like him, thank God. Thinking back about Jenkins, knowing what I know now, I suspect he mostly hated himself. I'm sure he didn't know that, at least not then, he being too young and immature to have developed any personal insight. Maybe years from now, if he lives long enough, he'll figure it out, maybe not.

Blackie, as I'll call him, now that I'm a safe distance away from his relentless intimidation, even hated his mother. I know this only from the tirades he directed at any young recruits who made the mis-take, the offense in Blackie's mind, of talking about their letters or phone calls home to their mom. "Moms are for wimps and pussies. You got that! You're a soldier mister, not a pussy."

As I write this, I'm surprised at how much I know about Bart Jenkins. It's mind boggling that I sat in front of him, day after day, listening to his tales of debauchery. I must have been horribly bored or incredibly lonely. That is until Tommy came along. I'll tell you about Tommy a little later.

Bart was a huge, hulking man. Calling him a man seems inappropriate; he was a thing that stood well over six feet, and I'd guess, weighed about two hundred thirty pounds. He wasn't fat. He was lean and mean, with large, well-defined muscles. He liked to parade around the barracks, bare-chested, shouting out challenges, daring anyone to compete with him in feats of strength, especially anyone he could find who was bigger than he was. His favorite competition was arm wrestling. I never saw him lose, always winning by shear strength or by technique, such as breaking his opponent's fingers.

Despite Bart's heavy musculature, he wasn't muscle-bound, as were a lot of the guys who pumped iron, an activity Jenkins thought was absurd. I never saw him lift anything he absolutely didn't have to. Blackie didn't need to body build; muscles were just him, a genetic gift, probably from his father.

Apparently, he was good at sports, if you could believe his tales of high school athletic endeavors. Bart told numerous stories about his outstanding performance as a football linebacker, baseball out-fielder, and star basketball player. He reveled in detailed descriptions of his late hits and hidden punches in football and his mean elbows in basketball. He liked to brag about the number of opposing baseball infielders he'd taken out by sliding into base with metal spikes held high, aiming for any appendage that got in his way. He even claimed to have sharpened his spikes with a file, hoping to inflict serious injury. I don't doubt that.

Sergeant Jenkins often spoke kindly of his father, whom, as I've said, he called, daddy. His father, who he unfortunately tried to emulate, taught him how to be a man, how to, 'kick ass and take names,' as Bart said. At a young age, he witnessed Daddy's relentless beatings of his mother, whom Bart grew to think of as a wishy-washy doormat, undeserving of her husband.

Bart openly talked about his father, telling of his frequent drunken rages during which he would beat his poor wife senseless. Unbelievably, the sergeant bragged about it, saying it was how he learned to handle women.

The whole thing was incredible, leaving me dumbfounded—thinking of someone abandoning his mother to idolize the man who mercilessly beat her to the brink of death. Once again, I thought it had to be genetic. I figured Black Bart, by some biological fluke of nature, had received most or all his chromosomes from his father, and virtually none from his mother.

Jenkins didn't mind talking about the ridicule and humiliation he went through at a young age. To our surprise, he admitted he'd been a weakling, small for his age, and a target for teasing taunts and derision from his classmates. As he proudly explained, "Later, in high school, everything changed." I suspect he had a massive overflow of testosterone at puberty, resulting in what Bart described as "an incredible transformation into a real man!"

He told us about the eighth-grade experience he went through—a growth spurt associated with profound muscle development, the appearance of a heavy beard and chest hair, and what I must believe was third-degree, pustular acne, which Bart must have left untreated as evidenced by his horribly pock-scarred face.

Men in close quarters tend to brag about their sexual prowess: past girlfriends, one night stands, prostitutes, even wives. If you were to believe Blackie's tales, his only sexual encounters were with the plethora of hookers hanging out around military bases and with four women he claimed to have raped.

His first attack was on an unfortunate teenage woman, an eighteen-year-old in Pensacola, about whom Bart braggingly said he had *taken* right after he graduated from high school. He liked to boast that the police never came close to catching him. His remaining three victims were residents of the Middle East: two during his Persian Gulf tour and one during his tour in Iraq.

I think Jenkins liked to spout off about his escapades because of the intimidating effect it had on the platoon. Every one of us believed we'd be beaten to death if we ever mentioned his violent, illicit past.

Of course, that was before Tommy came along. Bart quit talking about his criminal activities after Thomas Archambeau showed up. I'm sure he knew Tommy wasn't afraid of him and wouldn't tolerate his tales of immoral activity; Bart knew Tommy would have vehemently challenged the veracity of his tall tales, challenging Bart's motives and honesty.

When Bart thought he could get away with it, he engaged in killing, actual murder. Unfortunately, in the Iraqi desert, he felt he could get away with anything, including murder, and he didn't bother to hide the fact.

Near the end of my tour, just before I shipped out, despite having previously seen the joy Bart took in killing, I saw just how pathological he truly was. Sergeant Bartholomew Franklin Jenkins was a consummate menace to society, just a hairs-breadth shy of a whacked-out, homicidal sociopath.

•

Thomas Aquinas Archambeau, quite a heady name, which in his case was well deserved. Tommy hailed from Escanaba, a small town in

Michigan's upper peninsula, populated with descendants of French fur trappers. He was and remains the best friend I've ever had.

In Iraq, I learned a lot about Corporal Archambeau, not because he blabbed like Bart Jenkins but because he and I became close friends. Tommy was a self-confident gentleman with rock-solid integrity and a self-awareness you rarely find. He knew who he was, and he didn't have to seek approval for it; he didn't need permission to be a member of the human race. Tommy was confident of his abilities and sensitive to his weaknesses.

Life in my platoon had been lonely; I was forlorn and depressed until Tommy came along. It took some time for our friendship to develop, Tommy, at first, keeping to himself and I being too insecure to approach him. He had spoken to me a few times, but I was always too busy thinking about myself to return his kindness. A few weeks later, that all changed.

At first, he told me a little about himself; then he started asking about me. The amazing thing—the thing that blew me away—was his obvious, genuine interest in me. He honestly wanted to know about my past: my likes, my dislikes, and my dreams for the future.

It was hard for me to talk about myself. After all, no one had ever asked before. Everyone I'd ever known had basically ignored me, talking about anything but me. Mostly, they talked about themselves: how great they were, what they had done, and what they were going to do. Not that I hadn't tried telling my story, but after seeing so many bored faces and glazed-over eyes, it became too embarrassing and pointless, so I quit trying. Embarrassment kind of sums up my youth. I never would have admitted that if I hadn't met Tommy. Certainly, I never would have put it down in writing as I have here. If it weren't for Tommy Archambeau, I wouldn't be the least aware of who I'd been in the past or who I am now.

I think Corporal Archambeau must have bolstered my self-confidence; after a few conversations with him, the floodgates opened. I talked endlessly about myself: my past, my present, my family, my best memories, my worst memories, and most importantly, me. I'm referring to the real me: my shame, my fears, my faults, and even my few achievements.

Tommy listened intently, I mean really listened and understood, occasionally offering his insights, his empathy, and his helpful suggestions. He knew so much about human nature. When he talked about himself, he did it passionately, honestly admitting his past mistakes, along with his accomplishments. He'd tell me about himself from the inside, not like some people whose self-descriptions are aimed at showing up others with a façade of self-importance.

The most amazing point of all was Tommy's ability to sincerely convey details of his fears, his wants, his weaknesses, and his secrets—things he was ashamed of and things he was proud of. He did it all in a matter-of-fact way with no hint of shame or embarrassment, no boastfulness or pride.

Since I've been home, I've done some reading on psychiatry. Now I think I know what Tommy possessed, what made Tommy, Tommy. It was self-esteem, an often-misused term and misunderstood entity—a specious label when used to describe weak people with exterior self-confidence, usually arrogance.

Tommy Archambeau was the embodiment of self-esteem. He could accept compliments graciously and accept criticism with an open ear, without retaliation, taking it to heart, analyzing its accuracy, and doing his best to change his behavior accordingly. He neither criticized nor inappropriately praised others. He stood out in our environment, a platoon with many ill-tempered sycophants, doing their damnedest to please anyone of authority.

Tommy would offer constructive criticism but only if he perceived the need to help someone, and it always came across as kind advice. He also complimented others in an honest way, without exaggeration or superlatives and with no favors or compliments expected in return.

On rare occasions, he said unkind words or participated in gossip, something that was otherwise rampant in our unit. After such an exchange, Tommy would consider what he'd said, usually commenting that he'd not been at his best. He wouldn't show disabling remorse—instead, he'd analyze what he'd said, examining his motives, saying things such as "I wonder why I did that" or "I'll have to think about that."

I could go on about Tommy Archambeau for pages, not to glorify him with accolades, which he certainly wouldn't want, but to convey his qualities as an example of appropriate self-confidence and true inner awareness—one of the rare people who know who they are. Instead, I'd like use him as a case study—an entity to be psycho-logically dissected in order to separate the emotions, all the traits that fall together to make a human being. I present him as a person to be examined and understood, a person who I believe exemplifies true self-esteem.

Tommy once told me about his being a star hockey player in Escanaba. He was an All-American. Once again, he relayed this information without a hint of arrogance or a trace of embarrassment. In addition, he pragmatically stated he'd been popular in high school, having had many friends, and despite, by his own admission, being average in the *looks* department, more than a few girlfriends, one of whom he eventually married.

As he relayed his good fortune, considering his somewhat homely, acne-scarred face, I made a comparison between him and Bart Jenkins, realizing Bart's problem with girls in high school wasn't his appearance; it was his was his terrifying personality. That's all I'll say about Tommy now, Tommy Archambeau, my friend.

•

I've told you about Bart Jenkins and Tommy Archambeau. Now you get to hear about me.

I'll start with this. From the time I was a young child until now, people have been telling me how intelligent I am. I've never believed them.

So, who am I? That's a good question. I thought I knew the answer until I met Tommy. He made me realize I didn't have the slightest idea of who I was, but that was okay. It didn't scare me; it inspired me to work on finding myself.

I needed to figure out what made me tick—figure out who I'd been, deep on the inside. Until you know that about yourself, it's pointless to work on who you want to be. You don't have a starting point, a starting line for your venture into the future.

I can tell you, recite to you, who I was in relation to what I'd done and how I'd behaved. I don't think I can tell you why I did what I did. I don't yet have that degree of personal insight. Tommy tried to help me with that. I hope he gave me some foundation for the future, some building blocks to construct my self-identity, maybe even build a bit of self-esteem. So, I'll tell you about my past. Perhaps you can help me piece it together from a psychological point of view.

This autobiography will be mercifully brief, mainly because I don't remember much of my past. I don't know why my memory's so poor; maybe I don't want to remember. Here's a quick summary.

I was born and raised in Cincinnati, Ohio. Interestingly, from a geographic standpoint, Cincinnati is smack dab between Escanaba and Pensacola. Realizing that reminds me I have a blend of behavioral traits similar to both Tommy and, unfortunately, Bart Jenkins.

My family lived in an average neighborhood, not anything special but not in the rough parts of town either. I lived with my parents, two older brothers, and a younger sister.

I went to school. I was a smart kid. I was scared. I didn't do well in school. I was afraid my classmates would think I was an egghead, so I hung out with the losers. The losers seemed to like me, which made me wonder why they always used me as a target for their jokes. I was their verbal punching bag. I didn't mind being a punching bag for my friends—if not for them, I would have been alone.

The alternative to my derelict, so-called friends would have been the academic students, the other eggheads who didn't mind being eggheads. Even though, I knew, or at least had been repeatedly told, I was innately as intelligent as they, I remained, for unknown reasons, terrified of the mere thought of associating with them, the school's intelligentsia.

In my grade school years, I'd blush furiously if someone, like a teacher, gave me a compliment. I don't know why I was so embarrassed by being worthy of praise. I learned to under-perform to avoid compliments, thereby avoiding red-faced embarrassment. I guess I was full of shame.

My high school friends and I did a lot of stupid stuff—vandalizing, stealing, and, most importantly, drinking. I drank a lot in high school. I never liked the taste of beer or liquor, but I drank it anyway.

I had good parents. I think they loved me, but I'm not sure. I never told them I loved them, and they never said they loved me. I was too insecure to tell my parents about my fears, my frequent blushing embarrassment, and my feelings of shame. Of course, I never told them of my vandalizing, stealing, and drinking either.

During my last two years of high school, I had a girlfriend. She was okay. She wasn't very pretty, but I didn't mind. We never had sex, even though she wanted to. I was probably worried I'd embarrass my-self, somehow screw it up. No pun intended.

I was a pretty good athlete, but I never joined any teams, maybe because it wasn't the cool thing to do, more likely because I was worried— worried I'd be a burden to my teammates.

I went to church because my parents made me. I quit going when I graduated high school.

As I've told you, throughout my life, people have told me I'm very, VERY intelligent. That always surprised me and always made me blush like crazy. Despite my supposed profound intellect, I never did well in school.

After high school, I worked in a grocery store. I hated it. I think that's why I joined the military, but I'm not sure.

Okay, that's it in a nutshell—back to Iraq.

•

Tommy and I spent six months together in the Middle East. We talked nearly every night. I loved it. We talked about everything—what he'd done and what he wanted to do. He taught me how to analyze my feelings, how to assess my emotions, how to understand being happy at one moment and sad the next. It was great.

With three obvious exceptions, namely Bart Jenkins and his two sycophants, Tommy and I were friends with or at least acquainted with every guy in our platoon.

As a sergeant, Bart was one rank higher than Tommy, a corporal. Bart hated Tommy, taking every opportunity to give him dirty, back-breaking detail assignments, which Tommy always took in stride, never complaining.

A few of our platoon members, knowing Tommy and I were close friends, thought we were gay. I remember one of them, a buck private, boldly taunting Tommy, the higher ranked corporal, calling us a pair of faggots.

Tommy calmly blew the guy away, looking him straight in the eye with neither anger nor the outburst the repugnant private was hoping for. He quietly said, "No, I'm not gay, and my friend's not either. You'd probably like him if you ever got to know him. Besides, why would it matter if we were?" The private turned and walked away, looking like a scorned child.

We'd get packages from home every three to four weeks, or I should say, they would get packages, most of the other guys, Tommy included. The boxes usually contained food, cigarettes, and occasionally, liquor. I never got any packages. Since I didn't want to bother my parents, I made them promise not to send anything but letters if they wanted.

Tommy received one or two mail deliveries every three weeks or so—big boxes full of toys and candy he'd hand out to the Arabic kids, and there were swarms of kids. When we patrolled through town, they'd come out from everywhere, especially if they saw Tommy. There were also a lot of children who hung out around our camp.

Corporal Archambeau was their favorite American. A crowd of youngsters, even teenagers, would gather around him wherever he went. The kids loved him. He never complained about their begging for candy bars or toys, which he gladly handed out.

One of the children in town, a nine-year-old girl, became close friends with Tommy. She introduced him to her family. Her father, Mohammed, once invited Tommy to their home for dinner; that's when he gave Tommy permission to call him Mo. His daughter's name was Amira; she liked it when Tommy called her Ami.

We went on patrol nearly every day. Sergeant Jenkins usually split us into squads of four to five men, each group being dispatched to different reconnaissance assignments. He never once put Corporal Archambeau in his squad. Unfortunately, Bart nearly always took me. I never understood that; I hated it.

Black Bart would lead us around town, demonstrating how to rough up civilians and, sometimes, if there were no bystanders in sight, severely beat them. "This is called mandatory interrogation, you guys. Stick with me, and you'll learn how to beat information outta these sand niggers."

I saw him pummel men and women, even young boys, for no reason at all. I'd stand there in silence, ashamed of myself, afraid to say a thing, while Bart's disgusting stewards, his two acolytes, laughed, goading him to beat his victims senseless. "Go, Blackie, go! Give it to 'em, Sarge. You're the man."

I witnessed things I'd never repeat to anyone, assured Black Bart would exact horrid revenge, possibly having me taken out while on patrol, reporting I'd been shot by a sniper.

To make matters worse, Bartholomew Jenkins was an expert shot, a skill he often demonstrated with pride. Bart had an uncanny ability to assess crosswind velocity, target distance, and gravitational effect. The guy could hit a bull's-eye from five hundred feet.

On one of our patrols, Jenkins had the audacity to brag about the number of Iraqi civilians he'd killed 'just for kicks'. I suspect he did it to impress his boys.

As I've said, I often wondered why Bart routinely assigned me to his patrol section, especially knowing I'd witness his illicit, despicable activity. Over time, after Tommy helped me gain some personal insight, I realized what the sergeant's motives were in taking me with him to observe his murderous addiction.

I think he simply sensed my insecurity, my apprehensive, timorous nature, and he took advantage of it, forcing me to witness his bar-baric deeds, knowing I lacked the courage to report him. Bart knew he had me under his thumb; he knew he scared the shit out of me.

About three months after Tommy arrived, Jenkins crossed a line. As usual, I was on patrol with him and his two boys. We were in a High Mobility Multipurpose Wheeled Vehicle, otherwise known as a Humvee, driving through the outskirts of Baghdad. I saw a young Iraqi woman walking alone in a park. Unfortunately, Bart saw her too.

"Pull up next to the park and stop. Look at that, what a fine piece of Iraqi tail!" He told the driver, one of his boys, to go straight across the park's sandy lawn, heading toward the woman, who appeared to be no more than twenty years of age. "Let's go catch that bitch before she gets away."

The girl looked terrified as the hulking sergeant stepped out of the vehicle. "Where you goin'? I need to ask you a few questions."

The young woman, speaking broken English, replied. "I go home; I go to family."

The boys, apparently knowing their positions, were standing on either side of her. I could only assume they'd been through this routine before. I stayed in the Hummer.

Black Bart started looking around, panning the area for bystanders—there were none. Without warning, wham, he slapped the girl across the face. Falling back, she was caught by Bart's asshole friends, one pinning her arms to the ground as the other locked his hand over her mouth. "Good catch men. Now watch this!"

I was appalled. Bart ripped the poor girl's clothes off, and savagely raped her as his pathetic, evil servants chuckled with delight.

"Let her have it, Blackie."

"Yea, this bitch is fine. She needs a good fuckin'!"

The next thing I knew I was out of the Humvee, running toward them. It just happened— I had no idea what I was going to do. I was scared shitless. "Hey, what's goin' on?" What a ridiculous question, I thought. I felt like a fool.

Bart paused his attack and looked up. "What do ya think's goin' on, you lazy piece of shit? Stay right where you are and wait your turn."

Wait my turn, I thought. *He's out of his mind.*

When Blackie was through, each of his loathsome, reptilian friends took his turn atop the broken, helpless girl.

Bart addressed me. "You're next, ass-wipe."

I stood there, emotionally paralyzed, not responding, thinking, *God, please help me outta this mess.*

Jenkins yelled, "What's wrong with you? Get over here and ride this bitch."

"I… I don't want to." My fear was obvious. "You're a fuckin' homo pussy, ya know that? You're not a soldier, not even a man."

Thank God, he let me off the hook. I fell flat on my back when Jenkins smashed me in the chest with the heel of his hand. "Get up! We gotta get the fuck outta here before someone sees us."

As we drove away, I looked back at the girl, struggling to her feet, trying to cover herself with shredded clothing, hobbling away toward home. I spent the remainder of the day nauseated, crippled by shame and guilt—ashamed of my fear and helplessness, guilt-ridden for not having the courage to act or even report the incident.

That night I talked to Tommy. Engrossed in my story, he quietly listened to descriptions of the day's repugnant events. When I finished, he said, "I'm not surprised to hear this. Jenkins and his two servile friends are dangerous people. You need to be careful around them, especially Jenkins."

I asked what he thought I should do.

"This is a tough situation. If I confront Jenkins, he'll know you told me about it. I don't want to put you at risk; I honestly think he'd kill you. On the other hand, I can't let this go on. Let me think about it; we'll talk tomorrow."

We spoke the following night. Tommy had some good ideas. "I thought you might put in for a transfer. Then I could deal with Jenkins by myself. But a transfer would take weeks, and Bart might hurt you before you leave."

"Yeah, I don't like that idea."

Tommy chuckled, "No, I didn't think you would. This has to be done anonymously. If Jenkins knows I reported him, he'll go after you first. I pretty sure I can deal with him, but you're too close, always with him on patrol. You'd be an easy mark."

I said, Yeah, I'm glad you realize that."

Tommy laughed again. "I thought of writing an anonymous letter, reporting the incident to the first lieutenant. But he doesn't seem to have the backbone to challenge Jenkins. So, my plan is to go higher up. I'm going to report this to the captain."

"The captain! How can you make an anonymous report to the captain? I don't think I like that plan either, Tommy."

"Don't worry. The last thing I want to do is jeopardize your life. I'll figure it out."

Tommy made his report. One, two, three weeks passed, and nothing happened. Bart Jenkins went about business as usual. Tommy and I talked about it. "Tommy, nothing's happened. Do you thing the captain got your letter?"

"I know he got it. Here's the problem. Most people back home are against this war, and the last thing the military wants is more bad PR.

I'm sure they're worried about the media getting wind of this. I don't think they'll pursue it."

"Shit! What if Bart knows we ratted on him? I'll be a dead man."

"I've been watching him closely, and I haven't seen any change in his behavior. If he knew, I'd be able to tell. Don't worry, he's clueless."

"I hope you're right!

Tommy put his arm around me. "I'll keep watching. If he were going to find out, he would have by now. Just stay on guard; you'll be okay."

•

The day of my last patrol, it happened. Four of us, Black Bart, his friends, and I were riding in a Humvee on the edge of town. That was the day Sergeant Jenkins saw what he considered the perfect target. An Iraqi man was standing in the middle of a Baghdad street. The big, round man—a Muslim, as evidenced by his attire—had his back turned to us. A light rain had cleared the streets, leaving the sole Iraqi in the roadway two or three blocks from us.

Bart said, "Stop right here." Stepping from the Hummer, he turned with a cold stare, saying, "Watch this!"

Raising his M-16, Jenkin's said, "Hey, you morons, pay attention. You just might learn something. This one's goin' right in the back of the fat man's head." Leveling his rifle, he drew a bead on the Iraqi. No one said a word.

Just before Black Bart pulled the trigger, I took a long, hard look down the street, realizing who the man was. It was Tommy's friend, Mo, the father of Amira, the nine-year-old he'd befriended.

Jenkins, peering through the gun's scope, gently squeezed. He missed, that is he missed the Iraqi's head. The tumbling bullet tore into the man's back, knocking him flat to the ground. Bart's two shit-head friends broke out in raucous laughter.

I just sat there feeling sick. We finished our patrol, I having to listen to endless compliments on the sergeant's precision shooting, despite his having missed his mark by at least a foot.

That afternoon, after we returned to camp, I was informed that Tommy Archambeau was missing. His patrol had returned without him. Members of his reconnaissance group, having separated for a few minutes, couldn't find Tommy; he'd simply disappeared. A search patrol was sent out. I volunteered to go along.

Entering town, finding Mo, still lying in the street, our patrol went over to investigate. Of course, I didn't mention anything about what I'd previously witnessed. That's when we found out—found out what Bart had done.

I watched as two of my friends rolled Mohammed's body face up. Incredibly, there were two more bodies lying beneath him. I screamed, "My God, it's Tommy!"

Tommy Archambeau's body had been hidden from view, lying beneath Mohammed's obese corpse. Tommy was lying there, his arms still wrapped around Amira, who was wedged between her father and her friend. Sergeant Jenkin's bullet had ripped right through Mo and his daughter, lodging deep in Tommy's chest.

Initially, I thought Tommy's death was a tragic coincidence, despite the fact it was the one guy whom Bart truly hated. I assumed Bart had no idea the corporal and young girl were there, hidden from view, behind Mohammed. But, I did wonder how much Sergeant Jenkins saw through his telescopic sight—maybe he did know.

Certainly, Bart knew we—his friends and I—couldn't have possibly seen Corporal Archambeau from that distance without using a sight or, at least, a pair of binoculars. I wanted to think Jenkins didn't see him either.

But days later, after having thought long and hard about the whole terrible event, I remembered something Black Bart had said just before he fired his rifle. I didn't think much of it at the time, but now I do. As the sergeant looked through his scope, just before he squeezed the trigger, he said, "Well, well, well, look who's here." We all thought he was surprised to see the Iraqi was Mo, someone he knew. Now I think otherwise.

The army doesn't waste any time when disposing of dead soldiers. Tommy Archambeau took off in a body bag the very next day. His family buried him in a cemetery just outside Escanaba, next to his grandfather. I know because of the letter.

Three weeks after Tommy's death, I received a letter from his wife. I was elated when it arrived, elated to hear from someone who knew

Tommy better than I did. She thanked me for being such a good friend to her husband.

The unbelievable part, the part that hit me like a sledge hammer, was Mrs. Archambeau writing that Tommy once told her his time in Iraq would have been much more difficult if he hadn't met me, his good friend. I was stunned to hear he'd been talking about me in letters and phone calls to his wife. Tommy apparently told her that he would have had a hard time living in the desert, in makeshift homes with hundreds of men and women, if I hadn't been there. I, having never experienced any close friendships, was astonished.

My tour ended about three weeks after her letter. Now I'm back in Cincinnati, the Queen City on the Ohio River. Since being home, I've thought a lot about my tour, wondering if I'd truly learned any-thing from Tommy. I do know one thing for sure, I want to be like him. It's not envy; I don't want to be him; I want to be like him, as emotionally, behaviorally, and psychologically normal as he was.

I hope I've gained something from Tommy, absorbing some of his wonderful qualities. I'd love to be as mentally fit as he was. I crave having at least a modicum of personal insight and self-esteem. However, despite our months of friendship, I doubt I've truly gained much.

•

It's been eight years since I came back from the Middle East. I'm still in Cincinnati and I'm in graduate school, which surprises me.

After returning home, I went back to work at the grocery store. I didn't hate it as much as I had in the past when I was right out of high school. However, I was bored, feeling I could do better. I quit that job and spent a few months unemployed, taking time off to think about my life.

During that interval, I started going to church. I'm not sure why I did; it just seemed to happen. Maybe it had something to do with Tommy's belief in a supreme being. I remember our conversations as though they were yesterday. We talked about God, Christianity, Juda-ism, and many other things. Even as a young man, Tommy was convinced there was some external power, some source of creation that controlled or at least designed the universe. He called that force God.

Tommy had been raised as a Catholic. He'd been skeptical of the divinity of Jesus Christ, finding it easier to believe in a God, an all-knowing, omniscient, omnipresent entity, while questioning the divinity of a living man who claimed to be the son of God. Despite that, he told me he tried to emulate the behavior of Jesus, believing Christ was the best role model one could have.

Tommy also told me some interesting stuff about Albert Einstein. Apparently, as Einstein delved deeper and deeper into physics, specifically the science of matter, energy, and gravity, he eventually became convinced of the theory of intelligent design, the theory the universe and the laws of physics are too spectacular to have come about by chance. I was surprised when Tommy said Einstein hadn't been religious.

I said, "Tommy, I thought the guy was Jewish."

He replied, "He was born into a Jewish family, and I'm sure he practiced Judaism when he was young."

"Isn't that why he left Germany, to flee the Nazis?"

"Yeah, that's right. My point is this. Later in life, his writings indicated he gave no credence to any religion, Jewish or otherwise. He knew all religions were man-made entities, having little if any basis in divinity."

"Really?"

"The fascinating point is Einstein's conclusion about the creation of the universe. After studying and understanding so much about the atom, gravity, and relativity, he believed the universe was too in-credible to have come about by chance. The further he progressed in science, the more convinced he became of an external source of creation."

"Tommy, that's amazing. I would have guessed just the opposite. I would've thought the more he explained through science, the more he would deny the existence of a divine creator. Wouldn't you?"

"Sure, that's what set Einstein apart from many other scientists, at least at the time. I guess the magic of it all, the astounding way it all fits together, was too much for him to accept as coincidence. Einstein was an amazing man."

"Yeah, sounds like it to me."

Tommy continued attending Catholic mass every Sunday, even in Iraq. I asked him about the contradiction, his faith in God but not Jesus.

"I use Catholicism as a weekly reminder of my dedication to a Christian lifestyle. The Catholic Church has laws and rituals of questionable value—many having developed during centuries of corruption in the Middle Ages. Despite that, I still benefit from attendance, not from adherence to dogmatic rules but from the Christian atmosphere and comradery among devout parishioners.

"Don't get me wrong. The Catholic Church is a wonderful institution, giving millions upon millions of dollars to the poor and suffering, building hospitals and nursing homes, and providing hope for countless numbers of poverty-stricken, disenfranchised inhabitants of planet Earth. And, there's one more thing. Catholics believe in salvation through good deeds and good works. In contrast, when Martin Luther broke away from Catholicism, he advocated *sola fide*, salvation by faith alone. It's a major point, doing good deeds versus simply having faith. I prefer the former."

Tommy said his being Catholic was simply based on his child-hood experience, having been raised in a French Catholic community. He admitted any religion based upon benevolence and love toward your fellow man would be appropriate, be it Christianity, Islam, Judaism, Buddhism, Hinduism, and so on.

Thinking of our role in Iraq, I asked the obvious question. "You mentioned Islam. We're here fighting Muslims right now."

"I think Muslims, in general, are getting a bad deal. I haven't read the Koran, but I'd like to believe Mohammed's teachings were just as benevolent as Christ's. Unfortunately, the religious fanatics, the Muslim extremists—the jihadists are a problem."

"How's that? If they're motivated by Mohammed's teachings and the Koran, how can they be a problem?"

"Yeah, unfortunately, that's the message they're sending to the rest of the world. They want us to think that. They claim to be reacting to the words of Mohammed, but I suspect they function on a gross misinterpretation of the Koran. As I said, I haven't read the Koran, so I may be wrong. It's something for us to think about while we're here in the Middle East. That's part of the reason I enlisted. Someone has to help these poor people defend themselves from the extremists and dictators like Hussein. However, as I've said, I've never read the Koran or much about Mohammed's teachings. So, I may be wrong."

Tommy's enlistment in the army raised another issue. "Tommy, if you're trying to follow a Christian lifestyle, why did you join the army? You may have to kill someone."

"That's a good question, and believe me, I've given it a lot of thought. I'm patriotic in the sense of firmly believing in the importance of preserving democracy—not just for the United States but for the world. I studied sociology and government in college. From what I know, it appears democratic societies usually turn out the best in the long run."

"Would you kill to preserve democracy? It's still contrary to Christian teaching, or most religions for that matter."

"I've reconciled that contradiction by making a commitment to myself."

"What commitment?"

"Historically it's often been necessary to put down evil for the good of mankind. I hope I never have to take a life. However, if taking the life of a murderer is required for the protection of the innocent, I'll do it. I'd prefer to not be in that situation, wishing diplomacy could prevail, but that's not working here."

"Would you kill someone purely to save your own life?"

"Another pertinent question. You impress me. The answer is yes. That doesn't sound very Christian, does it? "No, it doesn't."

"I'm here out of a sense of obligation. I'm here not to harm others but to protect the innocent. I also have an obligation to stay alive for my wife and children."

"Of course."

"That reality could put me in a position of self-preservation. Yes, I'd kill someone who is trying to kill me. Without such dedication, the world would be chaos. There are always going to be those who seek power for their own benefit, rather than the good of all. Those people have to be stopped."

The possibility of Tommy's death, or my own, raised another thought. "Tommy, do you believe in an afterlife, heaven and hell?"

"I want to believe there's something more than just life on Earth. I suppose most of us do. Of course, the concept of heaven and hell is fairly well laid out in the Bible."

"So, you think heaven and hell exist."

"Who knows? I guess no one knows until they're gone. How-ever, I want to believe there's something more than this. It's difficult to think of the countless millions who suffer their whole lives, from birth till death, without receiving some reward in the end. That's a philosophical answer to an impossible question."

I continued, "What about hell?"

"Regarding hell, I don't lend any credence to the concept of eternal punishment. If there's a benevolent God, the thought of him sending any of his creations to eternal torture is impossible to reconcile. I guess my short answer is simply that I hope heaven exists; otherwise, our brief life on Earth seems rather pointless. Don't you agree?"

"Yeah, having heard your explanation, I do agree. Tommy, what are your thoughts on atheism?"

"I sometimes wonder how an atheist, a true atheist can live through life's ups and downs, expecting nothing in the end. But, who knows? Maybe atheists are right. I hope not."

"Please, go on."

"Okay, thank you, I will. An atheist may logically argue that the idea of a divine creator and, more importantly, the prospect of an afterlife of eternal bliss are simply the product of man's wishes—those wishes and hopes being the expected result of a painful, essentially meaningless existence on Earth, a life replete with pain and suffering, interspersed with brief interludes of happiness. In other words, hu-man beings naturally want to believe there's more to come, something better than life on Earth, something wonderful waiting for us."

"Wow, that was a mouthful. Tommy, you've got some crazy vocabulary, man."

"Thanks, I appreciate the compliment." "And?"

"And, what?"

"What about hell, from an atheist's viewpoint?"

"Hell's another story. I suspect, if speaking from an atheist's standpoint, the concept of hell came about after early man developed moral behavior—the idea of hell being necessitated by the kill-or-be-killed environment people lived in. The thought of spending eternity in unspeakable agony may have initially been used to keep the renegades in line. An atheist might argue that the notion of eternal damnation was propagated as an attempt to control man's evil nature, thereby allowing the development of civilized society."

"Tommy, my head's spinnin'."

"That's okay; so is mine."

Thinking about all I'd heard, I replied, "Tommy, I'm exhausted." I truly was.

Tommy politely agreed it was time to for us to take a break. "There's one last thing I'd like to clarify."

"Sure, what's that?"

"Well, after all I've said, I don't want you to think I'm an atheist; I'm absolutely not. Also, after recently thinking about it, I've come to the conclusion that Jesus Christ was and is divine."

"I'm glad to hear that, Tommy." I gave him a hug.

Two weeks later, Tommy Archambeau was dead.

•

I think I'll get back to my post-Iraq experience. As I was saying, I started going to church soon after returning home. My parents are Lutheran; they made me go to church when I was a kid. I hated it back then. I'd sit there daydreaming, bored out of my mind. I quit going the day I moved out of their house, the day after I graduated high school.

But now, ten years later, I'm back in church. Our pastor is a bright guy, and I enjoy his sermons. He has a lot of good advice about living right. I bet Tommy would have liked him. The Lutheran church would have been okay with him. For Tommy, the message was the important thing.

During the three-month hiatus between quitting my job and starting college, I spent hours upon hours pondering the world. Using the word "hiatus" reminds me of another change I've had since returning to Cincinnati. For some reason, and I have no idea why, I've started reading, something I rarely did. Consequently, my vocabulary has expanded by leaps and bounds. I've never been one to read the newspaper, magazines, books, anything relevant. My favorite literature was the TV guide. I preferred hours of TV over a brief trip to the library. Anyway, I never would have used the word "hiatus," let alone know what it means or how to spell it.

As I was going to say, after my three-month hiatus, I decided to go to college. I'm not sure why I did, probably because it was free. Since I'd served my country, the government paid for all of it. I had no idea what I was going to study. I wound up in psychology, not because I thought psychology was something special; it was just by chance if you ask me. When I randomly opened the college curriculum catalog, it was right there staring me in the face, Psychology 101. I thought, what the heck, and enrolled as a psych major.

Oh, yeah, one more thing about my time off, my hiatus. I like saying that, hiatus, that is. Anyway, it was during that time that I stopped drinking. I can't believe I did. I'd been a pretty heavy hitter for many years, especially in high school and, of course, during my military tour in Iraq where drinking was rampant. I liked getting smashed; it helped me quit thinking about myself, helped me quit worrying about everything, especially me.

I don't know why I went on the wagon, so to speak; I simply quit. I think I didn't need it anymore, maybe because I don't worry as much as I used to.

I just realized something; I don't feel nearly as insecure as I did in the past. Anyway, I don't need alcohol or any mood-altering sub-stance, probably because my mood is just fine the way it is. On occasion I do have a glass of wine if I'm out with friends—just one glass.

Speaking of friends, I can't believe how many good friends I have now. Real friends, not like the losers I hung out with in high school. These people seem to truly care about me. But the amazing thing is this—I care about them, too.

And another thing, I quit smoking. I was up to a pack and a half a day. Tommy never said much about it, other than once asking why I did it. I think I responded with something inane like, "Because, I like it." I did; I really liked it. Then it got old and seemed like a dumb thing to do. I haven't had a smoke for three years, and I don't miss it a bit.

I'm engaged now; I met her in one of my classes. She's wonderful, not a beauty queen, but my girl is everything I've dreamed of. I love her so much it hurts. That degree of love, or any love for that matter, is a new experience for me. She and I can sit and talk for hours, and she truly listens to me and responds. More importantly, I listen to her and respond. It's fun.

I never was much of a listener; I guess I was too busy thinking about myself to pay attention to anyone else, such as my girlfriend in high school. I can't remember a thing she said. All I remember is being nervous when around her, asking myself things like: *Do I look okay? Does she think I'm stupid?* Then I'd think, *I am stupid. I hope she doesn't think I'm a dork like my buddies do. Does she like my clothes? Am I cool enough for her? Maybe I should kiss her, maybe not. What if I have bad breath!*

Stuff like that used to spin around in my head. Oddly enough, I haven't felt that way in years. Being a good listener and having a clear head must be a habit I developed with Tommy.

After starting college, I stopped putting people down behind their backs. Tommy never did that. Maybe I learned more from him than I realize. I also quit telling dirty jokes, especially racial jokes. My friends in college didn't seem to think I was humorous. They would politely smile, but never laughed the way my friends in high school did. We were always cracking jokes back then, the raunchier the better. We'd all bust a gut laughing at racial slurs and put-down jokes.

Since I've stopped the inappropriate jokes, I've noticed I quit putting my foot in my mouth, a formerly common occurrence. I used to exacerbate my humiliation with self-deprecating humor, which my pseudo-friends in high school greatly enjoyed (exacerbate, self-deprecate, pseudo—I can hardly believe my new vocabulary).

Friends in college didn't seem to like it when I tried to entertain them at my expense, criticizing myself. They kindly told me I shouldn't put myself down, saying it was self-destructive and totally inaccurate. I didn't argue with them, and it's helped me feel better about who I am.

I used to wish Tommy had been here to tutor me in college, but I guess I did all right on my own. The truth is I surprised myself and did quite well. I graduated with a bachelor's degree in psychology. I worked hard and enjoyed learning, quite a change from high school. I even got an award for an essay I wrote on self-esteem and was given a plaque at a Psychology Department ceremony. I walked on stage, graciously accepted the honor, and simply said thank you.

I shudder to think what it would have been like getting an academic achievement award in high school. I probably would've fallen all over myself with embarrassment. I can only imagine what my high school buddies would have done, maybe hit me over the head with my plaque.

After graduating, I had to find a job, something that in the past would have been quite difficult, my only qualifications having been for bagging groceries. I found a part-time job as an assistant to a clinical psychologist, after which my girl and I got married.

While working with Dr. Hammond, the psychologist, I decided to go to graduate school for a master's degree. Now I'm out on my own with my own practice.

This is my fourth year as a clinical counselor, and I'm amazed at how much my clients seem to benefit from my advice. When I started, I'd wished Tommy had been there to guide me along, helping me analyze my patients' problems. But I've done all right. I've learned a lot over the years, and I'm proud of my work.

My wife and I are doing wonderfully, and we're anxiously awaiting the birth of our first child. I've been able to save enough money to put a down payment on a new house, which truly amazes me. In the past, I'd blow my paychecks as fast as I could, buying booze and cigarettes and spending money on material things I was sure I needed to make me happy.

I've quit trying to buy happiness. My car, for instance, is a used Ford Taurus. It runs great, I like it, and its purchase was practical. Years ago, I'd dream of having a convertible Mercedes or a Jag. That showy stuff doesn't seem to interest me anymore. I think it's more important to save for the future than spend money on meaningless luxuries. My wife and I have developed a budget, which we adhere to without difficulty.

I still miss Tommy, and once in a while, I send a letter to his widow, just to see how things are going up in Escanaba. She always writes back, thanking me for my concern, telling me she's doing well. She's been dating, but she's having trouble finding the right guy.

•

I can't believe it! I almost forgot to give you follow-up on Bart Jenkins. I'm proud to say that the more I thought about Sergeant Jenkins's abuse of Iraqi civilians and his murder of my best friend, the more determined I became to seek justice for that pathological son-of-a-bitch.

I'm convinced Tommy's death was intentional. Besides remembering Bart's comment, "Well, well, well, look who's here," there was also the fact he missed his target. I remember being astonished when the bullet struck Mo in the middle of his back, not in the head, as Bart had intended.

It was hard to believe Jenkins, being such an expert shot, could have missed by that much. Now, I'm convinced it was no accident. I believe Blackie knew exactly what he was doing, aiming low to take out Mo and Tommy with one bullet. I'm sure he didn't know Amira was there, she being so small, hidden behind her father.

Whether he intentionally killed Tommy or Amira, is a moot point, his long history of criminal activity, raping young Iraqi girls, and killing innocent civilians was more than enough to have him put away for life.

I decided to write some letters, describing what I'd witnessed in Iraq and what I'd overheard during hours of Bart Jenkins's incessant bragging. I sent letters to the Pentagon, my senator, and my representative in Congress. I even sent a letter to the president. I wasn't expecting much of a response, knowing the military's hatred of bad publicity. However, with persistence, after follow-up with more letters and phone calls, Bart Jenkins finally went down. I gladly testified at his court martial, which took no more than an hour. Jenkins essentially hung himself right in front of the review panel.

His display of violent arrogance started when he lunged from the witness stand, trying to grab the prosecuting officer by the throat, resulting in the placement of two MPs on either side of the stand.

As questioning progressed, Bart kept staring at me with threatening looks. I waited for the right moment and added the *coup de grâce*. I winked. That was all it took.

Black Bart leapt from the witness stand, screaming obscenities as he ran toward me. He didn't get far. The MPs tackled and cuffed him right in front of the judicial panel. The obvious verdict followed soon after. Bart Jenkins was sentenced to life in prison without parole. He was sent to Leavenworth. I know because I got a letter from one of my former platoon members who became a military prison guard after returning to the states. He told me he often saw Bart sitting in his cell crying and whining, acting like a heartbroken child. Jenkins reportedly had a habit of relentlessly groveling for favors from the guards.

My friend tells me Black Bart was terrified by most of the in-mates. The MP, having witnessed Bart's behavior in Iraq, wasn't surprised by his wretched, servile performance. It's what he expected from a guy so morally weak and pathetic

After word got out about his behavior in Iraq, some of the prisoners threatened to teach him a lesson.

Bart Jenkins, to no one's surprise, antagonized most of his fellow inmates. His immoral, psycho personality eventually became his undoing. My MP friend told me Bart's death was reported to be very slow and incredibly painful. Apparently, a trio of prisoners got a hold of Bart in the facility's laundry room. A guard found his mutilated, partially dismembered body a day later.

I don't feel bad about my role in sending Bart to his death chamber. I never would have had the guts to do anything like that before I met Tommy. Things are different now.

Thinking of how Tommy has changed my life reminds me of a question raised by one of my psychology professors. The question was this: "Are we products of nature or nurture?" The professor, continuing with his inquiry, added, "Is our identity, our inner-self with all our emotions and behavior, the product of genetic inheritance from our parents, i.e., nature? Or, have we all been molded from infancy by our exposure to parents, siblings and peers, i.e., nurture? Being a product of nature may imply our character traits are fixed, unalterable. Being a product of nurture would imply we have control over who we are and can change if we so desire."

I distinctly remember the professor's subsequent question to the class. "Is it possible to consciously change who we are as a human being, or are we stuck with what we have?" The class had difficulty with that question, as did I.

Initially, I thought it was likely impossible to voluntarily change one's inner-self.

Having pondered the question, I feel differently now, realizing the tremendous effect Tommy has had on my life. In fact, I'd like to use myself as an example of someone who once floundered due to low self-esteem and is now, by comparison, doing extremely well. Some-one who hated being at all like Bartholomew Jenkins and is now much closer to his dream of being like Tommy Archambeau. Whether it's nature or nurture may be irrelevant. I'm living proof that significant change is possible.

A month ago, my wife and I drove to Escanaba to visit Tommy's widow, Cynthia, a delightful, kind, and attractive woman. We had dinner at her house and got to meet Tommy's children, who are all teenagers now. They were pleasant, well-behaved, and a pleasure to talk to.

Before we left, Cindy took us by the cemetery. As we walked to Tommy's grave, I felt a tightness build in my throat. I thought of my past, how I'd never cried in public, fearing shame and embarrassment. None of that seems to matter anymore. I stood at Tommy's grave and openly sobbed. I'll never forget how good that felt.

Einstein Was Right— Everything's Relative

They hadn't seen each other in twenty years. Deborah was completely caught by surprise when he called; she couldn't figure out how Robert got her telephone number. He told her he wanted to get together, just to talk about old times. She thought that would be fun, so she agreed to meet him for dinner.

Over the past two decades, Deborah had dated a few guys, but nothing seemed to work out. She wondered about Robert, if he'd been more fortunate, perhaps attached, or even married. She didn't ask on the telephone, not wanting to know, not wanting to hear he had someone, not wanting to feel lonelier than she already did.

Robert hadn't been very lucky with romance either. The truth was he had made the call hoping to find Deborah was still single, hoping the flame was still there, hoping they might get back together.

As Deborah drove to the restaurant, she thought about how handsome Robert had been. She was anxious to see if he'd changed, praying she'd find him as attractive as she used to, with consideration of his age of course. Both she and Robert were now fifty years old. She reminisced about their past love affair, dreaming about his lean, muscular body and the passionate love they'd made so often. She hated to admit she'd never been with such an incredible lover, having since been disappointed with nearly all her relationships.

Robert arrived at the restaurant ten minutes early. The *maître d'* escorted him to a table, where he sat reminiscing, thinking about old times with Deborah. *She'd been so beautiful back then: slender, petite, and sophisticated.* He envisioned her sexy but tasteful outfits: chic sweaters, short, stylish skirts, nylon stockings, and high heels. She'd always looked good, sometimes stunning, and he'd been deeply in love with her and their romance. He knew he'd been immature back then, not nearly as urbane or polished as Deborah. He thought that was why she'd left him.

Deborah parked her car. As she walked to the front of the restaurant, she tried to remember why she'd ever broken up with Robert. She hadn't a clue. Perhaps she'd been thinking the grass was greener, leading her to search for some fantasy romance that didn't exist. For years, she'd been kicking herself for leaving him.

Robert sat watching the front of the restaurant, waiting to see the *maître d'* bring a pretty blond woman to his table. A mirror across the room caught his attention. Being so excited about seeing his old lover, he had purchased a new suit for the occasion. Checking himself in the mirror, Robert was pleased with how he looked. He thought, *I'm still a forty-regular, not bad for a guy my age.* He'd gained only a few pounds over the years and still faithfully exercised three times a week.

A minute later, he saw the *maître d'* bringing Deborah his way. His heart sank. *She looks so different, so much older.* Robert assessed her appearance. *She's nicely dressed but looks nothing like she used to.*

Deborah was wearing a high-collared blouse, buttoned at the neck, along with a blue blazer. Her skirt, hemmed just above the knee, was longer than those of years past. She was wearing heels but not as high as before, and she had gained weight. Though not fat by any means, she had certainly lost her sexy, hourglass figure. In low heels, she was almost frumpy.

The *maître d'* escorted her to the side of their table.

Robert stood and walked to her. "Debbie, you look great. It's so nice to see you."

"Bobby, I'm so glad you called. I think this will be a lot of fun." He assisted her to her chair. They talked about old times.

Deborah, shocked by how much Robert had aged, thought, *My God, he used to be so trim and muscular. It's so sad to see how he's let himself go. His hair, it's so thin with a receding hairline. It's not nearly as bright and blond as before. He's prematurely gray, and his suit, it's too small. He has to leave his jacket unbuttoned to make room for his paunch.*

Robert gazed into Deborah's eyes, amazed at how they'd lost their sparkle. *She has deep crow's feet around her eyes. I can't believe it. And she used to be so diet conscious, always watching her weight and exercising. She's gained at least ten pounds. Her hair is so short, barely past her shoulders. It looks like she perms, too!*

The waiter served their dinner. Conversation lagged while they quickly ate, both anxious to get it over, both horribly disappointed by the appearance of their former lover.

Robert spoke, "Debbie, it's really been nice to see you, and I've enjoyed talking about the past. We've had a few good laughs tonight, haven't we?"

"Yes, we have. It's been wonderful seeing you again, Bobby. It was a lot of fun reminiscing. We really should have done this sooner." Deborah looked at her watch, "Oh my, it's much later than I realized. Bobby, if you don't mind, I have to get back to watch my favorite TV show."

"Sure, that's fine, Deb. I understand perfectly. I have some favorite shows I hate to miss as well." Robert went around the table and pulled her chair back as she stood. "I'll walk you to your car."

"No, that's all right. It's still light outside; I'll be fine. I don't mind walking alone to my car."

"Whatever you say, Deb. I've got to tell you, it's been fun. I'm glad we got together. Okay if I give you a call sometime?"

"Of course, that would be nice. I'll look forward to it."

As Deborah walked across the parking lot, she wondered if he'd been serious about calling her—she hoped not.

Robert got in his car and started the engine. *Maybe I shouldn't have said that about calling her. I don't want her to get her hopes up. No way am I calling her again. It's heartbreaking to see how she's aged. I wish I'd never arranged this meeting; it's been such a disappointment.*

Actually, neither of them had a favorite television show. Instead of going home, each drove to a bar to drown the sorrow of their disheartening reunion.

•

By coincidence, both Deborah and Robert had previously agreed to go on blind dates the very next weekend. After seeing Robert, Deborah was not looking forward to her date with a gentleman named Jeffrey, nearly sixty years of age.

Likewise, Robert had some trepidation about his upcoming date. He'd been told the woman he was to meet, named Kathryn, was at least fifty years old, possibly older. He usually dated much younger women.

•

As usual, Robert arrived at the restaurant ahead of time. He was escorted to his table, where he sat, feeling bored, berating himself for agreeing to this. *I'll probably blow fifty to sixty bucks for dinner with some woman I'm never gonna see again.* He impatiently waited for her to arrive, anxious to get the whole thing over.

•

Deborah, on her way to a different restaurant, envisioned a balding, old man with a pot belly, sitting at a table waiting for her. *At least I'll get a free dinner out of it. I'll probably order the most expensive thing on the menu, rush through my meal, and politely say goodbye, never again agreeing to a blind date, especially with some old man.*

•

Robert saw the waiter escorting an attractive brunette in his direction. He crossed his fingers, hoping she was his date but thinking it was impossible. *She can't be fifty years old!* Pleasantly surprised when the waiter took her directly to his table, he jumped up, nearly running to introduce himself and help her to her seat. The couple made small talk while waiting for a server. A waiter came by asking if they would like to order. Robert blurted out, "Please, not yet. We don't want to rush through this. Perhaps a bottle of wine?" He looked across the table and smiled. "What do you think? Would wine be good?"

"Sure, that sounds like fun."

The bottle soon arrived, and as they talked and sipped on Chardonnay, Robert gazed into her eyes, silently noting their beautiful, deep-blue color and sparkle. *I love her hair, it's short—proper for her age. It looks as if she's recently had a perm. I like it; it gives her a pretty, classy. sophistication. When she smiles, the crow's feet around her eyes enhance her delightful look of maturity.*

He loved her attire; her sweater had a high neckline, not too showy, not overly provocative. Her wool skirt was neat and stylish, not too short, hemmed just above the knee. She was wearing flats, which Robert appreciated since she was a bit taller than average.

•

Deborah arrived to meet her date, and a waiter escorted her to her table. Walking across the room, she noticed a very refined-looking man sitting by himself. She hoped he was the one. *He doesn't look anywhere near sixty. He's so handsome, with a look of intelligence like an executive.*

To Deborah's delight, he *was* waiting for her. The gentleman rose, walked to her side, extended his hand, and introduced himself. He assisted Deborah to her chair, where she sat admiring him. Wanting to spend as much time with him as possible, she hoped he would order a bottle of wine and postpone dinner a bit.

Jeffrey, was bald, especially on the top of his head, but his remaining hair glistened silver with pure white at the temples. Deborah looked him over. *His face is very attractive, a bit droopy from age, but certainly not bad. And his little double chin is adorable. I love his hair; the silver at his temples gives him a distinguished look, and bald is so sexy!* She went on examining her date. *His suit is immaculate and looks very expensive. He's got a cute little pot belly, but at least he doesn't try to hide it by squeezing his suit coat around it. He appears to be in good shape, a little overweight, but what would you expect for a man his age?*

•

Robert's date, Kathryn, was pleasantly surprised by his appearance. *He's so handsome. His blond hair is thinning just a bit, but I love the gray at his temples. He looks so fit and muscular, hardly any belly, unlike most men his age.* As she sat there, working on her second glass of wine, she thought about what she would order. *I better be careful; I'll order something inexpensive. I don't want to offend him. I really hope we can meet again.*

•

Deborah's date, enthralled with her beauty, thought, *Nicely-arranged blonde hair, sparkling eyes and hardly any wrinkles, just a few, fine crow's feet when she smiles. And her figure's incredible, a little extra weight around the middle, but she still has a youthful, hourglass silhouette.* As they sat sipping wine, he anticipated their next date, hoping she would agree to see him again.

•

It took nearly two hours for Robert and Kathryn to finish dinner. Wanting to prolong her company, he ordered dessert. When they finally left the restaurant, he practically insisted on walking her to her car. She responded with, "I'd like that. I hate walking to my car by myself. You're such a gentleman."

As they stood in the parking lot, Robert considered giving her a kiss goodnight. A moment of awkward hesitation passed, at which point she smiled, looking him directly in the eyes, as if to say, *Please, go ahead. I'd love to have you kiss me.*

He gave her a short kiss on the lips, said goodnight, and asked if it would be okay to call her. Kathryn nearly dropped her purse as she hurriedly searched for a pen and paper to write down her number. They parted, both anxiously looking forward to their next date.

•

Deborah and Jeffrey finished dinner, and the gentleman, so excited about possibly seeing her again, asked, "Would you mind giving me your number? I'd love to see you again."

She whipped a pen out of her purse, grabbed a napkin from the table, and quickly wrote her number. Jeffrey smiled and asked if he could walk her to her car.

Deborah responded, "Yes, I'd love that. I'm always a bit leery of doing that alone."

An awkward moment occurred after they reached the car; her date pondered giving her a kiss. Deborah didn't wait; she puckered up and laid one right on his lips.

The Ceiling Fan

"*I*sn't this place just lovely? I'm especially attracted to the German woodworking; I've been told it's authentic. It all came from Germany nearly fifty years ago. I'd love to live here myself if I could only afford it."

"What do you think, honey? It is beautiful, isn't it?"

Brian nodded in agreement but added, "It is a gorgeous place, but I'm not sure we can afford it."

The realtor, Margaret, quickly jumped in, "Dr. Jamieson, don't worry about that. My boss has given me permission to negotiate. In addition, I'll be glad to adjust my percentage if we have to. You're such a beautiful couple; you deserve a place like this. Besides, Doctor, aren't you about ready to open your practice?"

Brian, irritated by Margaret's forward attitude, responded with a terse, "Yep."

The realtor, a dumpy, pushy woman, dressed in a wrinkled, blue blazer and tan slacks, proceeded to further aggravate her client. "Well then, I'm sure you'll soon be rolling in the bucks."

Smirking, Brian didn't say a word.

Margaret escorted them through the three- story home. Many of the rooms had expensive-looking hardwood furniture of German design. There were beautiful tables, chairs, wooden chests, and freestanding bookcases, even a huge armoire, still standing in the living room. The couple didn't ask about it. Brian was tired of Margaret's mouth, and Jenny assumed it would all be moved out when the house sold.

The place was magnificent. Thick oak door casings, carved crown moldings, and striking pine appointments, supposedly from the Black Forest of Germany, accented every room. The huge kitchen was spectacular, with walnut cabinets and oak-plank flooring.

Margaret took them up a wide staircase to the second floor, where they found five large bedrooms, two of which had walk-in closets. She delighted in showing them the master bedroom, a huge suite with a twelve-foot-high ceiling, bordered by a wide, sculpted-plaster crown. Suspended from the center of the ceiling was a large antique fan.

"Look, honey. It looks like the fans in *Casablanca.*"

The fan's long mahogany blades emanated from a shiny, polished brass housing encasing its motor and bearings. Margaret led them out to the hallway.

"Wait till you see the third floor!" She escorted her clients up another long staircase. A short way down the hall, Margaret opened a heavy oak door to reveal the largest room of the house.

Greeted by a glossy, parquet floor, the trio entered the massive room, well-lit by sunlight beaming through a pair of leaded-glass windows. The home's Mansard roof, partially visible through the windows, was adorned with beautiful, gray slate.

Brian strolled to a window. "Margaret, there's a walkway with a wrought-iron railing out here."

"Oh yes, isn't that charming? It's a widow's walk."

Jenny, brimming with excitement, said, "A widow's walk? I've never heard of that."

"It's an old tradition from the New England coast. Legend has it that sailor's heartsick wives, awaiting their husband's return from sea, would stand on the highest point of their homes, their widow's walk, longingly peering out over the ocean, hoping for the sight of a ship's sail. Unfortunately, since many sailors succumbed to the violence of the seas, the rooftop walkways became known as widow's walks. I believe that railing came from Marblehead."

"Honey, isn't that interesting? It's so romantic. Don't you just love this house?"

Brian, not wanting to sound too enthusiastic in front of Margaret, walked to his wife's side and in a soft whisper said, "Jenny, not now."

Seeing a smile appear on Margaret's face, Brian knew the realtor had heard him. He immediately regretted making the remark.

The sales agent went on, praising more of the splendid features of the house. "A few years ago, this area was renovated into a recreation room." She pointed to a long, slate billiard table with dark green felt. The sides of the table had ornate carvings with wood inlays. Pouches, woven from thick strips of dark leather, hung from each pocket. Two Tiffany lamps, suspended from the ceiling, were centered over the table.

"Does this come with the house?" asked Brian, referring to the table.

"It sure does. This and all the other furnishings you've seen. They've all been here since the original owner passed away. I apologize. I should have explained that earlier. That's part of the deal. You get all these gorgeous German antiques; however, you must agree in writing to leave everything if you ever move out."

Jennifer hugged her husband. "Brian. That's amazing. I can't believe it!"

Brian, relenting to his wife's emotions, couldn't conceal his feelings. "Well, I have to admit, this house is a pleasant surprise. In fact, I'm shocked. The place really is something. It'll be hard to turn down."

His comment was music to Margaret's ears.

Margaret showed them the last room on the third floor, a paneled library with an enormous walnut desk at one end and long shelves, packed with old books, at the other. The room had a ceramic tile floor with intricate designs along its border. An enormous wool rug, with woven images of German street scenes, covered the center of the room. The library's side wall, facing out to the yard, had a knee-wall breaking into a slant at four to five feet from the floor, the angled wall extending up to an elegant, cathedral ceiling, crisscrossed by immense, rough-hewn beams. Two large dormers, extending from ceiling to floor, had beautiful French doors opening to the widow's walk.

Margaret, assessing her clients' faces, smiled and thought, *Oh, my God, I've got a sale!*

They walked back to the first floor and spoke for a few minutes. Brian admitted to Margaret that he was interested. He and Jenny would talk it over in the evening. He promised to call her with their decision first thing in the morning and then asked the question Margaret hated to hear. "Margaret, Jenny and I have heard through the grapevine that the previous owner of this house met with a rather tragic death. Is that true?"

Margaret thought, *How the hell do they know about that?* She hesitated, smiled, and reluctantly replied, fabricating as much as she dared. "Yes, it's true. It was so sad. She was a pretty, young thing, but I heard she was very troubled. She hardly lived here more than a month or two."

"What happened!" begged Jenny.

"She jumped—jumped from the widow's walk. It was horrible, but as I said, I think she was a very depressed young lady, never married." The realtor went on with her deception. "I was told she had some medical problems."

Jenny spoke, "Oh, that's horrible!"

Brian added, "Yes, it is. I'm sorry to hear that."

Margaret, anxious to change the subject, quickly interjected. "Well, I have to be going. I think you would truly like it here, Dr. Jamieson, you and your lovely wife. I'll look forward to your call."

Brian had one more question, "We've also heard there've been many previous owners, some moving after only a few weeks. Why would that be?"

Damn it! thought Margaret. *I've gotta get outta here and get away from these questions.* She hesitantly responded, "Yes, Dr. Jamieson, I guess there have been a few. However, this is a special place, and it takes special people to live here—people like you, intelligent and motivated. Just think of what you could do here. The decorating opportunities are endless!"

"I think she's right, honey. We could do wonders with this house."

"Pardon me for asking," said Margaret. "Do you plan children?"

Jennifer loudly responded. "Yes, we do; we're hoping for a big family."

"Well, there you have it. Just think of it, a five-bedroom home full of little ones. And the recreation room, it's a virtual playground."

Jenny looked up to her husband with hopeful eyes. He smiled and gently squeezed her arm with reassurance. "Well, Margaret, as I said, I promise to call you first thing in the morning."

Margaret, her hands buried in the pockets of her blazer, crossed her fingers. "Okay then, we'll talk in the morning." As she turned to leave, she couldn't resist adding, "And remember, you're not the only ones interested in this house. I know of at least three showings scheduled for next week. I think you'd hate to miss out on this opportunity. You'd be kicking yourselves later." She walked to her car, leaving the newlyweds standing on the porch.

Brian turned to his wife, "I hate that woman!"

Jenny nudged him in the ribs, "Come on, she's not that bad. Everyone's gotta make a living."

Dr. and Mrs. Jamieson moved into their new home one week later, which, by coincidence, was exactly one year from their wedding day. They settled in on their first wedding anniversary.

•

Brian Jamieson and Jennifer Rosman had met years earlier when he was a third-year medical student and she was working as a nurse in a large training hospital. The son of devout Catholics, Brian had five siblings. In contrast, Jennifer was an only child, the sole child of orthodox Jewish parents, who, during their daughter's adolescence, repeatedly emphasized the importance of maintaining a traditional, Jewish household after marriage. They assumed Jenny would wed a Jewish man, not a gentile, certainly not a Catholic.

Initially, Jenny's parents wanted nothing to do with Brian. However, over time, the Rosmans came to enjoy Brian Jamieson's company. Eventually, to Jennifer's glee, a mutual sense of love evolved between her parents and the man she adored. Demands for a Jewish son-in-law faded and disappeared.

In contrast, Brian's parents, the Jamiesons, immediately attached to Jenny, elated their son had found such a lovely, kind, and attractive partner. Furthermore, to both Brian's and Jenny's surprise, both sets of parents, when they eventually met, got along wonderfully; they genuinely enjoyed each other's company.

A week before their wedding, Brian and Jenny had a serious discussion regarding the choice of religion for their anticipated family. They made a pact to postpone their decision until Jenny became pregnant, solemnly agreeing that a child would require a spiritually consolidated family. Until then, they would each maintain separate religions.

•

After an exhaustive day of moving, the Jamiesons retired to the master bedroom. The house had one major drawback, no air conditioning. It was midsummer, a hot, sticky night. Brian opened the bedroom windows and turned on the ceiling fan. They crawled into bed and snuggled. Having worked so long and hard moving, they quickly fell asleep. Moments later, Brian was awakened by Jenny, shaking his arm.

"Honey, do you hear that?"

He groggily answered, "Hear what?"

"That voice. I hear someone talking, it sounds like German. It woke me up."

Brian faced his wife with a puzzled look. "I don't hear a thing." "Listen. I still hear it. It's coming from above. I think it's coming from the ceiling fan."

Brian chuckled, giving his wife an incredulous look. "Come on, babe. Voices from the ceiling fan? I think you're just exhausted from working so hard."

Jennifer shot back in a serious tone. "No, that's not it. I still hear it. Someone's calling out, '*Fräulein.*' It's coming from that fan."

"All right, all right, if you insist, I'll turn the fan off, even though it's like an oven in here; I'll turn it off." The fan blades slowed to a stop as Brian crawled back into bed. "Is that better?"

"Much. But I'm still spooked. You've just proven it was coming from the fan. The voices are gone."

Brian rolled his eyes, "Let's get some sleep." The couple slept soundly the entire night.

The following day, Brian spent long hours at the hospital, returning home just after eight o'clock. "Jenny, I'm home."

His voice echoed through the monstrous house. Jenny ran out from the kitchen and gave him a big hug. They had dinner, watched a little television, and went to bed.

It was another sweltering night. Brian turned on the ceiling fan and got into bed. "Brian, I hear it again."

Jenny's husband, a bit irritated, was hot and tired. "Jenny. This is crazy!"

She responded with a tone of disappointment and hurt. "You think I'm crazy? You don't care about me, do you?"

"Honey, you know I love you. I'm just beat, and this whole story about German voices coming out of the ceiling fan is ridiculous. Don't you see that?"

She lay back on her pillow, listening to the heavily accented voice. *"Fräulein, kommen Sie zu mir. Kommen Sie zu mir. Kommen Sie schließen sich mir beim paradies an."*

Covering her ears, Jenny could still hear it. She sat up, teary-eyed, and said, "Brian! I can't take this. I don't care if you think I'm nuts. You have to turn the damn fan off!"

Brian closed his eyes, too tired to argue anymore. "Okay, okay, I'll turn it off."

He switched off the fan, got back in bed, turned away from his wife, and did his best to fall asleep in the stifling room. In no more than a minute, Jenny was snoozing away.

Brian tossed and turned for an hour, unable to sleep in the oppressive heat. He got up and walked to the window, "Not even a breeze." Going to the fan switch near the bedroom door, he whispered, "She'll never know." He flipped the switch and quietly returned to bed, quickly falling asleep. A short time later, he awoke, feeling a tap on his shoulder.

"Brian, why did you turn it back on?"

Jenny's husband was beside himself, exhausted to the point of distraction. "Because it's like a sweat box in here!"

She ignored his outburst, "I hear it again! I'm sure it's in German. I can't stand it."

Brian couldn't take anymore. "Jenny, just go to sleep." "I CAN'T."

"All right, I'll turn it off, but it's pretty silly. I'll be so tired I won't be able to think straight tomorrow, but I'll turn it off."

Jennie lay back on her pillow, pleased to have gotten her way. "Thank you, Brian."

Gently shaking his head, Brian whispered to himself, "Women."

The sequence repeated itself, over and over, for a full week—Jenny on the verge of tears about the voices, Brian on the brink of hysteria, trying to reassure her. His use of logic was to no avail. Jenny remained convinced the fan was talking to her while her husband developed critical sleep deprivation from endless nights spent rolling around on a soggy, sweat-soaked pillow in a room heavy with humid air and incinerating heat.

After two weeks, Dr. Jamieson could barely function. "Jenny, this lack of sleep is killin' me. I've gotta do something and do it soon. I'll move to another bedroom, buy an air conditioner, sleep in the basement, anything to get some rest."

As he lay in bed, a thought crept into his mind, a new outlook regarding his wife's insistence about the voices. It worried him. *Jenny's not crazy, I know that. But this whole thing is just too hard to believe.* Thinking of the young woman who leaped from the widow's walk and numerous previous owners staying no more than a few months, Brian decided to give his wife the benefit of the doubt. He wasn't one to believe in ghosts or haunted houses, having had little, if any, interest in the paranormal. However, his wife's seemingly genuine fear and her obvious sincerity, along with his love for her, drove him on. He had to call Margaret.

•

"Hello."

"Yes, this is Dr. Jamieson. Could I please speak with Margaret Reynolds?"

"Surely, Doctor. I'll transfer you."

"Hello, this is Margaret."

"Margaret, it's Dr. Jamieson."

"Doctor, how nice to hear from you. How are you enjoying your new home?"

"It's fine. Listen, I have a question. You told us the antique furnishings in the house came from Germany. Do you happen to know who arranged that?"

"As a matter of fact, I do. It all came from an antique shop here in town."

Brian eagerly replied. "Really, do you know where the shop is?"

"Yes. It's owned by an old German woman. I think she calls it Décor de Deutschland. Kind of a silly name if you ask me. Seems to mix French with German, but then again, I'm no language—"

"Do you know where it's located?" Brian said, cutting her off. Margaret was used to being interrupted by impatient clients and answered, "Sure, it's right downtown near the corner of Third and Madison."

"Thanks."

"Doctor, are you going to buy some furnitu—"

The doctor hung up.

"Geez, why are people so rude?"

Brian Jamieson left the hospital in mid-afternoon, knowing he would have to return later to finish rounds. He drove downtown, parked in front of Décor de Deutschland, and hurried into the shop. A small woman with blond hair, gray at the roots, was standing next to the sales counter. She was wearing a tight, low-cut sweater with an equally tight, surprisingly short, red wool skirt, and shiny, black high heels. "Can I help you, sir?"

"Yes, ma'am. My wife and I just bought a new home. I think you know of it. Our realtor told me you provided all the German antiques."

"Ah, Margaret, no doubt. Kvite a talker, isn't she?" Brian was surprised. "Yes, she is."

"You're referring to zee house on Trondheim Street, yah?" He nodded.

"Yah, I know zee house vell, Dr. Jamieson."

She knew his name. He was shocked. He and Jenny had just moved in. They had been in town only a few weeks. "How do you know my name?"

"Dis is a small town, Doctor. Verd gets around. Yah, every-zing in zat house came from Germany. Every-zing is authentic."

"Can you tell me how you came across all of those antiques?"

"Vye, of course. I acquired all of zem from Germany, right after zee voar. Even zee voodvorking, all of zee pine, oak, unt mahogany vas shipped here. Most of it from estates in Baerlin."

"You have a pleasant accent; certainly, you must come from Germany."

"Yah, I do. I lived in Baerlin during zee voar. Aftervard, I realized how valuable zee German artifacts vould be. Back zen, things ver being sold at absurdly low cost. People's ver destitute unt broken, some of zem starving."

"And you brought all of it here, to the States?"

"Yah, I had to. I tried verking a shop in Europe, but no one vould buy. Zey hated us, you know, vee Germans. Zey vanted nothing to do vith any-zing German. So, I shipped it all here, more zan fifty-years-ago, in 1951 to be exact."

"How did it happen to end up in that house?"

"Ven I came here, a builder, a construction man met me. He fell in love vith zee German furniture, moldings, rugs—every-zing I had. He built zat house, unt I helped decorate it. I made kvite a bit of money, thank goodness. It's kept me going through all zee years, through zee rough times."

"All of that stuff comes from Berlin?" asked Brian.

"Yah, mostly from Baerlin, some from uh-der parts of Germany, too. Such as Munich and Frankfurt. Some of my most beautiful finds ver in Bavaria."

"May I ask your name?"

"I am, Frau Schmidt, Helga Schmidt. Doctor, you may call me Helga." "All right, thank you."

The old woman showed Brian around her shop. Gorgeous German antiques, armoires, chests and tables, lined the walls. Many exquisite lamps were hung from the ceiling. "Doctor, vould you like to see my back room?"

"Sure, why not?"

They walked to a heavily paneled oak door at the rear of the shop. Frau Schmidt pulled a set of keys from her skirt, unlocked the door, and pushed it open for the doctor. Brian stopped short, stunned by what he saw.

The small room was full of Nazi artifacts: military helmets, German uniforms with swastikas, rifles, bayonets, and military boots. Across one wall was a large Nazi flag. A long wooden plaque, below the flag, had something spelled out in thick, brass letters—"Das Dritte Reich."

Brian exclaimed, "Oh my, God, I can't believe this."

"Yah, kvite impressive, isn't it? I only show dis room to special people like you, Doctor. Since you are living in my home, I thought you vould appreciate it. Excuse me for calling your house my home, but zat's how I feel since I supplied most of zee materials for zee interior.

Your house holds a very special place in my heart. You can understand, yah?

Brian didn't say a word. He felt uneasy in her Nazi museum. "Why do you have this stuff? It's a little frightening."

"Oh, Doctor Jamieson, zare is nothing to be afraid of. Since I lived zare—zare in Germany, during zee voar, I find these items to be very fascinating. You may be surprised, but I have fond memories of zee voar; Baerlin vas vunderful ven zee voar began. I vas a young girl zen, and zare ver many exciting parties unt balls, much gaiety. I had zee good fortune to have been invited to many of zee military balls. I vas, as zey zay, 'kvite a looker' back zen. I have danced vith many of zee high-ranking German officers. Of course, zare all dead now."

An armchair in the corner of the room caught Brian's attention. The upholstered chair had red velvet cushions on its seat and back. Its arms and legs were made of ornately carved wood that glistened with a gilded gold finish. An embroidered swastika adorned the center of the back cushion.

"Ah, Doctor, I see you are admiring his chair."

Brian, reluctant to hear about *his chair*, hesitated in silence. "Yah, it vas one of his favorites. He sat in it often, mostly ven quietly thinking. I sit zare sometimes when I vant to listen to music and reminisce about zee good times."

An old gramophone with a tarnished brass cone amplifier was sitting on a small table adjacent to the chair. Several 78 rpm records were filed on the table's lower shelf. The doctor responded. "Music, yes. I see you have a collection of records."

"Oh, yah, I love zem all: Beethoven, Bach, Handel. There are so many great German composers. I have some Strauss and Mozart, too, but of course zay ver Austrian."

Jamieson turned away from the chair and the old woman, facetiously thinking, *Yah, Austrian, not kvite as good as a German, but close enough.*

Looking around the room with both fascination and contempt, Brian noticed a framed photograph of Adolf Hitler with his arm around an attractive, blond woman wearing a dinner gown. Pointing to the photograph, he asked, "How did you ever get that?"

"Oh, zat is my prized possession. Zat photo brings back vunderful memories. Zat's me, ven I vas eighteen years old."

Brian was flabbergasted. "Are you serious? You knew Adolf Hitler personally? That's you standing next to him in his arms?"

"Yah, vasn't he a handsome man? He vas very kind unt loving to me. I suppose you find zat hard to believe, don't you, Doctor?

"Yes, I do!"

"I understand zat. The vorld is so full of misinformation. Millions blame him for zee voar, but I don't. He vas a brilliant man. You could never understand, unless you had lived in Germany at zat time." Brian, although thoroughly disgusted, remained intrigued by the old woman's story.

"Ven I vas a young girl, vee had nothing. After zee first voar, zee country vas broken, held under zee thumb of zee British and you Americans. We lived in poverty. Adolf brought us out from all of zat. He vas truly a hero."

The doctor, without saying a word, walked around the room, examining military artifacts and photographs of soldiers celebrating in huge beer halls, one of which showed a long banner, "Deutschland für Immer." There were photos of opulent ballrooms and elegantly dressed women.

While inspecting the room, looking at swastikas, photos of smug officers with arrogant, statuesque posing, and pictures of lavish par-ties, Brian thought of his wife and her Jewish heritage. It made him physically sick. Hiding his repugnance from Frau Schmidt, Brian asked, "Do you mind if we go out—back up front?"

"Vye of course not. I understand. Many peoples, except zee older Germans, find dis room upsetting. Unfortunately, zare are only a small number of surviving Baerliners here in town. They still stop by, now and zen, to reminisce in zee back room—reminisce about zee old times."

Brian couldn't believe it. The arrogance of this woman. He want-ed to slap her. Staring hard at the old frau, he examined her graying, dyed-blond hair, the deep, makeup-covered creases in her skin, and her awkwardly applied lipstick, eyeliner, and mascara. To the doctor, her vain attempts to look young were sad, almost pathetic.

His voice took a stern tone. "Listen, I want to ask about the ceiling fan, the fan in the master bedroom at our house. Do you know it?" "Of course, it's vun of my favorite pieces. It also holds a special place in my heart."

"Why is that?"

"Because, I still remember it from Baerlin. You know, zare was no air conditioning back zen. That fan made such a pleasant breeze in his bedroom."

Dr. Jamieson was almost afraid to ask. "Who's bedroom?"

"Vye, Adolph's of course. Der Fuhrer's bedroom. I had been zare many times."

Brian felt a sense of urgency. He thought of the voices, the messages Jenny had heard from the fan, a German voice, a man's voice, calling her fräulein. He was terrified. He wanted to punch Frau Schmidt in the face. He ran for the door and stopped, remembering a written message Jenny had given him.

Pulling a piece of folded stationery from his pants pocket, Brian turned back to Frau Schmidt. He would have enjoyed jamming the note down her throat but, instead, politely asked if she would translate the message his wife had written, doing her best to decipher what she heard coming from the fan.

"Could you please translate this?"

"Surely."

"I know the spelling's wrong. My wife had to do it phonetically."

"Yah, your vife, *sie ist eine dreckige Juden.*"

The word "Juden" caught Brian's attention. His eyes shot wide as he glared back at the wrinkled, old woman. "What did you say? I heard 'Juden.'"

The evil old spinster smiled, exposing teeth yellowed by age. "I apologize, Doctor. Every so often I slip, speaking in zee old language."

Brian, angrily repeated his question, yelling at the old bitch. "What did you say? Tell me—now!"

"Please, why are you so upset? I only said, 'Your vife, she is Jewish? Yah.'"

"How do you know that?"

Smiling again, she said, "I have my ways."

Tempering his anger and disgust, Brian bit his lip, concentrating on the message he'd handed her. He demanded, "Translate the note!"

"Zat's fine, Doctor. Let's zee here." Frau Helga examined the writing for a moment. "Dis is very interesting. It says, 'Frauline, come to me. Beautiful frauline, come to me. Come join me in paradise.'"

Brian clenched his jaw. The look of rage on his face quickly morphed into one of terror.

"Doctor, you look frightened. Vere did dis note come from?"

He was gone, out the door, running to his car—running to save his wife.

I've gotta get home! In his car, racing down the street, he thought of Frau Schmidt. *I could kill that bitch!*

Speeding down city streets, he quickly arrived home. His car careened up the drive and screeched to a stop. He ran to the house, yelling, "Jenny, where are you?" Bolting through the front door, Brian caught his toe on the edge of an area rug, falling flat on his face. He jumped up and ran to the kitchen. "Jenny!"

No one answered.

Sprinting to the stairway, Brian called out, "Jenny!" He flew up the steps. "Honey, are you up here?"

No response.

He went to the master bedroom. The mahogany blades of the antique fan were spinning, and the bed covers were pulled down. "Oh, my God, where is she?"

Thinking of the widow's walk, he bounded up to the third floor to the library. The French doors to the walk were open. Terrified, he stood near the railing, afraid to look down. Brian closed his eyes and said a prayer. "God, please don't let this be!" Forcing himself to lean over the rail, he opened his eyes and sighed with relief. *Nothing... there's no one there. Thank God.* He left, searching every square foot of the immense house. It took a while; there were many rooms. His beautiful wife was nowhere to be found.

The doctor pause, then said aloud, "Maybe she went out." He went to the garage and flung its door open. Her car was there. "Shit! Where the hell is she?"

Out of breath, breathing heavily, Brian Jamieson pushed on, running back to the house, up two, exhausting flights of stairs, returning to the widow's walk, where he again peered over the railing. She wasn't there. Glancing down, toward his feet, he saw a drop of blood on the walkway.

Startled by a low-pitched groan, Brian spun around.

There she was, in her nightgown, huddled against the wall in a corner of the walk. She was moaning, softly crying.

"Jenny! Thank God."

She didn't respond.

He shook her by the shoulders. "Jenny, baby, wake up."

Slowly, she raised her head and, with her eyes barely open, groggily mumbled some slurred words, as if in some sort of trance.

Brian yelled again, "Jenny, wake up!"

She softly mumbled and looked around, "Brian… where am I?"

"You're outside, on the walk—the widow's walk. What are you doing out here, hon?"

"I don't know; I don't remember how I got here."

"Jenny, please try to remember."

His wife took a few deep breaths to clear her head. "Ouch, my butt hurts, and my ankle." Brian looked down at her foot. A small line of blood from a scrape on her ankle dripped to the concrete surface of the walkway. Brian, taking some tissue from his pocket, wiped the blood from his wife's foot.

"Come on, let's go inside." They sat together, on the couch in the library. He waited, giving her time to regain her thoughts. "Okay, Jenny. Can't you remember anything? Try hard."

"I'm trying… I don't know what happened. I remember being tired. I think I went to bed to take a nap, so I wouldn't be sleepy when you got home."

Brian said, "The fan, the fan's running. Did you turn it on?"

"I'm not sure. It's so hot; I guess I did."

"And… then what?"

"I must have gotten out of bed, I don't remember… wait, I do remember. I remember the voice. It was louder than before. It was speaking to me. I was so frightened, Brian. I ran out of the room to call you on the phone. But I guess I didn't, did I?"

"No, you didn't. I didn't get a call."

"I vaguely remember walking to the library. I went out to the widow's walk, maybe to find a cool breeze, I guess." Jenny closed her eyes and leaned back on the couch.

"Please, keep going, Jen. What did you do next?"

Her eyes shot open. "Oh, my God, Brian. I remember now. I climbed up on the railing. He was calling me, calling me and telling me to jump! Oh, I was so scared, honey." Jenny hugged her husband.

Speaking softly, lovingly, Brian went on. "Jen, honey, thank God you didn't jump. Thank God."

"I fell. I remember falling when my foot slipped off the railing. I fell back on my butt and scraped my ankle on the walk. I guess that's why my rear-end hurts." She reached back and rubbed her behind.

"That's fantastic, you fell the right way, honey, back onto the walk. I hate to think what could have happened."

"My ankle hurts." She looked down at her foot. "Brian, look!"

While they'd been sitting on the couch, the blood from her injury had trickled down again. Brian shuddered as he stared at the red figure atop his wife's foot. The drips had formed a distinct pattern, a blood-red emblem, looking like a tattoo. It was a swastika. He reached down and wiped it off.

That night they stayed at a motel. No ceiling fans.

In bed, Jenny quickly fell asleep; Brian stayed awake. He had a secret task to perform—a task he'd pondered for hours. Finally, being certain it was something that had to be done, he quietly slipped out of bed, dressed, and left the motel room, locking the door behind him. He drove to the house. An hour or so later he returned, undressed and got in bed.

Early the following morning, a moving van pulled up to the old, German house. The movers were told to pack only Dr. and Mrs. Jamieson's belongings, having received specific instructions to leave all other furnishings behind. Brian and Jenny, waiting until the movers pulled away in a fully loaded truck, left their nightmarish house, immediately heading for Décor de Deutschland to confront Frau Schmidt.

Brian entered the shop, leaving his wife in the car to await his signal.

•

"Vell, Doctor, so nice to see you again. How is your lovely vife?"

He paused, glaring at her with an angry sneer. "You know damn well how she is!"

"Vye, Doctor, vut do you mean? Has some-zing happened to your young beauty? I hope not."

"You hope not, do you? Then you'll be pleased to know she's fine." Brian walked to the door and waved to Jenny, who entered the shop moments later.

"Jenny, this is the woman I've told you about. Frau Schmidt, this is my wife, Jennifer."

The old woman could not conceal her emotions. A look of bewilderment and anger draped her face. "I'm glad to meet you, dear." Her expression and tone belied her statement. "Mrs. Jamieson, are you here to buy some of my antiques?"

Brian interrupted with a terse, "No, we are not. We're here to talk about the ceiling fan in our home—the one from your lover's bedroom."

"Oh, yah, that fan is precious to me. Vut do you vant to know about it?"

Jenny yelled out. "That's fan is evil."

"Evil? Vut ever do you mean? I zink zat fan is beautiful. It's very valuable."

Jennifer angrily shouted, "Your fan tried to kill me!"

The Frau's expression did not change. Brian could tell Jenny's outburst hadn't surprised her in the least; she'd been expecting it. "That fan is a vunderful verk of art, my dear."

Jenny's outrage peaked. "You know goddamn well what that fan is, you old witch!"

Helga Schmidt looked smug, satisfied with Jenny's accusation. Brian went on. "You know why the prior owner of that house, the young woman, killed herself, don't you?"

The wrinkled old Frau paused, sternly staring at the young couple. "You Americans zink you are so special, so smart. You, young lady, zink you are so beautiful. I vas once young unt beautiful—more attractive, more glamorous zan both of you. You people know nothing of power, glory, or love. You are pathetic!"

Jenny stepped back, frightened by the irrational attack from the old Nazi. Brian Jamieson stepped between the two women, using incredible restraint to keep from grabbing Helga by the throat. "You're crazy, Frau Schmidt."

"Yah, you zink I'm crazy. You ver not zare—zare in the midst of zee Reich, bathed in zee glory of it all. None of you know about living life to the fullest. You Americans destroyed zat for me—you deserve to die."

Brian took a step forward. The Frau stood her ground, looking as though she wanted to spit in his face. Brian, coming within inches of her, screamed. "You are a delusional psychopath!"

"Oh, you people are zee mentally veak ones. Yah, you zink I am crazy; you zink zat because of my power unt conviction. He taught me zat. You zink he's gone, but he remains. Der Fuhrer lives on from zee darkness. Your house has proven zat. I told you he vas a great man. His power goes beyond the grave. It is here, in this city, in zee house, stored within his personal belongings."

Dr. Jamieson stepped back, composed himself, and smiled. "His belongings are no more. His power is no more."

The Frau cackled. "Vut are you saying? You know nothing of vut I am speaking."

Bryan, retaining an air of quiet confidence, repeated, "His power is gone—gone forever."

"Stop it. Shut up! You know nothing, you stupid man."

"I know more than you think I do, you despicable bitch." He smiled broadly, glaring straight at her.

Frau Schmidt, seeing his wide smile, paused for a pensive moment. Seconds later she erupted. "You ignorant, naïve man; you can do nothing. I will report you to zee Gestapo!"

The doctor, laughing aloud, mockingly retorted. "Zee Gestapo! You are delusional, you old piece of shit! Go ahead, tell the authorities I destroyed your precious ceiling fan. I'll tell them how you murdered the prior owner of that house, the young woman."

"Oh, Doctor, are you zat stupid? Be my guest, please call zee police and explain to zem zat Adolf Hitler is living in my ceiling fan and zat he tried to kill your lovely young bride. I'm sure zey will think you are kvite insane."

Brian and Jenny turned to the blare of a siren. Two fire trucks raced up the street, passing the antique shop. Brian looked back to the Frau and grinned. Her mouth shot open wide as she screamed. "Vut have you done, you fool?"

Laughing again, Brian said, "Old houses have old wood, layers of old paint, and old, unreliable wiring. They burn like tinder, burn to the ground, consuming everything."

"You monster! I'll report you to zee police. You are an arsonist. You have destroyed me." The broken old woman fell back, catching herself on the display counter. Her despair led her to shout, *"Ich werde den Heimlichen Dienst nachdemSie senden. Die Gestapo wird Sie töten!"*

Brian snickered. "Did I hear Gestapo again? You still think the Gestapo can help you? You really are psychotic." Mocking the old Nazi for the second time, he said, "Go ahead. Tell zee authorities zat I purposely burned down my new home because of a possessed ceiling fan. I'm sure zey vill zink you are kvite insane!"

As the couple was leaving the shop, Brian turned back, finding Frau Schmidt on her knees, sobbing—mascara streaming down her cheeks. She looked up with a blank stare and a face devoid of emotion but for a subtle quiver in her lips.

The doctor, with facetious sincerity, waved goodbye as he walked out and slammed the shop's door, shattering its full-length pane of glass into pieces, which slid across the foyer's tile floor, coming to rest at the knees of the satanic old woman.

•

Frau Schmidt, without her prized possessions from the Third Reich, her only remaining contact with her lost love, envisioned a lonely, destitute future of solitude. Slowly raising herself from the floor, she walked to the rear of her shop.

Entering her secret back room, she retrieved a key hidden on a shelf and unlocked the bottom drawer of a large, mahogany cabinet. A folded, Third Reich flag was lying far back in the drawer. Wrapped within it, was a German Luger, one of many previously owned by der Fuhrer. A small box of bullets next to the gun was labeled with a pro-duction date, Dresden, May 14, 1941.

Helga set the gun atop the cabinet and poured three bullets into the palm of her hand. The shells, manufactured more than sixty years before, had dulled brass casings, tarnished with time.

She wondered if the Luger had ever been fired. Never once had she seen der Fuhrer fire a gun or even pull one from his holster. She doubted it had ever been used and was certain it hadn't been cleaned in decades.

Taking one shell from her hand, she gently slid it into the chamber of the pistol and returned the remaining bullets to the box, which she placed in the drawer, along with the flag. She closed the drawer, locked it, and returned the key to its hiding place. Frau Schmidt walked with the pistol to her armchair.

Placing the gun on her lap, suspended on her wool skirt, she leaned back, closed her eyes, and thought about the house. Another siren sounded, more distant than the first. *My precious house, my lovely belongings, all burning.* Hating the thought, she opened her eyes, leaned forward, and fingered through the collection of phonograph recordings beside the chair. Despite his Austrian origin, she chose Johann Sebastian Strauss's *The Blue Danube Waltz.*

After carefully positioning the player's stylus on the recording, she relaxed, again closed her eyes, and listened. The music took her back. It was 1943. She was twenty years old and was accompanied by a handsome young military officer. They were in a huge, elegant ballroom. Frau could see the room: the glossy dance floor, the chandeliers, the hanging tapestries, and the exquisite artwork. She could smell the room, the distinct scent of wood paneling, burning candles, and the smell of gourmet food mingled with the fragrance of women's cologne. She could taste the saltiness of the caviar and feel the titillation of champagne bubbles popping in her mouth and tickling her nose.

Strauss's waltz progressed. The beautiful young blonde in the ballroom danced with her attractive escort. They moved together, turning, spinning as they traveled, floating across the floor, carried by the rhythm of Maestro Strauss's masterpiece.

The old frau turned her head to the side of the chair. Her eyes still closed, she smiled—smiled to the magic of her daydream. The scent of the young officer's hair, his cologne, even the clean smell of his uniform filled her with erotic urges. She could feel the strength of his body, the firmness of his back, the muscles in his shoulders and arms, and the power of his legs as he skillfully took command of her, gliding her across the room.

Her dreams carried her eyes around the ballroom. He was there, Adolph was there, standing with his arm around Eva, his companion, well known to be his mistress. Helga dared not look at them. If his eyes met hers, Adolph would be angry; she was sure of it. She was his secret possession. If Eva knew, it would be awkward, even dangerous, perhaps mortally so. Helga turned back to her escort and danced on.

At the completion of the Strauss recording, the stylus slid across the bare, center portion of the disc, producing a monotonous, scratchy sound. Frau Schmidt's daydream sadly ended as all good things do. She thought, *Life's pleasures always end too quickly.*

Removing Strauss from the player, she pulled another record from her collection. She wanted to feel the power, the might of the homeland, the dominance the Third Reich had wielded over Po-land, Czechoslovakia, Belgium, and France, the weaklings of Eu-rope. She longed to feel the glory of the time and the admiration she had held for the man who could have—should have—ruled the world. Her record selection, Wagner's "Flight of the Valkyries," was the perfect choice.

Again, Frau Schmidt put her head back, closed her eyes, and resumed her time travel. The thunderous power of the orchestra's horns, strings, and drums took her back. She was in der Fuhrer's office, his command center. She could feel his presence, his strength, his brilliance, and the magnificence of his authority. Her heart ached with a deep, romantic patriotism for the homeland. Tears rolled out of from her closed eyes, streaming down the heavy makeup concealing her age-weary face.

Helga's mood changed in synchrony with the cadence and power of Wagner's orchestral masterpiece. Captured by the rhythmic pulsations of the music, she repositioned herself in her seat and waved her arms with clenched fists, pounding on her thighs as the symphony came to its inspired, glorious conclusion.

Exhausted from the exhilaration of the music, she took a deep breath, sighed and slumped back to recover.

The finality of it all, the abrupt termination of her daydreams at the completion of each piece, Strauss and Wagner, left her in a deep state of melancholy. A horrible sadness overwhelmed her—the sad-ness of knowing what once was could never be again.

Frau Schmidt took the pistol from her lap, set it on the table next to her chair, and cautiously stood. She stretched her aching back, moving slowly around the small space of the room. She rubbed her elbows and bent forward to massage her knees. Never had she felt so old or so alone.

Turning back to the phonograph, she caught a glimpse of her face, her reflection in a small mirror hanging on the wall behind the armchair. Removing it from the wall, she sat, holding the mirror with both hands. Staring intently at her image, the frau saw her true self, who she was and what she had become.

Her bleached-blond hair was thin, so thin as to reveal spots of bare scalp. Gray roots, in dire need of coloring, rose from her fore-head. The deep creases of her hollow cheeks, caked with thick smears of makeup, were stained with streaks of black mascara— trails left by tears running down her face. She held the mirror closer, examining her loose, droopy eyelids and the dull color of her aging eyes. Seeing how her trembling hands had erratically applied her lipstick, she began to cry.

A tear fell from her nose, splashing on her wrist. Looking down at her hands, she was shocked. The hands she had always considered beautiful and delicate were bony, old hands, covered with wrinkled skin, speckled with large, brown spots and bulging blue veins. The ancient appearance of her thin, arthritic fingers belied the youthful beauty of her manicured, glossy red nails.

Leaning over the side of her chair, Frau Schmidt gently set the mirror on the floor, face down. After a moment of silent meditation, she took a deep breath and wiped the tears from her face. Having already listened to more than two hours of music, she decided one more piece would be all she needed.

Considering which symphony would be best as a finale, the old woman deftly pulled her favorite of all. She placed Beethoven's spectacular *Ode to Joy* on the turnstile. After gently positioning the stylus, the frau took the Luger from the chair side table and once again set it on her lap, suspended by the wool skirt stretched between her old, withered legs.

Helga turned the phonograph's volume to its highest level. Leaning back in her chair, her eyes fell shut as she indulged herself, captivated by the music and her memories. She thought of Adolf, his be-longings, the house, the furnishings, the woodwork, the huge Persian rugs, and most of all, his ceiling fan, the fan that spoke to her. The look, the feel, the scent of her beautiful house, spun around in her head. For an enchanting, but mercilessly brief moment, she forgot what had happened—forgot her home was gone, destroyed by that Jewish woman and her insane husband. Her pain was palpable.

While the chorus of Beethoven's masterpiece thundered through the shop, Helga Schmidt's despair intensified. Early into the symphony's third movement, she realized her private concert would soon end. She could not bear the thought of the approaching, heartbreaking silence that would be her life. The lonely solitude of a future with-out der Fuhrer would be impossible to bear. She thought of the gun, the Luger that was nearly as old as she. Once again, she wondered if the powder in the shell casing had outlived its usefulness, as had she.

Both Beethoven and Frau Schmidt were nearing their finale. She raised the Luger from her lap, inserted its barrel deep in her mouth, put her index finger on the trigger, and waited. As she took in the very last bit of the very last verse, she again fretted over the age of the gun and the bullet. Once more, reminiscing about dancing with the handsome, young officer, she reveled in memories of his virile, muscular body and the passionate sexual encounter they'd shared that night. She smiled, recalling her beauty, her youth, and her past sexual prowess.

The symphony ended. Again, she wondered about the gunpowder and squeezed as hard as her frail finger would allow.

The Luger, the shell casing, the gunpowder, and the lead bullet all performed to der Fuhrer's exacting specifications, as though they had been manufactured that very day.

Henri

*H*enri loved his home. The old woman upstairs kept to her-self, giving him full reign of the basement. Everything was fine until she bought that darn cat. Henri despised cats. *Time to move out,* he thought. *This house just isn't big enough for me and that cat. The smell of that litter box makes me sick.* He decided to leave the next morning.

The old woman was up and about early. Henri heard her walking across the kitchen, her clunky, old-lady shoes banging on the linoleum floor. *She'll go out soon, as she does every morning, to water her stupid petunias. When she opens the door, I'm outta here.*

A while later, when he heard the door open, he scrambled up the steps, stopping just short of the landing. Henri nearly swallowed his heart when he saw a monster feline sitting on the landing. He dashed for cover in a corner of the stairway. *How am I supposed to compete with that animal? A four-ounce mouse, against a ten-pound cat. It's like sending Peewee Herman in the ring with Mike Tyson!*

He cautiously peeked over the edge of the landing with one eye. The inside door was partly open, but the storm door was closed. The old woman was talking to her cat, telling him to stay inside. *As if that dumb cat understands anything,* thought Henri. The cat turned, climbed two steps from the landing to the kitchen, and sat down, precisely as he'd been instructed. *Okay, so maybe he does understand her. Maybe he's not so dumb, but he sure is fat and ugly.*

The woman opened the inside door farther, pushing it flat against the wall. Henri took another peek. *Fatso seems bored with all of this.* The cat turned and walked away. *Time to make my move!* Henri dashed up to the landing, his claws making a screech on the linoleum floor. He murmured, "Oh my God, he heard that; I just know it!"

Sure enough, the cat raced across the kitchen, skidding to a stop at the edge of the steps. Henri scurried behind the door, terrified, heart pounding like a steam engine. *Oh, no, oh God, please, get me outta this fix!* Shivering from fear, he stood up with his front paws on the back of the door. Looking down, he saw his hind paws were visible under the door's bottom edge. He was so nervous his toes were wiggling. *Dear God in heaven, please, don't let that fiend see my feet.*

The old woman opened the storm door. Henri shot out like a bullet, tumbled over the sill, and went into a long roll on the sidewalk. He heard the cat scrambling down the steps, close behind. Darting down the sidewalk, shrieking hysterically, he screamed "Help me! For the love of God, somebody help me! Mouse in trouble here! Someone call 911."

While frantically running in circles, and bellowing at the top of his lungs, Henri remembered something his father once told him. "Son, if you're ever up against the wall and doom is imminent, act like you're insane. It works for me every time. No cat wants to eat a mentally deranged mouse."

Henri went into his performance, flipping around and slobbering as though he were out of his mind. He started screaming, "I'm crazy! Look at me. My squash is rotten!" The cat sat back with amusement. Henri squealed louder. "Stay back! The doctor says I'm schizophrenic. He put me on medicine. It's not working!"

Unfortunately, the cat had once encountered Henri's father. He'd seen this routine before.

The mouse continued. "I think I have rabies! Be careful or I'll bite ya."

Sitting there, entertained by Henri's nutty charade, the cat thought, *I've seen enough, I'm not gonna fall for this trick again.*

Seeing the cat stand and lick his chops, Henri thought, *Oh, oh, he's not buyin' it. I'll give it one last shot.* Standing ram rod straight, he yelled, "Timber!" as he fell flat to the pavement and started banging his head on the concrete. "I must have spinal meningitis. It's unbearable. My head's gonna explode." From the corner of his eye, Henri saw the cat's claws protrude from its furry paws.

Knowing his charade had failed, Henri took off like a bottle rocket with the hairy beast right behind. The mouse, tripping over a crack in the sidewalk, flipped in the air and went into another roll. His eyes nearly popped out of his head when a massive paw came crashing down next to him. Springing to his hind legs, he flexed his muscles and leapt a full foot in the air just as the cat pounced.

Henri flew down the sidewalk with the predator right behind. His frenetic brain was swirling as he screamed, "I'm not gonna make it. I'm not gonna make it. No place to hide. No place to hide."

From out of nowhere, it appeared—a big wooden pole, right in front of him. He jumped, digging his tiny claws into soft wood as a pair of pearly white fangs clamped shut a mere hairs-breadth from the tip of his tail. He tore up the pole, smacking his head into a metal box. With horror-struck eyeballs, he peered back at the cat.

In a state of hysteria, Henri's head frantically shot back and forth looking for a safe hiding spot. His eyes set upon a quarter-size hole in the bottom of the box. Hurling himself up, he caught the edge of the opening with one paw and yanked himself inside. Tabby was foiled.

"Whoa, that was way too close!" Henri sat down to catch his breath. Peeking back through the hole, he saw the enemy still standing on the walk below. Henri, now feeling brave and secure, thought he'd have a little fun.

Pushing his snout through the porthole, he hollered, "Hey, you stupid cat, take this." Henri's tongue fluttered as he blew raspberries at his adversary. "You-hoo, cat, you're a lousy excuse for a feline. Your breath stinks, and to top it off, you're a jerk! You couldn't catch a quadriplegic mouse, let alone a master escape artist like me. Come on up here, and I'll kick your butt, you hear me?" He went on and on. "Go on home to your old woman and your smelly sandbox, you moron."

Henri rolled around in the bottom of the box, laughing his head off. "Oh, man, am I funny or what? I crack myself up." He peeked out another porthole just as the woman snatched up her cat and took it home.

Looking around the box, Henri exclaimed, "Hey, this place isn't bad. I could hang out here for a while, maybe even make it my new home. It's dark, warm, and most of all, safe. Not too shabby. This could be my new bachelor's pad."

That night, Henri discreetly ventured out to gather nesting materials. *No sign of the dummy*, he thought. *He's probably home, wallowing around in his poop-filled box.*

By morning, the mouse had a nice, cozy nest in the darkest corner of his new home. As daylight broke, he snuggled in for a snooze. *I've been working hard all night—time for a nap.*

He quickly drifted off but was soon awakened by clicking sounds. Every two to three minutes, "Click—click." In all his bustling around, he hadn't heard it. Now that he was trying to sleep, it was driving him nuts. "What the heck is that?" He got up to investigate.

Sunlight was shining through holes near the top of the box. Henri counted a total of four, two portholes in each side of his house. "Hey, what's the deal? This place isn't as dark and cozy as I thought." A beam of sunlight illuminated a bunch of machinery he hadn't noticed. He thought, *What's all that stuff?*

There were wires, gears, shiny metallic clips, switches, and a transformer. Henri spoke aloud. "This is awesome—look at all this junk. I can't believe it." He saw it move! Two metal plates snapped shut with a loud click. He watched intently. A short time later, the plates popped apart with another click. "So, that's what's makin' all the racket. I'll put an end to this, right now."

Climbing up on a large wire coil, Henri steadied himself and gave the metal plates a quick jab with his snout. The plates snapped shut. Startled by a loud screech from outside, he lost his balance, tumbled off the coil, and rolled down to the bottom of the box, bumping his head. "Ouch!" Henri jumped up, ran to one of his lookout portholes, and stuck his head out to see what had made that horrible noise.

Two automobiles on the street had crashed into each other. He saw some men arguing, one of them was pointing to the street light. Henri yelled out the hole, "Hey, you clowns, knock it off! A guy's tryin' to sleep in here!"

His tiny voice was drowned out by the sounds of the city. Pulling his head back, he said, "What a couple of bozos." He crawled back into his nest, tore some small hunks of cotton from his makeshift bedding, and stuffed a piece in each ear. As he lay down, Henri said to himself. "Okay, that's more like it. Maybe now a mouse can get some well-deserved peace and quiet." He slept like a baby.

When darkness fell, the mouse awoke and crawled out of his box, down to the sidewalk. *Time for some munchies,* he thought.

Henri saw a doughnut shop on the corner. *I'm amazed I missed that.* He could smell the doughnuts being cooked for the early morning rush. He softly spoke. "Well, roll me in flour, boil me in oil, and sprinkle on some powdered sugar. I can't believe it. I'm in mouse heaven!"

He ran to the shop, jumped up on the windowsill and peered through the glass. There were two large display cases right in front of him, one packed with doughnuts and pastry, the other with buckets of ice cream. Looking to a corner of the room, he saw it. "A cat— they have a cat in the doughnut shop! Darn cats are comin' out the woodwork."

Covering his eyes with his front paws, he threw his head back and groaned, "My dreams are shattered!"

Henri left the shop and daringly ventured down the sidewalk looking for food. After searching more than an hour, he'd found barely a crumb. On his return home, he quietly snuck along the curb, safely hidden from the walk, hoping to avoid any pesky nocturnal predators, such as cats.

When he reached his corner, Henri was surprised to find dough-nut crumbs scattered all around the walk. He whispered, "There's plenty of food right here, just a few feet from home. Talk about stupid. Food right next to my house and I'm travelin' all around town." He ate every morsel he could find and ran up the pole to his bachelor's pad.

As dawn arrived, the mouse, fatigued from his night-time excursion, settled in for a nap. He was getting used to the machinery's clicking sound and no longer needed the cotton earplugs. As Henri lay in bed, he thought of how dark and desolate it was in his new home. Feeling a bit melancholy and forlorn, he started thinking. *It's kinda lonely in here. Maybe I should find a lady friend.* Henri immediately reconsidered. *I don't know, though. You meet some babe, invite her in, and a few weeks later, ya got baby mice runnin' everywhere. I've never understood that.*

He thought of his parents and how they struggled; caring for more than thirty children wasn't easy. "You finally hook up with the right chick, you're happy, and the next thing you know your place is swarmin' with kids squealin' and crawlin' all over ya. I wonder why that happens."

Henri thought about it. *Darn kids just seem to pop outta nowhere. I'll have to think that one over. Anyway, in my opinion, women just aren't worth the trouble. I like my solitude.*

Henri's supposed love of solitude went down the drain that very evening. He awoke from his snooze at dusk and slipped out for his nightly rounds. As he crawled past the doughnut shop, he saw her. She was just sitting there, about five away, smiling at him. He nervously snuck up closer to check her out. *She is gorgeous! Petite body, little round ears, squinty eyes, full lips, and a beautiful set of fangs!*

He loved the smallness of her paws and her finely trimmed claws. *She even has a cute little curl at the end of her tail. And check out that figure. What a knockout!* It was love at first sight.

Henri could feel his heart pounding as he approached his new-found love. He was nervous—so nervous, his voice cracked when he introduced himself.

"Hel-hel-lo… I… I'm Henri."

"Glad to meet you, Henri."

"And you are… ah… your name is… my dear, my… uh—"

She broke in to save her new acquaintance from further embarrassment. "My mama named me Henrietta."

Her response made Henri's heart soar. His mind raced. *Surely, this was meant to be. Surely the God of all rodents has shined upon me. Her name is undeniable proof.* Henri squealed with delight, "Henrietta, I can't believe it. It's perfect. It's splendid. Henri and Henrietta; what a match!"

With a coquettish tilt of her head, Henrietta peered straight into Henri's eyes and smiled. She seemed to have similar feelings for the formerly avowed bachelor. The pair embraced and shared a long kiss. In the mouse world, they were now officially married.

They spent the night gathering more nesting materials for their honeymoon suite. Henri worked hard at nest expansion, which he completed just before sunrise, at which point they snuggled in for some well-deserved daytime slumber.

Henrietta couldn't sleep. Henri, long since accustomed to the clicking noise, rarely ever heard it. But Henrietta was beside herself. She woke her husband, "Honey, what's making all that noise. It's keeping me awake."

"What noise?"

"That clicking noise! What is that? I'm sorry, sweetheart, but I can't sleep with all that clatter goin' on."

Henri facetiously responded, "Okay, okay, honey buns, I'll see what I can do, but the last time I tried, I damn… I mean, I darn near killed myself. I fell off that dumb machine, scraped my knee, and bumped my head on the floor."

"Well, for goodness sakes, Henri, please be careful. I don't want you scraping those cute little knees of yours." She batted her eyelashes and smiled. Henri, detecting a hint of sarcasm in his new bride's voice, gave her a stern look. Henrietta responded with a wider smile, exposing two long, sparkling white incisors.

"I'll see what I can do, sugarplum." Henrietta's husband grumbled under his breath as he climbed the wire coil to the switch plates. He whispered, "I knew women weren't worth the hassle. She may be cute, but she can be a real pain in the—"

"What did you say, Henri? I didn't catch that."

"Oh, nothing, my sweet. I was just clearing my throat."

Early morning sunlight, beaming through the box portholes, lit Henri's way to the switch plates. Figuring he'd give one more try to stop the darn clicking noise, he positioned himself securely on the coil and slammed the metal plate with his nose. "Ouch, that hurt!" He heard a loud screech outside, just like the other day. A moment later, he heard a crowd of people around the box, complaining.

One of them said, "What's going on with these lights?" Another responded, "Yeah, what's the holdup? I gotta get across the street today, not tomorrow!" A third exclaimed, "That crossing signal is screwed up."

Henrietta lifted her head from the nest. "What did you do, Henri?

"What did I do? I didn't do nothin'—did I?"

"You better take a look, honey."

Henri clambered down from the coil, heading to a bottom porthole facing the sidewalk. He stuck his head out to evaluate the situation.

A number of people were gathered right next to the box, at the corner, impatiently waiting to cross the street. Many of them were eating doughnuts. There was a little girl with an ice cream cone. Henri started salivating.

He noticed the longer they waited to cross, the more crumbs they dropped. The girl's ice cream started to melt; a big beautiful drip fell from her cone, landing on the concrete right next to Henri's house. He exclaimed, "Wow! What a smorgasbord." He ran back to his nest. "You should see it, babe. There's food galore out there. Tonight, we feast!"

He jumped back in the sack with his wife and thought about what had just happened. Henri told Henrietta about the loud screech he'd heard the first time he'd nosed the metal plates and described the scene outside with the people stuck on the corner. He asked, "Hennie, do you think I had something to do with that?"

Henrietta rolled her eyes, "Of course you did, you dummy... I mean, darlin'. That switch must control the street lights and the cross-walk signals."

"Oh, yeah, maybe. Yeah, that's it! I figured it out. That's why those big cars got in a wreck. *Voilà*, my dear, I have solved the puzzle." Henri lay back in his nest with a self-satisfied look.

Henrietta, gently shook her head, "Oh, honey! You're a genius, you are."

"I must agree my love; I must agree."

Henri slept soundly while Henrietta did her best to ignore the continued, infernal clicking. Her husband went into a deep sleep and began dreaming about the treats awaiting them on the sidewalk. Images of gigantic glazed donuts, foot-long éclairs, and buckets of vanilla ice cream spun around in his head.

The pair woke in the evening and gleefully devoured piles of crumbs and ice cream drippings on the walk. Having their fill, they returned to the metal box and crashed in bed to digest their huge meal.

Over the ensuing weeks, Henri nose-punched the machine's switch plates every three or four days—whenever their food supply was running low. Henrietta would keep watch through a porthole to give Henri the all-clear signal, indicating there were no approaching cars. Henri didn't want to hurt anyone by causing another car crash. He just wanted to make the doughnut shop customers wait on the corner for a while, dropping crumbs.

Thinking about the crash he'd caused, Henri wondered about the drivers; he wondered why he cared about them, especially in light of what humans had done to his uncle Norman. His poor uncle had his head smashed by one of those wire contraptions with cheese on them. Henri's mother had told her son about those gadgets. She taught him how to gently remove the cheese without making the thing explode in your face.

Henri thought, *Uncle Norm's mom must not have taught him about that. I bet that's why he got his head crushed.* Despite that tragedy, Henri felt it wouldn't be right to hurt any humans, even if they had murdered his favorite uncle.

Life for Henri and Henrietta was going well. They had a nice home, a comfortable nest, and plenty of food. Henri was starting to think marriage wasn't so bad after all. Then it happened. He awoke one morning to find a nest full of youngsters—cranky little mice, crawling all over him. He couldn't figure it out. Two weeks later, another batch came along. His bachelor pad had been turned into a nursery swarming with tiny rodents.

Henri's life changed drastically. He had to work hard to feed his kids, hauling sidewalk crumbs up the pole and into his house. He complained to his wife. "Hennie, this job is killin' me. It's a lotta work feedin' all of those starvin' monsters."

Henrietta grimaced, and said, "Come on, honey. You're a father now, and you have to deal with your new responsibilities."

Henri moaned and walked away.

After a few weeks, he decided it was time to send the kids out into the real world. They simply had to go make it on their own. He told his wife how he felt. She knew he was right, but she sadly thought of how much she would miss the children and how she'd worry about them.

Henrietta had an idea. "Henri, I just thought of something. Why don't you show the children how to operate the switch? Then they can get food the same way we do."

"Hey, that's not a bad idea, Hen. I wish I'd thought of it."

She grinned, "I'm sure you do."

Henri demonstrated switch-plate nosing to each of his children, all nineteen of them. One by one, they were shown how to slam their snout into the metal plate. After thorough training, Henri sent them out into the world to find their own box.

He told them to look for busy street corners and explained that humans like to eat doughnuts in the morning and sandwiches in the middle of the day. He told the kids they had to stay awake in the morning, long enough to hit the light switch when the sidewalks were busy. Then they could sleep for the rest of the day and collect their goodies at night.

After sending his children out to find their own box, Henri was more relaxed. However, the following morning he awoke to find eleven new babies. He was devastated. "Hennie, I don't think I can stand much more of this. How do we stop these kids from showin' up outta' the blue? I'm a little tired of running a daycare center."

Henrietta was astonished. "Henri, do you mean to tell me you honestly don't know where babies come from?"

"Yeah, that's right. What's so strange about that? Do you know where they come from, smarty?"

Henri's wife instantly recognized an opportunity. "Henri, sweetheart, I'm sorry I said that. I don't know how these kids get here either. I guess we'll just have to put up with them for now. I'm sure they'll quit showing up sooner or later." Henrietta didn't want to stop having children, and since Henri was so naïve, she could carry on with more babies, acting as though she had no clue as to how they got there.

Thirty-six children later, Henri was contemplating suicide. "Look at these bags under my eyes, Hennie. I can't sleep, I can't eat, I'm wastin' away. I'm tellin' ya, these kids are gonna be the end of me!"

Henrietta took sympathy on her husband. "It's gonna be all right, honey. I think the babies will stop coming now."

"Do you mean it? How do you know?"

"I just have a feeling about it. I think we've already had more than our share."

"Oh, thank God. I hope you're right."

Henrietta loved her husband dearly. Not wanting to deprive him, or herself, of their intimacy, she thought of a solution. The following night Hennie went out alone to find the necessary items. After a long search, she found a discarded blouse decorated with sequins. Chewing through a thread, she freed a single sequin and carried it home.

That night, while Henri napped, she fashioned the tiny piece of plastic into a diaphragm. She plugged the center hole of the sequin with a bit of chewing gum and tried it out. It fit perfectly. Henri never knew the difference. The baby production line came to a halt. Henri was elated.

Within two weeks, Henri had trained and sent out all their remaining children. Two months later, he and Henrietta learned from a few of the kids they now had over two hundred grandchildren. Six weeks later, they had nearly five hundred great-grandchildren.

Each of these descendants had been shown by their respective parents how to operate traffic-light switch plates. Within six months, practically every switch box in the city was home to one of Henri and Henrietta's offspring. "It's incredible, Hennie. We've started a movement; our family controls the streets of the city!"

Henri, due to his copious supply of food, had gotten fat, so fat he would occasionally get stuck in the porthole entry to their home. He apologized to Henrietta for his appearance. "I'm sorry I'm so fat, babe."

"It's okay, Henri. I love you either way. Skinny or fat, I love you just the same."

"Thank you for the kind words, dear. I'll go on a diet, I promise."

More than a year had passed from the time Henri had left his home in the old woman's basement. In mouse years, he and his wife were getting old. Henrietta was well beyond childbearing age. It was time for them to settle back, relax, and wait for the inevitable. A few weeks later, they both sensed the end was near.

As they slipped into their nest for the last time, Henrietta softly spoke to the love of her life. "I think it's time for us to go for a long sleep, Henri." A tear rolled down her cheek as she gazed into the eyes of her husband. "I love you very much, Henri. I think we've had a good life together, don't you?"

"Yes, Hennie, it's been very good. My life with you has been wonderful. I never knew I could love someone so much. I'll never forget the first night I saw you, Hennie. You took my breath away. I'll remember you always, even after we're gone."

Henrietta cried harder as they hugged, "Dear, you're a very special mouse. I'm so glad I met you."

"So am I, babe, I'm very happy we met. At first, I wasn't so keen on havin' all those kids runnin' around, but it's all worked out for the best. You and I have made history, Hennie; never before has a clan of mice had so much influence on a city."

The couple rolled to their sides, face to face, snout to snout, and wrapped their arms around each other for the last time.

After a minute or so, Henrietta whispered to her love. "Henri, there's something I want to tell you before we go."

"What's that, hon?"

"Well, it's something important, but I'm afraid I might embarrass you."

"Come on, Hennie, how could you embarrass me after all this time? Go ahead."

"It's about babies, honey. I told you a fib, Henri. I actually do know where they come from."

"What? And you never told me. I can't believe it!"

"Please, don't be upset. I thought it was adorable you didn't know."

"Adorable, really? Then please fill me in. It's now or never." "Okay, honey." Henrietta whispered in her husband's ear.

Henri shot bolt upright in bed and screamed, "No frickin' way! You gotta be shittin' me. You can't be serious!"

"I'm very serious, Henri."

Henri, lying back in their nest, paused to take it all in. Moments later, a huge smile appeared on his face. Turning to his wife, he said, "I must have been pretty good, eh? Just think of all the babies I've made— or, uh, we've made, you and me, together." He paused again and then sheepishly added, "Was I okay, Hennie? You know, uh, at makin' babies?"

"Henri, you were spectacular. I mean it. You were the best ever."

He replied, "Awe babe, you're the best."

The best ever, Henri thought. He paused, thinking about his wife's comment, realizing the implication, thinking, *The best ever suggests a comparison, but with what, or more importantly, who?*

"Hennie, babe, uh… I've never asked you this, but I was just wondering, uh… Hen, was I the first, you know, the very first?"

Henrietta immediately recalled a one-night stand she'd had at the age of two months; it was an interlude with a handsome, young, wild thing, who truly meant nothing to her then or now. She erupted with, "Henri, my God! How could you ask such a thing? I'm shocked."

Feeling like a fool, Henri, struggling with a response, blurted out, "I'm sorry, Hennie. It's just that you said I was the best EVER, and I... I thought, *ever*, well... maybe the word *ever* could mean you were comparing me to... like comparing me to someone else... some guy you might have, uh... you know."

Henrietta, hearing Henri's angst-filled response, knew she had reacted appropriately by lying instead of hurting her loving husband with the truth. Before she could utter a word, Henri jumped back in.

"You know, maybe you could've said somethin' like... uh... you might have... somethin' like, honey, you were the best I could *ever* imagine, or maybe said... uh... for instance... uh, there couldn't be anyone better or somethin' like that... maybe."

Henrietta, tired and irritated, responded with, "Henri, my love—shut up!"

"Okay, whatever you say, babe."

"I love you, Henri, always have and always will."

"I love you, Hennie."

"Henri, you were spectacular. I mean it, you were and are wonderful."

They hugged for the last time and fell asleep, snout to snout, tightly wrapped in each other's arms. Henri, proud of fathering so many children, dozed off with a wide smile on his face.

•

By the end of the year, the city's traffic light debacle had gotten way out of hand. Most intersections were daily chaos, and the city was on the brink of shutting down.

Despite numerous attempts to identify the problem, the city workers were unable to find anything wrong with the light switches. In desperation, the director of Streets and Highways, ordered all traffic switch mechanisms be replaced with new, switchless digital equipment.

Thousands of Henri's children, grandchildren, great-grandchildren, and great-great-grandchildren scrambled from their homes as workers opened switch boxes across the city.

One of the last mechanisms replaced was at the corner of Washington Street and Second Avenue, near the center of town, adjacent to a doughnut shop. When a city employee opened that box, he noticed some straw and torn paper in the back behind the equipment. Reaching behind the switch mechanism, he found a small nest, which he carefully slid from the box.

There were two mice lying in the nest—one was chubby and the other was thin with a curly tail. The worker took a close look. He couldn't believe it; it looked as if the mice were hugging each other. On closer inspection, he was even more surprised, convinced the chubby one had a big grin on his face.

Dreams Can Come True

*H*e wasn't the most handsome guy around; then again, she wasn't exactly a beauty queen, so he was probably as good as she would ever have. In the beginning, he'd been kind and generous, but over the past few weeks, she had become disappointed with his often irritable and sometimes downright rude behavior.

April was a dreamer; since early adolescence, she had fantasized about wild romance and unending love. She dreamt every night, imagining her phantom lover, a chivalrous, dauntless man who would rescue her from loneliness and rejection.

Men, apparently interested only in external beauty, seemed oblivious to her kind, loving nature and generally ignored her. She often dreamt of a tall, tanned blonde who treated her like a princess, not only at the beginning but forever.

Gary was tall enough, and he did have brown, almost blond hair, but he certainly didn't treat her like a princess. After their last date, a movie and dinner, he dropped her off at home, leaving without as much as a goodnight kiss. That night she had a long, wonderful dream about her ideal man, a romantic lover who was never irritated, never rude, and always a gentleman.

Three days later, she and Gary went out on another dinner date. April was shocked when he pulled her chair back, assisting her with her seat. He'd never done that before. Peering across the table, she noticed his hair was getting lighter, now having blond streaks. Though politely, softly asking if he had dyed his hair, she received a harsh response.

"Dyed my hair, of course not. Do you think I'd be so superficial? I've got better things to do than worry about my looks."

They finished dinner with only one or two more irritating comments from Gary. He gave April a kiss goodnight in the car, after which she had to open the car door herself and sadly watch him drive away, leaving her standing on the sidewalk.

That night, she again dreamt of her flawless, ideal mate. Her mystical imaginings continued for what seemed like hours as she reveled over a *Castle in the Sky* lover. It all seemed so real, making her awakening to reality that much more agonizing.

Over the weekend, she and Gary went out for a movie and dessert. His hair looked more blond than before. In addition, his hands were different, cleaner looking, even manicured. There was no dirt under his nails and no red marks from chewing on hangnails. To her amazement, he even looked taller, more muscular, and slightly tanned.

Recalling his irritation on their prior date, April certainly wasn't going to ask him about his hair being lighter. She did, however, muster the courage to ask if he'd been going to a tanning salon. Gary smiled, not at all upset by the question. He calmly said he'd never been in a tanning booth, but he'd been outside a little more than usual and must have gotten some sun.

April thought that was odd, considering it was February. She didn't comment on his hands, thinking he'd be embarrassed if he had gone to a manicurist. After they finished dessert and were ready to leave, he surprised her by again walking around the table and pulling her chair back as she stood.

Gary drove her home and parked in front of her apartment. He kissed her, this time more passionately as they made out in the car. Wishing she could have stayed there for hours, April reluctantly told Gary it was getting late and she had to get up early for work. She would have preferred being there all night, in Gary's arms, captivated by his newfound passion.

To her surprise and delight, when she was about to open the car door, Gary stopped her, saying, "I'll get it, honey."

She couldn't believe it; he got out, walked around the car, opened her door, and walked her to the front porch. He even kissed her again, a goodnight kiss, followed by "I had a wonderful evening, April." To her glee, he whispered, "I love you."

Their relationship progressed, improving by leaps and bounds over the ensuing months. April's dreams about a fantasy mate gradually became dreams about Gary, who had become a perfect gentle-man and an incredible lover. They made amorous love in her apartment nearly every night.

It wasn't long before Gary presented her with a diamond engagement ring, which she enthusiastically accepted. Two months later they married.

After the wedding, to April's surprise, her dreams about an ideal lover stopped. She figured it was because her fantasy had been fulfilled. Gary had become her chivalrous, romantic savior.

Their first year of marriage was wonderful bliss. Gary was a loving, kind companion, always going out of his way to help his wife any way he could. A child was born ten months from their wedding day.

The good life continued. Gary's job was going well, he had a good income, and he loved his work. After a second baby, the family moved into a new home. With her increased responsibilities, caring for two children, April decided to quit her part-time job. Gary, recalling the number of women he knew at work who insisted upon having their own career, sending their children to daycare, was pleased with his wife's dedication to family and had no objection.

A year later, a third child came along, making April's life exhausting. Gary helped her as much as possible, as much as his work allowed. He often had to spend long hours at the office, arriving home late in the evening, tired and ready for bed.

April understood her husband's dedication to work but wished she could have more help with the children and her homemaking chores. Despite her fatigue by day's end, she was having difficulty falling asleep. Anxiety and worry about the kids kept her awake. The more she worried, the more difficult it became to sleep. She soon developed severe insomnia.

Gary, being sensitive to her dilemma, started coming home from work during the day, for an hour or so, to help out. He would change diapers and help with housework. He even went so far as to change positions at work to allow more time at home in the evening.

It was Gary's idea to have April ask their family physician for a sleep aid. The doctor prescribed a pill that must have been quite potent, making her sleep like a baby the very first night.

The following night she took another pill and quickly fell asleep but had a bad night, tossing and turning as she suffered through a horrible nightmare, something she hadn't done in years. Her dream was about the despicable man she'd lived with before meeting Gary. She awoke in the morning full of anxiety from her dream and a bit hungover from her sleeping medication.

That afternoon, April was plagued by recurrent thoughts of her dream about the dreadful, cruel, chain-smoking alcoholic with whom she'd suffered a painful and tumultuous three-year relationship. The immoral tyrant, whom she eventually abandoned, was a belittling, hateful, frequently violent man.

April's awful dreams continued, and her disrupted sleep made her days with the children more tiring. Despite Gary's help, she was bushed and done-in by bedtime every night. In desperation, after weeks of relentless nightmares, she doubled her dose of sleeping pills.

To her dismay, the nightmares only got worse. On the first night of taking two sleepers, she had another horrid dream about her old boyfriend, an unattractive, overweight man, with a pot belly, frontal balding, and repulsive greasy, gray hair. In her dream, he was berating her for burning his dinner, slapping her across the face, and screaming at her with a long, humiliating diatribe.

A few weeks later, Gary informed April he had decided to return to his prior position at work. He wasn't happy with the change he'd made and would no longer be able to leave work during the day or come home early in the evening.

April, though saddened by the news, understood and appreciated her husband's dedication to his job, thankful for the income and security Gary provided to support her and the children in their beautiful home. Over the following weeks, as her nightmares progressed, April continued her double dose of sleepers.

A short time later, she became concerned about Gary—thinking he was working too hard. He seemed to be letting himself go regarding his appearance and health. She was stunned when she caught him smoking a cigarette in the basement, trying to hide his new habit.

Afterward, having nothing to conceal, Gary started smoking in the house, often in front of the children. When she complained about it, he became irate, telling her to mind her own business. "It's my life and my choice, and I enjoy it!"

Gary was gaining weight; he'd quit working out at the gym, and had developed a paunch hanging over his belt.

April's nightmares continued with horrendous recreations of her tragic, past relationship. A recent dream resurrected memories of the ogre's wrath—blowing smoke in her face, slapping her and twisting her arm as she screamed for help. Her nightly imaginings recalled visions of his drunken, ranting tirades when he would call her an ungrateful, lazy bitch.

These terrifying dreams relentlessly progressed as April became increasingly addicted to her sleeping medication. During her endless months of nightmares, Gary appeared to prematurely age with thinning hair and a receding hairline. His beautiful blond hair gradually changed to an odd, gray color. He'd become a chain-smoker, and in contrast to his prior dedication to work, he often called in sick, spending the day on the couch in front of the television. Gary would sit there all day, smoking cigarettes and drinking beer, not lifting a finger to help April with anything.

Eventually, April's dreams became terrifying recreations of her past. Crippling images of her old boyfriend beating her, punching her in the face, leaving her with a bloody nose, bruised cheeks, and finally a broken jaw, filled her head every night.

She called her physician, telling him about the dreams, inquiring if there was some medication to help. Her doctor, hearing of April's double, sometimes triple, dose of sleeping pills, was aghast. He knew the pills were the culprit, the source of her vivid, appalling night-mares, and he instructed her to immediately stop taking them.

A day later, Gary came home from work with bad news. He'd been fired because of poor attendance and the deteriorating quality of his work. Drinking heavily that afternoon, he started strutting around the house in a rage at the world for being unjust. He yelled in his wife's face, "None of this is my fault. It's the damn company. They're a bunch of ungrateful assholes!"

April did her best to console her husband. "It's gonna be okay, Gary. You'll find another job."

Her words simply made him more infuriated. He blew smoke in her face and, incredibly, smashed her in the jaw with a closed fist, knocking her flat to the kitchen floor. Nonchalantly walking to the refrigerator, he grabbed a beer and kicked his wife in the side as he walked back to the living room. Sitting on the couch, he turned on the television, popped open his beer, and lit a cigarette.

The following day, April made an appointment with a divorce attorney. She told her story to the lawyer who listened intently to her tale of woe. She described how her husband had been such a wonderful, attractive man who seemed to love her deeply—treating her like a queen and going out of his way to help with their children.

April tearfully conveyed how Gary had turned into an angry, violent slob: a chain-smoking, beer-swigging, couch potato who often skipped work.

The lawyer, having handled hundreds of divorce proceedings, had never heard of such a sudden, drastic behavior change in a spouse. He sadly explained, "I'm sorry, but since your husband is un-employed, it's gonna be a battle getting child support, and alimony is out of the question."

As April, quietly crying, got up to leave, the attorney made one last comment, "I think you and your children should move out." April agreed and soon made the necessary arrangements.

She and the children moved into a small, two-bedroom apartment. Her lawyer arranged a court order restraining Gary from coming within five hundred yards of her or the children, and guaranteed April she'd get sole custody of the kids.

April was forced to find work to support her family. Having only a high school education and needing the freedom to leave work to drive her son to school, she started employment as a house cleaner. Her two younger children were placed in daycare.

It wasn't long before April started dreaming again. She didn't have nightmares. She resumed her wonderful fantasies about a glorious knight in shining armor who would rescue her from her horrific plight. After three to four months of romantically exciting dreams, she was introduced to just such a gentleman. They immediately started dating.

The Epiphany

Frederick Barrows knelt in the dirt to pray as he'd done every day for countless months. After finishing his long recitation, as always hoping for the epiphany that never came, he walked up a weed-covered hill to his car. Placing his foot against the rear door, he pulled hard on the driver-side handle. Struggling against a jammed, sprung door hinge, he managed to make a small opening, just wide enough to squeeze his skinny frame through. Fred slid in behind the wheel, found the loose end of the rope he'd tied to the door's armrest, and yanked the door closed—almost closed, securing it by tying the rope to the headrest.

A cloud of blue smoke blew from the rear of the Honda as it rolled onto the street. Fred headed for a gas station, any gas station. When he reached one, he was nearly out of fuel. As he pulled in, the front bumper of his junk car, with worn-out shock absorbers, struck the entry drive's pavement. The car stalled out, rolled the last few feet to the side of a pump, and stopped. After untying the door of the rusted-out Honda Civic, Fred walked in to pay the service attendant. Scrounging through his pocket, he found a handful of change, care-fully counted out one dollar, and placed it on the counter. "I'll have a buck's worth on number three."

The attendant, a young woman, smirked in response to the request for such a small amount. She preset the pump.

Fred walked back to his car, removed the gas cap, and inserted the nozzle handle. He watched the machine's digits click by, waiting for it to stop at one dollar. It didn't make it, stopping at ninety-eight cents. He was astounded. The exact same thing had happened just a week ago at a different station. He banged on the glass window of the pump and squeezed the nozzle. The price didn't move.

Walking back to the station, he requested his two-cent refund. The attendant grabbed two pennies from a tray and grinned as she handed them to her customer. Fred responded, "Two cents is two cents. Thank you."

Now he had enough fuel to make it to the junkyard that agreed to pay him fifty dollars for his Honda. Pulling into the yard, the Honda stalled again. Fred spoke with the owner, received his fifty, jammed it in his pocket, and set out for the long walk home.

Forty minutes later, he arrived at his residence, a sturdy cardboard box, an old refrigerator box he'd found behind an appliance store. Three months ago, he had dragged it back to his sleeping place, a ravine beneath an expressway overpass on the outskirts of town.

Prior to that, Fred had lived amongst the homeless men who populated the back streets and alleys of the city. He preferred being by himself, not pestered by other bums who hounded him for money, booze, and cigarettes. More importantly, he had once been severely beaten by another of the dispossessed—an enraged nomad strung out on cocaine. It was safer being alone.

Fred recited another prayer and crawled into his box for the night. He had a grimy old pillow and a urine-stained blanket he'd brought with him from town. Now that his car was gone, the clothes he was wearing, the pillow and blanket, a deck of cards, and the cardboard box were his only possessions.

•

Fred Barrows was guilt-ridden, plagued by shame and remorse, emotions that cost him his job, his life style, and his self-respect. Filled with unrelenting thoughts of the accident, consumed by self-reproach, Fred was barely able to function. Four years ago, being a liability to his employer, he'd been fired.

Since then, the twenty-eight-year-old hadn't seen or spoken to his parents, siblings, or nearly anyone else. When he left his girlfriend, he told her he was no good, saying she deserved better. He never saw her again.

As Fred lay in his cardboard house, he thought about the accident. He'd been driving drunk that night, something he rarely did. It was raining, and a blinding glare was coming off the road when it happened—when he felt a thud, a thump against the car's front fender.

Pulling over to stop, thinking he might have run over something lying in the street, Fred staggered up the road. A young child, a girl, was lying flat on the pavement. Fred saw blood dripping from her nose and mouth. One of her legs was pushed behind her in a grotesque, bizarre position.

Kneeling to the pavement, he felt for a pulse and, placing his ear against her mouth, listened for a breath, finding neither.

Fred panicked. Looking around, realizing there was no one else on the street, no one to have witnessed the accident, he ran, jumped in his car, and sped away, returning to his apartment. The following day he read a front-page article in the local newspaper about an eight-year-old girl's tragic death from a hit-and-run accident. It said the police were looking for a maroon-colored car as determined by paint chips found on the child's body.

According to the paper, there were no witnesses, and the authorities were asking for anyone having information about the accident to please call. The article described the girl's family—young parents with one child.

•

Fred returned to his prayers. Kneeling next to his box, he begged God for forgiveness, reminding God he had forced himself to quit drinking, achieving total abstinence from the day after the accident. Knowing he deserved to be in prison but was too frightened to turn himself in, Fred pleaded with God to grant him atonement for his horrible deed.

If he did confess to the authorities, then his parents, his prior fiancée, his siblings, everyone would know. The prospect of being exposed wasn't the real issue. He sincerely wished he hadn't run from the scene, but now, having long pondered the thought of incarceration, Fred had developed an unrelenting, terrifying, claustrophobic fear of being imprisoned. Turning himself in had become a psychological impossibility.

He asked God to forgive his only remaining addiction, nicotine. Aware of the self-destructive nature of smoking, knowing he was harming his body, a body created in God's image, Fred bore a long-standing commitment to quit but simply lacked the will.

After he finished conversing with his redeemer, Fred crawled into his cardboard home and fell asleep, his hands folded across his chest in an act of prayer.

When he was penniless, which was frequent, Fred would walk to town to panhandle. Hunger was his constant companion, relieved only when he'd resort to rummaging through dumpsters behind restaurants, searching for thrown-out surplus food. Surprisingly, there was an abundance to be found, making him wonder why restaurants were so wasteful, trashing piles of perfectly good food, rather than giving it to shelters for the homeless.

Before the accident, Fred had been very charitable, making a habit of volunteering for social projects at church and frequently donating a portion of his paycheck to feed impoverished children around the world. Now, when praying, he would remind God of his past benevolent, giving nature. At times, he felt foolish reminding God, as if He were unaware of the fact.

Fred thought, correctly so, that he'd been a good person prior to that horrible night; he had been—and still was—a kind, understanding, responsible man.

These moments of self-satisfying reminiscing provided comforting but painfully short-lived relief from his agonizing, relentless guilt.

•

The fifty dollars Fred received for his car was gone in three days, after which, as usual, he returned to town to panhandle—the first day, pocketing only two dollars and fifty cents. Early the following morning, he smoked his last cigarette. A few hours later, his nicotine craving forced him to walk back to town to beg for more money, hoping to get enough for one pack of smokes.

Standing on his favorite corner, looking forlorn and destitute, holding his dirty baseball cap out as a receptacle for spare change, Fred occasionally encountered a kind individual or two who would dig into their pocket, emptying its contents into his hat.

There was a light rain falling this day, and the streets were vacant of pedestrians—only one stopped to drop change into Fred's hat. At the end of the day, he counted it: two quarters, three dimes, three nickels, and three pennies, a whopping total of ninety-eight cents, not nearly enough for a pack of cigarettes. He bummed a smoke from a passerby and walked to his favorite dumpster for dinner. Back at his refrigerator box, he said many prayers and fell asleep.

The next morning, again consumed by his nicotine addiction, he became agitated and irritable, frantic for a smoke. He went back to town to beg.

It was a bright, sunny day, and the solicitation business was much better. That afternoon Fred counted his receipts: four one-dollar bills and a pile of change, a total of five dollars and ninety-eight cents. He walked to the nearest carry-out to buy a pack of Camel straights, placed his four dollars on the counter, and pulled the change from his pocket, dumping all the coins on top of the bills.

Fred asked for one pack of Camels or, if he were short of cash, the cheapest cigarettes available. The clerk handed him the Camels and counted his money. "This is too much. You've given me too much money, sir."

He was surprised to hear her call him sir, a rare event. The cashier continued, "Those cigarettes are on sale; with tax, they're five dollars even. Here's your change, ninety-eight cents."

Fred returned the coins to his pocket, left the store, and immediately lit up, inhaling three deep drags in a row. He walked home.

Arriving at his box, he retrieved a piece of lemon meringue pie and a dried-out hamburger he'd brought back from the dumpster the day before. After eating, he sat in his makeshift home, playing solitaire. An hour or so later, while lying on his blanket, Fred recalled his past, thinking how ill-fated and regrettable his life had become. He had no friends, no house, no money, and no hope of ever finding a job, especially now, reeking of body odor, urine, and garbage. On rare occasions, having the nerve to enter a public establishment to request an application for employment, he would usually be escorted out by management. On his last attempt, he was called "a dirty, lousy tramp, who was stinking up the office."

Sometimes he'd stand on a corner with a cardboard sign reading, "Will work for food or money." He'd watch cars endlessly pass by, some honking their horns with disdain and a few drivers politely giving him the finger or yelling out the window with four-letter words or slurs about the worthless, lazy, filthy bum. Only once did someone hire him; a kind, older woman asked him to mow her lawn, subsequently paying him twenty dollars, an amount he anxiously, graciously accepted.

Before falling asleep, he prayed long and hard for an hour or more, as usual, begging God for redemption, reconciliation within himself, and relief from his life of shame -driven agony. He prayed for a divine message, a sign, the epiphany that would save him from his plight.

That night, after praying, he thought about his cigarette purchase earlier in the day. He had received a total of five dollars and ninety-eight cents from a number of charitable pedestrians and was given ninety-eight cents change by the store clerk. It reminded him of the prior day's panhandling receipts of only ninety-eight cents. The number started to stick in his head, further reminding him of the faulty gas pumps at two separate stations, both freezing at ninety-eight cents. He passed it off as a bizarre coincidence and fell asleep.

The following morning, having endured a near sleepless night in sweltering heat, Fred awoke soaked with sweat. It was mid-Au-gust, and the temperature, even in early morning, was unbearable. He spent most of that day playing solitaire, on one occasion breaking down in tears as he thought of his past and pondered a dismal future.

Fred awakened early the next day. He lay in his box for an hour or so, thinking and praying. At 8:00 a.m., he left the shade beneath the expressway and walked to town for a bath. When his stench got so bad, reeking so much he was disgusted with himself, he would stake out a public restroom. After locking himself in, he'd completely dis-robe and do his best to bathe in the washroom sink, drying himself with paper towels, only to dress again in his filthy clothing.

After his makeshift bath, he collected a dumpster breakfast, placing it in an old paper bag. On his way home, the heat was ghastly. Walking past a time and temperature sign outside a bank, he noted the digital reading, "Time: 9:08 AM, Temperature: 98°."

It struck him, more ninety-eights, everything was ninety-eight. Ninety-eight degrees at nine-o-eight in the morning. He thought, *This is unbelievable.* He turned a corner, walking down a side street toward the expressway, passing a carry-out. A sign in the store's window read "State lottery hits all-time high, $98 million."

Fred was shocked, thinking this had to have some significance, maybe being an answer to his heartfelt prayers—possibly being his long-awaited epiphany.

It seemed absurd, even to him, but he believed it was a message from God. He wondered out loud, "What could it mean?" Looking back at the lottery sign, it hit him—hit him like a sledgehammer. "Oh, my God, it's the lottery."

Reaching into his pocket, Fred pulled out his last bit of change. Incredibly, he was holding ninety-eight cents in his hand. *This can't be a coincidence,* he thought. *I have exactly ninety-eight cents!*

He entered the carry-out, hoping to get two pennies from the store's spare change tray. There was a long line at the register, mostly customers wanting to buy lotto tickets for the giant prize. When he reached the head of the line, he saw an ashtray full of pennies sitting next to the register.

A surly-looking, overweight man behind the counter bellowed, "Okay, what do you want!"

Looking up, Fred reluctantly asked, "Any chance I could have two cents from your tray?"

"Yeah, just make it quick. What do ya need?"

"I'd like to buy a one-dollar lotto ticket." Fred placed his pile of change, his ninety-eight cents, on the counter.

The truculent clerk scoffed as he counted the coins and threw in two pennies. "Listen, you need to be wasting your last buck on a lottery ticket like I need a hole in the head."

Fred further irritated the nasty, fat-man by saying, "I've never done this before. I'm not sure how it works."

The exasperated clerk, responded, "What the hell's wrong with you? You give me a buck, and I give you a ticket. Got that?"

"Do I get to choose my number, or is that automatic?"

"Listen, pal, you're a real pain in the ass. You see the line a people behind ya? They all want a lottery ticket, too."

Fred was embarrassed. "Yes, sir, I know that. I'm sorry about the delay. Can I choose my own number?"

"Yes! You give me a number, or you let the machine pick one."

Fred sheepishly asked, "How many numbers are you allowed?" The clerk looked as if he were going to punch him. "You get eight numbers, buddy: one, two, three, four, five, six, seven, eight. I put 'em in the machine, give you a ticket, and you get the hell outta here."

Hearing grumbling from the line behind him, Fred anxiously faced the clerk and said, "I want to play 98989898. Is that okay?"

You're a real piece a work, ya know that? Yeah, you can play that number, but it's the craziest number I've ever heard. You win with that, and I'll give your dollar back." The clerk handed him his lottery ticket. Fred immediately checked to see if the numbers were correct. Everything was in order, 98989898. He walked home.

•

That night, Fred Barrows prayed harder and longer than ever before. Once again, he felt ashamed for asking God to grant him his wish— his new wish—his hope of winning the lottery. He repeatedly promised God he would use the money for a good cause, not squander it on himself. If he won, he swore he'd use the prize to pull himself up from the depths of despair and dedicate his life to helping others. He promised God to use his winnings to benefit mankind, to help his kindred homeless, the poor, and the hungry.

After nearly two hours of prayer, Fred lay back on his blanket, mentally reviewing his life. *The parents,* he thought. *The parents of the little girl, I could help them; I could give them millions. Money's no compensation for what I've done to them, but it's the best I can do.*

He went on thinking about the girl's parents, hoping they were doing as well as possible, hoping they'd had more children, hoping they hadn't divorced, as so often happens after such a tragedy. The risk of contact with them came to mind. *I'll have to do it carefully, giving them the money anonymously.*

For the first time in years, Fred had a pleasant dream, one replete with gratitude and love.

The following morning, he awoke excited, feeling his earnest prayers would be answered. He ran to town, begged for a quarter, and bought the morning paper to find the winning number.

•

Decades later, an obituary appeared in newspapers around the world.

> Frederick L. Barrows, the world-renowned philanthropist, passed away yesterday. He is survived by his wife of sixty years, Elizabeth Barrows, and their five children. Mr. Barrows, famous for his Foundation 98, was responsible for the establishment of thou-sands of charitable institutions, providing shelter for the homeless and food for the starving, in 98 countries around the globe.
>
> The humanitarian was well-known to have risen out of abject poverty after winning a large state lottery in his home state of Michigan. Shortly after winning his fortune, to the amazement of Wall Street, he astutely transformed his $98 million prize into billions.
>
> Mr. Barrows' uncanny ability to choose stocks, rarely losing as much as a dime, induced a Wall Street analyst of the era to write, "Frederick Barrows' flawless market investing is miraculous, as if directed by the hand of God."
>
> Frederick Barrows, known to have an obsession with the number 98, by coincidence or fate, died on his 98th birthday. The generous humanitarian will be sorely missed by millions who have benefited from his charitable endeavors.
>
> Fortunately, Foundation 98 fully intends to carry on with its work under the direction of Mr. Barrows' eldest child, Frederick L. Barrows Jr.

The Oak Tree

A baby cried. Virginia Dare, the first white child born in the New World was alive—her date of birth, August 18, 1587.

Four hundred miles to the west, in the dense virgin forests of North America, an acorn fell. Torn from its mother by a blast of wind gusting through a massive grove of stout, white oaks, the premature seed's good fortune was to land on moist, fecund soil. Nurtured by Mother Earth, the acorn survived and took root. By mid-September, while millions of acorns still clung to the vines of the great oak trees, a seedling broke through its mossy cover.

•

Samuel McCauley was exhausted, destitute, and ashamed as he walked home to face his wife with more disappointing news. Two years out of work, his daily excursions for employment were becoming pointless. He went to the back of their small, one-story frame home and yanked the rusty screen door open. His wife, Katie, was standing in the kitchen.

"Hi, honey. Any luck?"

Sam didn't respond. He sat at the kitchen table and buried his face in his hands. "Course not."

Katie, relentlessly optimistic, sat next to her forlorn husband. "It's all right, Sam. You're doin' your best, and it's not your fault. Everyone's outta work; you know that. You're no different from them. These times are real hard for most folk. We're gonna be fine, you, me and the boys."

"I'm not so sure 'bout that. You looked at those boys of late? Skin and bones. I can't even provide for my children. I'm ashamed, Katie."

"It's goin' to get better, Samuel. The paper says President Roosevelt is gonna make it better. He's got a plan called the New Deal. It's gonna put people back to work."

"Roosevelt can't do anything about this; nobody can."

As Katie started to offer more assurance, her husband stood and walked away. He went to the yard, screen door slamming behind him.

•

The McCauleys lived in rural Virginia, a few miles outside of town. Thick woods extended for miles behind their yard. Sam sat in his old wicker chair behind the house, his thinkin' chair, as he called it. Pulling paper and a matchstick from his shirt pocket and a pouch from his pants, he rolled a smoke, scraped the match across his heel, and lit up.

Sam's paternal great-grandparents had emigrated from Scotland to the United States in the 1800s. He was a third-generation American who remained proud of his Scottish heritage. Tall and thin with strong, sinewy muscles, he was adorned with brilliant red, nearly orange hair with freckles over his face and arms. At thirty-eight years of age, his hair was thinning, creating a deeply receded hairline with frontal balding. Years of sun exposure on his bared scalp had produced more freckles extending back on top of his head.

•

Sam sat, head hung low, feeling hopeless about what he knew would be a dismal, impoverished future. "Just don't know what I'm gonna do." He thought of the mill, the paper mill he'd worked at for years. He'd loved that job and had a lot of friends at the mill back then. It broke his heart thinking about it. "Damn market crash, I don't know a thing about stock markets. Never owned any stock, don't really know what stocks are. Stocks are for rich, high society people. Bunch of crooks they are, ruined my life."

The mill closed in 1931, and Sam had been looking for work ever since, two years now. "Money gone, damn bank wants to take my house; world just ain't right. The wealthy run us around expectin' us to keep makin' money for 'em. Then they ruin the economy and try to take your home. I hate those people." He looked up to a clear blue sky. *Beautiful day,* he thought. *Doesn't matter to me; just another wasted day.*

Sam went back in the house to find Katie still working in the kitchen. Walking down the hall to their bedroom, he locked the door behind him and went to the closet where he found his tackle box buried under a pile of clothes that had fallen from their hangers.

He sat on the side of the bed, placed the fishing box on his lap and pulled out his fillet knife. The knife had a carved ivory handle and a long, narrow blade curved at the tip. "Family will be better off without me. Katie's a good woman. She'll find a new man in no time, hopefully, a man with money. The kids will be better off, too."

The blade glistened as he held its razor-sharp edge to his wrist. He thought it over. *That'll be too messy and too slow. They might find me before I'm gone.* Holding the knife's point to his chest, he thought, *Right through the heart, that'll be quick, no mess, no turnin' back.*

"What ya doin', Sam?" He heard Katie coming down the hall. The door knob moved. "Honey, are you okay? Why's the door locked?"

Sam hid the knife in his top dresser drawer and shoved his tackle box under the bed. "I'm okay." He opened the door. "I was just resting, Katie. Where are the boys?"

"They're in the parlor."

After saying hello to his children, Joshua, his fourteen-year-old, and Jeremy, Josh's younger brother, two years his junior, Sam went back out to his chair. A moment later the back door opened. "Honey, your friend wants to visit."

Their dog, Keeper, ran out and sat next to the chair. Jeremy had found the dog about three years ago when she wasn't much more than a puppy, wandering in the woods. The boys attached to her instantly. Their father reluctantly agreed to let them keep the stray. The boys named her Keeper.

Reaching down, he gave his friend a pat on the head. Keeper licked his palm and looked up with loving eyes. Of medium size, around thirty pounds, with black fur, a long snout, and pointed ears that always stood at attention, Keeper had become a permanent member of the family. All four of her paws were white, along with a patch of white encircling one of her striking blue eyes. Her long, full tail seemed to be in constant motion.

"You're a smart girl, aren't ya, Keeper?" She was indeed a talented dog: intelligent, obedient, and devoted. Her obvious love for the boys and her protective nature made her a fond member of the McCauley household. She was especially attached to Jeremy, the twelve-year-old, and she slept in his bed every night.

Sam gave the dog a stroke across her back. Keeper jumped up and ran off to explore the woods where she could run free, never going far and always bounding back when called—one quick whistle was all it took.

As he watched the dog run through the woods Sam's eyes settled on his oak tree. A monstrous white oak stood tall at the back of his lot, surrounded by small trees and brush. The Virginia State Department of Agriculture had come out to his house four years ago to assess the tree. Sam had watched them make measurements with surveying equipment. They told him if their calculations were correct, his tree was over two hundred feet tall, with a gigantic canopy well over a hundred feet wide. They measured the trunk circumference at thirty-two feet and figured the trunk's widest diameter to be just over ten feet.

"Your tree's gotta be at least three hundred years old, Mr. McCauley, maybe closer to four hundred. Mighty old tree. Gotta be the biggest oak in the state, could be biggest east of the Mississippi."

He sat thinking about what the surveyors had told him. "That tree's the only thing I got, only thing I own to be proud of."

The white oak was well-known in the territory. Sam used to charge people a dime just to look at it. "Those days are gone. Most people don't have a dime, let alone want to waste it to gander at some old tree."

Then it hit him. "That tree's worth money!" He sat bolt upright, speaking aloud. "A lumber mill could get tons of oak from it. Good, white oak lumber." He thought of the sawmill down the road. "The mill in town is still operatin'. They could cut huge planks of clear, white oak from that trunk, probably get boards six to eight feet wide."

Looking up to the tree's branches, he thought, *Darn branches are huge. The mill could cut two-foot-wide planks outta them. That lumber would be worth a lot, surely enough to keep us goin' for a few more years. It might be worth as much as two thousand dollars, plenty to pay off the bank with some left over.* He jumped up and ran to the kitchen to give Katie the news. "Katie I'm gonna sell the oak tree."

"Sell the oak tree? What do you mean, Samuel? How can you sell a big tree like that?"

"Not the tree, darlin', the wood. I'll cut it down and sell it for lumber. Gotta be worth a fortune, thousands of dollars."

"Sam, what will the state say? Are we allowed to do that? That tree's famous."

"It's my tree, our tree. We can do what we want with it—hell with the state. We need the money, Katie."

"Honey, that tree's so big. How can you cut it down? I'm afraid you'll get hurt."

"Maybe I'll have the mill do it. Their loggers can cut it down for us; then I'll sell 'em the lumber. They can chop it down and pay us for the wood."

Katie looked relieved. "That's good, Samuel. Let them do all that work. I don't want you gettin' hurt."

Sam left to inspect his tree. He walked around it, thinking about where it could fall. *They gotta make sure it falls back toward the woods,* he thought. *That tree could crush our house if they're not careful.* Seeing a clearing in the brush in the woods behind the oak, Sam thought, *That's the spot. They can crash this giant right there, cut the branches off and haul her away. It's gonna be a lot of cuttin', a real big job. Bet they're gonna charge me a lot for all that work. Probably have to give 'em a sizeable bit from the proceeds. It's gonna take 'em some time, too.*

Time, he thought. *Time's all I got. Maybe I shouldn't pay those boys for doin' a job I can do. I got plenty of time.* He thought about Katie. *She won't like it, but I'm gonna do it.*

Sam was anxious to get started. It was late afternoon, but he still had three to four hours of daylight. "I'm startin' right away."

He walked to his shed, found his ax, and went back out to the tree. Holding the ax blade against the side of the tree, he laughed. "This little thing ain't gonna do the job. It would take me months to pound through that trunk."

His enthusiasm pushed him on, "Might as well get started any-way." Sam drew the ax back, high overhead, and swung with all his might. A chip of bark flew by his head as heavy vibrations shot up the ax handle, through his hands and up his arms to his shoulders. He dropped the ax. "Holy Jesus, this tree's hard as stone."

Sam looked down at his ax. The handle was shattered and had a long, protruding splinter. Examining the cut, he saw the ax had gone through the bark and about a half-inch into the wood. "This will never work. Gonna need a saw, a big saw." He ran back to the house.

"Katie, that tree's as hard as a rock."

"What tree?"

Sam looked puzzled, "What do you mean 'what tree'? The oak tree." "What about the oak tree, Samuel?"

He paused, giving his wife a perplexed look. "Katie, what's wrong with you? The oak tree, remember, the tree we're gonna sell."

"Honey, I've never heard of sellin' a full-grown tree."

He sat down at the kitchen table, resting his forehead on his hands. *What's goin' on with her?* he thought. "Katie, don't you remember the talk we had just a bit ago?"

"No, honey, I'm sorry, I don't. How did your day go, Sam? Any luck on the job hunt?"

His eyes opened wide with astonishment. Sam stood and walked out of the kitchen, shaking his head with confusion. "Crazy woman—wasn't even payin' attention when I told her about the tree. Guess I don't have to tell her about my plan to cut it myself; she won't know the difference."

•

Sam's brother-in-law, Patrick Cleary, lived up the road. A few years ago, Sam had helped him clear trees from his lot. *Paddy's got one of those two-man saws, a lumberjack saw. It's gonna take both of us to handle it. I could give him a share of the money for supplyin' the saw and the manpower. Better to keep the money in the family than give it to the mill. Patrick's been out of work as long as I have; he'll appreciate it.*

Sam met with his brother-in-law that evening, promising 40 percent of the proceeds for his help. Patrick agreed without hesitation. He'd sharpen his saw that night, and they'd start working early the next day.

The following morning, the pair walked across the yard. It was early fall, September, a cool, crisp day. "Good weather for workin', eh Paddy."

"Aye, it is. And I be quite anxious to get startin'." Walking through the yard, they passed Katie's flower garden. Sam noticed her flowers were starting to wilt and dry up. They'd been beautiful all summer.

The men approached the tree, looked it over, and decided where to cut. They'd cut at a steep angle, from high to low, making the tree fall into the clearing in the woods behind.

They started cutting, pushing and pulling the long saw blade as it passed through the bark and into the meat of the tree. "Sam, this tree won't be goin' easy. Darn things awful hard."

"It's white oak. That's why it's so hard and why it's so valuable. Years back, ship builders would come out here to harvest these trees. Apparently, they don't grow back east. Old Ironsides was made from white oak. Got her name from havin' such a hard hull—darn British cannon balls would bounce right off her."

"Old Ironsides?"

"Sure, you must a learned about it in history class."

"Sam, be ya forgettin' I was in Ireland at the time?"

"Well, I guess I did. Sorry about that."

•

Patrick was raised in Ireland. He lived there until age sixteen when he and his parents emigrated to the states. His parents settled in Boston, where Patrick lived until he met Sarah, Katie's younger sister. He fell in love with Sarah at first sight. They married soon after and moved to Virginia to be closer to Sarah's family. They now had three children.

Patrick kept a strong Irish accent and dialect. He was a stocky, muscular man, close to six feet in height. His dark, nearly black hair, light skin tone, and sparkling yellow-green eyes affirmed his Black Irish ancestry. His wife was a petite woman with brown hair and a strong resemblance to her older sister. People often confused them for twins.

Despite that resemblance, Sam's wife, Katie, wasn't quite as pretty as her sister. She was petite and had brown hair. Katie was a wonderful woman whose strength and determination contrasted with her demure size. She was a dedicated wife and mother, and she worked tirelessly to keep up her household. Sam, not being the most handsome man around, cherished his relationship with Katie. She was much more than he'd ever dreamed of.

•

"Sam, thanks for the history lesson on American battleships, but I think it's time we be gettin' back to work." They kept going, slowly cutting through the ancient tree. The sky abruptly filled with clouds, and the sunlight dimmed. "Sam, do you believe this? Those clouds come outta nowhere."

"Odd weather to be sure," said Sam. As he looked around the yard, the flowers in Katie's garden caught his eye. "Look at that, Paddy. A minute ago, those flowers were dyin'. Now they're bright, in full bloom. How the heck did that happen?"

Patrick shrugged, "I have no idea, Sam. Let's keep cuttin'; I'll be lookin' forward to my 40 percent." They took another three or four long strokes and stopped in amazement. The ground was covered with snow. Patrick chuckled, "Don't this be the damnedest weather ya ever seen, Sam?"

Sam ran through the snow to his house, yelling as he crossed the yard. "Katie, it's snowing. Come on out here; you won't believe it." He burst into the kitchen and stopped with a halt. The house was beautifully decorated for Christmas. Looking through the doorway to the front room, he saw a Christmas tree.

Katie ran into the kitchen. "What's all the commotion, Sam?" She was wearing heavy winter clothes but had been wearing a summer dress just twenty minutes ago.

Her husband stood there, sweating, dressed in jeans and a cotton shirt.

"Samuel, what are you doin' out there without your coat?"

"What?"

"Honey, it's cold."

"Yeah, that's why I was yellin'. Have you ever seen such crazy weather?"

Katie didn't know what to say. Sam glanced back at the Christmas tree. "Katie, what's that tree doin' in the parlor?"

"What are you talking about? You put it up yesterday, remember?"

Sam was confused, dumbfounded, and a little frightened. He asked, "Where are the boys? Are they okay?"

"Of course they are. They're in the front room, doin' their studies."

Sam walked to the parlor doorway. His boys were there.

"Hi, Papa."

"Hi, Papa."

"Hi, boys. You two all right?"

"No," said Joshua, the older boy. We're doing school work, and it's no fun."

Jeremy giggled, "Yeah, we hate it."

"You boys be good now. Listen to your mama." He walked back to Katie in the kitchen.

"Sam, what's wrong with you?"

Not wanting to get into a long discussion, he said, "Nothing's wrong, Kate." He walked back out to see Patrick.

"Samuel, somethin' real strange be goin' on here with this weather."

"I know; I don't understand it." He didn't tell Patrick about the Christmas decorations in his house; it was just too outlandish, and he feared it would scare him off. Instead, he thought about the money they'd get for the tree and decided they had to go on. "We have to keep sawing, Patrick. Don't want a let this weather stop us."

They took a few hard strokes with the saw and stopped again. The snow was gone and they were standing ankle-deep in brown oak leaves. They stood there, stunned, as thousands of leaves floated down from the giant oak. Patrick looked terrified. "Sam, somethin' bad be happenin' here. I don't be feelin' so good about cuttin' this tree."

"Paddy, I'm as frightened as you are, but I think we have to keep sawing."

"Why? Why don't we stop right now?"

Irritated, Sam yelled back, "Because we need the money! You want to keep lookin' for work? Keep disappointing your wife and children? We don't have a choice, Paddy."

"Aye, I be with ya on that. I'm sorry, Sam. I didn't know how determined ya was about it. I suppose you be right. The money's the important thing, ain't it? I'm willin' to keep goin' if you are, Sam."

"Thanks, Paddy. I apologize for yellin'. Please—just keep thinkin' about the money we're gonna make. The sooner we bring this thing down the sooner we get rich."

Sam and Patrick had been close friends for years. By heritage, they could have been arch enemies, Scot against Irish, Mack against Mick, orange versus green, but heritage and old customs were meaningless to them. The furthest it went was Sam's habit of wearing a bright orange shirt on St. Patrick's Day, in mock defiance of Patrick wearing a bit o' the green.

The pair pulled hard on the saw, cutting as fast as possible. Seasons flew by as they cut—summer heat, followed in seconds by rain, followed by sun, followed by rain, followed by snow. After a few minutes, they stopped, shocked by what they had seen. Sam pulled the long saw blade out of the tree and laid it on the ground as Patrick looked around the yard. "My God, Sam, look. Sam, your house!"

Sam spun around, looking across his yard. His house was gone. Katie's flower garden was gone, and the yard was overgrown with trees and brush. He trembled as the corners of his mouth drooped in a look of terror. "What in the name a Jesus. My house, my family!" He fell to his knees next to the tree. Patrick went to him, grabbing him by the shoulders.

"Sam, what have we done?"

"Paddy, if I tell you what I'm thinking, you're gonna figure I'm touched in the head."

"What? Sam, tell me."

"We're goin' back. The further we cut this damn tree the further back we go."

"Goin' back where? What do ya be talkin' about?"

"Going back in time. We're goin' back in time, Paddy." Sam told him about the Christmas tree and Katie's winter clothes.

Patrick gasped, "Sarah! Sam, what about Sarah and my children?" He took off running up the road to his house. Minutes later he was there, there where his house should have been. It was gone, nothing there but trees. Terrified, he sprinted back toward Sam, who moments later saw his friend stomping through the brush surrounding the oak tree. Patrick looked scared, on the verge of tears.

"They all be gone, Sam. The house, my family, nothing there. What have you done to us? What have ya done, Samuel?"

Sam, exasperated and exhausted, tried to console his friend. "I'm sorry, Patrick. I don't know what to say. I don't understand it either, and I'm as shaken as you are. My family's gone too."

"What would we be doin' now, Sam? Can ya tell me that?"

"We don't have a choice, Patrick. We've got to keep goin'. We gotta cut this damn tree to the ground and hope for the best, hope for salvation from the Lord. It seems like an evil thing's happening here, Patrick. It's taken over our lives, takin' our families and all. Paddy, I think we should pray over it. Pray hard and long for the Lord's direction."

The men knelt at the tree to pray aloud.

Sam went first. "Dear Lord, me and Patrick, we know we're sinners. We're God-fearin' men, and we attend Sunday meetin' regular. You know that, Lord. We're doin' the best we can in this world. We love our wives, and we love our children. You know times have been bad for us. We ask for your loving forgiveness, and we ask for your divine, holy guidance. Patrick and me are goin' to finish this job a cuttin' this tree. If you don't want that, Lord, please let us know. Give us a sign. Please give us salvation, Lord… Amen."

Patrick followed with "Amen."

"Your turn, Patrick."

"Sam, I don't know what I'd be sayin'. I don't be much at prayin'; besides, I think you said it all."

"Just add a bit more, Paddy. You'll do fine."

"All right, if you be insistin'." Patrick began his prayer. "Dear Lord in heaven, please help us. Sam and me be mighty frightened. You surely know how scared we are, and we pray for your help. Like my friend Sam said, we know we be sinners. Please, Lord, we just want our families back… Amen."

While Patrick prayed, Sam thought about his recent desperation, his fishing knife, and his family. He knew he had acted like a coward, and he knew taking his life would be wrong. "That was good Patrick. I've got one more thought to add. Dear God, forgive me for my recent fear and my cowardly plans. I know I was wrong in thinking that way. I know

I should have been askin' you for guidance. I pray for your forgiveness, Lord. Amen."

Patrick gave his brother-in-law a puzzled look. "What would that prayer be about? You aren't a coward, Sam; don't be sayin' that."

"Never mind now, Paddy. We have a lot to do."

They resumed sawing, slowly working the blade through the hard oak. As they cut, the seasons raced by. Daytime light was rapidly followed by nighttime darkness by daytime by nighttime, on and on. Sam noticed the sun was rising in the west and setting in the east. "Do you see it, Paddy? The sun's movin' backward. That proves what I thought. We are goin' back."

"Ya needn't be remindin' me, Sam. I'll be scared enough already."

More trees appeared in Sam's lot. In a short time, the men were in a thick forest. Hot summer days intermingled with rain were followed by crisp spring days, freezing cold winters, and mellow autumn days.

Samuel and Patrick watched in amazement as the trees came and went in reverse. Oak, elm, and maple trees shrank down to seedlings before their eyes, only to be instantly replaced by their full-grown ancestors. The men worked frantically. After thirty minutes, they were exhausted. They slowed their pace, stopping for a break on a clear summer day.

"Sam, when we stop sawin' we stop goin' back, ain't that so?"

"Sure, I think so. It makes sense."

"Then what if we stop right here and now and wait. Wouldn't we be catchin' up with them? Wouldn't we be headin' back to our families?"

"I don't think so, Paddy. They'd be movin' ahead just as fast. We'd never catch up."

"Then we should go lookin' for 'em, Sarah and Katie. Maybe I could find Sarah in Boston again."

"Patrick, we don't know how far back we've gone. Sarah and Katie may not even be born yet."

Patrick looked baffled, his mind challenged by the nuances of time travel. "Aye, I guess that's right. I guess it is. I'm not quite certain a that, but I'll take your word for it, Sam. I'll have to mull it over a bit."

"Don't be embarrassed about it, Paddy. It's real confusin' for me, too. We better start cuttin' again."

They took a few more, long, hard strokes. It was slow going. The men got soaked by a downpour. Slowing to a leisurely pace, they watched the rain storm.

Then they saw it.

When they were cutting hard and fast, it hadn't been evident. As they slowed to a snail's pace, cutting only millimeters with each stroke, they saw it. It was raining BACKWARDS! Small puddles at their feet disappeared, as droplets of water flew up to the sky. They continued, advancing the saw blade as slowly as possible. It was mesmerizing. Sparkling drops of water were rising up from everything, flickering up to the clouds. Patrick started laughing.

"Glory be, Sam. Would ya look at that? Can ya believe it, Sam? Have ya ever seen anything like it, anything so beautiful?"

"It's a sight, ain't it, Patrick? It's breathtaking, Paddy. Breathtaking. I could watch this for hours."

"Sammy, it's almost as beautiful as Ireland, almost."

Sam chuckled. "Patrick, I would love to watch this all day, but we ain't got the time."

"I hear ya, Sam. Best we be back ta cuttin', but you're spoilin' it for me. Ya know that, don't ya?"

Sam laughed again. "All right, let's get to it, Paddy."

The men resumed sawing at a fast pace. Moments later they were standing knee-deep in snow. They slowed their pace to watch, astounded as snowflakes rose to the heavens and the deep snow dwindled away.

"This is too amazing, Sam. I don't know if I can take much more of this magnificence."

"Kind of fun to watch, isn't it, Paddy?"

"Fun ain't the word for it. I ain't got the word for it. I don't know if I'll survive all this splendor. Aye, splendor, that's the word, Sam. And you think you're the smart one. How's that for a word, splendor?"

Sam smiled and shook his head in response to his friend's humor.

They cut two more strokes and stopped, once again standing in brown oak leaves. "Sam, this saw would be gettin' real dull. I brought my file. We should stop and sharpin' her up."

After sliding the saw out of the twenty to thirty-inch groove in the tree trunk, Sam inspected the cut. "It's gonna take us days to get through this, maybe weeks."

"Days is all we got, Sam. We'll be doin' it."

"Paddy, if this is gonna take longer than a day or two, we're gonna have to find food and water."

"Samuel, I'm glad you're here. I never would have thought a that. You're a genius, Sammy" They both laughed as Patrick sat down to deal with the saw. He pulled his file from his back pocket, placed the long saw blade across his lap and started filing each tooth, one at a time.

Sam watched. "Sharpenin' that big saw's gonna take forever."

"Oh, it's not that bad. I'll be knockin' her out in a quarter-hour or so."

Sam was just about to sit down when he heard a noise. "You hear that."

"No, Sam, my friend, I didn't hear a thing. You wouldn't be gettin' spooked now, would ya?"

"No, I wouldn't, and I'm sure I heard something."

The sound of cracking branches and rustling leaves echoed through the forest. "I hear it now, Sam. What would ya be thinkin'? A deer, maybe?"

As the men peered through the trees the noise got louder; it was coming toward them.

A man shouted. "They're over here, Captain. We got 'em." Two short men in gray uniforms, carrying muskets, appeared between the trees.

Patrick whispered, "Would they be Confederates?"

The soldiers looked little more than children. No more than five-six in height, with young, teenage faces. Their muskets looked huge in comparison to their size. One of them raised his gun. "What you boys be doin' here? You Yanks, are ya?" They approached, both with guns raised. The taller of the two yelled out, "Captain, think we got ourselves some runaways here, maybe Yanks!"

Patrick tried to stand, only to be knocked down as the butt of a musket smashed into his shoulder. Sam froze and raised his hands as the second boy shoved a gun barrel against his belly. "Sit." He slowly sat down.

A Confederate officer on horseback appeared. "Bring those men to camp, Sergeant, and keep your guns on 'em." The captain rode away as Sam and Patrick were pushed through the woods, gun barrels jammed in their backs.

The Confederate camp was huge, with hundreds of white tents, wagons full of ammunition, stacked barrels of gunpowder, numerous cannons, and hundreds, perhaps thousands, of Confederate soldiers. As the supposed runaways were pushed through the camp at gun-point, they saw the horrors of war.

The troops had just returned from battle. Sam and Patrick walked across the camp, past bloodied, moaning, sobbing men, lying on blood-drenched cots. Many of the wounded cried out in agony, awaiting their trip to the surgeon's tent.

Sam heard screams coming from a large tent displaying a brilliant red cross. As he and Patrick went by, he gazed over to the make-shift operating room. Bloody piles of amputated feet, legs, and arms were piled high in front. A soldier inside screamed as a doctor, wearing a white, blood-covered gown, sawed away at the young man's leg. The surgeon's assistants held the soldier down, pinned hard against a blood-drenched surgical table.

Sam looked away, sick to his stomach, sickened at heart. *Such misery,* he thought. He'd read about war; he'd heard many stories of the appalling, unspeakable horrors of the Civil War. Seeing these ghastly casualties first hand was terrifying, gut wrenching, and nearly unbearable.

The captive men were taken to the far side of the camp, near the officers' quarters. The taller soldier spoke, "Sit on that log, both of you. Percy, you watch 'em. If they move, shoot 'em. I'll get Captain Tucker."

"Yes, sir, I'll watch 'em good."

Sam looked at the young soldier who was pointing a musket at him. He had a smooth face, barely any growth of whiskers, just some stubble on his chin. *Can't be more than fifteen years old,* thought Sam.

Patrick, having heard the young man address his partner as sir, took a closer look at the taller one walking away. He thought to himself, *He has stripes on his sleeve. He's a sergeant, and he's no more than a young lad.*

The boyish soldier guarding Sam and Patrick looked frightened. His hands trembled as he raised his heavy gun. "You hear the sergeant?

I don't wanna have to hurt no one, but I'll shoot ya if you move. I swear I will."

Sam detected a lack of conviction in the boy's voice. He thought, *Poor kid, must be scared out of his wits.*

Patrick leaned over and whispered in Sam's ear. "We gotta get back to the tree. Gotta cut it." Sam nodded in agreement.

"Hey, no talkin'! You hear me?"

Sam nodded a yes to the boy as Patrick tried to befriend him. "Sorry, laddie, I mean private, Private Percy? Would that name be right?

"Yeah, that's right."

"We won't be talkin' again, Private Percy. I'll be promisin' that, especially with you lookin' to be such a fine soldier." The boy couldn't help but smile.

Patrick, being a good five years younger than Sam, figured he had the best chance of making a run for the tree. He dreaded the thought—thinking of how a mini-ball in the back would feel. The private turned away, just for a second, looking around the camp. Sam spoke under his breath. "They're gonna hang us or shoot us. I'm sure of it."

Patrick's eyes shot open wide as he envisioned himself dangling from the end of a rope. He thought about Sarah and the children. The young soldier turned back to his prisoners. *It's now or never,* thought Patrick.

"Excuse me, sir."

"You ain't gotta call me sir, mister. I ain't nothin' but an enlisted man, and you look old enough to be my daddy."

Sam and Patrick felt some relief in the boy's candor.

He doesn't want to shoot anybody, thought Sam. *He's just stuck here in a bad spot.*

The youngster, who appeared happy to meet someone who wasn't a soldier, someone who wasn't bossing him around, kept talking "Where you men from?"

Sam and Patrick didn't know what to say. Patrick finally spoke. "We'd be from Virginia, southern Virginia, down near—"

"You ain't from Virginia with that accent," the private interrupted. "You sound Irish—must be a Yank."

Patrick quickly responded, "Aye, you're a smart lad. I am Irish, but I been livin' in Virginia for years now. Samuel here's my brother-in-law."

"Why aren't you men enlisted? Why you outta uniform?"

They were speechless, surprised by the young man's sudden aggression. They couldn't think of a good answer. Patrick took a quick look behind the log, seeing they were sitting on the very edge of the camp. Thick woods with heavy underbrush was right behind them.

He started squirming around, putting one hand down on his crotch. "Soldier, Private Percy, I gotta make water. That be all right? Would it be all right if I go in the bushes right here?" He pointed to the edge of the woods.

"You ain't gonna run, are ya? Like I said, I'll shoot you if I have to."

"No, no, I be promisin' ya; I ain't runnin' nowhere. I just gotta be goin' really bad. Don't wanna mess me pants and have the captain see it, that bein' so embarrassin' 'n' all. Could be the captain would be offended, too. Besides, me and Sam here ain't done nothin' wrong. We ain't worried. We'll be explainin' everythin' to your captain. No reason for us to be runnin'."

The soldier hesitated for a moment. "I guess it's all right. Don't you go far. You do your business right there behind that bush—hear me?"

"Aye, I hear you." Patrick stood and looked over to Sam. As their eyes met, Sam responded with a subtle nod of understanding. The boy raised his musket and held it on Patrick, who walked through the brush toward the woods. Patrick went behind a bush, stood for a few seconds, and took off running, never looking back.

"Hey, come back here!" Private Percy raised his musket to eye level. Sam jumped up and grabbed the barrel of the gun just as it went off. A mini-ball whizzed by Patrick's head. Heat from the gun barrel seared Sam's palm as he struck the soldier hard in the chest with the heel of his hand. Percy let go of his gun and fell to the ground. Sam, still clinging to the hot barrel, dropped the gun and took off running.

"Bang, bang, bang." A group of Confederates fired as they ran across the camp in pursuit. Sam saw his brother-in-law, fighting his way through the brush about a hundred yards ahead. He heard rebel soldiers crashing through the woods, hootin' 'n' hollerin' as they went. Sam, hearing the soldiers gaining ground, called out, "God-speed, Paddy." He watched as Patrick took off like a rabbit, leaving him far behind.

A mini-ball hit a tree trunk, pelting Sam with splinters. He ran harder, heart pounding, sucking deeply with each breath. More musket reports, sounding dangerously close behind, rang out, echoing through the woods. Thumping feet and cracking branches were closing in.

A soldier yelled, "You two get this one."

Sam changed direction, taking a sharp turn to a dense grove of trees. *For God's sake, Patrick, I pray you make it.* His boot caught an exposed tree root, and he flew head over heels, landing hard on the ground. Lying there, groaning, staring straight up at the treetops, Sam let out a deep sigh as he tried to catch his breath. Seconds later they were upon him. "We'll get 'im, boys. Rest a you go after that Irish fella."

A soldier, standing directly over Sam, raised his musket high overhead, butt end down. Sam shut his eyes and crossed his arms over his face, preparing for a crushing blow. He took a deep breath and waited.

Nothing happened.

He let his breath out, slowly uncovered his face, and opened his eyes. The soldier was gone. Sam's back felt cold—he was lying in shallow snow. Snowflakes were rising all around him, creating a festival of twinkling flakes. He yelled out, "He made it! Patrick made it." Sam could have lain there forever, watching the snow float away. Seconds later, the snowflakes reversed direction, falling to the ground, covering Sam in a white, powdery blanket.

A moment later, Patrick appeared through the brush. "Sam, you alive? Sammy, it's Paddy." He saw his friend lying in the snow, struggling to get up. "Thank, God, Sam—did they hurt ya?"

"No, I'm fine, thanks to you, Paddy. I think they woulda killed me. Boy, Patrick, you're quite the runner, aren't ya?"

"Only when I'm scared outta me mind, Sam. Otherwise, I can barely move."

The pair laughed with relief as they walked away, returning to the tree. To ensure they had rid themselves of the Confederates, the men cut three long strokes and then stopped to finish sharpening the saw. It was late fall, and the ground was covered with dry, oak leaves.

•

A short time later, they resumed cutting. Their first few strokes were slow, purposely slow, allowing them to watch leaves flutter up through the air. The men watched with wonder as thousands of autumn leaves rose, attached to tree branches, and turned green. Patrick let out a big laugh. "This is spectacular, eh, Sam? It's splendorous, if that's a word."

Yeah, Paddy, I agree. We might as well enjoy it while we can. I'm sure we'll never see anything like it again."

Patrick laughed. "Aye, I sure hope not."

Having cut so far into the trunk, Sam noticed he couldn't see his brother-in-law on the opposite side of the oak, its huge trunk between them. He yelled out, Patrick, how ya doin' over there?

Silence.

Sam yelled louder, "Paddy, are ya there?"

Not a sound.

"Boo!"

Sam shot around to find Patrick standing right behind him. "Paddy, you scared the livin' bejesus outta me." Patrick, laughing loudly, made a facetious apology to his friend and returned to his side of the tree.

When the ground was clear of leaves, they increased their pace. The cutting went easier with the sharpened saw. Quickly passing through the seasons, they occasionally slowed the saw to watch rain drops rise to the sky, snowflakes float up to the heavens, and autumn leaves flutter up to their mother trees, filling the overhead tree tops with greenery.

After another hour or so of sawing, the men stopped, completely exhausted. Sam pulled out his pocket watch. "Paddy, we've been workin' on this tree for more than twelve hours. What do ya say we cut a few more strokes and stop on a nice summer night to get some sleep?"

"That sounds grand, Samuel."

They found a soft spot of ground to lie on. Besides being physically spent, they were hungry and thirsty, having had nothing to eat or drink all day. Despite that, they slept like babies, resting their aching arms and backs.

Awakening early the following morning, they each dreaded another day's work without food or water. As the men were about to start sawing, they heard a voice.

"*Asgaya sagawu!*"

Startled, both Samuel and Patrick turned, finding two Native Americans standing no more than ten feet away. The Indians, frighteningly silent on their approach, stared quizzically at the time travelers.

Both Indians had jet black hair, one wearing it tightly pulled back in a long braid, the other, who appeared older, was donned with spiked hair projecting straight up from atop his head. They were wearing deerskin pants and moccasins. The older, more powerful-looking man had a bare chest adorned with beads and paint. His partner wore a deerskin shirt and carried a spear tipped with a Clovis head, a spearhead chipped from stone. Patrick saw they both had stone-blade knives tucked in roughly cut leather belts. Each had a skin pouch slung over one shoulder.

"Sam, I think this may be worse than the Confederates."

"*Nagadan nij asgaya.*" The bare-chested visitor pointed to the tree as he pushed his young friend ahead to investigate. The braided one walked to the oak, sliding his hand across its sliced trunk. Turning back, he shrugged with a perplexed look as the fierce-looking Indian approached Samuel and Patrick, who stepped back, leaning hard against the oak tree.

Patrick spoke softly, "Sam, I think we should be makin' a run for it."

Sam leaned over and whispered. "No—we'd never outrun them. Look at 'em; they're solid muscle, and they live in these woods. We wouldn't have a chance."

"What if I grab the saw and make a quick cut?"

"Patrick, you can't do that. They'd be on you in a second. You see those knives and that spear? We'd be dead before you even picked it up."

The older Indian was standing a mere five feet away from the terrified men. He pointed at the tree. "*Sagawayu animoki?*" It sounded like a question.

"What do they want, Sam?"

"I don't know—just don't make any sudden moves."

The Indians walked slowly around the tree. The younger one looked at Sam and spoke with an accusing tone. "*Asgaya sagu an-imoki hulaka.*"

His senior partner grabbed him by the arm and spoke with sounds of reproach. *"Nadim talu asgaya. Lonti hu ma chaka."*

The young Indian made a gesture of apology and sat on the ground; the older one sat next to him and motioned to Sam and Pat-rick to join them. The men slowly, reluctantly went to their knees, practically crawling over to their visitors, slowly making their way across the ground, stopping a few feet from them.

The Indians spoke to each other. The young one removed the skin from his shoulder and opened it. He pulled out a square of folded deer skin, spread it on the ground, and went back in the pouch to find dried meat and small cakes of cornmeal, which he placed on the makeshift tablecloth.

The other took a skin from his shoulder, turned it to his mouth, and took a long drink. He handed it to Sam, saying, *"Gado ka mida."*

Sam turned to Patrick. "Paddy, what should I do?"

Patrick's eyes opened wide as he stifled a laugh at what he thought was an absurd question. "What should you do? Drink it! And save some for me!"

Sam eagerly gulped down water and passed the skin to Patrick.

The older Indian smiled with approval.

"Sam, they're giving us food and water."

The Indian smiled again. *"Oho, oho."* The younger man picked up what looked like dried deer meat and pushed it toward Patrick.

"Midjin, midji... micidin."

Patrick slowly, politely extended his hand, picked up the food, and took a bite. He turned to Sam. "Sam, it's good, kinda dry but tasty."

All four of them sat together eating. The Indians ate very little as they forced more and more food on their dinner guests. Sam and Patrick gladly took all that was offered.

Feeling more at ease, Sam spoke freely to Patrick. "I think they may be Algonquian or Powhatan." The elder Indian perked up, cocking his head and smiling in response to Sam's statement.

Patrick, seeing the smile, said, "I think our friend here agrees with ya, Sam."

Sam looked to the Indian and said, "Powhatan, yes?

The pair of visitors both nodded, the younger one saying, *"Oho, awani gia?"*

He must have asked a question, thought Sam. *He looks like he's waiting for a response.* Sam shrugged and turned his hands palms up, as if to say, "I don't understand."

When the food was gone, and the pouches were packed, the elder Indian stood, saying to his partner, *"Alsoda."*

Sam spoke, attempting to thank them for their hospitality.

The Powhatans looked at each other and shrugged. The younger man stood, and the pair started toward the woods. At its edge, they stopped and looked back, saying, *"Amadi,"* which Sam thought at first meant goodbye. But the older one waved his hand, obviously motioning Sam and Patrick to go with them.

"Should we go, Sam.?"

"They've been incredibly friendly, but I don't think we should go with them, Paddy. We don't know what could happen. We better get back to cutting, right now. Sam raised his hand, palm out as if to say, no thanks. The older Indian shrugged again and said something to his partner. They walked away, disappearing in the woods. Patrick spoke first.

"Samuel, me friend, that was, without any doubt, the most amazing experience of me short life!"

"I gotta agree, Paddy. It's something we'll never forget as long as we live, which may not be much longer the way things are goin'."

Patrick laughed out loud. "So much for the vicious savages told of by your American historians. Those two were magnificent: clean, muscular, healthy, kind, and generous."

Sam chuckled, "I think we happened to meet the right ones. Bet some of 'em weren't so friendly."

The men started their new day revitalized by sleep, food, and water. Working hard, making good progress through the tree, they saw seasons fly by at a dizzying pace, each lasting mere seconds. Approaching the center of the tree, its widest diameter, their sawing had to slow.

The tree's trunk was nearly as wide as their saw blade was long. They had only inches of bare blade exposed on either side of the tree, forcing them to take very short, quick cuts with the saw's handles banging into tree bark with every stroke.

The men stopped after an hour of hard work. Sam wanted to assess the depth of their cut. He estimated they were about eight to ten inches from the center of the trunk.

Patrick looked around the woods. They were surrounded by an incredibly dense, thick, dark forest with a menagerie of wildlife. Rabbits and squirrels scooted by. A few deer, seemingly unaware of the visitors, ran past, nimbly darting between tightly packed trees. The woods rang out with a chorus of hundreds, perhaps thousands of singing birds. It was louder and more beautiful than Sam and Patrick had ever heard.

They went back to cutting at the slow pace necessitated by the tree trunk's great width. After a half-hour, the men had to take a break. Unknowingly, they had stopped just millimeters from the center of the tree.

When they resumed sawing, the blade's edge passed through the tiniest of rings, a ring at the exact center of the trunk, the ring left by the seedling that had sprouted through the ground hundreds of years ago.

•

Four hundred miles to the east, on the shore of the new world, a baby cried. Virginia Dare had survived her first month of life in the severe, desolate conditions of Roanoke Island. It was late September 1587. Her mother cradled her baby and calmed her with a milk-engorged breast.

•

The men cut farther. The tree's immense weight was now pinching down on the saw's blade, making it nearly impossible to move. Sam and Patrick stopped sawing and gathered fallen tree branches— branches appropriately sized to act as wedges.

Leaving the saw blade deep in the sliced trunk, they jammed wooden wedges in the sawed groove, pounding them in with large rocks. Placing a wedge every foot or so, Sam counted fifteen in all and rammed into the cut. "Sam, I don't think this tree's moved a bit. This is hopeless."

"All we need is a tiny bit more room for that blade, Patrick. A thirty-second of an inch could make a big difference."

"How much ya figure this monster weighs?"

Sam did some quick calculations in his head. "I gotta' believe a five-foot length of that trunk weighs at least a ton. I've been told this tree's over a hundred feet tall—that's close to twenty tons. Throw in all those huge branches and I figure you're talkin' thirty tons of tree. That's a lotta weight pushin' down on those wedges."

They commenced cutting. Their wedges must have widened the cut by at least a hair; the saw slid easier. They cut furiously, anxious to finish the job, anxious to get back to their families. After another hour of arduous, bark-banging strokes, the trunk's width narrowed, making the sawing easier and the cutting faster.

It began to rain; the men slowed their pace but kept cutting. Sam called out to Patrick, who was still hidden from view on the other side of the massive trunk, "Patrick, look at the rain. It's falling from the sky."

Patrick yelled back. "Sam, how interesting. Have you never seen rain fall from the sky before?"

Sam shook his head and chuckled. "Hey, Patrick, maybe you're not as smart as I thought. What I'm telling you is the rain's not goin' backward anymore. We must be goin' back!"

Patrick called out again. "I know were goin' back. That's the problem. So, Sam, tell me something I might wanna hear."

"Paddy, what I'm tellin' ya is we're headed back out, goin' forward in time. Our prayers have been answered."

Delighted with the news, Patrick burst out laughing. "Sam, isn't that grand? I don't know what I'd do without you. You just keep figuring things out for me, Sammy."

Sam yelled to Patrick one more time, telling him it was time for a break. They sawed slowly and stopped on a summer afternoon. Meeting at the front of the tree, they hugged each other in celebration, delighted by the prospect of returning home.

Their backs and shoulders ached severely, their forearms and biceps were tight, and their hands were blistered. They didn't care—they lay down to rest. While lying on the ground, staring up at the sky, they heard a loud crack from deep in the woods.

"What was that, Sam?"

The men sat up, looking back through the dense woods. Seeing some movement, they got up to investigate, cautiously walking through the darkly shaded forest.

It was a hot day, and the woods were heavy with humidity. A clearing ahead of them was lit by sunlight. They saw a dirt path, a trail about a hundred yards ahead. Horse-drawn wagons, stacked high with huge logs, were slowly rolling by on the trail. Numerous men, carrying saws and logging equipment, walked behind the wagons.

Sam and Patrick got as close as they could without being seen. Getting down on their bellies, they crawled a bit closer, no more than twenty feet from the path, close enough to hear the loggers talking as the pair safely hid from sight, lying behind thick undergrowth in the dark shade of the forest's towering trees.

Mosquitoes, disturbed by the intruders, swarmed up from the damp, warm turf. Patrick was frantic, soaked with sweat, lying on the ground in the heavy, sweltering air of the forest, covered with mosquitoes. He was just about to slap one of the pests when Sam grabbed him by the wrist and whispered. "They'll hear that. Just rub 'em off and put up with it."

Patrick quietly but vigorously rubbed his arms and face, leaving smears of blood all over his skin.

Peering out through the leafy brush, Sam looked farther down the trail. He saw a team of Negro slaves bringing up the rear of the procession. The barefoot slaves stumbled along the rocky, dirt path, shackled together at their ankles in a long line. The wagons stopped, and some men jumped down to the muddy path.

Patrick gulped and whispered to Sam, "They see us. We best run for it, Sam."

Samuel, not making a sound, held his friend's arm to the ground. "They don't see us. They're just stopping. Who knows why?"

The loggers were wearing unusual clothes, billowing cotton shirts and tight-fitting pants, buttoned just below the knee. White stockings covered their calves down to their black leather boots. They were speaking with odd accents. Patrick whispered, "Who are they?"

"I think they're colonials—look at their clothes. They're talkin' in old English."

"Aye, they sound a wee bit like me."

Sam put a finger to his lips.

Patrick softly whispered, "Aye, I'll shut me trap."

No more than seconds later, Patrick opened his trap. "What are they doin' way out here?"

Sam gave him a disappointed stare. "I'll tell ya later, Paddy. Now please be quiet."

Looking back to the line of slaves, he saw they were hurrying through ankle-deep mud, trying desperately to catch up to the wagon. Some tripped over their shackles, falling face down in the mud.

The slaves had bare chests and legs, clothed only in filthy, ragged shorts. Their sweat-drenched bodies glistened in the hot sun. The Negroes were huge, muscular men, dwarfing the white colonials who dominated their lives.

An ugly colonial with a pock-marked face, long, greasy hair, and a large paunch drooping over his belt, walked to the front wagon to speak with one of the drivers. Sam faintly overheard their conversation.

The wagon master was complaining about the slaves. They were too slow, holding up the long trip home. Sam heard the man mention Newark and something about ships. He saw a whip stuck in the fat one's back pocket. The whip's tail was dragging on the ground.

"Must be the slave foreman," Sam whispered. "That's what we heard, Paddy, the crack of a whip."

The foreman walked back to the slaves who were all sitting in the dirt. Sam listened intently. "I'll be teachin' ye, ye good for nothin' filth. I'll teach ye to move faster!"

The slave master randomly chose a victim, a big, hulking man with shining, deep black skin. "Ye stand, ye worthless animal." The slave slowly stood, nearly falling as his ankle chain tightened and strained, pulling on the ankle of the man behind. "I said stand!" The foreman pulled his whip from his pocket and cracked it in the air above his head.

Patrick, who had barely been watching, his thoughts consumed with killing mosquitoes, quickly looked up when he heard the loud

CRACK! The men watched as the foreman mercilessly flogged the poor slave. It seemed to go on forever.

The unfortunate Negro screamed as the whip tore skin from his back. By the time the flogging stopped, strips of bloody flesh hung from his body. The blood running down his legs formed a puddle at his feet. The foreman walked away without a word.

Patrick nervously whispered "Sam, did ya see that? I really think we should be goin' now."

Sam, saddened and horrified by what he'd witnessed, didn't say a word, only nodding in agreement. They crawled back a few yards, got to their feet and quietly left. Quickly making it back to the tree, they grabbed the saw handles and made one, hard swipe and looked back through the woods into the sunlit clearing. The loggers were gone.

The men cut furiously, inspired by going forward in time with the prospect of seeing their loved ones soon. They decided against taking any long breaks—breaks were dangerous; they never knew who or what would come along. They cut for more than an hour, taking only short, five-minute rest periods when needed. They encountered no one. After a full two hours of sawing, they were spent, nearing total exhaustion. Sam heard a splintering sound. "Paddy, did you hear that?"

"Aye, I did. I think I felt her move."

They stopped to inspect the cut. The sawed groove in the massive tree trunk had widened. A few of the wedges had loosened, falling to the ground.

"Sam, she's leaning. We'd be gettin' close!"

The men rallied, sawing with all their might. The tree moved again, slowly at first, leaning just a bit. As they continued sawing, they again heard an exciting cracking sound.

"Stand back, Patrick. I think she's comin' down." They ran back from the monstrous tree, a good fifty to sixty feet away. As they watched, the saw groove slowly widened. Splinters of oak shot out in all directions as the tree leaned farther. The huge canopy of leaf-covered branches swayed from side to side.

Crack! Pop! Pop! Crack!

It sounded like a volley of gunshots as wood chips, splinters and chunks of oak flew from the tree. Leaning past the point of no return, it accelerated, falling through the dense forest with a thunderous, seemingly endless roar.

The massive tree tore its way through branches and trunks of neighboring oak, taking countless smaller trees with it. It smashed to the ground with a tremendous, earth-shaking thud. The men felt the ground move beneath their boots as the heavy trunk drove itself deep into the soft, boggy ground of the forest. A cloud of dust, dirt, leaves, and twigs filled the air. Sam and Patrick looked at each other and yelled out with delight, hugging and dancing around like drunken teenagers. They spun around together, suddenly coming to a halt.

"Sam, it's your house!"

Samuel McCauley turned to see his white frame house, screen door, and wicker chair. He could have cried as he ran to find his family. He left Patrick standing there, exhausted. Sam flung the screen door open and ran inside, "Katie, Katie, I'm back." Katie appeared from the parlor.

"Honey, you're home early. Why aren't you at the mill?"

"Katie, I'm home."

"Yes, Sam, I see that. Why are you so excited? Did something happen at work?"

"Work, what work?"

Katie cocked her head with a look of confusion. "You all right, Samuel?"

Sam looked around the kitchen. It looked different, not the way it was two days ago. His eyes set on Katie's calendar hanging on the wall—May 1927.

"Katie, what year is it?"

"Sam, you're scaring me. What's wrong with you?"

He yelled out again, "What year is it?"

"It's 1927, you crazy man!"

"Wait here, Kate." Sam ran out to the yard just in time to see Patrick wielding the long saw blade, holding it across the gigantic surface of the oak stump, preparing to cut the last remnant of intact trunk, a wide strip of bark-covered wood that was still clinging to the stump, holding the massive weight of the nearly severed trunk a few feet above the ground. "Paddy, wait!"

Patrick turned to his friend's call and dropped the saw. "What's wrong? I thought I'd be finishin' the job before I went to see Sarah and the wee ones."

"No, we can't do that. Paddy, we still have jobs. We have our jobs, Paddy. It's 1927."

The men inspected the remaining uncut wood at the far side of the stump. The fallen tree hadn't torn all the way through; four to six inches of wood was bent over, still attached to the trunk. "Look, Paddy, there're still some tree rings we haven't cut. We started this job in 1933."

"Aye, that would be for sure."

"Katie's calendar says it's 1927; that's six years ago. There must be six years of time left in that bit of trunk where it hasn't torn through."

"Aye, Sam. So, let's cut on through her and get back where we belong."

"No, Patrick, I think we're better off here. I think the Lord has answered our prayers, Paddy. He's given back our lives, our jobs, and our families."

Patrick's eyes opened wide as he realized what Sam was saying. "Oh, Sam, could ya be right about that? Could it be true, our jobs? Is it true, Sam?"

"Yes, Paddy, it's the truth."

"Oh glory, the Lord's blessing has fallen upon us, eh Sam?"

Before Patrick left for home to see his family, he and Sam talked, agreeing to both show up for work in the morning, just as though nothing had changed.

After visiting with Katie and the boys, Sam went out to his thinking chair. He wasn't satisfied. *After all, we've been through, there's gotta be more—more to this than just gettin' our jobs back, workin' the mill again.*

He sat for a while thinking about it. Sam got up and walked out to the tree. He sat on the gigantic stump, trying to figure the significance of it all, wondering what opportunities could be gained from their return to 1927.

Walking back to the house, he saw his old, rusted pickup truck, the one he'd had to sell after losing his job. The truck was parked on the gravel drive next to the house.

"Looks like I can start drivin' to work again."

The next morning Sam drove to Patrick's house; they rode together to the paper mill. It was as if they'd never left. Their old friends were there, all acting as though they'd seen Sam and Patrick the day before. Sam asked Patrick to meet him for lunch. He had something to talk about. He had a plan.

The men sat together in the mill's small dining area. "Patrick, how much money do you have in the bank?"

"None, of course. Why are ya askin'?"

"Patrick, you're forgettin', it's 1927. Didn't you have money in the bank back then?"

"Oh, yeah, I forgot. I'd be thinkin' about five hundred dollars."

"I've got about seven hundred," replied Sam. "Listen, we're gonna be outta work in a few years, right back where we started. Nothing's gonna be any different, Paddy. We're gonna wind up right where we started, unemployed and flat broke."

"Aye, Sam, but we at least gotta a few extra years to enjoy."

"Paddy, a few years is nothing. We have an opportunity here, a chance to change our future."

"And what might that be, Sam? How do we change our future?"

"Gold, Patrick, we gotta buy gold. After the market crash, paper was worthless. Gold is safe. If we work hard and save our money, we can buy gold. It'll get us through the rough times ahead. Patrick, I think it's what the Lord has given us. It came to me last night, and I think it's a gift from God."

"Sam, I'd like to be agreeing with ya, and I think it's a grand idea, but is it safe? Spendin' all our money on gold—it sounds a wee bit risky."

"It's not, Paddy. It's the best thing we could do."

Patrick leaned forward, his head held in his fingertips. He was silent for a moment. "All right, Sam, you're the one with the brains—I'll do it."

"You're makin' the right decision, Paddy; I guarantee it. Maybe we should get our money together soon and get started."

"Now, there ya go, Sam, impatient as always. But I guess I'd be the same, bein' it were my idea. I suppose we can go to the bank tomorrow, right after work."

Samuel smiled and placed an arm around his friend as they shook hands on their agreement.

As he was about to leave, Patrick spoke up, "Sam, I been meaning to ask ya—how is it a man with an eighth-grade education knows so much? I'm quite impressed with your knowledge of all that stuff regardin' the Algonkos and the the Powhatoos, the Civil War and the colonials with their slaves and such."

Samuel turned to his friend with a quizzical look.

Patrick continued. "I'm especially keen on that talk about early American ship buildin' and the vast importance of white oak and the Old Ironsides thing. Where'd ya come up with that, Sam? Ya haven't been fabricatin' with me now, have ya?"

Sam smiled in response to the compliment. He sarcastically answered, "Paddy, me lad, might ya be accusin' me a bein' a liar?"

Patrick laughed, "Aye, I might be. But I prefer the term fabricatin', it bein' much less offensive, as they say. And by the way, that accent was pretty good; I liked it. You should keep it up, kinda reminds me of me home. I've been a wee bit lonely in Virginia, bein' the only Irish-man for miles around."

Sam chuckled and gave his Irish brogue one more try. "I understand ya bein' a bit put out, Paddy, me boy. These parts bein' so loaded with Scotsman, hardly a bit o' the green to be found."

The men laughed together as Sam explained. "I may only have an eighth-grade education, Patrick, but I read books. You may want to try it sometime."

"Books? I'd sooner die! I'm quite happy bein' the ignorant Irish-man I am."

Sam placed a hand on his friend's shoulder. "Paddy, you're anything but ignorant. You're a good man and a good friend."

•

The next day, Sam drove Patrick home from work. In preparation for their trip to the bank, Patrick changed into his best dress clothes. They drove to Sam's place, so he could change clothes. As the men walked around to the back door, Sam saw Joshua, Jeremy, and Keeper playing in the yard. He was still shocked at how young his boys were, six years younger than a few days ago.

Joshua was now eight and Jeremy would turn six in a few weeks. Keeper looked the same, a bit sprier, but otherwise no different. Sam went in the house, returning minutes later wearing his Sunday best.

He saw Joshua attempting to climb on the huge, fallen tree trunk, fingers dug into the bark, straining to pull himself up. It was impossible; the top edge of the trunk was more than ten feet off the ground. Meanwhile, Jeremy had crawled beneath the fallen trunk where it was elevated on the three-foot-high stump. He thought it made a nice fort.

Keeper was running around, barking. Sam yelled out. "Stay away from the tree, boys—it's not safe." He walked across his yard to the edge of the woods, pulled Jeremy out from his hiding place and reprimanded him. "Jeremy, this tree falls, it'll kill ya!" He snapped his fingers, "Just like that." He addressed Joshua, "Get down from there, Josh. Please, boys, stay away from this tree, all right?"

"Yes, Papa."

"Yes, Papa, we will."

Sam and Paddy jumped in the truck and took off for the bank. They bounced around in the old, rusty pick-up, heading down the dirt road toward town. When they reached the edge of the city, the truck rolled onto smooth pavement. They parked in front of National City Bank.

The bank was bustling with business. The economy was booming; people were investing, saving, and spending. Asking to speak to someone who could help them invest in gold, they were directed to a middle-aged man, Mr. Snead, sitting at a large desk.

"Hello, gentleman. Please, sit down. How can I help you?"

Sam introduced Patrick and himself as they took a seat. "Yes, sir, we'd like to buy gold," said Sam.

"Ah, gold, a wise investment gentleman. How much would you like to invest?"

"Mr. Sneed, if you'll check our accounts, you'll find I have seven hundred thirty dollars, and Patrick here has a little over five hundred. We want to invest the entire amount."

"Really, the entire amount, eh? I'll be right back." Sneed left to check the accounts with one of the tellers. He returned a moment later. "Mr.

McCauley, you have a bit more than you thought, seven hundred sixty dollars, and Mr. Cleary here has five hundred thirty-five. Are you sure you want to invest all of it?"

"Yes, sir, we're positive."

Snead pulled a gold transaction application from his desk drawer and picked up a pen. When he began to write, it happened.

Mr. Snead disappeared. People were racing around, faster and faster. The front door of the bank flew open and closed like a revolving door out of control. Sam looked up to a large clock on the wall; its hands were spinning around in a blur. The lights in the bank quickly switched on and off as night and day shot by. Patrick ran to the window and stood motionless as he stared at the familiar sight of rapidly changing seasons. Rain, sunshine, rain, snow, all passing at an incredible rate.

It stopped as abruptly as it had started. Sam was sitting at a dust-covered desk. Paper was strewn around the bank floor. Except for the two men, the bank was empty. Huge cobwebs hung from the corners of the ceiling and light fixtures.

Looking at the front entrance, Sam said, "Paddy, the doors are locked, chained together."

Seeing Patrick's clothes had changed, Sam, glanced down at himself, expecting to see his suit and tie but instead found he was wearing a shirt and jeans, the same he wore the day he started sawing the tree. Patrick turned to Sam and screamed, "Sam, the tree!"

A second later, Sam thought of the boys. "Oh, my God, Patrick, the boys. Jeremy was playing under the tree."

The men broke their way out of the bank, smashing a window to get outside. Sam's truck was gone. They took off running, up the street to the dirt road toward Sam's house. It was a four-mile run, taking them just over a half-hour. As they ran, Sam prayed, "Dear, Lord, please protect my children. God, please help me. I love my family so much. I can't live without them, all of them. Please don't let my boys be hurt."

Arriving at Sam's house, they ran up the gravel drive to the yard. Katie and Joshua were in the yard. Katie was loudly sobbing, her face buried in her hands. Joshua was hugging her. He looked older—taller than a few hours ago; he was back to age fourteen.

They were standing next to the tree's stump with Joshua staring down at the ground near the fallen trunk. It was torn away from its stump.

Sam, terrified, yelled, "Katie, where's Jeremy? Where's Jeremy?" He ran to his wife's side, grabbing her by the shoulders. "Katie, where is Jeremy!"

Katie pulled her hands from her face, tears streaming down her cheeks. "Oh, Sam— Keeper's dead."

"Kate, for the last time, where is Jeremy?"

Katie didn't respond.

Joshua, tears rolling down his face, looked up at his father. "Papa, Jeremy's in the house; he's crying; he's in his room."

Sam's hand went to his chest, covering his heart, "Oh, dear, God, thank you!" He walked to the edge of the fallen tree trunk. Seeing a single black-and-white paw protruding from beneath, he knelt to the ground to stroke his friend. "You're a good girl, Keeper, such a smart dog."

Katie stopped sobbing when Sam returned to her side. He asked, in a soft voice, "Katie, tell me what happened."

"Sam, I was in the house when I heard Keeper barking wildly. I went out to see what was going on. Keeper was darting around the tree trunk, barking at Jeremy. She was uncontrollable. It was as if she knew something bad was about to happen. Just as I got there, the tree started to move. Jeremy was under there, Sam; he was right there, under that tree. I heard cracking wood. Then Keeper ran under the tree. She jumped up on Jeremy, pushing him out from under the trunk just as it fell. She saved our son's life, Sam—it was a miracle!"

Patrick extended his condolences about Keeper and told Sam and Katie he had to go home to see his family. Sam, Katie, and Joshua returned to the house. Sam went to Jeremy's room to console him. He told Jeremy how much he loved him, how frightened he was, and how sad he was about Keeper. "She was such a smart girl, and she loved you; she saved your life. Jeremy cried and hugged his father.

Sam spoke again with Katie and Joshua and then, being exhausted from the day's events, took a seat in his wicker chair. He mentally reviewed the unbelievable experience he and Paddy had shared over the past week. Realizing their adventure, in addition to costing Keeper's life, and jeopardizing his son's life, had simply put him and Patrick right back where they'd started. "We've gained nothing. I've gained nothing, and I've killed our beautiful dog in the process."

Now, so disgusted with the outcome of his project, Sam had no interest in selling the oak tree. "That tree is evil; it's too damn dangerous to mess with." He vowed to have it cut to small pieces and hauled away. "I'll never touch that thing again."

I'm no good—I'm worthless, he thought. *I put Patrick through all that work and we haven't achieved a damn thing.*

Sam sat in his chair for a while, pondering his future. *What future? There is no future for me. Just as I thought, Katie and the boys will be better off without me.*

Walking back to the house, he went to his bedroom, locked the door behind him, and opened his top dresser drawer. After finding his fishing knife, Sam, sat on the bed, staring at the knife's long blade.

He thought about their adventure, what he and Patrick had just experienced, a miraculous occurrence, the event of a lifetime. Nothing else would ever come close. The rest of his life would pale by comparison. "Why should I bother? I've already seen more than any man ever has or will."

Sam thought about the soldiers and the grisly, horrific scenes he'd witnessed in the Confederate camp. "Those young men. Such misery— dying before their time—wanting to live, but goin' through such torture."

He remembered his near-death encounter with the rebels, chasing him through the woods.

He thought of the Indians and the simplicity of their lives. *They were so strong and healthy, living off the land. They had nothing compared to what I have. They lived in thatched huts, struggling through long, cold winters—doing' their best to keep their families alive.*

His mind drifted back to the colonials, the downtrodden Negro slaves, and the misery of their lives. Robust young men, forced to abandon their families to work for vicious white barbarians, being beaten and flogged until blood dripped from their bodies.

Looking back at his knife, Sam spoke, "What right do I have? God's given me a second chance. Maybe he wanted me to see the horrors of the war camps, the misery of the slaves, and the simple life led by the

Indians. I'm so much better off by comparison. I have no right to do this." He thought of Katie and the boys and how terrified he'd been, thinking Jeremy had been killed.

Sam pulled his flannel shirt tails from his pants, held his knife in his right hand and rolled the blade in the flannel-covered palm of his left. He flexed his arm, snapping the blade off at the hilt of its ivory handle. Tossing the handle to his top drawer, he knelt to the floor, dangling the long, shiny blade between two fingers.

Samuel McCauley peered through the space between his bedroom's floorboards, looking down to the blackness beneath his home; he pointed the curved tip of the knife between the boards and dropped it. The glistening blade fell to the darkness, landing on cold, barren earth.

Omar's

This story is a chapter taken from my novel, *Caduceus*. Mounir Arafa is the son of Arabic parents who emigrated from Lebanon to Detroit, Michigan, in the early 1960s. The family resides in East Dearborn, Michigan, an enclave of Arabic immigrants, which today represents one of the largest Arabic populations outside Indonesia and the Middle East.

*M*ounir (moo-NEAR) Arafa and Salim (suh-LEEM) Naheed walked through the rear entrance of Omar's. They liked to stand in the back and scan the room before choosing a table. Most of the tables were already taken, mainly by Arabic guys from the neighborhood. Mounir knew nearly all of them, at least casually.

There was a mix of Arabic Orthodox Christians and Muslims throughout the room. Most of the Christians, including Mounir and Salim, drank alcohol, as did some of the westernized, second-generation American Muslims—those who didn't strictly adhere to Islam. This combination kept Omar's bar business well in the black.

In the far corner of the room, near the front door, Mounir noticed a big, blond-haired guy shooting by himself. A young woman was sitting nearby, drinking beer. The adjacent table was vacant.

"What do you think, Sal?" said Mounir as he pointed across the room.

"Looks good to me, Munie—we can take the table right next to 'em."

Omar's, the biggest pool hall in the area, was located on Michigan Avenue in the heart of East Dearborn. Being known for its serious players and high stakes, few women ever ventured in. Years ago, the building had been a restaurant.

Omar Khouri bought the restaurant in the early seventies and converted it to a pool hall. The room's ceiling, covered with black tin panels, was high, fifteen feet or more. The floor still had its original maroon linoleum, which was worn through to bare wood at numerous spots.

Lamps with translucent green glass shades were suspended from the ceiling—one centered over each table. The shades, hung below eye level, left the remainder of the room dimly lit by a faint, green glow. Led Zeppelin was playing on the jukebox. The song's heavy bass vibrated through the room.

The floor creaked as Mounir and Salim walked toward the bar to speak with Omar, who was standing behind the counter. He was a short, round man with a face framed by a neatly trimmed salt-and-pepper beard. His mustache was thick and heavy; his head was sparsely covered by thinning, black hair. He had a rotund belly, always covered by a white apron, which by this time of night was soiled with food and beer. Mounir loved this fat old man like a father.

"Hey, Munie."

"Omar, my man, how are you tonight?"

"Another day, another night—I'm happy; things are good."

"Good evening, chief," said Sal. "Kind of quiet in here for a Friday night?"

"It's still early, Salli. You know it'll liven up—just give it time. You two want the usual?"

"Sure, we'll be at the table up front," said Salim.

Omar facetiously responded. "No kidding. I never would have guessed."

Mounir and Salim didn't drink while shooting. Omar prepared a tonic on the rocks with a deceptive lemon twist for Mounir and a Coke with a slice of lime for Salim. Their drinks, giving the appearance of cocktails, contained no alcohol. This came in handy when they wanted to feign intoxication.

As Mounir walked past the end of the bar, Omar spoke up. "Munie, you want your stick now or later?"

"I better take it now."

Walking around the end of the bar, Mounir joined Omar in his office. The small room reeked of stale beer, the smell coming from stacks of cased empties lining one wall. A desk on the opposite wall was cluttered with piles of invoices, dirty coffee cups, and an ashtray full of butts. On the wall above the desk was a locked, steel case.

Omar took out his keys, opened the case, and pulled out Mounir's personal cue—two pieces of dead-straight maple locked together with a bright brass coupling, total weight: nineteen ounces. It had no carvings, no designs, nothing pretentious. Mounir liked a stick that didn't draw attention, something inconspicuous.

He thanked Omar, walked back to the bar, and handed his stick to Salim. Mounir wouldn't need it for a while. They took their drinks and walked to the vacant table at the front of the room.

•

Mounir had been shooting pool at Omar's since he was fourteen. His parents' apartment was close by, just a block away from the hall. At the time, Mounir, being under age, was only allowed to come in early after school and on Saturday mornings. Mounir would run errands and help clean up in exchange for free use of the tables.

Omar, having taken an instant liking to his young helper, was attracted to Mounir's intelligence, precocious maturity, and dependability. He also recognized Mounir's potential as a pool player. Even as a youngster, the kid had an incredible eye and an uncanny ability to position shots.

Through his high school years, Mounir and Omar became close friends. Mounir was an A student but had no interest in pursuing academics and no intention to go to college. Omar often tried, unsuccessfully, to push him toward a higher education.

Testing in the Dearborn school system had shown Mounir Arafa to be a true prodigy. In the second grade, his Stanford-Binet IQ was measured at 184. He was at the top of the genius range with scores higher than 99 percent of the population.

Schoolwork was a bore to Mounir. Despite expending minimal effort in school, he easily maintained a straight A record. In high school, having no interest in athletics or extra-curricular activities, he was thought of as a loner. Salim was his only friend. They had lived as neighbors in the same apartment building as children and became good friends in early childhood.

Mounir had known Salim as far back as he could remember. Salim's family moved to a newer building when Mounir was twelve, but he and Salim kept a close friendship as high school classmates. Salim was truly Mounir's only friend.

Shunning people and notoriety, Mounir did his best to remain invisible at school. Approaching graduation, he was informed he was the most likely candidate for valedictorian of the class of 1977.

Mounir's grade point average was a perfect 4.0. He was flatly against receiving the valedictorian honor and had no intention of giving a speech at graduation. His solution to this dilemma was simple; at the end of his senior year, he failed to show for a final examination. He was given an F, and his grade average dropped to 3.9. A female classmate with a 3.95 became valedictorian.

After graduation, Mounir and Salim were even closer friends. They moved into an apartment together and often worked the same jobs. Mounir, abhorring the thought of working for a living, especially at manual labor, could not tolerate being controlled by a supervisor. Consequently, his employment was generally short lived.

Determined to survive on income from games, Mounir chose to be a gambler, and he convinced Salim to do the same. They'd avoid high-risk games of chance, those with unfavorable odds, instead concentrating on honing their skills at blackjack, poker, and Mounir's favorite, billiards.

Mounir had a photographic memory and was adept at counting cards in blackjack. He developed a system of signals to tell Salim when to draw or stay. They played multiple hands and always came out ahead. The pair took frequent trips to Vegas and routinely came home with two to three thousand dollars in winnings.

At the age of twenty-four, they had successfully remained unemployed for more than two years. Independent, carefree, and financially secure, they, by Mounir's twenty-fifth birthday, had over twenty thousand dollars in savings.

The men dated women frequently but rarely had relationships lasting more than a few months. Salim was impressed by his friend's kind treatment of women. Mounir, always a gentleman, never made promises he couldn't keep and always treated his girlfriends with respect. It was a standard Salim found difficult to emulate.

•

The men arrived at the vacant table next to the blond guy. Mounir set the first rack for eight ball, and Salim broke using Mounir's cue. The six ball fell into the side pocket. Salim sank his first shot and scratched on the next.

Mounir took one of Omar's house sticks off the wall, chalked it, and called his pocket, "Fifteen in the corner." There was a lot of green and he missed. The fifteen came to rest at the lip of the pocket.

As they played, Mounir discreetly kept an eye on their neighbor. *He's pretty good,* thought, Mounir. *He has an air of self-confidence. I like that.* He assessed the guy's stroke and body language. *He's cocky— impressed with himself—showing off for his girlfriend.*

Glancing toward the girl, Mounir saw three empty beer bottles on the table in front of her."

•

Salim had three balls left: the eight ball, a solid, and a stripe. He called the solid in the corner and sank it. Trying to bank the eight in the side pocket, he missed.

While scanning the table, Mounir noticed the guy next to them looking his way. Mounir lined up a shot, a tough shot at an acute angle. When he was sure the blond was watching, he made his play, leaving the ball hanging a good six inches from the pocket as the cue ball scratched in the side. "I'm just not with it tonight, Sal."

"Too bad, Munie; I guess I'll have to kick your butt."

"Ah, a challenge; I like that—your shot, wise-ass!"

Salim pulled the cue ball from the pocket and took dead aim at the eight. He cautiously set it up as the guy next to them looked on.

"Eight ball in the corner." He timidly stroked the cue ball, barely sinking the eight.

"You lucked out, Sal."

"No luck involved, Munie—just skill, my man, pure skill."

The blond guy went back to his game and set a new rack. He was wearing a red flannel shirt and jeans. His sleeves, rolled up on his large biceps, revealed muscular, hair-covered forearms. He stood about six feet two inches and had a V-shaped upper body and a narrow waist.

Mounir figured the guy was an autoworker, probably got paid today, Friday.

As the big guy leaned forward to break, his right bicep bulged through his flannel. He took a powerful stroke. A loud crack rang out. The break was tremendous—balls scattered over the entire tabletop. Two solids fell in.

Figuring the guy was showing off for him, Mounir recognized an opportunity. "Nice break," he said as he took a step toward the adjacent table.

The man glanced up with a quizzical look. "Thanks."

Mounir took another step and extended his hand. "My name's Munie."

The guy hesitated, finally took Mounir's hand, and gave it a firm squeeze. "I'm Rick."

Detecting reluctance in the greeting, Mounir, thought, *It's either prejudice toward Arabs or suspicion of my motives.* He preferred prejudice. It made the game more fun. "Nice to meet you. This guy over here's Sal."

Rick acknowledged Salim with a nod. Mounir walked back to his table and set another rack. Salim broke. Rick's girlfriend got up and headed toward the restroom.

"Cindy, get me two more beers." The request sounded like a harsh demand. He pulled a wad of bills from his pocket and tossed some money her way. She returned minutes later with three beers. "Cindy, I want you to play," said Rick.

"Oh, come on, Rick. Please, you never like it when I play!"

He responded with an order, "Yes I do. Your shot. Shoot the stripes."

Mounir cautiously observed. Cindy couldn't shoot; she was petite with small hands. Placing her tiny fist on the table, she tried to rest the cue between her knuckles. There was no stability and she missed nearly every shot.

Her inability aggravated Rick. He criticized her after each missed shot and ignored her when she occasionally sank one.

"Cindy, you can't shoot for shit! Why don't you hold the stick right?"

"My hands are too small. I told you that. I knew you'd get mad."

"You're an embarrassment, girl."

"I can't help it if I can't play this game."

"You're uncoordinated, like all women."

"Okay, Rick, forget it. I'm not playing! You go ahead and play by yourself."

"Hey, playing against you is like playing by myself."

Mounir seized the moment. Looking at Salim, he gave him a nod. Salim took a few steps toward Rick's table. "I'll play you if you want. I'm getting bored. Munie here isn't much competition."

Rick paused with a suspicious look. After a few seconds, he spoke. "All right, I'll play you. Eight ball, I break."

"Sounds good to me," said Salim.

As Salim racked, Rick glared down the table and asked, "How 'bout five bucks?"

"Five bucks? Sure, why not?"

Rick delivered the same crushing break with balls strewn everywhere. The eight ball bounced gently off the back rail and returned close to its original position. The fifteen and six fell in. Rick chose stripes and sank two more.

As the game progressed, Salim played to his best ability and eventually won with Rick leaving only one ball on the table. Rick reached for his wallet with a mixed look of embarrassment and disgust.

Salim, spoke, "It's okay. Don't worry about it now. Another game?"

Rick stared at him for a second. "Okay, ten bucks this time."

"Fine with me—my break." Salim's break was adequate, but nothing compared to his opponent's. He lost the game with four balls remaining. Rick was up by five dollars. Salim asked, "You want me to pay you now or keep playing?"

Rick looked encouraged and confident. "We'll play. How about twenty-five?"

"Twenty-five?" Salim pulled out his wallet as if to count his money. He fingered through some bills, paused, and said, "All right, your break."

Backing off his game, Salim, not wanting to scare off his opponent, assured Rick's win. Eventually, Rick sank the eight ball on a long bank off the end rail.

Salim called out, "Good shot—your game."

Mounir, standing back, silently observing Rick's attitude, gave another quick nod to his partner. This was Salim's signal to pay Rick the thirty dollars owed. He laid a twenty and two fives on the table. Rick picked them up and said, "Want to keep going?"

"I guess so. I'll play one more, but if I lose, that's it. How about givin' me a chance to win my money back? Can we go for fifty?"

Rick hesitated. "You got fifty on you?"

"Yep." Salim set two twenties and a ten on the rail, securing them with a cube of chalk. "That good enough?"

Rick, staring at him, announced, "My break."

It was apparent Rick was feeling powerful and self-assured. Salim knew this was a crucial game. If Rick won, he might be tempted to leave with his eighty-dollar winnings. Salim had to win.

As usual, Rick produced a staggering break, pocketing one stripe and one solid. Salim scanned the table. Overall, the stripes were in best position. There were two solids in tempting, gimme spots—one at the mouth of a corner pocket, the other at a side pocket.

However, there were two more solids lying hard on the end rail, buried behind a stripe. It would be difficult to free them up. Salim, watching his adversary set up for his next shot, thought, *Come on, go for the solids, you sucker.*

Rick took the solids and sank the six. Mounir grinned, winking at Salim. Rick shot the second gimme, sank another solid, and ended up stranded with a bad leave. It was exactly what they'd hoped for.

Salim sank five of the remaining six stripes and, knowing Rick could never catch up, intentionally missed the final ball, the twelve. Rick missed his next shot. Salim sank the twelve and finished off his opponent by banking the eight ball into the side pocket. Rick glared at Salim with an odd, sheepish look mixed with anger. He went for his wallet.

Salim quickly said, "Hey, no problem, man. I'm only up by twenty dollars. I trust you."

Rick gave him a hard look. "Then I guess you wanna keep playin'?"

"It's your call, pal."

"Don't call me pal!" The muscles in Rick's neck bulged as he grabbed the rack, firmly set it to the table, and announced, "Fifty bucks! Nine ball."

Salim's eyes opened wide, "Nine ball? I haven't played it much."

"Nine ball or nothin'!"

"Okay, whatever you say. Nine ball it is."

Cindy was silent. Her boyfriend had already downed the two beers she'd bought. He sent her off for more.

For the next two games, Salim backed off. He and Mounir wanted to restore Rick's confidence. Rick won two games of nine ball, fifty bucks each, putting him up by eighty dollars. Salim paid him the eighty.

"Munie, this guy's killin' me. I'm down eighty bucks. You play him!"

Rick looked across the table with a grin and sarcastically said, "I guess you're up, Mooney!"

Mounir loved it, thinking, *This shit head is actually challenging me.* Responding with intentional hesitation, he said, "Okay, I guess I'll play." Mounir turned to Salim. "Sal, if I lose much money we can forget about Acapulco."

Cindy returned from the bar. Rick's growing confidence and the four or five beers he'd had were making him irritatingly talkative. "You guys are goin' to Mexico?"

"Yeah, we plan to."

"I've been to Acapulco. It's a blast—plenty of wild women."

Cindy looked up and rolled her eyes.

"That's what we've heard. We can't wait to go; we've been savin' up for weeks."

"You'll have a good time. Take my word for it."

Mounir thought, *I wouldn't take this asshole's word for anything.* He asked, "Still want nine ball?"

"Yep!" said Rick.

"Fifty?" asked Mounir.

"Yep!"

"I'll rack. It's your break, Rick." Mounir lost the game outright—sinking only two of nine balls.

"Sal, why don't you get us two more drinks. I need another one to straighten me out."

Rick chuckled and taunted Mounir. "Think more booze will help?"

Remaining silent, Mounir stared at Rick and smiled. Salim said he'd be right back. Mounir walked to the end of the table and racked another set for nine ball. "Hey, you mind if we drop the stakes to twenty-five dollars?"

Laughing, Rick said, "No problem. I'd hate to have you guys miss out on Acapulco."

Rick sank the nine and won the game just as Salim returned from the bar. Mounir pulled seventy-five dollars from his wallet and laid it on the table. Rick scooped up the cash and said, "You two losers ready to call it quits?"

Mounir, astounded by the guy's arrogance, ignored the comment. He and Salim stepped over to their original table as if to confer on the issue.

They pulled out their wallets, counting their money as Rick looked on. Mounir returned and said, "We'd like to keep playing. Winner names the stakes."

His face beaming, Rick let out a derogatory laugh. "No problem! I won! Next game's for a hundred dollars if you can cover it."

Rick, having had at least six beers by Mounir's count, was slurring his words. Cindy shouted, "Rick, are you crazy? You're gonna lose all your money!"

"Shut the fuck up, Cindy! These guys are the ones losin' money."

"Rick, you're drunk!"

"I said shut it, Cindy. You can leave any time."

"Yeah, right. What should I do, walk home?"

"Listen, just sit there on your pretty little ass and watch me in action."

Wondering why his hatred for Rick was so intense, Mounir thought, *I'm really gonna put this piece of shit in his place. Money's no longer the issue. This son-of-a-bitch needs a lesson in humility.*

Mounir had him right where he wanted him. Rick was cocky, sarcastic and bragging to his girlfriend. He'd never be able to back down now. To top it off, he was drunk.

Rick stepped to the head of the table and repeated the stakes. "Nine ball, one hundred bucks. My break!"

Mounir, nodding in agreement, racked balls one through nine in a diamond pattern at the far end of the table. The one ball was positioned at the head of the diamond with the nine ball centered. The remaining balls were placed randomly. Mounir, having surmised his opponent didn't understand the strategy in nine ball, watched Rick deliver his usual power break as if he were playing eight ball or slop. This could easily set up a run of the table by any decent player.

The rules of nine ball require the cue ball to first strike the lowest number ball on the table. The low-number ball may be pocketed directly or used to pocket a higher-number ball through a combination shot. Sinking the nine in proper numeric sequence or by a combination wins the game. A hard break could dangerously expose the nine to a combination shot, which could end the game early.

Rick sank the five and seven on the break. The nine was frozen on the far rail. He sank the one, ending up with a bad leave and no chance of hitting the remaining lowest ball, the two.

Mounir's strategy was to keep the game as close as possible without losing. He banked the cue ball into the two; it careened into the six, which fell into a corner pocket. Hitting the two again, as though he wanted to bank it into the side pocket, he purposely produced a near miss.

Pocketing the two and three balls, Rick inadvertently freed up the nine, which had been lying hard on the rail. Three balls remained: the four, eight, and nine. Mounir was concerned; he couldn't safely give Rick any more room. Rick shot a four-nine combination and missed.

Mounir stepped to the table, hesitating to create the appearance of uncertainty. He cautiously chose his next shot. The four ball fell into the corner, leaving the cue ball positioned for an easy shot on the eight. There was no chance for an eight-nine combination.

Feeling he could safely back off once more, Mounir changed his approach. He sank the eight and purposely positioned the cue ball for a tough leave on the nine. Pausing again before calling a bank shot to put the nine in the far corner, he skillfully missed, leaving the cue ball hanging close to the head rail with the nine resting at the far end of the table.

Rick, surprised Mounir had missed the bank shot by so much, stared at his opponent. Standing at the table, he paused for close to a minute to consider his options—there were none; there was too much green. He couldn't sink the nine, and he knew it. Rick gently tapped the cue ball causing it to roll only a few inches. This was an illegal move, a foul.

Mounir didn't object. He stepped to the table and aligned his next shot. Calling the corner pocket, he beautifully banked the cue ball off the rail with reverse English. It struck the nine, which quietly fell into the leather pouch of the far corner.

Rick stared at the enemy with disbelief. Mounir responded with a matter-of-fact, "My game. That'll be a hundred bucks." He wanted to make Rick pay the money now as Cindy watched. He wanted to piss him off.

Taking a wad of bills from his pocket, Rick tossed two fifties on the table. Mounir took the money, carefully folded the bills, and slid them in his shirt pocket. "Thanks. By my calculation, you're still up fifty-five bucks. Nothing lost so far; we'll go again. Nine ball, one hundred dollars. I break."

Mounir hadn't asked him to play—he'd declared they would play. Rick, with a look of rage, took the bait. With muscles tensed, he slammed the rack on the table and murmured under his breath. Cindy looked down without a word.

It was nearing midnight, and the room was packed with players and bystanders. All the tables were taken. Cigarette smoke filled the air, creating cones of light under each green lamp. The room vibrated from the beat of music, the crack of billiard balls, and the din of conversation and laughter. Omar busied himself serving drinks from behind the bar and entertaining customers.

Mounir stepped up to break. Stroking the cue ball with moderate force, he drove five balls into the cushions. As planned, the nine-ball remained motionless at its center position. He looked up to Rick. "Your shot."

As the game proceeded, Mounir loosened up, showing off just enough to get the muscle man riled.

Four balls remained on the table when Rick looked across to Cindy. "Don't just sit there lookin' stupid. Go get me a beer!" Mounir figured Rick didn't want her watching as he lost another game, but Cindy returned just in time to see Mounir sink the nine with a double bank shot.

"Rick, you lost again, honey. This guy's very good. He's a better player than you. You've gotta stop!"

Mounir loved her comment.

Rick yelled at his girlfriend. "Just give me the goddam beer, sit down, and keep your fuckin' mouth shut!"

Mounir felt the hair on his neck bristle. Rick looked back at Mounir, seeing an audience gathering behind him. Two Arabic guys, staring at Rick in response to his outburst, occupied a nearby table. Four or five more were milling around the area. They all knew Mounir, and they'd all seen him in action. They knew he was moving in for the kill, and they wanted to see the show.

Mounir, with an expressionless face, stared hard at Rick. "That'll be one hundred dollars!"

The veins in Rick's neck bulged as he reached in his pocket, peeled off two more fifties, and threw them on the table. Mounir picked up his money, folded it neatly, and placed it in his pocket. Grinning at Rick, he delivered the coup de grace. "Maybe you should listen to your girlfriend, pal. She's right, you know; I am better than you."

Rick looked as if he were going to explode. Grabbing the rack from the wall, he smashed it down on the table.

Mounir responded, "Okay, it's your money. Two hundred dollars this time."

"Two hundred dollars my ass!"

"Hey, I won. Winner names the stakes, remember? To make it fair, we'll lag for break and you can name your game."

"Eight ball! We go back to eight ball."

"Whatever you say, pal."

"I'm not your pal!"

Mounir smiled and said nothing.

To lag for break, each player banks a ball off the far rail, back toward the head rail. The one who gets closest to the head rail without hitting it, wins the lag.

Rick went first. The ball stopped about eight inches from the rail. Mounir, preferring Rick break, intentionally brought his lag up short, a full foot from the rail. Rick stepped to the table. "My break! Rack 'em for eight ball, pal."

The crowd was building; Mounir loved it. He was ready to shut this redneck down, and he wanted to do it with an audience. As anticipated, Rick delivered an awesome, shattering break. Mounir tensed as he watched the eight ball hit the back cushion, careen off the twelve, and come precariously close to falling in the corner pocket, stopping just at its lip. Two balls fell in—one stripe, one solid.

Salim walked over to Mounir and handed him his personal stick. Rick didn't notice the exchange. He was preoccupied, transfixed by the balls on the table; he assessed his possible shots. Mounir saw Rick stagger as he rounded the table's corner. *He's drunk.*

Choosing solids, Rick sank the five ball and, now too drunk to make even the simplest of shots, missed an easy play on the two.

Mounir, stepping to the table, checked the position of the remaining six stripes—envisioning every shot he would make and every leave he would need to clear the board. He'd do it with a flair to please the crowd.

He banked his first four shots, barely hesitating between each. All four balls hit the pockets dead center. Two stripes remained. He sank the first with a double combination— stripe to solid to stripe. For the last two balls, the stripe and the eight ball, he'd put on a show.

Mounir sank the stripe with a triple bank shot, cue ball off the far cushion, stripe off two cushions into the far corner. The crowd applauded and let out a yell. The cue ball came to rest about ten inches from the eight, which still sat at the lip of the corner pocket.

A solid, number six, was resting midway between the cue ball and the eight, obstructing any clear shot. Mounir could easily sink the eight with a straight bank off the side rail. Instead, he decided to use a massé.

A massé shot applies extreme English to the cue ball. The shot looks strange due to the position of the stick—butt end held high, tip pointed nearly perpendicular to the tabletop. A massé requires skill and a steady hand. The cue tip strikes down hard on top of the cue ball at an eccentric point, creating incredible spin, which causes the ball to move in a curved, semicircular course. The shot is used to curve around an obstructing ball, into the object ball.

Mounir, glancing up to the crowd, saw Omar standing a few feet from the table. Omar smiled and winked. The commotion around Mounir's table had attracted a larger crowd with fifteen or so people gathered nearby. Raising the butt of his stick high over the table—Mounir positioned the cue at a seventy to eighty-degree angle to the table top. The fingers of his left hand were fanned out—pressed hard to the felt. He struck down with a firm, sharp stroke.

The cue ball shot forward, suddenly curving a full 180 degrees around the six. It struck the eight dead center and stopped. The eight ball slowly rolled over the lip of the pocket and quietly fell in the pouch. The crowd went crazy, roaring with wild approval.

"Nice shot, Munie!"

"Way to kick his ass, Munie!"

Mounir looked up from the table, staring directly into the eyes of his prey. "Two hundred dollars, Rick."

The enraged victim glared back. His body went stiff, tense. He squeezed his stick with a tight, white-knuckled grip and bulging forearms. Speechless, he turned to scan the crowd. He knew he had been set up, and he wanted revenge.

"Fuck you!"

"Excuse me, what did you say?" responded, Mounir.

"You heard me. I said, fuck you."

Mounir laid his stick on the table and stepped toward Rick, stopping a few feet away. "I don't think you're in any position to be telling me what to do, friend." Three guys in the crowd stepped forward to emphasize the point.

Rick leaned his stick against the wall and turned to face his girlfriend. "Cindy, give me some money!"

"Damn it, Rick. I told you this would happen."

Rick walked to Cindy, grabbed her arm and yanked her around in her chair. His fingers dug into the skin of her forearm as she winced in pain.

Mounir's reaction to Cindy's physical abuse caught off him off guard. Though infuriated, he felt a degree of sadness, which came out of nowhere. Once again, he questioned the source of his emotion. He didn't understand it. Something deep inside him, something he couldn't identify, made Rick's behavior terribly frightening.

"I only got a hundred and sixty dollars, Cindy. Give me some fuckin' cash. Give me forty dollars so we can get the hell outta this shit hole."

Tears rolled down Cindy's face as she opened her purse and handed Rick the money. Rick pulled the remaining cash from his pocket and walked back to the table.

Mounir's eyes were on Cindy, who was quietly crying as she rubbed her arm. His emotions were consolidating into pure rage. His fear and sadness were gone.

Rick threw two hundred dollars on the table. Mounir ignored the money, took one step toward the big man, and stared into his eyes. "You're a real asshole, pal—an asshole who abuses women."

Rick placed his hands on his hips. His shoulders and arms bulged as his flannel shirt tightened on an expanded chest. "Who the hell are you to tell me how to treat women, you fuckin' greaseball?"

The last thing Mounir remembered was Rick moving toward him. The last thing Rick saw was the flash of a maple cue. With un-canny speed, Mounir grabbed his stick from the table and swung. The thick, butt end of the cue crashed into the big man's face as he lunged for Mounir.

The blow made a loud crack when the stick smashed squarely into Rick's mouth. The cue snapped in half at its brass coupling as Rick's front teeth snapped off at the gum line. He fell, spewing blood and chips of enamel as he crashed to the floor.

Mounir pounced on him, one knee on his chest, one hand at his throat. Squeezing Rick's windpipe between his thumb and forefinger, he yelled, "You need to die you piece of shit."

Rick, choking on blood pouring from his lacerated lips and gums, struggled to breathe. Salim yelled out, "Munie, stop it! You're gonna kill the guy."

Cindy, trying to pull Mounir off her boyfriend, was crying hysterically. Omar stepped in, attempting to console Cindy as Salim pulled Mounir's hand from Rick's throat. "Munie, you gotta stop!"

Mounir, looking as though he were in a trance, finally let go and stood up. To Salim, he seemed confused, not aware of what he'd done.

Omar grabbed Mounir by both shoulders. "Munie, are you okay?" What are you doing? I've never seen you this way!"

"Yeah… yeah, sure, I'm okay… I'm sorry, Omar."

"You and Sal better go. The police may be coming. You two go out the back. I'll take care of this mess. Don't worry, we'll cover for you. It'll be all right."

Mounir glanced back at the two hundred dollars lying on the table. He picked it up, pulled the rest of his winnings from his shirt pocket, and turned to Cindy, who was kneeling at Rick's side. Bending over, he gently helped her to her feet.

"You don't have to put up with that treatment, you know. You seem like a nice person. You deserve much better. Why don't you find a new boyfriend?"

He handed Cindy all the money, $250. She was speechless, simply staring in awe as she took the cash.

Salim, having often seen Mounir's kindness and generosity to-ward women, wasn't the least surprised by his friend's gesture. He put his arm around Mounir as the pair exited through the back of the pool hall.

"Munie, you're really something. You never cease to amaze me, my friend."

They left Omar's, entering the darkness and safety of East Dearborn.

Look at That Dude

"Look at that dude."

"Whoa, what's up with that?"

"Heck if I know."

"Man, that gives me the creepy crawlies."

"Me too. Just look at that."

"What do ya think's wrong with him?"

"I can't tell. Maybe he likes bein' that way."

"Likes bein' that way! You can't be serious."

"I am serious. Why else would a dude be like that?"

"Who knows? Man, that dude is one strange lookin' guy."

"Yep, he spooks me out."

"Oh, oh, he's comin' this way. We better scoot."

"No, wait, wait. He stopped. I think he's goin' back."

"You're right; he's turnin' around."

"Holy, God! What is that?"

"Sweet mama, that ain't nothin' if it ain't freaky."

"I think I'm gonna be sick."

"Don't you puke! He sees us barfin', he might get pissed."

"Oh, no! Now he's starin' at us."

"Look down, look down—look down at the sidewalk. Pretend we're just hangin' out, talkin'."

"We *are* just hangin' out, talkin'."

"Yeah, but he might think we're talkin' about him."

"We *are* talkin' about him."

"Of course, we are, but we don't want him to know. That dude looks dangerous."

"Yes, he does. He looks very dangerous."

"Ohoooo, mama, look at that. Look what's comin' down the street."

"Whoa, look at her go."

"She is fine!"

"You're not kiddin'. Shake it, shake it, baby."

"Oh, my God, she's walkin' toward that dude."

"She better be careful."

"Look! She's talkin' to him."

"Blessed mother in heaven, he just put his arm around her!"

"What is *that* all about? That chick is hot. What is she doing with that guy?"

"Man, I have no explanation for that. That is insane. That is troubling."

"Troubling! That is outrageous."

"You got that right. That is a seriously outrageous situation."

"I agree. And that lady is seriously fine!"

"Look at the hair on that woman. She might be the finest thing I've ever seen."

"Once again, I must agree. She is quite a fine woman—a smokin' hot, very fine chick."

"Uh, oh, now *she's* lookin' this way. She's turnin' toward us."

"My sweet Lord, look at her face!"

"Yow, she… is… beautiful."

"You are absolutely correct. She may be the most beautiful thing I have ever seen in my entire life."

"Yeah, her face is seriously nice."

"Her face is incredibly nice. Lookin' at her is makin' me kinda lightheaded."

"Don't you pass out on me. If you fall out, that dude might come over here and kick our butts."

"Okay, okay, I feel better now, but I can't quit lookin' at her."

"Of course, you can't. There ain't a man on earth could quit lookin' at our fine lady."

"Our lady? So now she belongs to us? That is nice. That is very nice."

"No, she don't belong to us, not yet. But she will as soon as that dude leaves."

"Really? I can't wait. How about you go over there and ask her out? I'll stay here."

"You don't ask chicks like her on a date. You just talk to them, cool like. A guy's gotta be sophisticated, cool, and mellow with a fine lady like that."

"Oh, of course, sophisticated. I guess I forgot who I was with."

"You gotta be cool and smooth, like Cool Whip on peach cobbler."

"Peach cobbler! That *is* sophisticated."

"Yep, cobbler's 'bout as good as it gets, my man."

"Hey, did she just smile at us?"

"I think she might have—she definitely might have smiled our way."

"You are right, I think I saw her teeth, and her teeth are super-white."

"Yep, the hot chick's teeth are super-white, and she definitely could have smiled our way."

"This is hard to believe. We've got a fine lady right in front of us, and she can't keep from smilin' at the magnificent, young men she see's admiring her super-fineness."

"My man, once again, you are correct. The hot lady can't quit smilin' at us. And that dude can't quit starin' at us."

"Hey, check out her lungs."

"Ohooo-yeah—WOW—I can't believe what my eyes are seein'.'"

"You can say that again; just look at those. They are nice." "Indeed, they are. Those lungs are fine and nice."

"I've never seen a pair as fine as those."

"Nor have I, my friend, nor have I."

"But what can that fine lady possibly see in that dude? That's not right."

"Yep, there's something seriously wrong with this picture, man."

"Very seriously wrong, this is some serious stuff we've encountered."

"Indeed it is; it's kinda scary."

"Yes, it is. It's very scary."

"My God, look at that button. That button's 'bout ready to pop."

"Oooooo baby, I'm prayin' it shoots right off."

"I'll tell ya what. We're not leavin' if that button goes."

"I am definitely with you on that, my man, definitely."

"Wait! Now she's turnin' back to that dude."

"Yowser, look at her rear end!"

"Whoooeeeeeyow—look at that. That is, without a doubt, the most beautiful thing I have ever seen in my life."

"Wait a minute. I thought her face was the most beautiful thing you've ever seen."

"It was, until I saw that."

"I gotta agree. And she's skakin' it again. Shake it, shake it, baby."

"That is a sight to behold."

"Yeah, I'd like to be holdin' it right now."

"Me, too, but that woman is too hot for guys like us."

"Yep, the chick's too smokin' hot for guys like us, but look at the dude she's with. Please explain that to me."

"As I said, there *is* no explanation for that—absolutely none."

"It probably don't matter much to him. He's the one with the smokin' hot lady hangin' all over him."

"Ain't that the truth? He's gotta be a happy man. A man or something else, whatever he is."

"Hey, why don't you go over there and ask him why he looks like that?"

"Sure, why don't you kiss my butt?"

"No way, I'd rather kiss *her* butt."

"You got that right. She is fine!"

"She sure is. She is a one-of-a-kind, super-fine and super-hot lady."

"You ain't lyin'; she is extreme, my friend, extreme."

"Know what? I think you should go over and congratulate that dude on his incredibly fine woman."

"Stop tellin' me to go over there! You go over there."

"You crazy? No way! But seriously, what the heck's wrong with that guy?"

"How many times I gotta tell ya? I DON'T KNOW."

"Not so loud; he's gonna hear you. He might come over here and kill us."

"He might. But if he does, I'll make one final request."

"Oh, and what would that be?"

"It would be that I get five minutes alone with his woman. That's worth dyin' for."

"For a second time, I must agree. She is nice; she is very nice!"

"Nice? She is on-fire super-hot. But her man, I don't know what to make of him.

"Me either. I'm surprised they even let him walk around in public."

"Yep, they should lock him up somewhere and leave his lady for us."

"Whoa, what is that? What did she just pull outta her mouth?"

"I don't know. Looks like some kinda… ooh, she threw it. You see that?"

"Yes, I did. I think it was some kinda… some kinda chewin' gum, maybe."

"No way! You tellin' me she's chewin' gum? What's up with that?"

"Man, I bet she likes chewin' gum."

"A gum chewer, that is hot—that is super-hot. Chewin' gum is a hot thing to do, and she's doin it right in front of us."

"Hey, what do ya think it means that she's chewin' gum?"

"What does it mean? You don't know what it means when a chick's chewin' gum?"

"That's right. I don't know."

"It means she is fine – super fine!"

"Yes, she is—she is a super-fine woman. But the dude she's with looks like some kinda alley monster."

"He does, but ya know, I feel a little sorry for him."

"I know, I know. Now that I think about it, he's not that bad.

"I gotta agree. He's kinda cool. In fact, he reminds me of my brother."

"Sure, I see the resemblance. And your brother's a good-lookin' guy."

"Yes, he is; he certainly is. My brother is a handsome young man. And he's got plenty of girlfriends, fine girlfriends—some are super-fine, and they all think he's smokin' hot."

"Yeah, that dude over there is all right."

"Yep, he looks like a nice guy—looks kinda gentle, especially the way he's treatin' his lady."

"You're right; he *is* treatin' her well. And, ya know, she's hot, but she ain't *that* hot."

"I was just thinkin' the same thing."

"She's fine, but she's not super-fine. Besides, there are *lots* of fine women around here."

"There certainly are. I see fine, hot chicks everywhere, every day."

"I know. She's not bad, but she's not *all that.*"

"Hey, what time is it."

"I've got five forty-five."

"Whoa, I gotta get goin'. If I'm late for dinner, my ma's gonna beat my butt."

"Yeah, I've gotta get up early. Gotta be at school for morning detention—I got caught cheatin' on a math test."

"I'll catcha tomorrow."

"Yep, see ya."

The Great Lakes Plaza

*T*he rig pulled into the Great Lakes Plaza entrance, following the signs for trucks only. It was a bit early for lunch, but Michael Walker was hungry.

Michael was an experienced trucker with more than fifteen years on a Columbus-to-Chicago route. Driving truck was his life, and he loved it. The hours were long, but the pay was excellent, and his route was short enough to allow adequate time with his wife and kids at home in Columbus, Ohio. Michael figured trucking was the salvation of his marriage. It kept Karen and him apart long enough to avoid arguments and conflict, provided plenty of honeymoon week-ends, and fulfilled Michael's wanderlust. They'd been married since high school, had three children, all boys, all doing well. Michael loved his family dearly, loved his job, and loved his life.

The company had recently transferred him to a new route, Cleveland to Chicago. Michael drove his car from Columbus to Cleveland, a two-hour trip, in early morning, five days a week. He'd load his truck in Cleveland and take off on the Ohio Turnpike, headed for Chicago, often staying overnight, sleeping in his cab, and returning home the following day.

This was his first visit to the Great Lakes Plaza, about sixty miles west of Cleveland. The turnpike plazas were nice, having been recently renovated and providing more than a few good choices for lunch.

Michael parked his truck and climbed out of its huge cab. He stood tall, just over six feet, with a handsome, rugged look. His denim jacket, jeans, Western boots, and hat gave him the look of a rodeo rider rather than a trucker.

Walking across the lot, he entered the plaza, finding a variety of restaurants: Starbucks, Panera, Sbarro, and Burger King. After buying a couple of slices of pepperoni pizza from Sbarro, he looked for a place to sit in the dining area, which was lined with long, Formica-topped tables. Smaller tables for four filled the center of the room. He took a seat.

Numerous travelers milled around. He spotted a few guys he pegged for drivers, no one familiar. His lunch was interrupted by some children making a disturbance a couple of tables over. They were loudly complaining to their mother, apparently unhappy with the food. Michael noticed they were eating Burger King. *That's unusual,* he thought. *Most kids love that BK junk.* He finished his pizza and left for Chicago.

The Great Lakes Plaza was a good location for Michael to get an early lunch on his way to Chicago, along with an occasional dinner on the way home.

A day later, on his return east, he stopped at the same plaza. He called his wife, Karen, to tell her he was running late, asking her to not hold supper for him; he'd grab some food on the road. After pulling his rig off the turnpike's eastbound lane, he slowly rolled to a stop in the truck lot, jumped out of his cab, and walked over an elevated causeway to the plaza on the opposite side of the expressway. Minutes later, he was carrying a sandwich, side of pasta, and a drink from Panera as he walked to his usual table in the dining area.

A commotion across the room caught his attention. A woman and her three children were having dinner. The mother was telling her kids, "Shut up and eat." It was the same family, the same kids from the other day, with the same complaints about the food.

Michael finished dinner, threw away his trash, and crossed the room toward the family. They were eating food from Burger King, just as before. *Poor kids,* he thought. *I bet she brings them here all the time, lunch and dinner, for the same lousy food—must not have enough sense to buy them something different. Panera would be better, but she probably can't afford it. By the looks of their clothes, they don't seem too well off.*

The woman was wearing a black T-shirt and tattered jeans. Her hair looked dirty. The children, two boys and a girl, looked disheveled and all of them, even the young girl, looked as though they could use a bath. *Must be rough for those kids.*

Michael left the plaza, climbed into his truck and took off for Cleveland, looking forward to seeing Karen and the boys that night.

The next morning, after an early start, he returned to the plaza for coffee and a snack from Starbucks. Intending to eat on the road, he walked toward the exit, passing the dining area on the way. He came to a halt, nearly spilling his coffee.

They were there again: same woman, same kids, same food, and same discontent. *They're even wearin' the same clothes. I'm sure of it. They must eat here every day. This is crazy. Who pays to get on the turn-pike to eat at Burger King?* He took a seat at a nearby table to observe.

As always, the kids were loudly bellyaching about the food. The oldest, a boy of twelve or so, was bitching to his mom. "Mom, I'm sick of this food. Every day's the same crap. You gotta get us outta here."

The girl was whining, "I wanna go home, Mommy! We've been here too long."

Michael's curiosity was piqued. After finishing his pastry and drink, he walked to their table, having no idea what he was going to say, but determined to find out what was going on—why they were there every day. Cautiously approaching the mother, seated at the end of the table, he said, "Excuse me, ma'am."

The woman shot around in her seat with a vicious glare and screamed, "Go away!"

Michael quickly stepped back, nearly falling over a chair. He forced a smile. "I'm sorry."

Spit flew from her mouth as she scream, "Leave us alone!"

He moved back farther and left. *What a bitch!* he thought. Glancing around the room, he was surprised no one else seemed to have noticed her outburst.

As he was leaving, he saw an old, black man, a janitor, pushing a mop bucket down the hall. The man was short, about five foot six. He had salt-and-pepper hair, cropped close, and a hint of gray whisker on his chin.

Michael approached. "Excuse me."

"Yes, sir. What you need?"

"Well, this is gonna sound like an odd question."

"That's okay. I get lotsa people askin' me funny questions. Go ahead."

"I'm curious about the family that's here all the time. I'm sure you've seen them, a woman and three children?"

"Well, they's plenty a folk come in here, some quite regular. What you wanna know 'bout 'em?"

"I'm not sure, I mean… I'm not sure what I wanna ask."

"Mister, I think I know who you be talkin' 'bout. How's if you point 'em out to me?"

The men walked back to the dining area.

"That woman over there in the black T-shirt. The one with three kids. I see them here all the—"

"Oh, Lordy!" The janitor's face broke into a big, toothy grin. "Just what I 'spected. Mister, you got the gift. Yes, sir, you got it. I'll be dog- gone if you ain't got the gift!"

"What gift? What are you talking about?"

"I'm talkin' 'bout the gift. The gift a gettin' to see them folk. It's what they call the supernatural."

"Supernatural? What's so supernatural about seeing some people eating lunch?"

"I don't see 'em."

"What? I just showed them to you. They're sitting right over there." Michael pointed across the room.

"I believe you, mister. But most folk can't see 'em. I bet you see a chubby woman, wearin' some black shirt, and three children, two boys and a girl, right?"

"Yeah, that's right."

"And they all be eatin' Burger King food, right?"

"Yes, that's exactly right. So, you do see them."

"No sir, I don't. Not a lick. I just know what they look like from talkin' to people with the gift—people like you."

Michael was silent, pondering what to say. "This sounds… this sounds crazy."

"Sure it do. You might think I'm crazy, too. But you the one all shook up 'bout it. You the one 'proached me with your silly question, right?"

"That's right."

"So who's crazy? You go ask other folk in here 'bout that family. Ask 'em if they see 'em sittin' there."

"I'd rather not."

"Why? What's the harm? Just go ask."

"Okay, okay. I guess I can do that. Will you wait here?"

"Shore nuf, I'll wait. I'm lookin' forward to it."

A minute later, Michael returned with a flushed, embarrassed look on his face. "All right, I believe you. I felt like a fool askin' those people. No one knew what I was talking about."

"Course they didn't. But don't you worry none 'bout that. People with the gift are special—you're special. You got somethin' they ain't got. You should be proud."

"How do you know about this?"

"I know 'cause I been workin' here at this plaza for years. I've talked with people like you before, people with the gift."

"Okay, so let's say I've got this gift thing. What should I do now?"

"I don't know what you should do. Way I see it, you ain't gotta do nothin'. Just 'cept it, and go on livin' your life."

"But this is incredible. It's an amazing thing. I'm having trouble believin' it."

"Course you is. All the people I meet with the gift is right shocked 'bout it." He hesitated. "There is one thing, though. One thing I should tell you, Mr..."

"Walker, Mike Walker. And what's your name?"

"You can call me Louis—just like old Joe Louis, the Brown Bomber. Anyway, I was gonna say, Mr. Mike, you best stay away from that woman. From what I hear, she's right nasty—mean 'n' nasty."

"Yeah, I know that already, Joe... I mean Louis. I tried talking to her, and she started screamin' at me to get away."

"You best leave them be. They ain't right. I think there's somethin' evil goin' on with that woman. So listen, Mr. Mike, I enjoyed talkin' with ya, but I'm gonna catch hell if I don't get back to work. I'm here every day, every weekday that is. If you stop back, we can talk some more."

"Sure, Louis, thanks. Believe me, I'll be back." Michael left the plaza and took off for Cleveland, certain he'd return the next day.

The following morning, he awoke early, sped to Cleveland, hurriedly loaded his delivery, and took off on the turnpike, heading west, arriving at the plaza at nine twenty in the morning. He quickly parked his rig and ran across the lot, boot heels clicking on the pavement.

They were there: same table, same food, same complaints from the kids, same rude remarks from their mother. He left the dining room and found Louis down the hall, sweeping the floor.

"Hey, Mr. Mike. You here early today."

"Louis, we have to talk. This whole thing is drivin' me nuts. I told my wife about it last night. She thinks I'm off my rocker. You gotta help me."

"I'll do whatever I can, Mr. Mike, but I don't think I can be a much help."

"Please, Louis. Tell me anything else you can think of about this gift."

"Let's see, well… I can tell you, like I did, you special and you not alone. Over the past few years, I met four or five people with the gift. So you not alone, Mr. Mike. Don't you worry 'bout that."

"Okay, so I'm not the only one. I guess that helps a little. Is there anything else?"

"Yeah, I can tell you two years ago, some fella with the gift made a big ruckus over it. He told some newspaper man 'bout it, and they got a bunch a investigators out here to the plaza."

"Investigators?"

"Yes, sir, what they call paranormal experts. Bunch a fools, if you ask me."

"What did they find?"

"They didn't find nothin', Mr. Mike, not a blessed thing. They brought in all this equipment: cameras, lights, microphones, tape recorders, and stuff. You shoulda seen 'em, all ooh-in' and aah-in' 'bout some little sounds they heard, some little spots a light they seen and such. One said he saw some kinda fog in the room. Said it looked like ghosts. I got a good laugh outta the whole thing. Like I said, bunch a fools. They didn't see nothin' like you see, Mr. Mike. None a them had the gift—and if you ain't got it, you ain't got it, and you ain't gonna see 'em. Simple as that."

"What happened afterward?"

"Nothin' happened. That was it. They left, and we ain't heard from 'em since."

"We? Who's we?"

"I mean us, here at the plaza. Lotsa folk who work here met people with the gift. I ain't the only one."

"Is there anything else you can tell me? Do you know how I could get in touch with one of the other people, people with this gift?"

"No, Mr. Mike, sorry, I can't help you with that. I never seen any of 'em again." Louis paused. "But I guess I should tell ya somethin' more, tell ya 'bou—"

"Tell me what?"

"I been hesitatin' 'bout it, but you bein' so persistent 'n' all, I guess I should explain."

"Please, go on, Louis. What is it?"

"Mr. Mike, there is one important thing I've left out."

"Please, what else?"

"Well, just about a month before those with the gift started seein' that family, there was a bad automobile wreck, right outside the plaza. And from what I hear, I think it was the same family. A mother and three children was on they way to Cedar Point, and they stopped in here for lunch. I hear the children was all hollerin' not to stop for lunch 'cause they was anxious to get to the park."

"Yes… and?"

"Bit later, when their mama pulled outta here, she was fussin' with them kids and not payin' no attention to her drivin'. As she was gettin' on the turnpike, she smacked right in the side a some big semi-trailer that was whizzin' by. That car flipped upside down and flew over the guard railin'. They was all killed, instantly. It was a horrible thing."

"Oh, God. That is horrible."

"'Bout a month later, I met the first person with the gift, like you, Mr. Mike. He described that family to me, and I figured it's them got killed. Figure they got stuck here somehow."

Michael was skeptical. "That story's a little hard to swallow, Louis."

"I know, I know, but it's what I think."

"Okay, Louis. I appreciate your talking with me. I gotta tell you, this whole thing's spookin' me. I don't know what I'm gonna do."

"Like I said, as I sees it, you ain't got to do nothin', 'cept maybe stay away from this place."

"Yeah, you're probably right, but I've got an urge to talk to that woman again."

"Mr. Mike, I wouldn't do it. All I know is she's right mean. My feelin' is she's some kinda witch. I'd be stayin' clear a her."

"Thanks for the warning, Louis. I'm sure we'll talk again."

Michael turned and walked away, headed toward the exit. As soon as Louis was out of sight, he returned to the dining room. As he walked in, the woman looked at him with an inhuman glower. Peeling her lips back over jagged teeth, she stuck out a swollen, black-and-blue tongue. Michael decided not to push his luck. He left for Chicago.

It was a hot, sticky night, and the rest stop in Chicago was packed with semi-trucks, all lined up with their engines idling to keep the air conditioning running. Michael spent a fitful night in his cab, desperately trying to fall asleep, rolling around in a sweat-soaked bed. His thoughts were consumed with the family, the woman, and his gift. He didn't want the gift.

It's not a gift! It's a curse, he thought. *A curse that's gonna destroy me. Karen thinks I'm out of my mind and wants me to see a doctor. I'm afraid to tell anyone else about it. They'll all think I'm nuts—I've gotta let it ago.*

As he lay on his cot, he convinced himself to never go to the plaza again—never. Having found some relief in his commitment, he fell asleep.

Michael's cell phone woke him early in the morning. The company had an unscheduled load for him to pick up in Chicago before leaving for Cleveland. It would be a long day.

Hours later, after completing his delivery and loading another, he was on the road, headed for Ohio. He promised himself he wouldn't stop. *I'll drive straight through to Cleveland without eating and hurry home to my family. There's no way I'm goin' in that plaza.*

The sun was setting behind him as he crossed the Indiana line into Ohio. It was dark by the time he drove by the turnpike sign reading, "Great Lakes Plaza 2 miles."

"Two miles!" His head was spinning. Fearing he would lose his resolve, Michael clenched the wheel and accelerated, speeding straight ahead, determined to race past the plaza. He began yelling out loud, "Don't stop, don't stop, don't stop!" Approaching the plaza entrance, consumed by an irresistible urge to turn, he did his utmost to stay on course, but the wheel started turning, as if controlled by an external power, a force Michael couldn't defy. "Shit, I've gotta take one more look!"

Rolling up the entrance ramp, he spoke aloud to himself. "I'm so weak. I have no will power. I just can't resist this-this thing."

After parking, he slowly walked over the causeway, praying as he went. He prayed to God, asking they, the family, not be there, asking this thing, this gift, simply be a bad dream, praying his gift would be gone forever.

Cautiously entering the dining area, he stood still with eyes closed and said one last prayer. He opened his eyes. No one was there, no family there. He yelled out, startling the diners, "They're gone! Thank you, God!"

Now he could leave and never come back. It was over. He wouldn't talk to Louis; he wouldn't talk to anyone. Telling himself, *Maybe it was all some crazy dream; maybe it never happened,* gave him a content sense of peace.

As he approached the exit doors toward the parking lot, he heard a voice behind him.

"Hey, Mr. Mike."

Michael stopped, reluctantly turning around. "Hi, Louis."

"How ya doin' tonight? Runnin' late, are ya?"

Michael smiled, giving his friend the good news. "They're gone, Louis. The family's gone. I don't see 'em anymore. My gift is gone."

Louis, seeing the relief on Michael's face, thought, *I should just let 'im go. Let him leave and forget 'bout it.* "That's wonderful, Mr. Mike. Now you can forget this whole thing. Maybe you ain't got the gift no more! You just go on home. I bet you lost the gift. Maybe you never had it."

Michael, detecting the insincerity in the janitor's voice, said, "Come on, Louis. Don't be bullshittin' me!"

"Oh, Mr. Mike, you shore is hard-headed, ain't ya?"

"Yeah, I'm real hard-headed. So, don't hold back on me."

"Mr. Mike, you never been here this late in the day, has you? Not like tonight."

"No, I haven't."

"Well, you don't see 'em cause they ain't there."

"You're confusing me, Louis. I know they're not there—that's what I said."

"What I'm sayin' is I hear those folk don't just sit there, eatin' all day. They move around the plaza. Right 'bout now they probably be down in the restroom or maybe at the gift shop. Other folk with the gift tell me they wander around the plaza, all day and all night."

Michael's face sank with a look of dread. "Oh, God, I didn't want to hear that, Louis."

"Mr. Mike, I'm right sorry for tellin' ya, but you always be pushin' me for the truth."

Michael took off running down the hall, toward the restrooms, leaving Louis standing there, shaking his head. He checked the men's room—no sign of the boys. He stood outside the ladies' room for a minute. No one came out. He ran to the gift shop.

There they were, all four of them. Michael nearly ran into the mother as she walked out of the shop.

"You again!" she screamed. "I warned you, mister. Now you're followin' us, aren't ya? I been watchin' you. You're a trucker—I hate truckers. Dirty truckers, always drinkin', poppin' pills, and cheatin' on their wives with hookers. You're gonna be sorry for messin' with me and my children!"

Michael stood, frozen, terrified by her look. He felt a tap on his shoulder. It was Louis, right behind him.

"Mr. Mike, you don't look so good. Kinda look like you seen a ghost. That family's here, ain't they? I'm tellin' you, you gotta let it go. Nothin' good gonna come a this."

Michael let out a deep breath. "You're right, you're absolutely right. I need help. Someone has to help me, Louis, help me get rid of this obsession. Maybe I should see a doctor or talk to my minister. But right now, I gotta get outta here and never come back."

"That's exactly what you got to do, Mr. Mike. I've enjoyed meetin' you 'n' all, but I think it be best we never see each other again. You know what I mean? I like you a lot, but it best you never come back to this plaza."

"I understand what you're saying. It's been a real pleasure meeting you, Louis. I wish you the best of luck."

"You too, Mr. Mike. I be wishin' good things for you in the future, for you and your family."

"Goodbye, Louis"

"You be careful, Mr. Mike"

Michael didn't look back. He headed straight out the door, over the causeway, and jumped in his truck.

Night had fallen. It was dark with a light drizzle of rain. Glaring headlight reflections shined off the wet blacktop as the giant truck pulled onto the turnpike.

Except for the subtle clapping of windshield wipers, the cab was quiet—barely illuminated by a soft, yellow glow from the instrument panel. The truck's wipers created a soothing rhythm as Michael sat back to relax.

The huge rig, weighed down by a heavy load from Chicago, slowly accelerated as Michael shifted through the gears, gradually reaching a cruising speed of fifty miles an hour. Hoping for some peaceful solitude, he left the radio off.

Unfortunately, Michael's thoughts soon drifted back to the woman's tirade and what she'd said about hating truckers for their immoral habits—drinkin', druggin', and whorin' around. Michael wasn't much of a drinker, but he knew many drivers who were. The woman was right about truckers poppin' pills to stay awake. He'd done that on rare occasions. Her last comment, about hookers, brought back bad memories. He'd only been unfaithful to Karen one time, years ago when he hired a prostitute in Muncie. Having always regretted it, Michael knew it would never happen again. He loved his wife, even more, after his single, unfaithful act.

Rolling down the turnpike, he thought about his years with Karen. Their twentieth anniversary was coming up next month. The years had flown by much too fast. He loved trucking, but for the first time in his life, he felt a deep yearning to spend more time with his family.

Over past years, even when he was home, he'd often find himself doing things, projects, yard work without his wife or children. He felt bad about it. *Karen and the boys deserve more than I've given. It's time for me to be a better husband and father.*

A thought came to him; *I should ask the company for a shorter route— one closer to home. If they won't comply, I'll find another dispatcher, a different outfit, one that can accommodate me.*

Excited about that prospect, he thought, *I'm nearly forty years old. I need a change, and my family needs a change.* Michael Walker had a new sense of contentment.

The front seat of the cab was wide, nearly six-feet across. Michael felt a cold chill run through his body. Reaching for the dash to turn up the heat, he heard a deep, guttural sound, right next to him. He screamed. Mouth agape with terror, body violently twisting away from the passenger side of the cab, he screamed louder, "Oh my, God!"

She was there, glaring at him, wild-eyed, head shaking, greasy hair flying. "I told you. I told you to leave us alone. Now you can join me in hell." She grabbed the wheel and yanked. The truck shot across the shoulder, ripped through a steel barrier and somersaulted down a steep slope. The cab was crushed flat on impact.

•

Weeks later, Karen Walker arrived at the Great Lakes Plaza. After burying her husband, she developed a horrible feeling, a sense that something or someone at the plaza had killed him. Michael's obsession with the whole thing made her want to look for herself. She was heartbroken and frightened about a future without her husband and deeply worried about her children growing up without their father. Karen entered the dining area and looked around. Many travelers and truckers were having lunch. No one she knew, no sign of any woman with three kids. As she turned to leave, she thought something or someone touched her sleeve. She turned back; there was no one there. An odd sensation took her, as if something was passing through her, something warm and wonderful.

Karen instantly felt a profound, deep love for her husband— deeper than ever before. She experienced a new sense of security; a bolstered self-confidence assured her she and her children were going to be all right.

She left the dining room to look for the janitor. She found Louis mopping the floor near the restrooms. "Excuse me. Are you Louis?"

"Yes, ma'am. How'd you know my name?"

"I'm Karen Walker, Michael's wife."

"Oh, Miss Karen, I'm surely glad to meet you. Your husband, Mr. Mike, was a real good man. I was tore up when I heard the news. I'm really sorry for your loss, Miss Karen."

"Thank you so much, Louis. I was wondering if we could talk."

"Sure we can. It'd be my pleasure."

"Louis, can you tell me anything about what was going on here? You know, with the family Michael told me about."

"I'm sorry, Miss Karen, but there ain't much more to say than what your husband done told you—told you 'bout his gift 'n' all."

"I was worried about him after he started talking crazy, talking about seeing invisible people."

"I understand how ya musta felt, ma'am. But I believe it's the truth. Mr. Mike had what I call the gift. I've seen a number a people in here like that, people with the gift."

"Louis, I guess it's not important if I believe you or not. I just wanted to make sure it didn't have anything to do with his accident."

"You're right, Miss Karen. It ain't important for you to believe. But I can tell ya, Mr. Mike was straight in the head. He weren't crazy. That's what I believe, and I don't think there was any kinda foul play goin' on here. I think the accident was nothin' more than that, an accident. Poor, Mr. Mike, I surely did enjoy talkin' with 'im."

"Louis, just in case—just in case you happen to get in touch with Michael somehow, I'd like you to give him a message."

"That'd be fine. I doubt that will ever happen, but if it do, I'd be happy to tell him whatever you want."

"Tell him I love him. Tell him the children love him and we all miss him terribly."

"I'll do that, Miss Karen."

"Also, and this is important, Louis, tell him not to worry about us; tell him we're gonna be all right—I know that now. Before I came in here, I was frightened and worried about a future without Michael. But something happened in the dining room just now, something beautiful. It was love, Louis. It was so wonderful; I felt Michael's love like never before. Now I know we'll be fine. Please tell him that if you can."

Louis, for the first time in many years, was speechless. Overwhelmed by Karen's words, he felt the love he'd had for his deceased wife—a love he still carried inside, a love for the kind woman he'd shared life with for forty-three years.

His eyes welled with tears as he spoke. "I... will, Miss Karen, I promise. I'll tell Mr. Mike just what you said if I see him. Thank you, Miss Karen; thank you for comin' by."

"Thank you, Louis. It's been nice meeting you."

"Goodbye, Miss Karen."

Karen Walker left the plaza and never returned. Months passed as she and the children recovered from their loss. Life went on. They did fine, just as she knew they would.

•

In Toledo, Ohio, a pair of young newlyweds, Brent and Julie Adamson, were moving into their new apartment. Brent Adamson had recently graduated from college and was starting a new career as a financial advisor. He was assigned to a half-day, five-day-a-week morning schedule at his firm's office in Sandusky, Ohio. Each morning he'd get on the Ohio Turnpike, travel forty miles to Sandusky, spend three hours in the office, and return to Toledo for the afternoon. On his daily drive back, he'd occasionally stop at the Great Lakes Plaza for lunch.

After a month on the job, Brent was eating at the plaza often. On nearly every stop, he saw a woman sitting by herself, eating food from Burger King. A tall, thin man, dressed Western style in a denim jacket, jeans, and cowboy boots, was always sitting a few tables over. Though they were there every day, Brent never saw the man and woman talk.

Brent, his curiosity growing with each visit, finally approached an older, black gentleman, the plaza's janitor, to ask him if he knew why those people were there so often.

"Excuse me, sir. I have an unusual question to ask."

"You go right ahead. I get lotsa silly questions at this plaza. I've been here for years, ya know. How can I help you?"

"It's about those people who are here every day. I've been in here about ten times this past month, and there's been a woman and some Western dude here every time."

Louis looked up at Brent with a broad, toothy smile, and said, "Oh, Lordy, I been waitin' for you, mister."

"You've been waiting for me?"

"That's right."

"You don't even know me. What are you talking about?"

"Sir, I might know you better than you think. You say you see a man dressin' Western style?"

"That's right."

"A tall guy, kinda slender?"

"Yea, that's him."

"I'm sorry to hear it. I'm real sorry for Mr. Mike."

Brent responded with a surprised look. "How's that? Who's Mr. Mike?"

"I'll tell ya later if that'll be okay with you."

"Sure, that's fine."

"I been waitin' for someone with the gift, someone like you."

"The gift? I don't get it, what gift?"

"Sir, I'll explain everythin' to you later. Right now, if you don't mind, I'd like you to point these folks out to me."

"Of course—no problem." The pair walked to the dining area, where Brent directed Louis to Michael's table.

"Is the Western fella here?" asked Louis.

"Is he here? He's sittin' right in front of you!"

"And the woman with the children. Where's she?"

"There's a woman's sitting over there." He pointed to an empty table, two rows down. "But I don't see any kids—just a woman in a black shirt."

Louis wondered where those kids might be. *Probably off gettin' candy at the shop,* he thought. "Listen, mister . . ."

"Adamson, Brent Adamson."

"Listen, Mr. Brent. This is gonna seem real strange to ya, but you're gonna have to talk to Mr. Mike for me. Like I said, I'll explain it all later."

Brent, thinking the old black man was very odd, reluctantly agreed. "Please ask him his name."

"Okay." Brent asked and turned back to Louis, "He says his name is Mike Walker."

That confirmation hit Louis with a pang of sadness. He'd been hoping it wasn't Michael. "Could you ask him if he can hear me?"

"He says he can hear you."

"Is he sittin' right here at the table?"

"No, he just got up. He's standin' right in front of you."

Louis extended his hands as if to touch his friend—nothing there.

"Mr. Mike, I'm right sorry to find you here."

Brent conveyed Michael's response. "He says he's sorry to be here too, but he's doing all right." Brent chuckled when he added, "He also says he's sick of eating pizza every day!"

Louis smiled and spoke again, feeling foolish as he addressed the void in front of him. "Mr. Mike, is there anything I can do for ya?"

"He wants you to tell him about his wife. He saw her here about a month after his accident. He saw her talking with you."

"Oh, my, I'm glad you reminded me. Miss Karen and I had a good talk. She's a real sweet woman, your wife is."

Brent, seeing Michael's response, gently took Louis by the arm. "He's getting a little teary eyed. Maybe you should change the subject."

"I'm sorry 'bout your sadness, Mr. Mike. But I can tell ya some good things Miss Karen told me."

Brent turned to Louis. "He wants to know what she said."

"Miss Karen, she said she and the children love you very much, Mr. Mike. They miss you a whole lot. You gotta know that. And she told me somethin' she said was important. She wanted you to know they all gonna be all right. She said she was frettin' 'bout that a lot, at first—bein' worried 'bout how the family was gonna get on without you. She said a strange thing happened the day she come here to the plaza. She had a real good feelin'—a feelin' of love and safety. When she left, she knew everythin' was gonna be just fine."

Louis saw Brent looking intently at the empty space in front of him. "Louis, he says he feels better now. He said something about staying here until he made sure his family was safe and says he's ready to leave now. Louis, I don't get it. Where's he going?"

"I guess he's goin' where he belongs." Louis turned back to talk to his friend. "I'm mighty glad to hear you gettin' outta here, Mr. Mike, mighty glad."

Brent spoke. "He says he's gonna miss you, Louis. He's been watching you work every day, and he's tried to talk to you without any luck."

Louis turned to face Michael again. "Mr. Mike—Mr. Brent here tells me the woman's children are gone. You know anything 'bout that?"

"Michael says he hasn't seen them for weeks. He thinks they paid their dues and got to leave." Brent looked even more confused. "What's he talking about, 'paid their dues'?"

Louis didn't answer. He looked straight ahead toward the vacant table. "I think you're right. And I gotta feelin' you done paid your dues, too, Mr. Mike, you bein' such a nice fella and all. I bet you been here long enough, Mr. Mike, plenty long enough. But that woman, I 'spect she's gonna be here for some time."

Brent paused a moment to listen to Michael's response. "He's smiling, Louis. He knows he'll be leaving soon. He's been feeling it deep in his bones for days now. He's glad he got this chance to talk to you before he goes. He wanted to hear what Karen said. He says he's okay now, thanks to you."

Louis took a long look at the space before him. "Mr. Mike, when you get there, how 'bout you put in a good word for old Louis. I'm gettin' up in my years, and I 'spect I won't be round much longer. If I'm figurin' right, I got a beautiful woman waitin' to see me. I'm kinda anxious to go."

Brent smiled. "Mr. Mike says to consider it done. It will be his pleasure."

BOOK REVIEWS

A VICTIM OF CIRCUMSTANCE
… wow!… captivated by your story from beginning to end… shirley t
… truly impressed with your writing!… marjorie d.
… a fine example of excellent prose . . .rhymer 1
… amazing story… held me enthralled from start to finish… freda
… a touch of brilliance… wonderfully done… Bravo!… marjorie d.

BASEMENT MONSTERS
… vivid ghastly scenes… liberty justice
… what an entertaining story… cmctarnahan
… absorbing, with vivid images… dark, slimy, smelly, and downright
   horrible… gruesome… I got a grin out of it… alvina

CARL AND LYNNETTE
… an incredible verbal picture of parental love, reciprocated in a
   fervent yet gentle manner… loved both Carl and Lynette… shy1250
… I'm teary-eyed!… love this story… saw every character and heard
   every word… I imagined I was there… annmuma
… loved it the whole way through… rosalita21
… I felt like I was watching a movie. Great job… onegirl
… an awesome story… keep writing these great stories… karenfay

CIAO
… I felt like I knew them both… super dialogue… intriguing…janet7053
… I love your writing… bjbarnes

DREAMS CAN COME TRUE

... loved it!... great characters, structure, and design... royowen

... fantastic story!... love weird stories like this!... very well written... flowed expertly!...can't wait for more of your work!...alexander3571

... man, what a story!... you have a strong style... your stories are interesting... I really enjoyed it... very good job!... look forward to more... balance

EINSTEIN WAS RIGHT—EVERYTHING'S RELATIVE

... oh, how I laughed when I read the last line... very well done... Einstein was right, indeed... Isn't that funny!... janilou

... captivating and imaginative... highly original... would love to see finished version of your book . . .it needs to be published... please finish it for me, lol... nmills

... brilliantly perceptive and observationally wise... royowen

... ten out of ten for originality... rebekah

HENRI

... great writing style... keeps the reader's attention... looking forward to more... freda

... One of the most enjoyable stories I've read for some time... well done... great characterization... good structure... a riveting read... royowen

... a sweet, cute tail... er, tale... it made me smile... adorable... would happily read to children, except the diaphragm piece - the funniest of all... whole heartedly give this an excellent rating!... samduck

AN OBSERVATION ON SELF-ESTEEM

... an outstanding story... very well written... worth a second read... awesome!... carolinasangel

... can't wait to read part two... it kept me glued to my chair... inmemoriam

... a bushel of kudos... damn, this is intense... so much tension... a nice hook at the end...

… can't wait for Part Two!… it'll be great… a gripping read… definitely liked the way this flowed…

… really excellent… spot on… characters so well developed one can see them… frogbook

LOOK AT THAT DUDE

… LOL!… goes on and on and gets funnier and funnier… a good laugh… LOL!… ps

OMAR'S

… filled with suspense… righteousriter

… another stupendous chapter . . .I'm in awe!… kintesiegel

… excellent writing… gambev

THE SHORT-ORDER COOK

… excellent… got a good laugh out of this one… prettybluebirds

… OMG!!!… makes you think twice about eating out!… very unique… flows well… kathleenspalding . . .

… clean… trimmed well… great flow… driven

… story is great… really enjoyed it… kept my interest all the way through… becky7777

STEVEN'S EDUCATION

… story is brilliant… never been so entertained… a travelogue for criminals… never boring . . .don't stop writing… mabaker

… Wow… how interesting… love stories that create critical thinking… great job!… wordspinner314

THE EPIPHANY

… captivating story… pulls the reader along… excellent… compelling… kmtracy

… great story!… loved reading this… amazing… creative… lokman

... wonderful story!!... sensitively written... cleverly thought out... a beautiful story with a twist... kimosphere123

THE CEILING FAN

... excellent... couldn't have been better... fantastic story... stnick

... great story... very descriptive... felt like I was on a tour!... the suspense mounted... held my interest... great read... LOVED the story! Very creative history-based fiction!... kimosphere

... a compelling story--I was totally engrossed the whole time!... mmichelle97219

... phenomenal story!... very creepy and ghoulish!... simply loved this creepy little tale... alexander3571

THE OAK TREE

... suspenseful . . .intriguing... vivid images, alliterations, and metaphors... in smell, touch, sight... such visual descriptions... the old oak tree symbolizes endurance and strength... well done!... liberty justice

TO LIVE IS TO SUFFER

... what an impressive story... oliver818

source: http://www.fanstory.com/